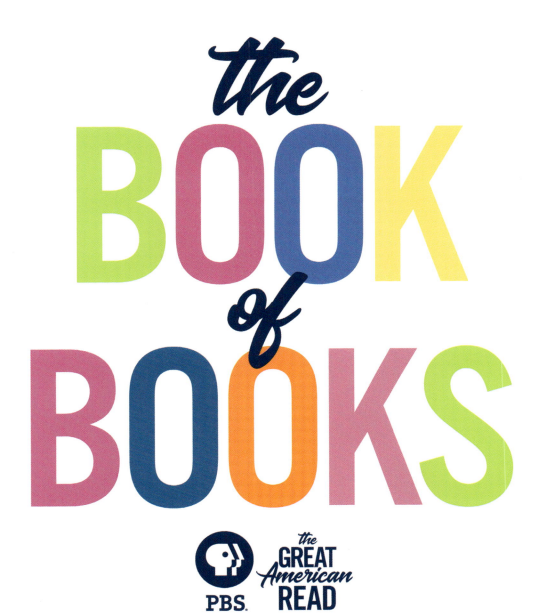

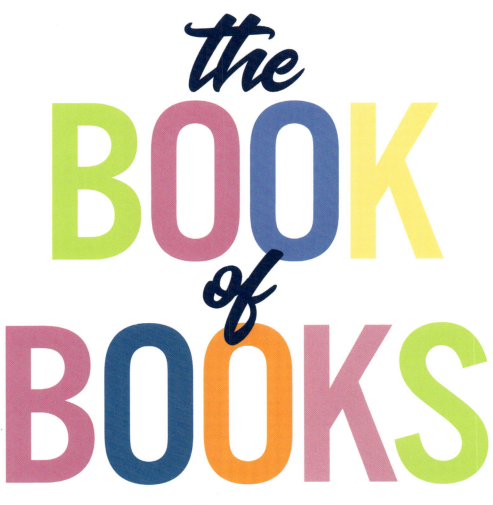

the BOOK of BOOKS

PBS | the GREAT American READ

FOREWORD BY MEREDITH VIEIRA
TEXT BY JESSICA ALLEN

BLACK DOG
& LEVENTHAL
PUBLISHERS

Black Dog & Leventhal Publishers
Hachette Book Group
1290 Avenue of the Americas
New York, NY 10104

www.hachettebookgroup.com
www.blackdogandleventhal.com

First Edition: August 2018

The Black Dog & Leventhal Publishers name and logo
are trademarks of Hachette Book Group, Inc.

The publisher is not responsible for websites (or their content)
that are not owned by the publisher.

The Hachette Speakers Bureau provides a wide range of authors for
speaking events. To find out more, go to www.HachetteSpeakersBureau.com
or call (866) 376-6591.

LCCN: 2018941274
ISBNs: 978-0-316-41755-6 (hardcover); 978-0-316-41754-9 (ebook)
Printed in the USA
LSC-K
10 9 8 7 6 5 4 3 2 1

CONTENTS

FOREWORD

There are few things as satisfying and as long lasting as a beloved book. My favorite books have become the touchstones in my life; I remember where I was when they found me, why they spoke to me at that particular time, and how I'd often passionately recommended them to my friends. Many of my favorites still sit on my bookshelves as a reminder of the wonderful experiences they've brought to me. In quiet moments, I pull them from the shelves and revisit them like old friends.

With *The Great American Read*, PBS has set out to unite America around one powerful idea: What if we could forget for a moment all of the things that divide us and remember the ideas, the characters, the stories that make up our common thread? What if by celebrating our favorite books together, and by learning the unique history behind them, we could rediscover the joy the finest storytellers have brought us?

The book you are holding is an essential guide to this wonderful PBS initiative. Extensively researched, *The Great American Read: The Book of Books* includes summaries and the little-known backstories of every book and every author featured in the television series, giving you a fresh perspective on how each of America's top one hundred novels fits into the fabric of our history, both in America and abroad. Best of all, you are likely to draft a new reading list of your own, either of books to revisit or to discover for the very first time.

As you'll soon see, the list of top one hundred novels America has chosen is intriguing in its scope—the earliest of America's favorites dates from 1605, and the latest is from 2016. The range of experiences the list captures is equally fascinating. From the sumptuous to the scandalous, from the toughest neighborhood to the grandest mansion, these stories are the mirror of our culture, never the arbiter, and as such they suggest to us who we have been as a culture and we may very well be now. They also span the range of our reading experience, from books we might have read as children to books we might have recently discovered.

Perhaps the most satisfying aspect of *The Great American Read: The Book of Books* is the history that surrounds both books and publishing—the stories behind the story—provided by author Jessica Allen. Jessica and her team have delved deeply into publisher archives to bring you fascinating details about the books: little-known information about first editions, the stories behind famous books to film, several original author manuscripts, the day jobs of famous authors (did you know Harper Lee was an airline ticket agent and Diana Gabaldon was a science professor?), and more.

I hope you'll join me and our friends at PBS in celebrating *The Great American Read* and that you'll find *The Book of Books* as wonderfully entertaining as I have.

—Meredith Vieira

INTRODUCTION

More than 300,000 books were published in the United States last year. This number encompasses romances, mysteries, Pulitzer Prize winners, true crime, thrillers, literary fiction, natural science, travelogues, and religious tracts. Memoirs, essays, pop culture. The book destined to become someone's best-loved, the book that turned a reluctant reader into a passionate one, the book that made a child want to become a writer. All of these, and so very many more, appeared on shelves and screens.

Even as television and social media compete for our attention, books remain. Indeed, they thrive. When I was a child, if my local library didn't stock a title, I didn't read it. Today we carry entire libraries around on a device no bigger than a paperback. We order titles published anywhere, to arrive on our doorstep within 24 hours. It's a glorious time to be a reader.

The technology behind this growth in accessibility is extraordinary, but so is the technology at the heart of reading itself. Reading began as listening, when our ancestors started telling tales to pass collective knowledge from one generation to the next. In time, this transmission begat writing, which furthered the capacity for progress and widened humanity's imaginative scope. The development of literacy has no serious competition as our species' most significant achievement.

A few years ago I attended a talk given by artist Chuck Close. Speaking about the purpose and power of his materials, he noted, "Even colored dirt can make you cry." So can

black marks on a white page. We weep with sorrow, or joy. Our cares disappear, as do our surroundings, and we are transported, as if by some supernatural sleight of hand, into other times, minds, and places—all by reading. To remind yourself of the mystery of this process of comprehension and imagination, have a look at a book in a language you don't know. You'll instantly appreciate the tremendous power of what amounts to just a bunch of lines and circles.

"Tell me a story," a little one begs, and we oblige. Like our prehistoric relatives, we continue to rely on narratives to entertain, to inform, and to instruct. Reading broadens our perspective. In a world fraught with conflict, where terrible news is always a click away, we can fall into a novel and find solace and hope. Writing the entries that constitute *The Great American Read* reminded me of the importance of reading to the development of civil society—in every sense of the word, from politeness at the post office to supporting a meaningful discussion of ideas and issues. Some books propose values or promote behaviors that I find less than praiseworthy, but I believe in not only the writer's right to espouse said views but also the absolute necessity of engaging with outlooks with which we don't agree. Personal and intellectual growth comes from reading widely and deeply, as well as from developing a willingness to push past the comfortable into the utterly strange.

Other books discussed in the pages that follow live within me, as much a part of myself as my very DNA. A quotation from *Wuthering Heights* formed the centerpiece of my wedding vows. *One Hundred Years of Solitude* changed the way I think about time. I can still remember how horrified I was by the climax of *Nineteen Eighty-Four* when I was a child, frantically petting my schnauzer to comfort myself, and how my friends and I, like so many teens before us, quoted lines from Salinger, Baldwin, and Vonnegut. A huge chunk of my graduating class used the conclusion of *The Great Gatsby* as their send-off quote in our high-school yearbook.

Some worthy titles did not make the cut. Depending on your sensibilities, you may rage against the lack of *Middlemarch*, *The Sound and the Fury*, or *Madame Bovary*, or search in vain for *Interview with the Vampire*, *The Golden Compass*, or *Kindred*. I unsuccessfully attempted to insert entries for *Mrs. Dalloway*, *Never Let Me Go*, and *The Constant Gardener*, but my editors caught on pretty quickly to this good-hearted mutiny. We bibliophiles have our beloved titles, no doubt, the books we think everyone else should adore as much as we do, and our go-to responses when asked to name which tomes we'd bring to a desert island. But still another pleasure of reading is the giddiness that stems from knowing that there are so many other books waiting to be devoured and explored.

Readers talk about cherished characters being as well-known as old friends. Such a statement would seem trite if it didn't feel so unassailably true. Yet we age even as they stay the same, and our relationship to Tom Sawyer or Jo March differs depending on whether we encounter them when we are children or as adults. Therein lies another one of reading's profound joys—how much a book appears to alter upon each rereading. Our books change with us.

It's our hope that the 100 books that make up *The Great American Read* encourage you to revisit old favorites and find new ones, to engage with challenging texts and hone your powers of empathy, to help raise readers and reach reluctant ones, to swap stories and share books with friends and family.

I wish you happy reading!

THE BOOKS

PRIDE & PREJUDICE.

CHAPTER I.

It is a truth universally acknowledged, that a single man in possession of a good fortune, must be in want of a wife.

However little known the feelings or views of such a man may be on his first entering a neighbourhood, this truth is so well fixed in the minds of the surrounding families, that he is considered as the rightful property of some one or other of their daughters.

"My dear Mr. Bennet," said his lady to him one day, "have you

VOL. I.   B   heard

ABOVE: Page 1 of the first edition of *Pride and Prejudice*, by Jane Austen. It begins with "It is a truth universally acknowledged . . . ," one of the most famous first lines in literature.

Once Upon a Time

THE BEST FIRST LINES IN LITERATURE

YOU CAN'T JUDGE A BOOK by its cover, but you can absolutely judge it by its first line.

A great first line grabs you by the shirt and doesn't let go. In some cases, a first line sets up the whole novel, and offers us exactly what we need to know in terms of tone, location, and the plot to come.

In other instances, the first line shows us the vast new world of emotions, characters, and actions we're about to explore.

Either way, the most extraordinary first lines compel us to keep reading.

Far out in the uncharted backwaters of the unfashionable end of the Western Spiral arm of the Galaxy lies a small unregarded yellow sun.
—Douglas Adams, *The Hitchhiker's Guide to the Galaxy*

It is a truth universally acknowledged, that a single man in possession of a good fortune, must be in want of a wife.
—Jane Austen, *Pride and Prejudice*

Our hero was not one of those Dominican cats everybody's always going on about—he wasn't no home-run hitter or a fly bachatero, not a playboy with a million hots on his jock.
—Junot Díaz, *The Brief Wondrous Life of Oscar Wao*

I am an invisible man.
—Ralph Ellison, *Invisible Man*

Many years later, as he faced the firing squad, Colonel Aureliano Buendía was to remember that distant afternoon when his father took him to discover ice.
—Gabriel García Márquez, *One Hundred Years of Solitude*

Ships at a distance have every man's wish on board.
—Zora Neale Hurston, *Their Eyes Were Watching God*

Last night I dreamt I went to Manderley again.
—Daphne du Maurier, *Rebecca*

Call me Ishmael.
—Herman Melville, *Moby-Dick*

124 was spiteful. Full of a baby's venom.
—Toni Morrison, *Beloved*

It was a bright cold day in April, and the clocks were striking thirteen.
—George Orwell, *Nineteen Eighty-Four*

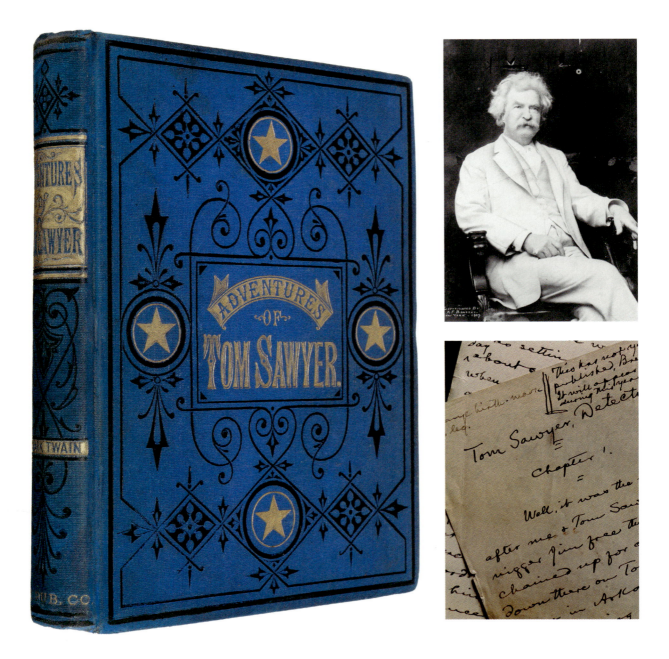

THE ADVENTURES OF TOM SAWYER

Mark Twain · 1876

Mark Twain drew on his Missouri boyhood to write *The Adventures of Tom Sawyer* (1876). Encapsulating the innocence and free-spiritedness of youth, it possesses an uncanny ability to make us nostalgic for early days that may in no way resemble our own. Tom skips school to go swimming, flirts with pretty girls, falls in love with Becky Thatcher, hangs around with Huckleberry Finn, gets into scrapes, and incurs the wrath of Aunt Polly. He's like a Norman Rockwell painting come to life, with an ever-present devilish grin and happy-go-lucky personality.

It's all fun and games until someone gets murdered. One night in a graveyard, Tom and Huck witness Injun Joe killing the town doctor. Terrible as they feel when the wrong man gets arrested and tried for the crime, they fear Injun Joe more. The truth comes out during the trial, setting off a chain of events that climaxes in a nearby cave. Tom saves the girl and gets the gold. At the end of this amusing novel, Tom convinces Huck to stick around in civilized society, at least for a while, by promising that they'll soon have a gang-initiation ceremony involving blood and a coffin.

The Adventures of Tom Sawyer represented a literary departure for Twain. He initially became famous for his travelogues and lighthearted tales, including "The Celebrated Jumping Frog of Calaveras County" (1865). But as a longer piece of fiction, *The Adventures of Tom Sawyer* enabled Twain to touch on broader themes about the way society stifles one's individuality as well as the hypocrisy of the adult world. He would bring these beliefs even more fully to the fore a few years later in *The Adventures of Huckleberry Finn* (1884). But without Tom Sawyer, there could be no Huck Finn: in *Tom Sawyer*, Twain broke ground artistically, creating what has been called "the archetypal comic novel of American childhood." Through this novel, readers were given a chance to see kids being kids; at a time when children were still expected to be seen and not heard, *The Adventures of Tom Sawyer* gave us children with personalities and drives, just like adults.

Born Samuel Langhorne Clemens in 1835 in Missouri, Mark Twain derived his pen name from a navigational term used to measure water's depth, a nod to his days piloting a steamboat up and down the Mississippi River. Twain labored too as a printer's apprentice and miner, educating himself in libraries. He married an heiress, fathered four kids, and lived next door to Harriet Beecher Stowe in Hartford, Connecticut. His house is a museum now, preserving roughly 16,000 objects, among them Twain's spectacles and bed.

Like a hapless character he might have created, Twain had terrible troubles with money. Though he earned a great living from his writing, he lost huge sums by repeatedly making foolhardy investments in newfangled technologies and start-ups. He went bankrupt by age 59. To pay back his creditors, he launched an enormously popular around-the-world lecture tour, performing in more than 120 cities from Buffalo to Cape Town.

No one performed Twain better than Twain himself. He'd stand onstage, dressed formally in a black suit. He'd speak ever so slowly and tell hilarious stories about his years on the water and on the road. Plenty of Twainiacs have tried to imitate the original in the years since he died in 1910, but none has come close to evidencing the staying power of actor Hal Holbrook. His one-man show ran through over 2,000 performances in 63 years.

The *New York Times* lauded Twain in his obituary as the "greatest humorist this country has produced," and he continues to be a touchstone for comedians and writers, among them Amy Schumer, Bret Easton Ellis, David Baldacci, and Bill Murray. He wrote quips on every topic for seemingly every occasion, but he took seriously his work of capturing American youth.

THE ALCHEMIST

Paulo Coelho · 1988

Written in Portuguese and first published by a small press in Brazil in 1988, *O Alquimista* initially sold just a few hundred copies. It went out of print fairly quickly. Undeterred and adhering to the very tenets he espouses in his work, Paulo Coelho began shopping the book to other publishers, and one took a chance on the passionate writer. Today, *The Alchemist*, as it's known in English, holds the record as the most translated book by a living author, published in some 80 languages from Xhosa to Vietnamese to Hebrew. It spent more than six years on the *New York Times* bestseller list. Devotees often call its author "maestro." Readers and critics have offered many explanations for the appeal of Coelho's novel, but perhaps none so best sums it up as the idea that Coelho "gives his readers a recipe for happiness."

Paulo Coelho wrote his story of fantasy and adventure in just two weeks. A shepherd boy in Andalusia named Santiago asks a Romani fortune-teller about a recurring dream. She interprets the dream as prophesizing that Santiago will discover treasure at the Pyramids of Giza, so he sets off to Egypt. Santiago encounters Melchizedek, the king of Salem, who explains the concept of the "Personal Legend," something that a person has always wanted to do. He meets and falls in love with Fatima, who promises to marry Santiago once he has completed his journey. Santiago then travels with an alchemist, who helps the boy discover his true self, and who helps him transform into a kind of windstorm called a simoom to escape opposing tribes. At last he begins digging at the pyramids, only to learn that the treasure he seeks is back home in Spain—and inside himself.

Technically, *The Alchemist* is a novel: it has characters, a plot, themes and motifs, and an imaginative narrative and style. However, it offers readers solace as well as a meaningful message about finding one's path, in a way that veers toward the self-help allegory. Once you discover your true destiny, the book argues, you will find that the entire universe will help you achieve your goals. It's an inspirational account of self-actualization that speaks to individual fulfillment and the oneness of creation. When you're smiling, as the saying goes, the whole world smiles with you.

By the time Coelho became one of the world's best-known authors, he was already a success of a different kind. In the 1960s, he wrote songs for Raul Seixas, sometimes called "the Father of Brazilian Rock," while participating for about two years in a sect that did drugs and practiced black magic. In time he developed his personal version of Catholicism, which includes symbolism, mysticism, and pantheism. His most famous work draws on these religious beliefs and shares lessons learned over a lifetime of spiritual study to help readers embark on their journeys of transcendence and devotion.

Coelho was born in 1947 in Rio de Janeiro. Along with songwriting, he worked as a journalist, theater director, and actor. In 1986, he walked the nearly 500-mile-long road to Santiago de Compostela, an ancient route through Spain to the shrine of the apostle Saint James the Great; this devotional pilgrimage changed his life. He published a novel based on his experiences, *The Pilgrimage*, a year before *The Alchemist*. Coelho continues to write and uses social media to communicate directly with his readers.

The book continues to resonate with fans young and old, famous and ordinary, bibliophiles and reluctant readers alike. When Devon Kennard, a linebacker for the New York Giants, decided to run a book club on his Instagram account, he selected *The Alchemist* and Harper Lee's *To Kill a Mockingbird* (1960). He sent signed memorabilia to people who asked especially insightful questions. Actor Will Smith has called the book "metaphysical, esoteric nonsense," but considers it to be one of his favorite books, in part because it espouses the idea that "we are who we choose to be."

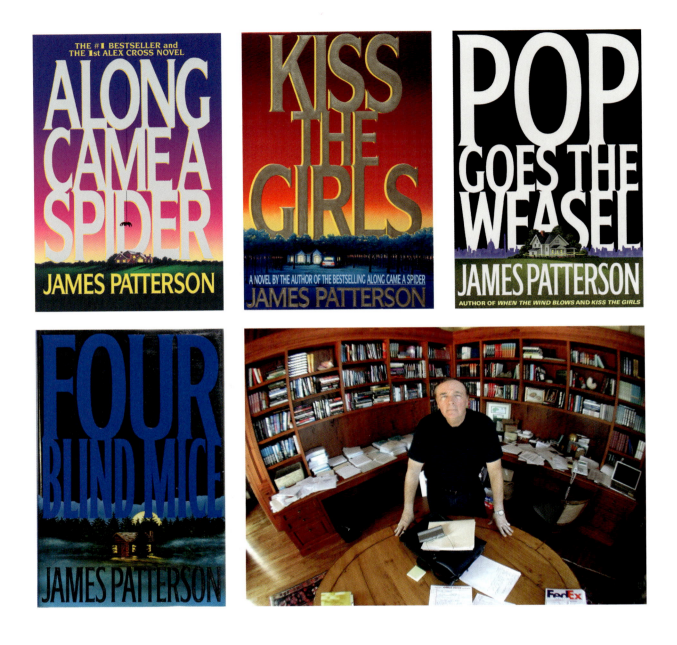

CLOCKWISE FROM TOP LEFT: Book covers from the Alex Cross mysteries: *Along Came a Spider*, *Kiss the Girls*, *Pop Goes the Weasel*, and *Four Blind Mice*, published by Hachette. | Author James Patterson at his home office in 2006. Born in Newburgh, New York, in 1947, Patterson graduated from Manhattan College and has had more than 50 *New York Times* bestsellers, a world record.

ALEX CROSS MYSTERIES

James Patterson · 1993–present

This *Publishers Weekly* headline from a 2016 article sums up the phenomenon that is James Patterson: "It Takes 16 People Working Full Time to Publish All of James Patterson's Books." The man averages nine hardcovers per year, along with children's books, YA, and middle-grade fiction. His publisher had to hire more people simply to keep up with editing, marketing, design, and publicity, as well as media and entertainment partnerships and the author's philanthropy. Such prolificacy is even more astonishing given that Patterson has had more than 50 *New York Times* bestsellers, a world record. So he doesn't just write fast, he writes well.

Patterson's first novel, *The Thomas Berryman Number*, was rejected 31 times before being published in 1976; it went on to win the Edgar Award for Best First Novel. But *Along Came a Spider* (1993), the first to feature Alex Cross, an African American homicide detective in Washington, DC, was his breakout book. Since then, Cross has appeared in more than 20 other thrillers and crime novels. Sales of the series approach 90 million.

An intelligent, rational hero, Alex Cross earned a PhD in psychology from Johns Hopkins, with a specialty in forensic and abnormal psychology. Over the course of the series, Cross leaves the DC Metropolitan Police Department (MPDC) to work as an agent for the FBI, then returns to private practice as a psychologist. In the most recent books, he serves as a consultant to MPDC's Major Case Squad. He struggles to balance his commitment to solving crime with his family obligations, including his three children and various love interests, some of whom are killed as a result of their relationship with Cross. His first wife died in a drive-by shooting before the action of *Along Came a Spider*, but later he meets and marries a fellow detective, Bree Stone.

The Cross mysteries share several characteristics: They drop readers straight into the action, with virtually no backstory or lengthy descriptions. They force Cross to confront a villain, or multiple villains, in a fast-moving plot. As a profiler, Cross specializes in particularly twisted individuals, and the novels can be graphic in their depictions of violence. He hunts serial rapists, hired assassins, corrupt officers of the law, members of the mafia, human traffickers. With short sentences, short paragraphs, and short chapters, these books are the very definitions of page-turners, hence Patterson's tremendous success—readers can't stop reading.

Patterson moved into the children's-book world after witnessing his son's struggles with reading, and he now writes books designed to foster a lifelong passion for literature in kids and teens. He also funds scholarships, donates to educational institutions, and runs a website for parents, teachers, and caregivers to help connect young readers to books they'll love.

Born in Newburgh, New York, in 1947, Patterson graduated from Manhattan College and entered the PhD program in literature at Vanderbilt University. Once he realized that he wouldn't be able to teach college and write at the same time, he left graduate school for New York City, where he worked in advertising until the mid-1990s and rose to CEO. These days, Patterson runs a veritable empire, employing a team of cowriters who craft manuscripts from his detailed outlines and often go through multiple rounds of revisions. "I look at it the way Henry Ford would look at it," he says when asked how he gets so much work done. Up-front and unabashed about his collaborators, Patterson continues to look for new talent with which to pair up, from a New York City doorman to a former US president—*The President Is Missing* (2018), a novel and character-driven series on Showtime about the disappearance of a US president, is a joint effort with co-author Bill Clinton. Nevertheless, Patterson writes 365 days a year. He told *Vanity Fair* that he wants his obituary to read, "He was slowing down at 101, and had only finished four novels that year."

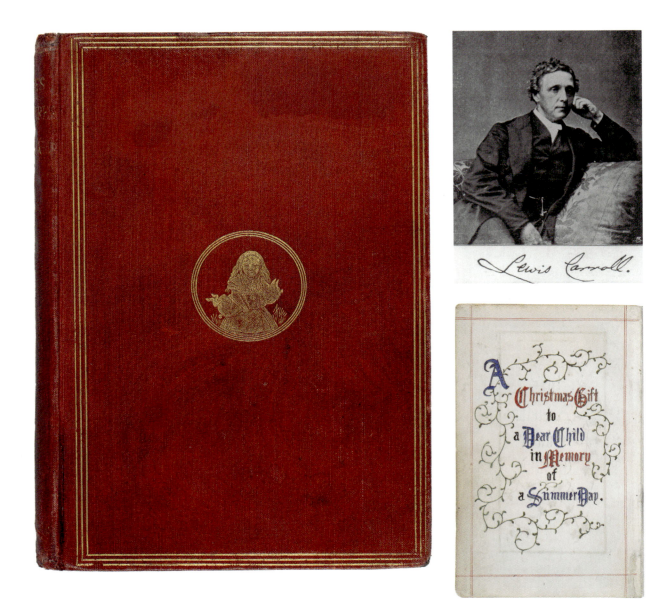

ALICE'S ADVENTURES IN WONDERLAND

Lewis Carroll · 1865

Going down the rabbit hole with Alice has been a childhood rite of passage for more than 150 years. *Alice's Adventures in Wonderland* (1865) encapsulates youth, a time when imagination reigns and frolicking is a full-time job. For many kids, reading Lewis Carroll's fantastical, nonsensical tale of grinning cats, mad hatters, and murderous queens marks the start of a lifelong love of literature. But adults can appreciate the absurdities and paradoxes at play on another level, as well.

The story opens with young Alice casting about for something, anything, to do as her big sister reads. She notices a white rabbit rush past, consulting his pocket watch and muttering about being late. A curious child who delights in good manners, she decides to follow—and enters an illogical world that challenges her profound love of order and her sense of self.

Everywhere she turns, Alice's notions about the way things work are upended. She holds a baby only to witness its transformation into a pig. She cries so much, she almost drowns in her own tears. She meets a cat who can appear and disappear; tastes a drink that makes her small, then eats a cake that makes her big; and plays croquet with flapping flamingos and squirming hedgehogs. She attends a tea party in which she's pelted with unanswerable riddles and later learns about "the different branches of Arithmetic—Ambition, Distraction, Uglification, and Derision." Eventually sentenced to a beheading, Alice wakes up and discovers she's been dreaming.

Although Lewis Carroll denied that there was a real-life analogue to his beloved protagonist, he never denied the story's origins: Rowing to a picnic one summery day with a group of neighbor children, his young companions begged to be entertained. Charles Lutwidge Dodgson, as he was known in real life, obliged with a twisty yarn about an inquisitive girl named Alice.

Dodgson was born in 1832 in Daresbury, England, to a family of clerics in the Anglican church. He followed in his father's footsteps to Oxford University's Christ Church, but focused instead on mathematics. After graduating, he was offered a teaching position at the college, where he remained for the next 26 years. By all accounts an awkward, shy man, Dodgson found comfort in his numerous friendships with children, forging bonds with them he was unable to create with grown-ups. He loved to take their photographs—at the time a painstaking process that demanded stillness of its subjects, so he would regale his sitters with elaborate fictions. When he met the Liddell family in 1856, Dodgson spent time with all four kids but grew particularly close to the three daughters. It was the middle girl, Alice, who requested a story on the boat that day.

So taken was she with the tale, Alice Liddell asked Dodgson to write it down. He obliged, and the manuscript made its way to a publisher in 1865. Critics were initially more impressed with the novel's illustrations by John Tenniel than its text. Nevertheless, Carroll convinced his publisher to let him write a sequel; *Through the Looking-Glass and What Alice Found There* appeared in 1871.

Both books became wildly popular. They continue to inspire adaptations, among them cartoons, television shows, musicals, anime, graphic novels, and a 1967 song about hallucinogens by Jefferson Airplane. Writers as diverse as Vladimir Nabokov and Franz Kafka also owe a debt to Carroll. Beneath the whimsy and the wit, the message of *Alice's Adventures in Wonderland* can seem a bit bleak: Try as we might, we can't command a chaotic world. Logic is fallible, authority arbitrary. Rules change. Nevertheless, waiting on every page are opportunities for us to rediscover magic and dreams we thought lost.

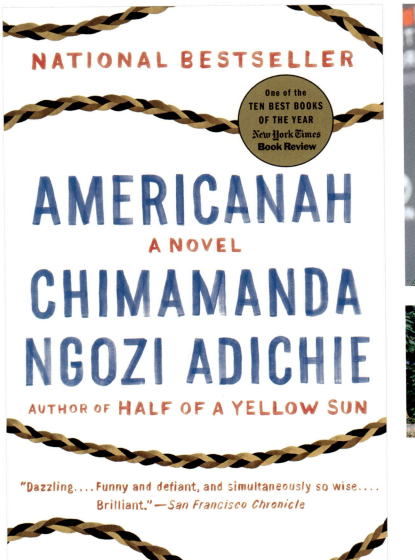

NATIONAL BESTSELLER

One of the TEN BEST BOOKS OF THE YEAR New York Times Book Review

AMERICANAH

A NOVEL

CHIMAMANDA NGOZI ADICHIE

AUTHOR OF HALF OF A YELLOW SUN

"Dazzling....Funny and defiant, and simultaneously so wise.... Brilliant."—San Francisco Chronicle

CLOCKWISE FROM LEFT: Hardcover edition of *Americanah*, published in 2013 by Penguin Random House. | Portrait of author Chimamanda Ngozi Adichie, who grew up in Nsukka, Nigeria, in a house once inhabited by another great African writer, Chinua Achebe. Her third and most well-known novel, *Americanah*, explores perceptions of race in the United States, Britain, and Nigeria. | Adichie studied at the University of Nigeria, Nsukka, pictured here, before continuing her studies in the United States. Her father was a professor there, and her mother was the first female registrar.

AMERICANAH

Chimamanda Ngozi Adichie · 2013

n one of the most watched TED talks of all time, Chimamanda Ngozi Adichie cautions against the "danger of the single story." Using examples from her childhood in Nigeria and her education in the United States, she demonstrates the insidiousness of the idea that entire cultures, or even single individuals, can be summed up in one narrative—that all of Africa is poor and troubled, for example, or that Adichie wouldn't know English because she grew up in Nigeria. Single stories lead to stereotypes. Instead, she argues, we must recognize a multiplicity of stories about one another, about other countries, and about the world; doing so promotes diversity and understanding.

The Igbo daughter of a professor of statistics and the first female registrar at the University of Nigeria, Adichie was born in 1977 in Enugu and grew up in Nsukka, in a house once inhabited by another great African writer, Chinua Achebe. She earned a scholarship to attend college in the United States at age 19, eventually receiving undergraduate and graduate degrees in literature, creative writing, and African studies from Eastern Connecticut, Johns Hopkins, and Yale, respectively. In 2010, she was named to the *New Yorker*'s prestigious "20 Under 40" list, which recognizes young writers of promise.

Adichie's third and most well-known novel, *Americanah* (2013) explores perceptions of race in the United States, Britain, and Nigeria. Ifemelu and Obinze develop a relationship as students in Lagos. Looking to escape Nigeria's military dictatorship, Ifemelu leaves for the United States. Obinze, unable to secure a US visa, goes to London but is eventually deported. Back in Nigeria, he grows wealthy through real-estate deals and marries a beautiful but conventional woman. Ifemelu, meanwhile, has become a prominent blogger about race in America, and has two long-term relationships with American men, both of which end poorly. Eventually, Ifemelu returns to Nigeria, and she and Obinze try to navigate the gulf of time and experience that has emerged between them.

Nigerians use the term *Americanah* to describe those who've fallen under the spell of American culture or who pretend to be Americanized. Arriving in the United States, Adichie realized the extent to which race is a construct, a lesson her characters learn too as they navigate being black outside of their homeland. Still, for all its serious treatment of serious themes, the novel is shot through with moments of humor, and at its core, it's a story about the mad, glorious thrill of first love.

In 2017, *Americanah* was selected as the inaugural text for One Book, One New York, in which the entire city was encouraged to read the novel, in effect constituting the world's biggest book club. The novel also won the National Book Critics Circle Award. A film adaptation, starring David Oyelowo and Lupita Nyong'o, is in development.

A year after *Americanah*, Adichie published *We Should All Be Feminists* (2014), a book-length essay based on another well-regarded talk. In this short work of nonfiction, she offers an updated, inclusive definition of feminism, arguing that the problems of gender are everybody's problems. The message is being heard: Beyoncé sampled lines in her 2013 song "***Flawless," and the government of Sweden mandated that every 16-year-old high-school student receive a copy to foster discussions about gender equality. In 2017, she published *Dear Ijeawele, or A Feminist Manifesto in Fifteen Suggestions*, written as a letter in response to a friend who wanted advice about raising a feminist after giving birth to a daughter. With wryness and warmth, Adichie's suggestions range from avoiding the exultation of marriage as an accomplishment to warning against promoting likability above all else to encouraging a passion for books. In her fiction and nonfiction, Adichie seeks to further gender equality and espouse human dignity, with the understanding that every experience is unique.

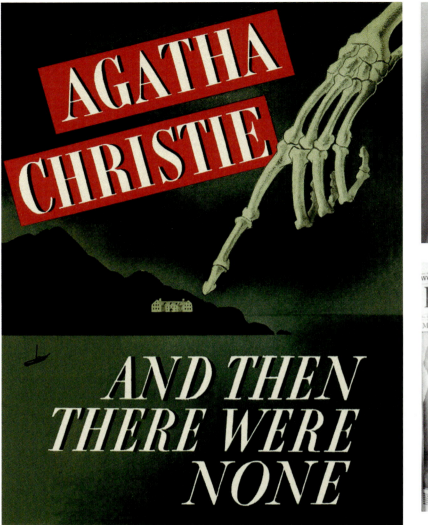

AND THEN THERE WERE NONE

Agatha Christie · 1939

One of the bestselling mysteries of all time, *And Then There Were None* (1939) begins with the arrival of eight strangers on a small island off the coast of England. Each has been invited in an extremely personal way calibrated to fit to their circumstances, with some coming to work and others to socialize. A framed copy of the nursery rhyme "Ten Little Indians" hangs in each guest room. That night, as everyone gets to know one another, a recording starts playing, detailing the ways in which each visitor has been involved in a murder. While some protest their innocence, others reveal their complicity right away. Regardless, none will escape a final reckoning.

Born in 1890 in England, Agatha Mary Clarissa Miller had little formal education until her teens, when she was sent to finishing school. Her childhood no doubt fueled her imagination, raised as she was to believe that her mother was psychic. Her first marriage, to Archie Christie, ended unhappily in 1928, but a second marriage to Sir Max Mallowan was cheerier and lasted until Christie's death in 1976. Christie traveled extensively throughout her life, drawing on her visits to places like Cairo and Istanbul in her fiction; she also developed a love of surfing in Hawaii and South Africa.

In 1926—shortly after the publication of her sixth novel, *The Murder of Roger Ackroyd*—while still married to Archie, Christie disappeared. Fifteen thousand volunteers turned out to help search, and the story made the front page of the *New York Times*. She was discovered, using the last name of Archie's mistress, at an English spa hotel, with no memory of how she'd arrived. The enormous popularity of *Gone Girl*, about another married woman who disappears, led to speculation that the strange case of Christie served as the basis of the 2012 novel. Despite rumors of amnesia, depression, and a nefarious plot to frame her cheating husband, Christie never spoke publicly of those lost days.

She just kept writing. In addition to stand-alone mysteries such as *And Then There Were None*, Christie wrote a beloved series of novels featuring Hercule Poirot, a genteel Belgian detective who rivals Sherlock Holmes in criminal deduction, as well as others starring the elderly amateur sleuth Jane Marple and husband-and-wife team Tommy and Tuppence. Her literary output astounds—some 65 detective novels, plus plays, nonfiction books, short stories, and romances, over the course of her career. She liked to think up plots while soaking in the tub. Her novels have been turned into radio plays, miniseries, feature-length films, and video games. All told, she has sold some two billion copies, earning Christie a designation in the *Guinness Book of World Records* as the bestselling fiction writer of all time.

Taking as its central concerns guilt and justice, *And Then There Were None* drives readers to consider whether punishment ever truly fits the crime. The eight guests, butler, and maid really have done some awful deeds, and the extent to which they feel remorse is revealed as they're picked off, one by one, according to the nursery rhyme: one man sips a poisoned drink ("One choked his little self and then there were nine"), someone else is given a lethal injection while sleeping ("One overslept himself and then there were eight"), and so on. The book was originally titled *Ten Little Niggers*, as the rhyme was then known in Britain, but was retitled by sensitive editors.

In addition to being deeply creepy, as the guests realize the murderer must be a member of their group, *And Then There Were None* pushes the boundaries of the mystery novel as a genre: no detective arrives on the scene, so readers are thrust into the same situation as the characters, with no expert to rely on and nothing but their own wits to lead them to the book's shocking solution.

Talk the Talk

IMPORTANT LITERARY TERMS

LITERARY TERMS give us a way of talking consistently and coherently about novels, plays, poems, short stories, and other written works. Using this vocabulary, we can make connections and uncover patterns within a text itself as well as across multiple texts.

ALLEGORY: A type of writing in which the characters and setting stand in for something else, such as abstract concepts or social institutions. Allegories tend to make their references very clear and are typically more concerned with making political, religious, or philosophical points than with providing realistic depictions of people and actions.

ALLUSION: A figure of speech that makes reference, either directly or indirectly, to another work, event, myth, person, or so on. An allusion suggests similarities between the main subject and what's being alluded to.

BILDUNGSROMAN: A work, usually a novel, that portrays the coming-of-age of its protagonist. A bildungsroman tends to follow the protagonist from childhood through young adulthood, with a focus on his or her psychological, moral, or spiritual development.

CANON: The body of music, art, literature, and other significant creative endeavors that scholars point to as the most influential in the development of a culture. In recent years, the Western canon has expanded to include works of art by previously underrepresented populations.

CLIMAX: The most intense or exciting part, or culmination, of a literary work. Generally, the climax marks a point of no return, in which the characters, plot, or setting have been irrevocably changed.

DICTION: The word choice or rhetorical style used by the author—or by the characters, whose diction may be entirely different from that of the narrator.

FIGURATIVE LANGUAGE: Words and phrases used in a nonliteral sense to achieve a particular effect. Literary devices such as metaphor, simile, hyperbole, understatement, and pun are all examples of figurative language.

FOIL: A character who stands in sharp contrast to another character, usually the protagonist. The foil helps underscore or highlight some aspect of the protagonist, often a particular characteristic or personality trait.

FORESHADOWING: The literary technique of hinting at or implying future events in the plot. Foreshadowing can be accomplished in a variety of ways, including through description, actions, and dialogue.

GENRE: A type of literary work. Romance, mysteries, Westerns, horror, and thrillers are all examples of literary genres, each with its own set of concerns and conventions. Great writers often expand the boundaries of the genres they work within.

IMAGERY: Figurative language that appeals in some way to our senses. Imagery frequently signifies an important idea, action, or motivation in the text.

IN MEDIA RES: Latin for "in the middle of things." This term is used to describe a literary work that begins in the middle of the story, often at a key moment in the action or plot.

IRONY: A strong contrast between surface significance (of a word or phrase, or of an action or situation) and underlying or "real" significance. In everyday speech, people often use the words *irony* or *ironic* to refer to mere coincidences or unexpected and undesired outcomes, but in literary analysis *irony* tends to be reserved for incongruities that reveal important ideas or perspectives.

NARRATOR: The person who tells the story. Sometimes the narrator is the main character of the literary work, often giving us "first person point of view." Often, however, the narrator is not part of the story, nor is the narrator the same as the author; instead, the narrator may be the voice the author assumes in order to convey the story, and this voice may or may not share characteristics with the author as an individual.

PLOT: The action or events of the story. The plot is everything that happens, and can usually be described as having a beginning, a middle, and an end.

PROTAGONIST: The main character or hero of a story. Sometimes the protagonist is also the narrator, or the person telling the story. While most novels have only one protagonist, some focus on two or more characters equally.

SATIRE: A literary genre that seeks to ridicule or expose the folly of a particular aspect of society, a government, or an institution. Satires often employ irony.

SYMBOL: An element, such as a physical object or location or phenomenon, that has a meaning beyond its literal significance. Some elements are understood as symbols only by readers, while others may be symbolic to characters as well. Allegory is symbolism taken to an extreme.

THEME: An important idea or value expressed in a literary work. A novel's themes are conveyed by a variety of features, including the plot, direct or indirect remarks by the narrator, and symbolism.

TONE: The attitude a character, narrator, or writer takes. Tone is conveyed through diction, dialogue, rhetorical style, figurative language, and description.

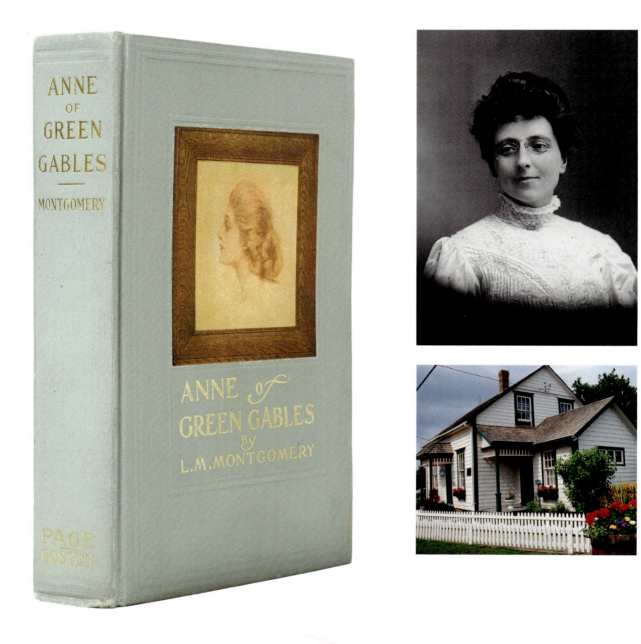

ANNE OF GREEN GABLES

L. M. Montgomery · 1908

Like so many memorable novels, *Anne of Green Gables* (1908) presents a seemingly simple scenario: In this case, what if a kindhearted couple requested a boy from the orphanage but got sent a girl instead? And what if this girl were spirited and spunky, with big dreams and a huge heart? Exploring answers to these questions required a novel and then some—a series of 11 books, as a matter of fact.

After a childhood spent shuttling around foster homes and orphanages, Anne Shirley is sent to live with Matthew and Marilla Cuthbert, a brother and sister. Getting on in years, the Cuthberts need someone young and spry to help run Green Gables, a stately house and farm in the fictional town of Avonlea, on Canada's Prince Edward Island. A skinny chatterbox with bright-red hair, Anne at first irritates Marilla but charms Matthew, so she stays. She goes to school and makes friends with whom she has silly adventures. Her imagination and bold spirit sometimes get her in trouble, but these qualities also enable her to find happiness. Though she fantasizes about being a writer, she earns a teaching degree, and eventually must decide between pursuing her ambitions and helping her family.

In subsequent books, Anne grows up, becomes a teacher, founds the Avonlea Village Improvement Society, gets engaged to her childhood best friend, transforms into a wife, mother, and (eventually) grandmother, and meets lots of new people. The series arcs over Anne's life, from her arrival at the Cuthberts' at age 11 to her late 70s. As she gets older, the themes get more intense, and the books mature along with their plucky protagonist.

Born on Prince Edward Island in 1874, Lucy Maud Montgomery was raised by her maternal grandparents. Her mother died when Lucy was an infant, and her father, heartbroken and grief-stricken, left his daughter to be raised by his wife's parents. It was a lonely childhood, and she, like Anne, coped by dwelling in her imagination. She published her first poem in 1890, then went on to write 20 novels and over 500 short stories before she died in 1942. Many interpret Montgomery's final piece of writing, found on her bedside table, as a suicide note; in the document she asks for God's forgiveness, and describes a feeling of losing her mind.

Montgomery cut out a photo of a beautiful woman and hung it on her wall as inspiration for her romantic, dreamy character Anne Shirley. The author was unaware that the woman in question was Evelyn Nesbit, a gorgeous chorus girl who gained notoriety after her rich husband murdered the man who raped her years before, the famous architect Stanford White. In the books, Anne looks nothing like the voluptuous model, a testament to Montgomery's imagination and romantic spirit.

So popular are the novels in Japan that the city of Hokkaido boasts a precise replica of Green Gables. Fans know her as *Akage no An* (literally "Red-Haired Anne"); superfans join the Buttercups, the country's largest and oldest fan club, and make pilgrimages to Prince Edward Island. *Anne of Green Gables* was published in Japan in 1952, and many people attribute Anne's popularity to the changes taking place in the country at the time: World War II not only left a lot of orphans, but fundamentally altered the society's concept of femininity.

Mark Twain called Anne "the dearest and most moving and delightful child since the immortal Alice." Even as Anne shows great spirit in the face of hardship, and even as she serves as a kind of protofeminist, willing to ask questions and probe conventions, she's really fun, the kind of girl who would have been a hit at a slumber party or perfect to take on a road trip, someone you'd be glad to call a bosom friend.

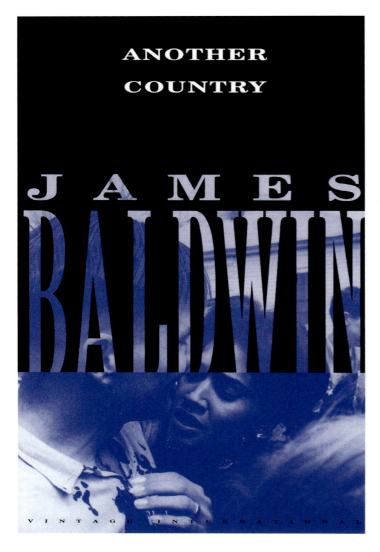

ANOTHER COUNTRY

James Baldwin · 1962

You were born where you were born and faced the future that you faced because you were black and for no other reason. . . . You were born into a society which spelled out with brutal clarity and in as many ways as possible that you were a worthless human being."

These stirring, still-relevant words were published in 1962. Back then James Baldwin sought to offer his nephew some guidance about the deeply prejudiced American society in which he lived, and his work continues to rouse and to motivate those who read it.

Born in New York City in 1924, James Baldwin fell in love with books as a child, when he would roam libraries rather than risk being abused at home by his stepfather. He was encouraged in his literary efforts by Countee Cullen, a writer who gained fame during the Harlem Renaissance; another early mentor was Richard Wright, whose incendiary *Native Son* (1940) broadened Baldwin's sense of the possibilities of African American literature. Disgusted by the racism he witnessed on a daily basis, and worried about its effect on his writing, in 1948 Baldwin left New York for Paris, an environment he thought might be more tolerant of his race and sexuality. He had just $40 to his name. With Wright's help he began publishing, and would live in France off and on for most of his life.

By the time Baldwin started working on *Another Country* in earnest, he had already published two novels, *Go Tell It on the Mountain* (1953) and *Giovanni's Room* (1956), and two books of essays, *Notes of a Native Son* (1955) and *Nobody Knows My Name: More Notes of a Native Son* (1961). He was close friends with key members of, and very involved in, the civil rights movement. (The award-winning 2016 documentary *I Am Not Your Negro*, narrated by Samuel L. Jackson, is based on Baldwin's relationships with three

pillars of the movement: Martin Luther King Jr., Medgar Evers, and Malcolm X.) Still, *Another Country* almost wasn't published. The novel took Baldwin more than a decade to write, and he lugged the manuscript on his travels around the world. He completed it at a friend's apartment in Istanbul in 1961; published the following year, it became a bestseller.

Another Country (1962) explores the interplay of romantic love, sexuality, race, and friendship among a loosely connected group of men and women in 1950s-era Greenwich Village. The suicide of Rufus Scott, a black jazz musician in a destructive relationship with a white woman from the South, brings together Ida, Rufus's sister; Vivaldo, his bisexual friend; Eric, an actor recently returned from France and the first man with whom Rufus had sex; and others who struggle to determine what drove Rufus to his death. While the characters sometimes seem to stand for segments of society—the white liberal, the pansexual, the tormented black man—Baldwin gave his characters experiences and traits that were then unusual in literature, including homosexuality and bisexuality. And the brotherly and passionate love that links them rings true.

In her eulogy for Baldwin upon his death in 1987, Toni Morrison said, "You gave us ourselves to think about, to cherish." Throughout his career, Baldwin sought to record the most difficult truths about racial inequality as he witnessed and felt them, while trying to help readers find their way back to one another, perhaps learning to even embrace those who espouse hate. This attitude pours off the pages of *Another Country*. He never stopped believing in the country that forged him; he concluded the aforementioned letter, published in the *Progressive* in the same year as *Another Country*, with an unsentimental appeal to patriotism: "We can make America what America must become."

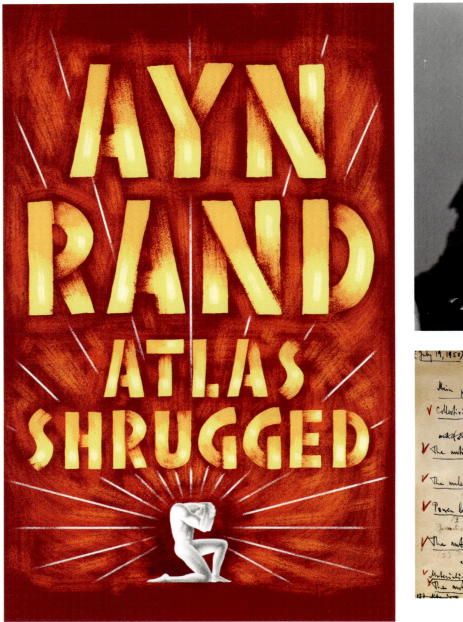

ATLAS SHRUGGED

Ayn Rand · 1957

As a work of fiction, *Atlas Shrugged* (1957) is a sci-fi fantasy about a collectivist society in a dystopian United States gone wrong. As a work of ideas, Ayn Rand's fourth novel argues for the importance of the individual over the group, the need for unregulated economics, and the benefits of selfishness.

Rand's hatred of collectivism began early: her father's pharmacy was appropriated by Lenin's Bolsheviks after the 1917 October Revolution, an act that sent the family into poverty, despair, and exile to Crimea. Alisa Zinov'yevna Rosenbaum was born in Saint Petersburg, Russia, in 1905. She started writing at a young age, and read deeply in the classics as well as the Russian and Western literary canon. Rand immigrated to the United States in 1926, landing in Hollywood with dreams of becoming a screenwriter; she served as an extra on a Cecil B. DeMille film and worked in the costume department for RKO Studios.

In some ways, plot and character in *Atlas Shrugged* are secondary to the novel's exposition of Objectivism, the ideology Rand created. John Galt's impassioned monologue in the novel summarizes its central tenets—its 50-odd pages proved so difficult that it took Rand two years just to write that section. According to Objectivists, individuals should pursue "rational self-interest," or their individual happiness. Laissez-faire capitalism offers the best economic opportunity for people to do so. Government intervention impedes the individual, so governments should be as hands-off as possible. For these and other reasons, the philosophy has been embraced by American libertarians and conservatives over the past several decades.

Atlas Shrugged opens with a society in disarray. When Dagny Taggart's railroad fails, she founds her own line. She and her lover discover a special motor, and she sets off to locate the inventor. Meanwhile, industrialists keep vanishing, offering Dagny another mystery to solve. The government moves to acquire all patents and further restrict the economy, creating more chaos and trouble. After a plane crash, Dagny learns that the missing industrialists have gathered under the leadership of John Galt—brilliant, handsome, and essentially the Platonic ideal of masculinity, he's also the inventor of the engine. Together, Galt and the industrialists are on a "strike of the mind." Things worsen until the economy collapses, forcing a showdown and a rebuilding.

The character of Dagny allows Rand to attack the so-called mind-body problem. In many works of philosophy and literature, the mind and the body are conceived of as separate entities, with the mind elevated and lofty, the body vulgar and gross. Even as Rand praises the power of the mind—showing what happens when creative brains go on strike and disappear—she nevertheless portrays Dagny as taking pleasure in her body's physicality and sexuality. She is smart, rational, and independent, with her two halves in alignment.

Rand stopped writing fiction after *Atlas Shrugged* to concentrate full-time on her nonfiction philosophical work. She lectured widely, accruing guru-like status and multitudes of impassioned followers. She died in 1982. A floral arrangement in the shape of a six-foot-tall dollar sign was placed next to the casket during her funeral.

As a young man, Ted Turner took over his family's advertising business and plastered "Who is John Galt?" on billboards across the south in 1967. There's something about *Atlas Shrugged* and *The Fountainhead* (1943) that particularly speaks to teenagers, and Rand is a staple of classrooms and dorm rooms alike. Remarking on her own youthful fascination with the book, journalist Lesley Stahl said, "Like the backseats of lovers' lane cars, Ayn Rand is for the young." But some adults may feel they need a Rand-esque reminder to question commonly held beliefs and to not passively accept the existing social order; others read it to try to understand how Objectivists justify the glorification of unfettered greed.

BELOVED

Toni Morrison · 1987

n Toni Morrison's *Beloved* (1987), the ghosts do more than inspire nightmares—they show up on the porch, murderous with rage, begging for love. Told through a series of flashbacks and stream-of-consciousness set pieces, the novel is a harrowing, horrifying account of America's past.

Beloved begins in 1873, when Paul D arrives at the Cincinnati home of Sethe, who lives with her eighteen-year-old daughter, Denver. Sethe hasn't seen Paul D since he helped her escape from Sweet Home, a plantation in Kentucky where, as slaves, they were subjected to vicious cruelty and degradations. As Sethe and Paul D attempt to overcome their shared traumas and form a family, an enigmatic young woman named Beloved appears, soaking wet, seemingly out of nowhere. Sethe takes her in and keeps her in the household, even as Beloved becomes increasingly destructive, because Sethe believes her to be the reincarnation of her dead daughter.

Eighteen years earlier, Sethe slit the throat of her two-year-old daughter, tried to murder her sons, and attempted to smash the infant Denver against a wall. Sweet Home's overseer and slave catchers had discovered the family living in freedom, and Sethe saw death as preferable to her and her children being forced back into slavery. Thanks to the efforts of abolitionists, she escaped prison, a return to slavery, and a death sentence, but not the contempt of her neighbors. Bartering with sexual favors, she could only afford to have "Beloved" carved on her daughter's headstone. Overwhelmed by these revelations, Paul D flees, sending Sethe and Beloved into a spiral of guilt and obsession that requires the intervention of the black community.

The book presents a world in which the unthinkably brutal realities of slavery have cracked open the boundaries between the natural and the supernatural. Morrison's lyrical prose heightens the novel's physical and psychological violence, making for a simultaneously beautiful and challenging reading experience. Its evocation of the emotional, moral, and spiritual wreckage of slavery stands as a stark reminder of the horrors that lie at the heart of American history.

Morrison dedicated her novel to "Sixty Million and more," a rough estimate of those who died as part of the slave trade. Sethe was based to some extent on Margaret Garner, a real-life woman who committed an unspeakable crime to prevent her family from being forced back into slavery in pre–Civil War Ohio. Garner was arrested for murdering her child, but the judge had trouble deciding whether to try her as a person or as property under the Fugitive Slave Law. She and her other children were re-enslaved and sent back to the South.

A single mother with two sons, Morrison would get up in the wee hours to write before going to work as an editor at Random House. She was born Chloe Anthony Wofford in 1931 in an Ohio steel town, the setting of her first novel, *The Bluest Eye* (1970). As she would later explain, she wrote the book she wanted to read—about an African American girl growing up in a prejudiced society who longs to have blue eyes—and she proudly embraces the label "black writer." The enormous commercial and critical success of *Beloved* (her fifth novel) changed her life.

When *Beloved* failed to win the National Book Award, more than 45 black writers and critics sent a letter of protest to the *New York Times*. The novel was awarded the Pulitzer Prize in 1988, and Morrison received the 1993 Nobel Prize in Literature, the first African American woman to be so honored, as well as the 2012 Presidential Medal of Freedom from Barack Obama. She continues to give voice to stories that cry out to be heard.

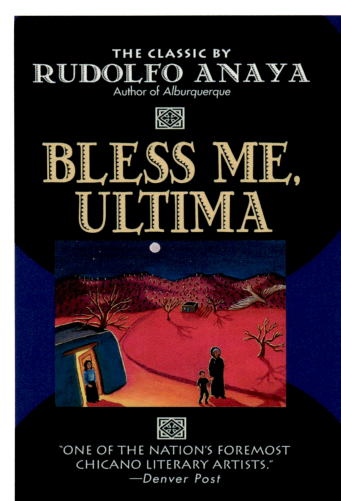

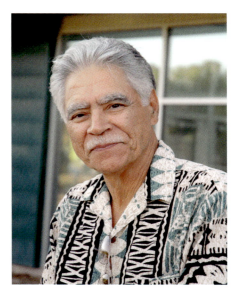

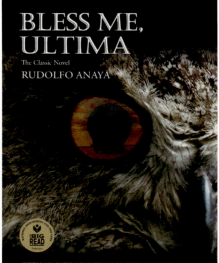

BLESS ME, ULTIMA

Rudolfo Anaya · 1972

Broadly speaking, Chicano literature centers on the experience of Mexican Americans, beginning in the years after the US annexation of large swaths of Mexico in the mid-19th century and continuing through today. Several significant works arrived on the scene in the 1960s and 1970s, an era of increased awareness of and interest in previously marginalized groups. *Bless Me, Ultima* (1972) was written during this period, and quickly became a Chicano—and American—classic.

Six-year-old Antonio Juan Márez lives with his mother, a devout Catholic from a farming family, and his father, a *vaquero* (cowboy) who cherishes his independence on the *llano* (plains) in rural New Mexico during the 1940s. His parents welcome an old *curandera* (healer) named Ultima and her pet owl into their home, and Ultima and Tony, as the young boy is known, grow very close. Ultima teaches Tony about medicinal plants and broadens his experience of the natural world. A flashback reveals that she midwifed at his birth and, as a result, believes that she alone knows his future.

Using magical realism, Anaya depicts Tony's coming-of-age as he is pulled in multiple directions: toward the Catholicism of his mother and the supernatural practices of Ultima, toward his friends at school who speak English and his friends who speak Spanish, toward his mother's hope that he'll join the priesthood and his father's desire for Tony to ride on the plains. Some of Tony's concerns are universal, such as endeavoring to escape from the weight of parental expectations, while others speak to a specifically Mexican American experience, such as reconciling Ultima's style of indigenous healing with religion imposed through colonialism.

As Tony explains, when Ultima arrives, "The magical time of childhood stood still, and the pulse of the living earth pressed its mystery into my living blood." Several events hasten Tony's maturity while deepening his sense of the unknown. He witnesses the fatal shooting of a deranged former soldier, an episode that leaves him unsure about the nature of sin. His older brothers return home from fighting in World War II, changed by what they experienced. They leave soon after, which constitutes another kind of loss for Tony. He hopes that his upcoming first communion will help address some of his concerns about retribution and penance, but when he fails to find the solace he seeks in the church, he has a vision of a golden carp, a pagan divinity. In time, Tony starts to discover that he can create an identity and belief system that blends elements from many cultures and religions. Tony thus stands as a symbol of multiculturalism, with its emphasis on "and" rather than "or."

Anaya grew up in New Mexico, where he was born in 1937, as the son of a vaquero and his wife, a farmer's daughter. He started *Bless Me, Ultima* while teaching public school in Albuquerque in the early 1960s. Initially the manuscript failed to find a home with publishers, who struggled with its blend of English and Spanish as well as its profanity, the latter a commonly cited reason for the banning of the book in schools. Anaya has since published many other novels for children and adults and has edited several anthologies featuring Latino writers.

Scholars point to *Bless Me, Ultima* as the first Chicano novel to enter the American literary canon. It's certainly one of the bestselling. Anaya and his important book cleared the way for other notable works that explore Mexican American identity, like *The House on Mango Street* (1984), by Sandra Cisneros, and *Aristotle and Dante Discover the Secrets of the Universe* (2012), by Benjamin Alire Sáenz. And in expanding the canon, we celebrate a more inclusive and representative idea of what it means to be American.

THE BOOK THIEF

Markus Zusak · 2005

n the aftermath of World War II, philosopher Theodor Adorno famously remarked that "to write poetry after Auschwitz is barbaric." And yet, in the decades since, people have continued to write and create, to turn to imagination to make sense of experiences, even the seemingly unimaginable experiences of the Holocaust. In *The Book Thief* (2005), Markus Zusak not only continues this tradition, but shows how literature can be one of our brightest lights in times of moral darkness.

Death narrates *The Book Thief*, a young-adult novel about Nazi Germany. By the end, readers feel sympathy for this character, who reveals himself to be far from the typical evil or creepy Grim Reaper–esque portrayals. In fact, as we come to discover, Death tries to be fair and gentle in his dealings. He reminds readers that mortality comes for everyone. What troubles him are not those who die but those who survive, "the leftover humans," damaged but alive.

Ten-year-old Liesel Meminger already knows quite a bit about death, growing up in Germany in the 1930s. Mourning the recent loss of her little brother, Werner, Liesel now lives with foster parents in southern Germany, where her mother felt she would be safer (her Communist father has already been taken away). She steals her first book, *The Grave Digger's Handbook: A Twelve-Step Guide to Grave-Digging Success*, from the men who bury Werner. When her foster father, Hans Hubermann, discovers that she doesn't know how to read, he begins to teach her. She steals another book during a town-wide book-burning celebration of Hitler's birthday. As the war moves closer, a young Jewish man named Max, the son of a man who saved Hans's life during World War I, arrives and is hidden in the Hubermanns' basement. Max paints over a copy of Hitler's *Mein Kampf* to create his own handwritten tome—a book within the book that proves a stunning experiment with form. Liesel continues stealing books, which she shares with Max, and she too begins to write her own.

Like Adorno, political philosopher Hannah Arendt wondered about the effects of the Holocaust on those who witnessed and participated in its events. In a series of articles for the *New Yorker* in 1963, she coined the phrase "the banality of evil" to underscore the role of ordinary people in the tragedy. Many people were simply obeying their bosses and doing their jobs, rather than acting out of sociopathy, murderousness, or rabid anti-Semitism. Some of these ideas are explored in Zusak's book. Although this novel is about the Holocaust, it isn't about concentration camps, prisoners, or perpetrators; it's about regular people caught up in a culture gone mad, and about those who were left behind once the tragedy was over.

Born in Australia in 1975, Zusak grew up in the shadow of the Holocaust, as the child of parents who emigrated from Germany and Austria in the 1950s. He began publishing books in 1999, and has released five novels to date for young-adult readers. *The Book Thief* was initially published for adult readers in Australia, but was promoted as a young-adult novel in the United States. His awards include the Children's Book Council of Australia Book of the Year Award in 2003 and the Best Young Australian Novelist of the Year Award from the *Sydney Morning Herald* in 2006. Zusak's books have been translated into over 40 languages, and *The Book Thief* (his fifth novel) remained on the *New York Times* bestseller list for 500 weeks. Geoffrey Rush and Emily Watson starred in the 2013 film adaptation.

Sensitive to his subject matter and solicitous of his impressionable readers, Zusak rewrote his novel over 200 times. He has repeatedly stated in interviews that *The Book Thief* "means everything" to him, and the novel amply demonstrates both his passionate commitment to his story and the centrality of books to our lives. Books save Liesel, books cement her relationships with other people, and books give her a lifeline in a drowning world. We need to keep writing and reading, Zusak tells us, so that we can keep living.

All Personality

THE MOST COMPELLING CHARACTERS

GREAT CHARACTERS leap off the page and straight into our lives. They become our friends, our role models, maybe even our fantasy boyfriends or girlfriends. As in a fairy tale, they appear more real to us than many of our actual acquaintances. We wonder what happens to them when we close the covers of the book, but we can take comfort in the fact that we can revisit them anytime we wish.

10 FAMOUS KIDS

1. ALASKA YOUNG: the complex, mysterious, wild, and unpredictable teen girl who captivates, challenges, and ultimately devastates the protagonist of *Looking for Alaska*, the "hurricane" to his "drizzle"

2. ALICE: the titular character of *Alice's Adventures in Wonderland*, whose elaborate, curious dream of an illogical, imaginary land reveals so much about all that is great, and all that is puzzling, about youth and adulthood

3. ANNE SHIRLEY: the plucky, dreamy orphan with a great imagination, known as *Anne of Green Gables*, whose comical misadventures give way to marriage and maturity across several books

4. HARRY POTTER: an orphan boy with a curious scar and terrific magical powers who faces his fate and saves the world from evil in the eponymous seven-book series, and probably the most famous literary child of the 21st century

5. HOLDEN CAULFIELD: an antsy, anxious teen who spends a long weekend ferreting out phonies and roaming around New York City in *The Catcher in the Rye*, and whose singular voice launched a thousand imitators

6. KATNISS EVERDEEN: the moody protagonist of *the Hunger Games* trilogy with fierce hunting and archery skills, as well as an admirable unwillingness to accept the terms of the dystopian society in which she lives

7. THE LITTLE PRINCE: the sprightly little fellow whose probing questions inspire the stranded pilot—and readers—in the book of the same name, boasting a kicky coif and jaunty scarf drawn by the novel's author

8. PIP: a complicated young man named Philip Pirrip whose coming-of-age in Charles Dickens's semiautobiographical *Great Expectations* forces him into dubious situations, challenging dilemmas, and moral quandaries

9. SCOUT FINCH: a girl who witnesses—and learns to despise—intolerance and racism, loses her innocence, and develops a strong moral sense of ethics and justice in *To Kill a Mockingbird*, and perhaps the most famous literary child of the 20th century

10. TOM SAWYER: a happy-go-lucky kid who gets into scrapes and escapades with his best mate, Huck Finn, and whose comedic adventures helped 19th-century readers redefine their conception of childhood

10 FAMOUS WOMEN

1. DAENERYS TARGARYEN: in an epic fantasy series full of fierce females, *A Song of Ice and Fire*'s Daenerys stands out for her passionate commitment to freedom and her devotion to her three dragon "children"

2. ELIZABETH BENNET: the intelligent heroine of *Pride and Prejudice*, who learns to temper her sense of pride, overcomes her own prejudices, and falls in love with the one man who is absolutely, positively right for her

3. JANE EYRE: the protagonist of the eponymous novel who overcomes one horrible circumstance after another while developing a laudable self-identity and the desire to choose a life that best suits her

4. JANIE MAE CRAWFORD: an independent woman who defies familial and societal expectations, wears overalls, and defiantly asks for—and even demands— what she wants in *Their Eyes Were Watching God*

5. MA JOAD: the steadfast matriarch, known as the "citadel of the family," who helps the Joads soldier on and survive during the Great Depression as they migrate from Oklahoma to California, in *The Grapes of Wrath*

6. JO MARCH: a thoughtful woman who, along with her sisters in *Little Women*, seems to embody various roles available to women in 19th-century America, with the literary Jo giving girls an alternative to the conventional roles of wife and mother

7. NATASHA ROSTOVA: one of three central characters in *War and Peace*, sometimes called "Tolstoy's ideal

ABOVE, TOP TO BOTTOM: "The Shower of Cards," an illustration by John Tenniel for *Alice's Adventures in Wonderland* by Lewis Carroll, brings Alice to life. | Tom Sawyer is one of the most enduring characters in American literature, pictured here on the title page illustration for the first American edition of *The Adventures of Tom Sawyer* by Mark Twain, published in 1876.

woman" for her sensitivity, grace, and emotional acuity, but who nevertheless falls into a disastrous affair

8. OFFRED: a handmaid in a dystopian society who, along with other fertile women, is forced into sexual servitude, but who manages acts of resistance large and small, including telling the story that becomes *The Handmaid's Tale*

9. REBECCA DE WINTER: despite lending the novel her name, the first Mrs. de Winter never actually appears, but figuring out what happens to her drives the second Mrs. de Winter—and the plot of this psychological thriller

10. SCARLETT O'HARA: quite possibly the most famous female character in American history, Scarlett O'Hara transforms from spoiled brat to a resilient, powerful force in *Gone with the Wind*, losing her man but saving her homestead

10 FAMOUS MEN

1. CAPTAIN AHAB: this egotistical maniac no doubt needs no introduction, but his obsession with the white whale known as *Moby Dick* in the novel of the same name gets pretty much everyone killed, except for the intrepid Ishmael, who tells the tale

2. MICHAEL CORLEONE: the youngest son of Vito, raised to "go straight," this young man takes over his crime family, becoming as hard and ruthless as his father ever was in *The Godfather*, and transforming into a villainous antihero

3. FITZWILLIAM DARCY: the yin to Elizabeth Bennet's yang in *Pride and Prejudice*, a wealthy gentleman who learns to temper his own sense of pride, overcomes his own prejudices, and falls in love with the one woman who is absolutely, positively right for him

4. DON QUIXOTE: a skinny middle-aged gentleman who becomes convinced that the chivalric romances he consumes and adores are real, leading him and his earthy squire, Sancho Panza, on a series of (mis)adventures

5. DORIAN GRAY: a handsome Englishman who enters into a terrible Faustian bargain, falls into depravity and debauchery, and watches as a portrait of his once-gorgeous visage gets as decrepit as his soul

6. ALBUS DUMBLEDORE: the wise, wonderful headmaster of Hogwarts School of Witchcraft and Wizardry, who mentors and guides Harry Potter and his friends as they grow up, learn to master their magical powers, and battle Lord Voldemort

7. JAY GATSBY: a tragicomic hero, a host of excellent parties, and a mysterious man with a nefarious obsession, whose longing for his first love, Daisy Buchanan, in *The Great Gatsby* came to epitomize the American Jazz Age

8. HEATHCLIFF: one-half of *Wuthering Heights'* great love story, as well as a man with no past who enacts cruel revenge and torture to ensure that everyone he encounters becomes as miserable and deprived as he is

9. JACK RYAN: Tom Clancy's morally upright hero, whose unflinching sense of right and wrong protects his family, the US government, and the country itself from terrible dangers in many novels like *The Hunt for Red October*

10. TYRION LANNISTER: unafraid to defy his family and unwilling to kowtow, lover of wine and women, and clever speaker of truth to power, this nobleman plays the "game of thrones" better than anyone in *A Song of Ice and Fire*

ABOVE, LEFT TO RIGHT: Mr. Darcy and Elizabeth Bennet, hero and heroine of the book, are introduced, as shown in the illustration by C. E. Brock for the 1895 edition of *Pride and Prejudice* by Jane Austen. | Don Quixote, holding a sword and a shield, descends into Montesinos Cave in this engraving by R. Chiswell, circa 1700.

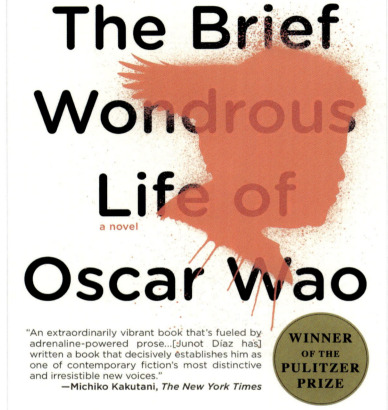

NEW YORK TIMES BESTSELLER

The Brief Wondrous Life of Oscar Wao

a novel

"An extraordinarily vibrant book that's fueled by adrenaline-powered prose...[Junot Díaz has] written a book that decisively establishes him as one of contemporary fiction's most distinctive and irresistible new voices."
—Michiko Kakutani, *The New York Times*

WINNER OF THE PULITZER PRIZE

Junot Díaz

author of *Drown*

CLOCKWISE FROM LEFT: The hardcover dust jacket for *The Brief Wondrous Life of Oscar Wao*, published in 2007. | Portrait of author Junot Díaz in New York City. | A page from one of the notebooks Díaz kept while writing *The Brief Wondrous Life of Oscar Wao*, part of a photo series about what inspires the writer, taken for the *New York Times*.

13

THE BRIEF WONDROUS LIFE OF OSCAR WAO

Junot Díaz · 2007

f there's such a thing as a literary rockstar, Junot Díaz is it. A well-regarded writer after the 1996 publication of his short-story collection *Drown*, Díaz rocketed into the stratosphere with *The Brief Wondrous Life of Oscar Wao* (2007), a wide-ranging saga about an immigrant family. The novel won major prizes, crested bestseller lists, and earned him legions of fans. "Everyone knows Junot Díaz is the man," says James Franco.

Said man was born in 1968 in the Dominican Republic, arriving in the United States at age six. He grew up in New Jersey, near a large landfill, with a strict disciplinarian father, then worked his way through Rutgers, pumping gas and working at a steel plant. At Cornell, where he earned an MFA, Díaz first began writing in the semiautobiographical voice of Yunior de Las Casas, who appears in other stories and narrates big chunks of *The Brief Wondrous Life of Oscar Wao*.

Yunior takes Oscar de León, a lonely, chunky "ghetto nerd," under his wing after Oscar spirals into a depression and twice attempts suicide. Oscar speaks Elvish, Spanish, English, street slang, and Dungeons & Dragons. He dreams of becoming the next J. R. R. Tolkien—and the first Dominican one—but fears that his interests in role-playing, comics, and sci-fi mean he'll never have a girlfriend and thus will die an unkissed virgin. He also blames his bad luck with girls on the *fukú*, a curse that followed the de León family from the Dominican Republic to their new home in the United States. In addition to Oscar and Yunior, the novel tracks Lola, Oscar's rebellious sister and Yunior's former girlfriend, as well as Oscar's extended family.

As a child, Díaz would walk for miles just to check out library books. He incorporated this voraciousness for the written word into *The Brief Wondrous Life of Oscar Wao*, which collages high and low culture, blends Spanish and English, and mixes elements of literary fiction with science fiction and fantasy. He opens the novel with two epigraphs—one from a Fantastic Four comic, one from a poem by Nobel Prize–winner Derek Walcott. Footnotes offer factual asides and explanations, especially with regard to Dominican history, but they also give Díaz a chance to play with readers' expectations. Like Oscar (and Díaz), Yunior knows pretty much everything there is to know about fantasy, and he peppers his sections with references to characters and storylines. For example, of the brutal, bloody reign of dictator Rafael Trujillo, Yunior notes, "Homeboy dominated Santo Domingo like it was his very own private Mordor."

Among the prizes won by Díaz for his debut novel were the National Book Critics Circle Award, the Dayton Literary Peace Prize in Fiction, and the Pulitzer Prize (he was only the second Latino to win that prize). *Time* magazine called it the best work of fiction published in 2007. In 2012, Diaz received a MacArthur Fellowship (also known as a "genius grant"), the same year he published another short-story collection, *This Is How You Lose Her*. Currently he teaches writing at the Massachusetts Institute of Technology.

Dangerous as it may be to too closely align creators and their creations, Díaz and his novel both come off as very real. They lack pretense; they have no interest in erudition for erudition's sake. They speak openly about the difficulties encountered by immigrants to the United States, and they speak plainly about being nerdy outcasts. They decided, consciously or not, to go their own way, rather than follow the more traditional, hypermasculine path encouraged in Dominican society. They hold themselves up as hybrids, more than the sum of their immigrant backgrounds or struggles to assimilate, able to shape-shift and do good like the most fantastic of superheroes.

CLOCKWISE FROM TOP: Cover of the first edition of *The Call of the Wild*, published in 1903. | Author Jack London, photographed in 1896. London was an intrepid traveler and adventurer, and he joined the gold rush in the late 1890s. | The Saint Bernard–collie mix on whom Buck, London's hero in *The Call of the Wild*, is based sits with his master Marshall Bond in a cabin in Dawson City, Yukon.

14

THE CALL OF THE WILD

Jack London · 1903

Suffering through a long Alaskan winter in 1897, Jack London hunkered down with John Milton's *Paradise Lost* (1667) and Charles Darwin's *On the Origin of Species* (1859); both would come to bear on *The Call of the Wild* (1903), the book that turned the impoverished adventurer from California into a household name.

John Griffith Chaney was born in San Francisco in 1876 to the wayward daughter of an aristocratic family and a traveling astrologer who abandoned his lover upon learning of her pregnancy. His mother married a Civil War veteran when Jack was an infant, and he was given that man's surname. At age nine, London left school to start earning money for his family, often through difficult, menial jobs. He toiled on the line at a cannery, stole oysters in San Francisco Bay, and worked in a laundry. He rode the rails as a tramp and went on sealing trips to the Far East. He longed to be a writer, and wrote whenever he could. In his first five years trying to get published, London received almost 700 rejections. He stabbed the notices onto a spindle, amassing a four-foot column of nos.

Like so many others, London decided to seek his fortune in the north, as part of the Klondike gold rush of the late 1890s. Although he returned home to California with nothing but scurvy to show for his efforts, he carried a wealth of knowledge that would come out in the array of works he published before his untimely death at age 40 in 1916. On his travels, he saw masters mistreating their animals as well as their fellow man, witnessed nature's tremendous power, and befriended a Saint Bernard–collie mix, on whom Buck, the canine protagonist of *The Call of the Wild*, is based.

Buck lives on a ranch in California. Part sheepdog, part Saint Bernard, he is kidnapped and sold to dog traders who beat Buck into obedience and send him north to the Klondike region of Canada. He is shocked and horrified by what he sees, including dogs killing and mauling other dogs. Now owned by two mail carriers, Buck works as a sled dog and does whatever he needs to do in order to survive. He starts to turn ferocious and wild, adhering to "the law of club and fang." In time he becomes the property of John Thornton, for whom he develops an intense affection after Thornton saves Buck's life. But eventually the pull back to nature, away from civilization, proves too strong, and Buck transforms into the leader of a pack of wolves.

The Call of the Wild was a massive success. With the publication of *White Fang* three years later, London became the highest-paid writer in the United States. These books represent a reaction to the rapid industrialization of the 19th century and an exhortation to return to nature. Once there, only those who are strong, physically fit, and mentally tough will survive, although being in touch with one's animalistic or atavistic instincts will help too. Buck represents the soul who cannot be tamed by civilization, an archetype central to American culture.

In recent years, London has become famous beyond his writing and his adventures: his Sonoma County farm, known as Beauty Ranch, stands as a model of sustainable agriculture. Borrowing methods for conservation and restoration he learned while living in Japan and Korea as a correspondent during the Russo-Japanese War, he disavowed pesticides, used green manure, and bred livestock that were suited to the climate. His love of farming dovetails with the love of wilderness he extolled in *The Call of the Wild*—nature has the power to kill, to wound, to destroy, but also to redeem and sustain us.

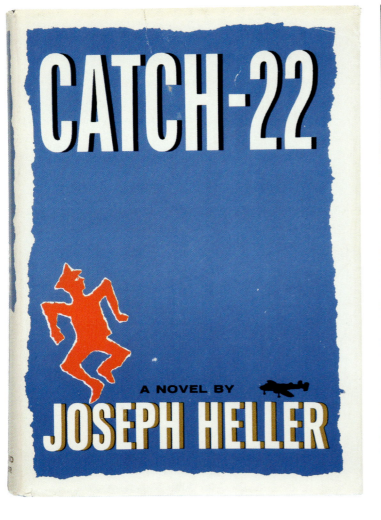

Left to right: Lt Clifford (P), Lt Chrenko (CP),
S/Sgt Rackmyer (TG), Lt Heller (BN), Pfc Zaboly
(X), S/Sgt Schroeder (RG) and S/Sgt Ryba (G)——
another 488th crew.

CLOCKWISE FROM LEFT: Cover of the first edition of *Catch-22*, published in 1961. The book's title coined the now-common idiom "catch-22." | Portrait of author Joseph Heller, photographed by Inge Morath in 1965. Heller was born in Coney Island, New York, and wrote from his experience as a bombardier during World War II. | A photo from the war diary of the 488th Bomb Squadron dated June 1944 shows Lt. Joseph Heller with this crew.

15

CATCH-22

Joseph Heller · 1961

A funny novel about war sounds like an oxymoron, or at least it did until *Catch-22* rolled onto the scene in 1961 and changed everything. With a penetrating eye and sarcastic wit, Joseph Heller radically altered how we write and talk about war.

The novel grew out of Heller's experiences as a bombardier during World War II, yet it's closely associated with later conflicts. Especially popular among young people in the 1960s, *Catch-22* seemed to embody that era's mistrust of authority, preconceived notions, and conformity. Indeed, as Heller later explained, the novel sought to figure out how a person is supposed to stay sane in an insane world.

Heller always claimed that the novel's first line appeared almost fully formed in his mind one day: "It was love at first sight. The first time he saw the chaplain, Someone fell madly in love with him." He didn't yet have the name for that "someone," but he very quickly had the plot, many of its characters, and the inimitable voice. That someone turned out to be Yossarian, and the novel centers on his experiences with an American Army Air Forces squadron on an island off the coast of Italy, near the end of World War II.

Angry that so many people are trying to murder him, Captain John Yossarian constantly tries to get out of flying bomb runs, as do his fellow soldiers. His superiors keep raising the number of runs the men must fly before being discharged, so no one ever leaves—unless they get killed. Many of his closest friends are driven insane by their wartime experiences, but Yossarian works to hold on to his humanity and his lucidity. The knowledge that everyone must die, somehow, someday, offers no comfort. The extent of Yossarian's trauma, stemming from the gory death of a fellow airman, is gradually revealed over the course of the book. It's a sad, horrific counterpoint to the absurdist, silly scenarios that constitute so much of the novel.

Bureaucracy rules Yossarian's world. The people in power refuse to listen to reason, in part because they're physically absent. The squad's major, for instance, only allows visitors to his office when he's elsewhere. The war seems to be guided by unseen forces, not by the people actually in the field. These observations were especially relevant to readers during the Vietnam War, and they continue to inform criticism of how war is waged into the 21st century, when drone strikes and other remote technologies have further stretched the chain of responsibility for violence.

Joseph Heller was born in Coney Island, Brooklyn, in 1923, to poor Jewish parents originally from Russia. Upon his return from the war, he attended New York University on the GI Bill and received a master's from Columbia University. He worked in magazine publishing, then switched to copywriting for an advertising agency, where one of his colleagues was Mary Higgins Clark, who would become a bestselling suspense author. After the massive success of *Catch-22*, Heller went on to write more novels, including a 1994 sequel to *Catch-22* called *Closing Time*, several screenplays, and two memoirs, before his death in 1999.

Not many novelists can be said to have invented a common expression. With *Catch-22* Heller not only created an enduring satire about human conflict, but he also coined an idiom describing the experience of being caught in a problem that forbids its own solution. The catch-22 that Heller's pilots face is that they can be excused only from flying missions if they are found to be insane, but requesting an evaluation of their sanity shows that they are concerned for themselves and thus must be sane. This kind of arbitrary double bind seems to permeate modern life, with its opaque bureaucracies and conflicting imperatives, and all we can do, as Heller shows us, is laugh and despair at once.

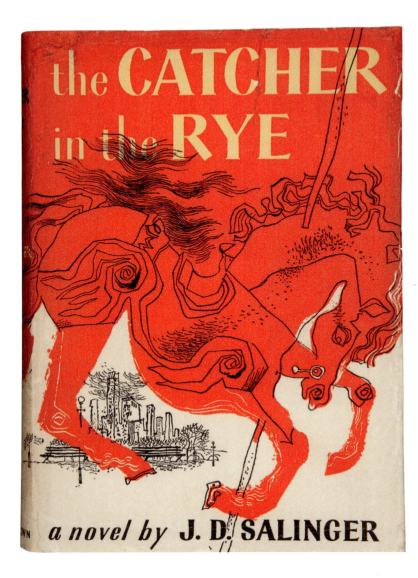

16

THE CATCHER IN THE RYE

J. D. Salinger · 1951

The Catcher in the Rye (1951) is the hub around which so many subsequent novels and movies turn: *The Outsiders* (1967), about a boy too sensitive for the world in which he lives; *Rushmore* (1998), about another young man who falls apart after getting expelled; *Less Than Zero* (1985), about wealthy kids who use drugs and sex to cope with isolation and alienation; *Turtles All the Way Down* (2017), about a teenage girl with obsessive-compulsive disorder. Indeed, when we contemplate adolescence and anxiety, it's likely Holden Caulfield who springs first to mind. In many ways, J. D. Salinger created the modern archetype of the teenager.

This debut novel focuses on 16-year-old Holden during a long weekend in New York City in the late 1940s or early 1950s. Recently expelled from Pencey Prep, Holden decides to leave school early, after a fight with his roommate. Roaming around Manhattan in a red hunting cap, he becomes mildly obsessed with finding out what happens to the ducks in Central Park during the winter, asking various people to weigh in. He has a disastrous date with a girl named Sally, tries to have sex with a prostitute, visits with his precocious kid sister and a beloved former teacher, and hangs out in some of the haunts of his youth.

In Holden's world, there are few things worse than being a "phony." He strives to be anything but. From his very first line, in which he lets readers know that he won't be offering any of the usual biographical details or "all that David Copperfield kind of crap," he speaks with a candor and forthrightness entirely his own. Even when he tells us that he's "the most terrific liar you ever saw in your life," readers believe every word he says, because of this honesty. The use of slang and profanity also heighten the novel's realism. Within two weeks of its publication, the book was a bestseller, and continues to sell around 250,000 copies a year.

The Catcher in the Rye is a very New York novel. Holden skates with Sally at the Rink at Rockefeller Center, sees a show at Radio City Music Hall, and takes his sister, Phoebe, to the American Museum of Natural History and the Central Park Zoo. The city fuels his interior monologue. Even today, visitors and locals alike continue to plan itineraries based on places Holden goes as he wanders, ruminating and reminiscing.

Jerome David Salinger was born in 1919 and grew up in Manhattan. He briefly attended New York University and Columbia, where in 1941 he wrote a story about Holden called "Slight Rebellion off Madison." A mentor urged him to put the character in a novel. Two years after *The Catcher in the Rye* catapulted him to stardom, Salinger left Manhattan for a farm in New Hampshire, where he would live out the remainder of his days as a recluse; as an obituary explained, Salinger became "famous for not wanting to be famous." He published no further novels after his first, but three collections of stories and novellas came out in the next decade: *Nine Stories* (1953), *Franny and Zooey* (1961), and *Raise High the Roof Beam, Carpenters and Seymour: An Introduction* (1963); a fourth collection, *Three Early Stories*, was published posthumously in 2014. Periodically rumors creep up about manuscripts locked in safes, but to date no further work has appeared.

Salinger once wrote, "Some of my best friends are children. In fact, all of my best friends are children." *The Catcher in the Rye* seems to see straight into the soul of everyone who feels conflicted about entering adulthood, which is to say, pretty much everyone. Picking up on the theme, Norman Mailer quipped that Salinger was "no more than the greatest mind ever to stay in prep school." Salinger's devotees would no doubt respond, "Yeah, so?"

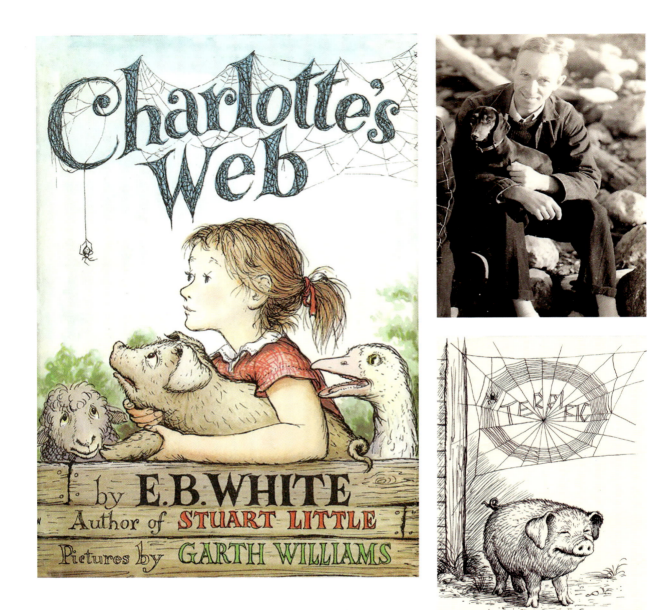

17

CHARLOTTE'S WEB

E. B. White · 1952

E. B. White thought up the central plot of *Charlotte's Web* (1952) as he walked through his barn to feed his pig. He'd purchased a farm in coastal Maine in 1933 and, as a lifelong lover of animals and nature, cherished the time he spent among the sheep, geese, chickens, pigs, and, yes, spiders who lived there. Even though he understood the usual cycle of life on a farm, White was nevertheless sad to think that an animal he'd bought to slaughter would have to die. So he began to consider alternatives. Around this time, he carefully cut down the egg sac of a spider he'd been observing in his barn and carried it in a candy box back to his Manhattan apartment, then allowed the newly born spiders to colonize his dresser. And thus the story of a special friendship between a pig and a spider was conceived.

The runt of the litter, Wilbur is initially spared on account of his smallness, thanks to the intervention of a little girl named Fern. Snubbed by other animals, he becomes friends with Charlotte, a wise spider who lives above his pigpen. When Wilbur discovers that he will be killed once he gets fat enough, Charlotte helps him develop a plan: she'll weave superlative statements about Wilbur—such as "Some Pig"—into her web. Call it arachnid marketing.

The publicity campaign is a success: Wilbur grows too popular to be butchered. However, shortly after spinning an egg sac at the county fair, Charlotte dies. Compounding Wilbur's grief, her offspring scatter, except for three who take up residence in their mother's original web near Wilbur. These three and their descendants ensure that Wilbur lives out his days in friendly company.

As in many great children's books, a vein of sadness runs throughout *Charlotte's Web*. Summer ends. Kids grow up, abandoning their parents in the process. Love is powerful but not powerful enough to overcome the forces of nature. Everything must die, no matter what. The effectiveness with which the novel delivers these hard but important truths comes from the book's humility: White never sets out to teach lessons, but rather allows readers to draw them from his simple, affecting tale.

White turned to children's fiction as a way of entertaining his niece, but he'd already been a successful writer for many years. He was born in upstate New York in 1899, edited the student newspaper while an undergraduate at Cornell University, worked in public relations and publishing, and wrote articles for the *New Yorker* for over 50 years. He even married the magazine's fiction editor, Katharine Angell. The "E. B." stood for Elwyn Brooks, but he was generally known as "Andy."

After publishing a piece about his Cornell writing teacher William Strunk Jr., White was asked to update Strunk's "Little Book" concerning grammar and composition. Strunk and White's *Elements of Style* appeared in 1959, inspiring generations of writers with such nuggets as "use the active voice" and "omit needless words." White followed his own advice; his lucid, perfectly controlled prose continues to beguile readers and has helped to make *Charlotte's Web* one of the most celebrated and bestselling children's books of all time. The novel has been adapted into multiple feature films, cartoons, a musical, and even a video game. White received a special Pulitzer Prize for his entire oeuvre in 1978 and died in his farmhouse in 1985.

Often asked whether his stories were true, White would demur: "They are imaginary tales, containing fantastic characters and events. . . . But real life is only one kind of life—there is also the life of the imagination." *Charlotte's Web* somehow seems like both—an imaginative story that becomes so much a part of ourselves as we read that it feels real.

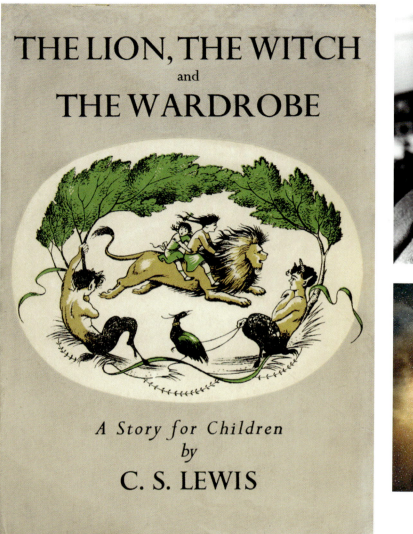

18

THE CHRONICLES OF NARNIA SERIES

C. S. Lewis · 1950–1956

Like a kaleidoscope, The Chronicles of Narnia (1950–1956) series changes color and contour, depending on how you turn it. On the one hand, the seven books of fantasy rank alongside The Lord of the Rings (1954–1955), His Dark Materials (1995–2000), and Harry Potter (1997–2007) as epic entertainment and classic children's tales. On the other hand, the books serve as primer texts for Christian apologetics, with allegories both covert and overt running throughout. Aslan may be a heroic lion of enormous proportions, for instance, or he may be an embodiment of Jesus—it's the reader's choice.

Lewis began conceiving of *The Lion, the Witch and the Wardrobe*, probably the best-known of the novels, in 1939, then picked it up in earnest in 1949. In the book, as the Blitz pummels London, the four Pevensie children are sent to live with wacky old Professor Kirke. Exploring one day, the youngest, Lucy, discovers a wardrobe through which she can enter another world, full of talking animals and mythical creatures. At first her siblings dismiss her claims about Narnia, as it's called, but eventually they make it to the strange land as well. Narnia is in the midst of a long winter, with the evil White Witch in charge. The aforementioned Aslan, gallant and beneficent, is her sworn enemy.

Six more books track the adventures of the Pevensies and explain the history of Narnia: *Prince Caspian: The Return to Narnia* (1951), *The Voyage of the Dawn Treader* (1952), *The Silver Chair* (1953), *The Horse and His Boy* (1954), *The Magician's Nephew* (1955), and *The Last Battle* (1956). Lewis wrote them in an order different from the one in which they were published, and readers disagree about whether they should be read in the order they were written, in the order they were published, or by sequence according to the plot's chronology.

Clive Staples Lewis loved mythology and animals from a young age. He was born in Ireland in 1898 and studied in England. During his tenure as a literature professor at Oxford, Lewis participated in an informal writing group called the Inklings, whose members also included his friend and fellow faculty member J. R. R. Tolkien. Referring to a draft of *The Lion, the Witch and the Wardrobe*, Tolkien noted, "It really won't do, you know." Whereas Tolkien went to great lengths to separate his staunch Catholicism from his fantasy novels, Lewis had no such compunction. His spiritual path contributed to his religious frankness: he was raised Protestant, but became an atheist as a young man. He started to return to religion after being wounded in battle during World War I, and converted back to Christianity in 1931. Most of his books, whether fiction or nonfiction, deal in some way with his religious beliefs. Lewis died in 1963.

After a successful, Emmy-nominated BBC television series that aired from 1988 to 1990, Disney produced three movies based on the books in the 2000s. *The Lion, the Witch and the Wardrobe* also remains a staple in children's live theater. But the biggest impact of Lewis's novels has been on literature itself. Of the four Pevensie siblings, the eldest daughter, Susan, stops believing in Narnia as she matures, becoming more interested in boys and clothes than talking beavers. Neil Gaiman wrote a story in 2004 called "The Problem of Susan," addressing this shift; the title has become a catchphrase for a feminist critique of the series and of fantasy as a genre. More broadly, Lev Grossman borrowed the trope of children escaping into—and rising to rule—a magical land for his Magicians trilogy (2009–2014). As he would later explain, *The Lion, the Witch and the Wardrobe* taught him how novels worked. You open a book, you fall through the covers, and you land somewhere else—only to look up and find you never really left.

Another Day, Another Dollar

WRITERS WITH DAY JOBS

DON'T QUIT YOUR DAY JOB. So goes the line we habitually utter to those who wish to earn a living through their imagination. Of course, it's the rare writer who can find super-success right away, or who can live off the proceeds of writing alone. Many writers worked a day job while writing on the side, and some kept the day job even as they began to find success by their pen. Still others found fame only posthumously, necessitating a fair amount of clock-punching to keep themselves and their families afloat.

JEAN M. AUEL: Keypunch Operator, Circuit Board Designer, Technical Writer
Throughout the 1970s, while raising five children, Jean M. Auel worked a variety of jobs at an electronics plant in Portland, Oregon, and earned an MBA from the University of Portland. She quit upon discovering that the plant wouldn't hire female managers, and turned her attention to her novel about a group of Paleolithic cavepeople. The gamble paid off, and *The Clan of the Cave Bear* (1980) set a new record for the largest advance ever paid for a debut novel.

CHARLES DICKENS: Factory Worker, Freelance Journalist, Editor
Charles Dickens was forced to work in a factory at age 12 after his father was sent to debtor's prison; this experience would haunt his novels, manifesting in children forced to grow up—and to toil—much too soon. A few years later, Dickens became a court reporter and stenographer, then started working as a freelance journalist. Eventually he founded and edited literary magazines, which would serialize many of his novels, as well as work by Wilkie Collins, Elizabeth Barrett Browning, and other contemporaries.

DIANA GABALDON: Science Professor
With a PhD in quantitative behavioral ecology, Diana Gabaldon taught scientific computation and other subjects at Arizona State University's Center for Environmental Studies, founded the journal *Science Software Quarterly*, contributed entries to the *Encyclopedia of Computers*, and wrote several scientific articles and textbooks. She also penned comic-book scripts for Disney. But she always longed to write fiction and in 1988 started writing a novel about time travel just for fun.

STEPHEN KING: High-School Teacher
After graduating from the University of Maine in 1970 with a degree in English and a teaching certificate, Stephen King could not find a job teaching, so he began working in a commercial laundry to pay the bills, writing all the while. In 1971 he was hired as an English teacher, which gave him plenty of material to work with as he began drafting *Carrie* (1974). When that novel about a telekinetic misfit who gets revenge on her tormentors became a bestseller, he devoted himself to writing full-time.

HARPER LEE: Airline Ticket Agent
The daughter of a prominent lawyer, Harper Lee grew up expecting to be a lawyer too; she even earned a place at the law school at the University of Alabama. She dropped out, however, in 1949, and moved to New York City with dreams of becoming a writer. To support herself, she worked as a ticket agent for airlines. One

Christmas, her friends got together and gave her a year's salary, enabling her to quit the job and focus on the manuscript that became *To Kill a Mockingbird*.

HERMAN MELVILLE: Customs Inspector

In 1851, Herman Melville published *Moby-Dick*; it was decidedly not a success. Nor were his subsequent novels. He launched a public lecture series in the late 1850s, in the hopes of supplementing his income, but that too failed. Thanks to the influence of his wife and her family, Melville secured a position as a customs clerk for the city of New York in 1866, a job he would hold for close to two decades. Despite his lengthy service, he never received a raise.

TONI MORRISON: Editor, Professor

Toni Morrison began working as a textbook editor at Random House in Syracuse after separating from her husband in 1964. She would wake up at 4:00 a.m. to write. A few years later, she transferred to the publisher's New York office and began acquiring and editing titles by Angela Davis, Muhammad Ali, Huey Newton, and James Baldwin, among other diverse authors; she would work at Random House for 19 years. In 1989, Morrison became a professor of creative writing and literature at Princeton University.

KURT VONNEGUT: Car Dealer

During a low point in his writing career in the 1950s, Kurt Vonnegut ran a car dealership on Cape Cod. He had been working in the public-relations department at General Electric but moved to Massachusetts to focus on writing. When business was slow, he would write or doodle on his official Saab stationery. He would draw on his days selling cars in *Breakfast of Champions* (1973), which features a Pontiac dealer as a protagonist.

ABOVE, LEFT TO RIGHT: Pulitzer Prize winner Harper Lee, photographed here in 1960, worked as an airline ticket agent to support her writing dreams. | Kurt Vonnegut used downtime during his job as a car salesman to write or doodle.

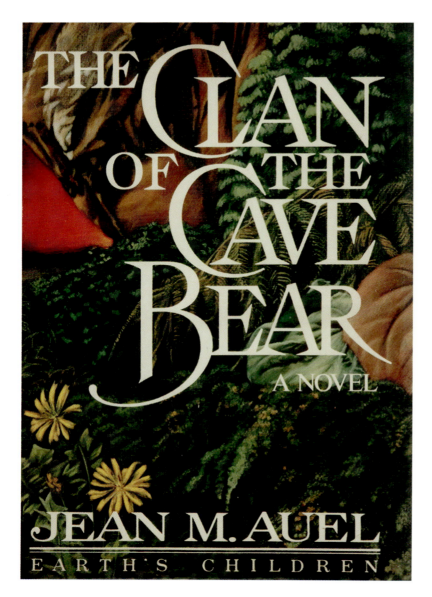

19

THE CLAN OF THE CAVE BEAR

Jean M. Auel · 1980

Jean M. Auel made Paleolithic cavemen sexy. Her bestselling Earth's Children series reimagines prehistoric times, roughly 35,000 years ago, when woolly mammoths and saber-toothed tigers walked the earth. While Auel's Cro-Magnon and Neanderthal characters fight, copulate, and strive to survive, as you'd expect, they also seek justice, display empathy, and fall in passionate love. As it turns out, our early ancestors really were just like us.

Auel was a 40-year-old mother of five when she began writing a short story about a prehistoric woman living among strangers. The more she researched and wrote, the more she realized that she wouldn't be able to say everything she wanted to say in a few pages, or even a whole novel. Indeed, she knew before she'd finished the first draft of *Clan of the Cave Bear* that the story's arc would stretch across six books. *Clan* came out in 1980—setting a new record for the highest advance paid for a debut novel—followed by *The Valley of Horses* (1982), *The Mammoth Hunters* (1985), *The Plains of Passage* (1990), *The Shelters of Stone* (2002), and *The Land of Painted Caves* (2011). Collectively, the Earth's Children books have been translated into 35 languages and have sold 50 million copies.

We first meet Ayla quietly playing near a stream. In a matter of seconds, a devastating earthquake destroys her family and her home, sending her alone into an unforgiving Ice Age world. She is discovered half-dead and badly wounded. Although the five-year-old is clearly an "Other," the clan's medicine woman, Iza, shields Ayla and, along with Iza's shaman brother, adopts and teaches the girl.

Unlike members of the Clan, Ayla has blue eyes and blonde hair. Her legs are not bowed; her brow is not overly pronounced. She uses speech, whereas the Clan members rely mostly on hand signals, and she is capable of inventing, learning, and expressing a range of emotions. When Ayla cries, Iza wonders if she might have an eye infection of some kind. Slowly it becomes clear to readers that Ayla is Cro-Magnon and the Clan is Neanderthal. Ayla's differences cause many conflicts, even as she helps the Clan find a new place to live, and her resilience in the face of adversity, including forced sexual servitude, keeps her compelling as a character.

Auel immersed herself in experiential research to ensure that her books were as accurate as possible. As a result, her characters can start a fire without matches, build a snow cave, and use animal brains to soften a hide. Readers the world over—including anthropologists and archaeologists—relish this attention to detail. But Auel didn't just have to learn about how our ancestors might have used tools; she also had to teach herself to write. By her own admission, she checked out almost as many books about the craft of fiction as about prehistory. She was born in 1936, married her high-school sweetheart at age 18, took night classes in physics and math, and climbed the career ladder at an electronics plant in Portland, Oregon, earning an MBA in 1976. She quit the plant upon learning that it wouldn't hire female managers, and focused on her strong female protagonist.

That same feisty determination marks Auel's lead character and helps explain the book's continuing appeal. Despite the vast gulf in time and circumstance, readers cannot help but feel for Ayla, a girl striving to build the best life she can in an often brutal and vexing world. Erotic as it may sometimes be, *Clan of the Cave Bear* also emphasizes the need for girls to develop strength, regardless of the era.

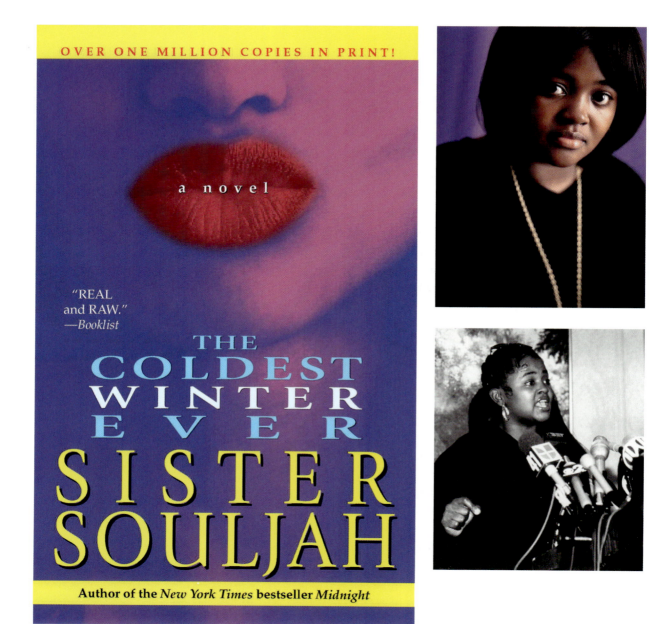

CLOCKWISE FROM LEFT: Cover of *The Coldest Winter Ever*, published in 1999. | Portrait of activist and author Sister Souljah. Her four novels are considered models of "street literature." | Sister Souljah speaking to the media after presidential candidate Bill Clinton's criticism of her controversial statements following the 1992 Los Angeles riots.

20

THE COLDEST WINTER EVER

Sister Souljah · 1999

At a young age, Sister Souljah had two significant revelations: first, she realized that the importance of Africa to world history, literature, and the creation of civilization was largely left out of school curricula in the United States. Second, she realized her voice was commanding enough to redress these and similar omissions.

The Coldest Winter Ever, Sister Souljah's debut novel from 1999, marks a turning point in what's often referred to as "street literature," or stories that take place in an urban environment, feature protagonists of color, and have emotional, sometimes sensationalistic plots. This literary genre initially rose to prominence in the 1960s during the Black Power movement, when prison memoirs began being published and circulated outside of the institutions. In recent years, street literature has been revitalized and popularized, thanks to the efforts and achievements of novelists like Sister Souljah, Zane, and Sapphire.

Named for the season in which she was born, protagonist Winter Santiaga lives a coddled life of relative luxury in the projects in Brooklyn, thanks to the criminal empire created by her drug-dealing father, Ricky. The family, which also includes Winter's mother and three sisters, Lexus, Mercedes, and Porsche, moves to a mansion on Long Island, where an FBI raid leads to the imprisonment of Ricky around Winter's 16th birthday. Winter eventually winds up in a group home, where she hustles and battles to hold on to the trappings of her lavish lifestyle.

In a case of art reflecting life, Winter meets an older female activist named Sister Souljah. Despite this mentor's encouragement and support, Winter continues to steal, betraying the trust of those closest to her. Through Winter, the author portrays the potentially corrosive effects of ill-gotten wealth. Winter's spoiled upbringing prevents her from developing attachments or being loyal, which contributes to her comeuppance in the novel's climax. She cares only about herself.

Told in the first person, the bildungsroman features a raw, bold voice. Like Tom Sawyer and Holden Caulfield, Winter doesn't suffer fools and uses the language of her world to offer her opinions on just about everything, from clothes to hair to African art. Of the fictional Sister Souljah, Winter says, "How is this bitch supposed to help the community when she don't know how to rock her shit? I checked her arm, no Rolex, not even a Timex, nothing. No weight on her neck, nothing. Her hairdo was phat but that don't mean nothing when you don't know how to accessorize."

Born Lisa Williamson in the Bronx in 1964, Sister Souljah moved to Englewood, New Jersey, as a child, and graduated from Rutgers University. In college she became active in the antiapartheid movement, which led to a lifelong commitment to activism, including supporting disadvantaged youth, Afrocentrism, and women's causes. She became a member of the hip-hop group Public Enemy in the 1990s.

To date, Sister Souljah has published four novels related to the Santiaga family and its New York City universe: *Midnight: A Gangster Love Story* (2008), *Midnight and the Meaning of Love* (2011), *A Deeper Love Inside: The Porsche Santiaga Story* (2013), and *A Moment of Silence: Midnight III* (2015). She has also published one memoir, *No Disrespect* (1995). *The Coldest Winter Ever*, which has sold more than two million copies, has been optioned for a movie.

Sister Souljah prides herself on speaking truth to power, especially to mainstream culture and its monolithic institutions. She rejects what she considers the "ghettoization" of her work, noting, "Shakespeare wrote about love. I write about love. Shakespeare wrote about gang warfare, family feuds, and revenge. I write about all the same things."

21

THE COLOR PURPLE

Alice Walker · 1982

The youngest of eight children born to sharecroppers in rural Georgia in 1944, Alice Walker grew up to be the first black woman to win the Pulitzer Prize for fiction. *The Color Purple* (1982) offers a searing indictment of white racist culture and patriarchal black culture. It also poignantly celebrates the bonds between black women and testifies to the strength of the human spirit.

The novel's main character, Celie, an uneducated 14-year-old girl in 1930s rural Georgia, writes letters to God chronicling rape and abuse at the hands of her father, Alphonso. She gives birth to two children by Alphonso, who takes them away. A man known only as Mr. _____ wants to marry Celie's beautiful sister, Nettie, but Alphonso gives him Celie instead. Mr. _____ agrees, and Celie enters into an unhappy marriage. Nettie flees Alphonso's house for Celie's but leaves when Mr. _____ advances on her. Celie assumes that her children and Nettie are dead. When Shug Avery, a nightclub singer and the mistress of Celie's husband, gets sick, Mr. _____ allows her to move into his house, where she and Celie become friends and eventually lovers. Celie learns that her husband has been hiding letters from Nettie, who has become a missionary in Africa, traveling with a white couple and their adopted children. In time, Nettie discovers that these adopted children are Celie's, and the novel ends happily.

As a student at Spelman College and Sarah Lawrence College, Walker became increasingly active in the civil rights movement. In later years she became an outspoken feminist, environmentalist, and political activist. Today, in addition to continuing to publish books, she remains involved in antiwar and Palestinian causes. In 1973, she discovered the unmarked grave of Zora Neale Hurston, who died penniless and in obscurity after being hailed as one of the great writers of the Harlem Renaissance. Thanks in large part to Walker's efforts, Hurston's work experienced a resurgence of attention.

One of the most noteworthy accomplishments of *The Color Purple* is the sympathy with which it treats its characters. Indeed, the novel demonstrates the insidiousness of violence, helping readers understand the difficulties of uncovering and eradicating the roots of sexism and racism. Victims, whether in the novel or among its readers, are encouraged to eschew guilt and shame, and to live their lives with dignity. Doing so takes courage. It's an undertaking that not only cultivates joyfulness in the world but irrevocably breaks a pattern that causes so much hurt.

In Steven Spielberg's 1985 hit movie based on the book, Whoopi Goldberg won much acclaim for her portrayal of Celie, and Oprah Winfrey, making her acting debut, was widely praised in her role as Sofia, Celie's daughter-in-law. At the time Winfrey hosted a local talk show in Chicago, which she would brand and take national the following year. It was nominated for 11 Academy Awards, and the *New Republic* called *The Color Purple* "perhaps *the* culture touchstone for black women in America, a kind of lingua franca of familiarity and friendship." The book was also turned into a popular Broadway musical, running from 2005 to 2008, with an even more popular revival in 2015–2017.

Walker credits a childhood accident that left her blind in one eye with teaching her to really see and to observe, and sight plays a key role in her novel. In a remarkable passage meant to encourage Celie to develop resilience, Shug reminds her to stop and look: "I think it pisses God off if you walk by the color purple in a field somewhere and don't notice it."

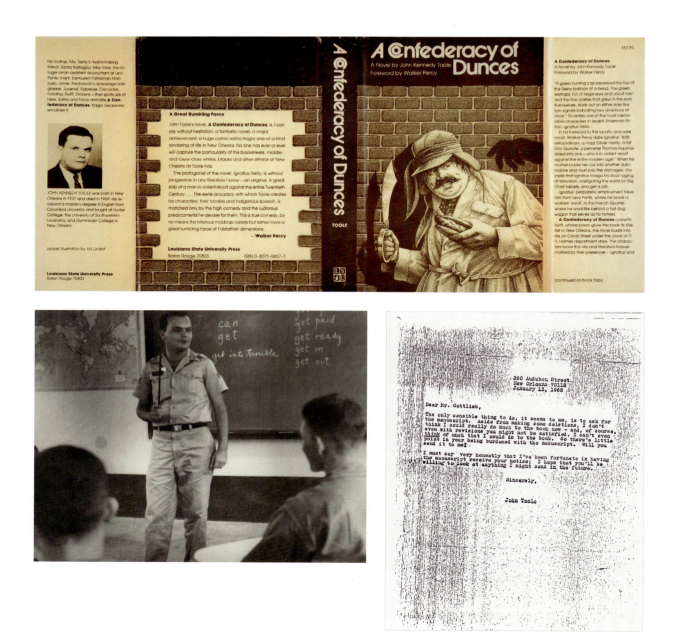

CLOCKWISE FROM TOP: Dust jacket from the first edition of *A Confederacy of Dunces*, posthumously published in 1980. | Author John Kennedy Toole taught English to Spanish-speaking draftees at Fort Buchanan, Puerto Rico, circa 1961–1963. He started writing *A Confederacy of Dunces* during his deployment. | A letter from Toole to Simon & Schuster editor Robert Gottlieb, housed with the author's papers at Tulane University.

22

A CONFEDERACY OF DUNCES

John Kennedy Toole · 1980

Everyone deserves a parent as loving and relentless as Thelma Ducoing Toole. After her son killed himself in 1969, she dedicated herself to making his dream of being a published novelist a reality. She sent his manuscript from publisher to publisher, the pages growing increasingly tattered along the way. Eventually, Thelma cornered novelist Walker Percy in his office at Loyola University in New Orleans. He began reading out of politeness, then out of enjoyment, and finally out of sheer disbelief: as he later wrote, "surely it was not possible that it was so good." He also helped get it published—*A Confederacy of Dunces* came out in 1980. The sprawling, funny novel became a bestseller and—amazingly, for a debut comedy—earned its author a posthumous Pulitzer Prize the following year.

Set in New Orleans, *A Confederacy of Dunces* stars Ignatius Jacques Reilly, an obese oddball who lives largely on hot dogs, wears a hat with earflaps regardless of the weather, hates contemporary culture, and adores medieval philosophy. He falls in love with Myrna Minkoff, a young Jewish college student, and much of the book consists of the strange correspondence between them after Myrna returns home to New York. The novel also focuses on the relationship between Ignatius and his overbearing, alcoholic mother, Irene Reilly.

Like Ignatius's favorite tome, *The Consolation of Philosophy* by sixth-century Roman philosopher Boethius, *Confederacy* is a mash-up of literary forms; it mixes prose, light verse, journal entries, and letters. The novel's structure reflects its action, which is less a single propulsive story than a jumble of amusing and revealing episodes. Despite his scholarly pretensions, Ignatius must work—often reluctantly—a series of mundane jobs in order to support himself and his mom, and these lead him into all kinds of fascinating encounters, adventures, and misadventures in and around the French Quarter. Many readers consider the novel to be a near-perfect rendering of the multicultural vibrancy that is New Orleans, down to the city's distinctive dialects.

John Kennedy Toole knew of what he wrote. Born in 1937, he grew up in New Orleans and entered Tulane on full scholarship at age 16. After graduating, he began studying for a PhD in English literature at Columbia, in New York City, but would return home to New Orleans periodically to teach, eventually settling there permanently. His students relished his sense of humor and admired his brilliance, and impeccably decked out in a suit and tie (in contrast to his protagonist), he was a very popular teacher.

Drafted into the army in 1961, Toole began writing this novel during his military service in Puerto Rico. Notwithstanding his efforts, including an intense multiyear correspondence with Robert Gottlieb of Simon & Schuster, he could not get *A Confederacy of Dunces* published. Increasingly isolated and depressed, Toole committed suicide in Biloxi at age 31, leaving his manuscript atop an armoire in his mother's house.

The work, with its huge cast of characters and satirical bent, might be compared to similarly hefty novels by Charles Dickens, who also envisioned novelists as holding up a mirror to society. Like Dickens, Toole had the knack for capturing a personality with just a weird tic or two: Mr. Clyde, for instance, sells hot dogs on the street and threatens people who irritate him with a rusty fork. From her vibrating exercise machine, Mrs. Levy tries to psychoanalyze her family and friends, simultaneously improving others and herself. Irene Reilly has magenta hair and a fondness for muscatel. Like Dickens and every beloved writer, Toole's memory lives on in all who have fallen for the book's comedic charms.

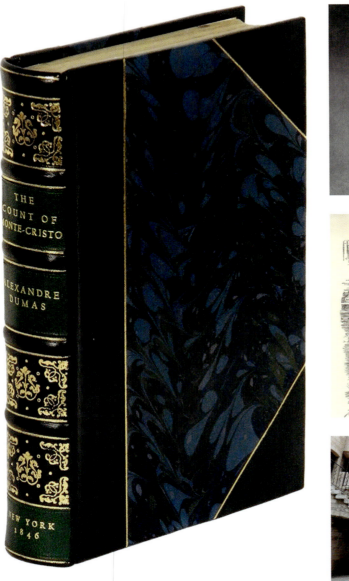

CLOCKWISE FROM LEFT: Cover of the first US edition of *Count of Monte Cristo*, published in 1846. | Portrait of author Alexandre Dumas, taken in 1846. The son of a French aristocrat and a slave, Dumas worked his way up through the military and became the highest-ranking black official of his time. | Illustration from *The Count of Monte Cristo*. The caption reads, "My name is Edmond Dantès." | Chateau d'If fortress prison, located in the Bay of Marseille, where the character Edmond Dantès was imprisoned in the novel.

23

THE COUNT OF MONTE CRISTO

Alexandre Dumas · 1844–1846

When we talk about the beauty of the Sistine Chapel, we praise Michelangelo and only Michelangelo. But the truth is that Michelangelo employed a team of assistants to carry out his vision. When we talk about *The Count of Monte Cristo* (1844–1846), we commend Alexandre Dumas for the classic tale of adventure, and only Dumas. But like Michelangelo, Dumas too had a veritable literary assembly line behind the scenes.

Although Dumas gets the credit, he collaborated on *The Count of Monte Cristo* and *The Three Musketeers* (1844) with Auguste Maquet, a writer whose job it was to generate outlines, plots, settings, and sometimes even drafts, while Dumas filled in the gaps, added a dollop of pizzazz, and slapped his name on the cover. As it turns out, Maquet was one of 73 collaborators who helped Dumas keep up with the demand, stay so wildly prolific, and generate the income he needed to support his lavish lifestyle. Without this team Dumas likely wouldn't have been able to produce the roughly 100,000 pages he's credited with writing in his lifetime, including novels, plays, romances, journalism, travel writing, history books, and true crime.

Dumas—or Maquet—probably based the Count of Monte Cristo on Pierre Picaud, a 19th-century shoemaker who was falsely accused of treason by three friends who lusted after Picaud's rich fiancée. All told, Picaud spent 10 years plotting revenge, which he eventually let loose on a massive scale, tricking one friend's daughter into marrying a criminal and poisoning someone else, among other acts of torture and destruction. Similarly, in Dumas's novel, Edmond Dantès gets sent to prison for life on charges trumped up by several friends who envy his good fortune. In prison he meets a priest who shares a secret about buried treasure. Dantès eventually escapes, finds the treasure, transforms himself into a count (among other aliases), and returns to his hometown, where the only person to recognize him is his former paramour, Mercédès. Then he systematically achieves vengeance by hurting or destroying every single person who wronged him.

In addition to Picaud, Dumas may also have been thinking about his father when creating the count. Born out of wedlock, the son of a French aristocrat and a slave, Thomas-Alexandre Dumas worked his way up through the military and became the highest-ranking black official of his time. Ultimately, however, he found himself imprisoned in Naples, feeling betrayed when his supposed friends back in France took far too long to come to his aid. Tom Reiss's book about Dumas (who was also known as Thomas-Alexandre Davy de la Pailleterie), *The Black Count: Glory, Revolution, Betrayal, and the Real Count of Monte Cristo*, won the 2013 Pulitzer Prize for biography.

The first cinematic adaptation of *The Count of Monte Cristo* appeared as a silent film in 1908. Since then, the novel has served as the basis for a Garfield cartoon, a Soviet miniseries, and an Argentine telenovela, as well as many other films. The movie *Oldboy* (2003), for example, changes the setting from 19th-century France to 21st-century South Korea, where a man has been mysteriously imprisoned for 15 years; he too exacts a violent retribution.

The swashbuckling tale satisfies in part because the good guy gets his revenge: a victim of circumstances, Dantès deserves a better life than the one he's led, and the people he kills are clearly villainous. Nevertheless, the novel poses interesting questions about the criminal-justice system and the moral defensibility of retaliation, leaving us to wonder what would happen to society if everyone sought vengeance when wronged. Dantès ultimately decides that it's God's job to offer punishment. Perhaps the story served as a cautionary tale to its writers: fed up with his treatment, Maquet took his case to court rather than taking matters into his own hands, and successfully sued Dumas for more money.

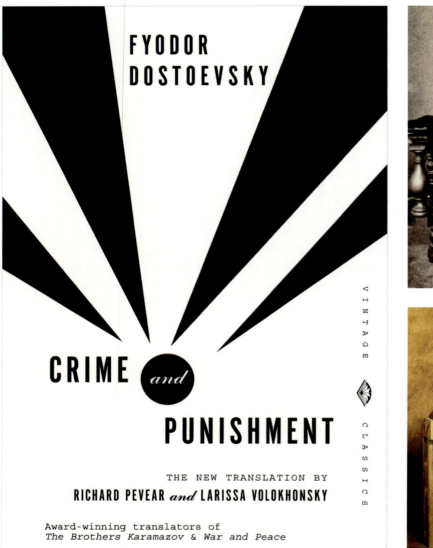

FYODOR
DOSTOEVSKY

CRIME *and* PUNISHMENT

THE NEW TRANSLATION BY
RICHARD PEVEAR *and* LARISSA VOLOKHONSKY

Award-winning translators of
The Brothers Karamazov & War and Peace

VINTAGE CLASSICS

CLOCKWISE FROM LEFT: The Vintage Classics cover of *Crime and Punishment*, published in 1866. | Portrait of author Fyodor M. Dostoyevsky, taken in 1865. Born in Moscow in 1821, Dostoyevsky was imprisoned for his socialist politics, reprieved from a death sentence, and sent to Siberia. After a decade in exile, he returned to Saint Petersburg and took up the pen. | Illustration for *Crime and Punishment* by artist Baron Klodt Mikhail Petrovich, from the collection of the Russian State Library, Moscow.

24

CRIME AND PUNISHMENT

Fyodor Dostoyevsky · 1866

When it comes to 19th-century Russian novels, readers tend to split along two lines: those who favor the high church of Tolstoy, filled with sweeping social epics, and those who worship at the altar of the more emotional Dostoyevsky, draped as it is with tragic tales of the individual. And no one is more tragic than Raskolnikov, the protagonist of *Crime and Punishment*, as he commits an awful act of violence and must suffer the spiritual, moral, and physical consequences.

Once a promising student, Rodion Romanovich Raskolnikov has fallen on hard times. He decides to rob and kill Alyona Ivanovna, a pawnbroker with whom he's transacted on occasion in his Saint Petersburg neighborhood. He meets a man on a drinking binge, who tells Raskolnikov about his daughter, Sonya, recently turned into a prostitute to support their family. Raskolnikov reasons that he'll be doing the world two good deeds with his murder: ridding the city of an evil creature, and using her money to benefit others—an almost-perfect encapsulation of utilitarianism, a philosophy that privileges any action that is useful and, on balance, promotes happiness. The plan goes awry immediately when Alyona's sister walks in, so Raskolnikov kills her as well, even though she's absolutely innocent. As he interacts with Sonya, his sister, his mother, and others, Raskolnikov must decide whether to confess.

True to its title, *Crime and Punishment* begins with a crime and concludes with an official punishment. The middle of the long novel, on the other hand, details the effect of the wrongdoing on its perpetrator, which itself constitutes a form of punishment. Raskolnikov believes himself to be superior to everyone else and therefore that society's norms, rules, and morality don't apply to him. Nevertheless, every time someone mentions the murder in his presence, he panics or faints, thereby telegraphing his guilt. At various points he slides along a spectrum of mental instability from a bit touched to totally insane, but continues to wrestle, rationally

and lucidly, with philosophy. Dostoyevsky balances the two halves of the book such that Raskolnikov transitions from a distant, proud misanthrope to a more humble man capable of empathy.

Born in Moscow in 1821, Fyodor Dostoyevsky wanted to be a writer from a young age. After becoming involved in socialist politics, he was arrested in 1849, thrown in prison, and sentenced to death. When he arrived at the execution, he and members of his political group discovered that it was a ruse meant to inflict psychological torture; instead of dying, he was being exiled to Siberia, where he would serve time in a labor camp. He returned to Saint Petersburg in 1859 a changed man, aware of "how much strength the human personality possesses to create the conditions under which it can survive amidst the worst adversity," according to biographer Joseph Frank.

Dostoyevsky wrote at a furious pace. *Crime and Punishment* was serialized in 1866, then later published as a stand-alone work. As he gained success and fame, he developed a gambling problem, forcing his family into debt, and suffered from a rare form of epilepsy. Versions of these twin torments manifest in many of his books, which feature characters plagued by mental and physical illnesses. In spite of their hardships, some manage to find dignity and even gladness in day-to-day existence, a possibility reinforced by Dostoyevsky's deeply held religious beliefs. Dostoyevsky died in 1881, at age 59, but left behind a huge body of work, including novels like *The Idiot* (1868–1869) and *The Brothers Karamazov* (1879–1880), along with journalism, essays, short stories, and poems.

Before the rise of psychology as a science, people turned to novels to learn about the personalities and proclivities of their fellow man. *Crime and Punishment* stands as one of the most masterful portraits of psychosis ever published. A cautionary tale, it tells you what you need to know about how an ethical and moral transgression might very well drive someone mad.

#RebelReader

FREQUENTLY BANNED BOOKS

"**THERE IS NO SUCH THING** as a moral or an immoral book," Oscar Wilde wrote in the preface to *The Picture of Dorian Gray*. "Books are well written or badly written. That is all." Not everyone agrees: banning books, or at least trying to, has a long history not only in totalitarian regimes but in societies that pride themselves on their freedoms. Books get banned for all sorts of reasons, from profanity to politics to religion. What some see as broad-minded and realistic, others see as offensive and damaging.

Some books are challenged even as they're celebrated. When *The Grapes of Wrath* came out in 1939, it received critical accolades, among them the Pulitzer Prize, and became a bestseller. But it was also banned in several parts of the United States, including Kern County, California, where the fictional Joads wound up after leaving Oklahoma. The California county's board of supervisors took issue with Steinbeck's portrayal of the migrants and their treatment, denounced the book as "libel and lie," and forbade it from being shelved in libraries and schools in the area. (The ban was lifted 18 months later.)

Being part of the canon never seems to preclude a book from censorship. Widely seen as a foundational text within Chicano literature, *Bless Me, Ultima* has been routinely and roundly criticized for its portrayal of homosexuality, its raw language, and its sensitive depiction of indigenous beliefs. People who seek to ban or censor books often envision themselves as protecting impressionable minds. Some parents, upon discovering that their children are being exposed to the violence of *Beloved* or *The Call of the Wild*, the racism of *To Kill a Mockingbird*, or the critique of racism of *Invisible Man*, complain to local school boards, sometimes resulting in the book in question being struck from classroom reading lists.

Few books come under as intense scrutiny as those written for children and teens. The Harry Potter series had to cope with charges of Satanism. Other books, like *Looking for Alaska* and *The Diary of Anne Frank*, are periodically deemed too sexually explicit, with some fearing that risqué content might encourage readers to experiment. Offensive language is another oft-cited reason for keeping a book out of the hands of a young person, as is the catchall category of "unsuited to any age group."

Yet banning books inevitably backfires. *The Catcher in the Rye* has been repeatedly banned, for reasons ranging from "antiwhite" bias to "excess vulgar language" to a lack of morality in its protagonist, Holden Caulfield. During its most intense censorship in the 1960s and 1970s, some teachers were fired for assigning the book to students. It didn't help when Mark David Chapman claimed that the novel influenced him to murder John Lennon in 1980. All this controversy has arguably cemented the novel's place on syllabi of high-school English classes, and it continues to sell some 250,000 copies every year.

More recently, *The Curious Incident of the Dog in the Night-Time* came under fire for "taking of God's name in vain." The Hunger Games trilogy has been kept off shelves for being "anti-family" and "anti-ethnic." *The Lovely Bones* has been criticized for "dubious morals" and its religious themes, the latter a reason some have given for taking both *The Handmaid's Tale* and *The Da Vinci Code* out of circulation. There are those who seek to ban the Koran and the Torah. In an ironic twist on Wilde's quip, *Fifty Shades of Grey* has been challenged for being "poorly written."

Responding to ongoing efforts to remove or limit access to titles, the American Library Association created

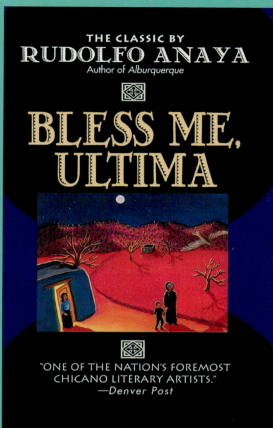

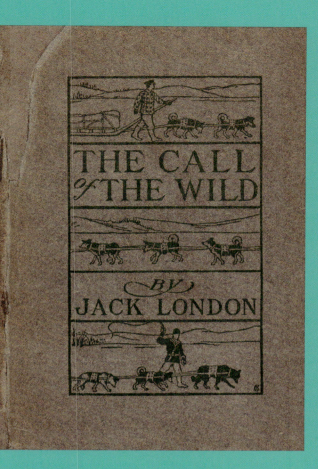

Banned Books Week in 1982. Participating libraries put up themed displays, promoting previously banned books and supporting "the freedom to read." The internet makes it easier than ever to find works that might be missing from the local library for whatever reason, and social media, with its hashtags like #RebelReader, encourages people to read widely and deeply. Without the lively discourse that comes from diverse viewpoints, even those that might be distasteful or troubling to us, democracy dies. George Orwell's *Nineteen Eighty-Four* goes into a fair amount of detail about just such a situation—probably why it's the fifth-most-banned book of all time.

ABOVE, LEFT TO RIGHT: Rudolfo Anaya's *Bless Me, Ultima* was banned for portraying homosexuality, graphic language, and depictions of indigenous beliefs. | Jack London's *The Call of the Wild* was banned after concerned parents complained about its violence.

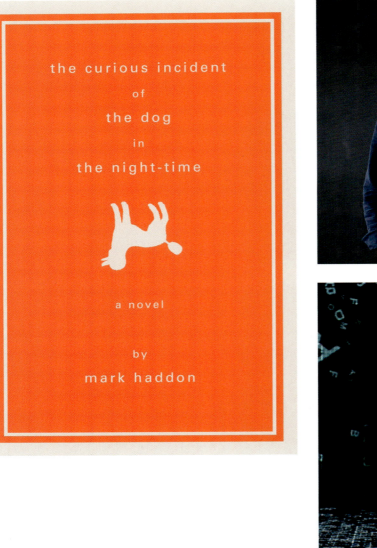

25

THE CURIOUS INCIDENT OF THE DOG IN THE NIGHT-TIME

Mark Haddon · 2003

Demonstrating sensitivity toward those with mental and physical disorders, Mark Haddon never names the precise condition that drives his main character's behavior. Readers of *The Curious Incident of the Dog in the Night-Time* (2003), however, might notice 15-year-old Christopher's differences starting from the book's first chapter, numbered as it is with a 2, rather than a 1. Christopher John Francis Boone knows every prime number through 7,057, as well as the name and capital of every country in the world, but he's unable to appreciate emotions beyond happy or sad, and he lacks the capacity for empathy. Haddon decided not to label Christopher as a way of showing that his protagonist is so much more than his symptoms.

The Curious Incident of the Dog in the Night-Time begins at seven minutes after midnight, when Christopher discovers the murder of his neighbor's poodle, Wellington. After suspicion falls on him, Christopher sets about trying to determine the true culprit, a project that forces him to interact with his Swindon neighbors and uncover the answers to other mysteries. He learns of his father's affair with Mrs. Shears, Wellington's owner, which heated up in response to the relationship between Mr. Shears and Christopher's mother, before she disappeared from Christopher's life. He thinks she's dead.

Christopher writes *The Curious Incident of the Dog in the Night-Time* as part of a school assignment. He takes his title from "Silver Blaze," an 1892 story about Sherlock Holmes. In it, the master detective realizes that a dog's silence offers the clue to the crime: the dog didn't bark because he knew the person sneaking around the horse stables that night. Like Holmes, Christopher values cool logic and precise deductions; he populates his narrative with facts about astronauts, technology, and other subjects that rely on such tools, and he greatly admires Holmes. Even as Christopher tries to use reason to solve Wellington's murder, he discovers, and starts to understand, the illogic of emotion and of life.

Haddon spent many years working with differently abled children before becoming a full-time children's-book writer. He also wrote for a popular UK television show. He was born in England in 1962 and graduated from Oxford in 1981. Since the publication of *The Curious Incident of the Dog in the Night-Time*, his first book written for an adult audience, Haddon has mostly continued to write books for grown-ups. In the United Kingdom, the book came out in two editions simultaneously—and unusually—with one marketed to adults and one to teens; both were bestsellers and award winners, taking home such accolades as the Guardian Children's Fiction Prize and Whitbread Book of the Year. The appeal of Haddon's book points to the now-blurred lines between YA fiction and adult fiction. Thanks to the massive success of novels by J. K. Rowling, Philip Pullman, John Green, and Stephenie Meyer, among others, books about teens are finding a much broader audience.

In 2012, the novel became a play, premiering in London's West End and winning seven Olivier Awards, before transferring to Broadway, where it won both the Drama Desk Award for Outstanding Play and the Tony Award for Best Play. During the course of its New York City run, the play employed some 20 puppies, all of which were adopted postproduction. The novel ends just as happily. Christopher may be unusual, but the world would be a better place if everyone were a little more like him—cognizant of their own strengths and weaknesses, determined to combat their limitations and achieve their goals, curious about and open to new, if occasionally scary, experiences.

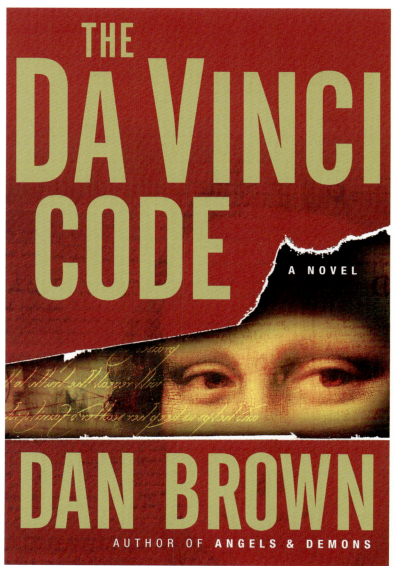

26

THE DA VINCI CODE

Dan Brown · 2003

Among the by-products of the blockbuster novel *The Da Vinci Code* (2003) are a rise in tourism in Rome and Paris, a spike in interest in early religious history, and—thanks to sales of his book as well as books denouncing its portrayal of Christianity—a big boost to the publishing industry. Dan Brown's thriller also sent readers searching for the Holy Grail.

On vacation in Tahiti in 1994, Brown experienced an "I can do that" moment while reading a thriller, and he started writing when he returned home. *The Da Vinci Code* was his fourth novel, and his second to feature Robert Langdon, Harvard professor of symbology (the fictional study of symbols). Its incredible success propelled his previous books onto the bestseller list. Today, Brown is one of the most popular and highest-grossing novelists in the world. He continues to write about Langdon, and has published three more novels to date featuring this protagonist: *The Lost Symbol* (2009), *Inferno* (2013), and *Origin* (2017). In 2016, he released a version of *The Da Vinci Code* aimed at young adults.

When the original novel begins, Langdon is at the Louvre to investigate the death of curator Jacques Saunière, who wrote a series of enigmatic messages in blood before dying. Sophie Neveu, a cryptographer and Saunière's estranged granddaughter, arrives and realizes that the police suspect Langdon. Together they interpret Saunière's strange clues, which force the pair to undergo a whirlwind hunt through France and Britain, art history and theology. *The Da Vinci Code* puts its protagonists through the proverbial wringer: car chases, gunfire, villains disguised as sympathetic friends. But it also offers a compelling mystery coupled with a tantalizing bit of romance at the very end, and the byzantine, centuries-long conspiracy at its heart appeals to readers' desire for an ordered world, even if that order is enigmatic and sinister.

The Da Vinci Code traffics in secrets. As Langdon and Neveu discover, Saunière belonged to the Priory of Sion—a clandestine society whose members also included Leonardo da Vinci and Isaac Newton, and whose job it is to keep safe certain documents entitled the *Sangreal*, or the Holy Grail. Langdon and Neveu must outwit bloodthirsty members of Opus Dei, a Catholic Church–approved sect trying to find the objects in question. In its controversial alternate history, the novel proposes that Jesus and Mary Magdalene procreated, and their descendants live on, covertly. Supporting evidence includes hidden signs in *The Last Supper*, Leonardo da Vinci's 15th-century painting of Jesus and his disciples, as well as other hidden messages in cultural touchstones. Readers interpret codes and uncover symbols along with the characters, and the thriller offers a goodly dose of erudition—or at least the appearance of it—in addition to cliffhangers and breathless action.

Daniel Gerhard Brown was born in 1964 in New Hampshire. His father, a teacher at Phillips Exeter Academy, would plan elaborate treasure hunts for the family. Brown graduated from Exeter and went on to Amherst College. After trying to be a singer-songwriter, he started writing full-time in 1996. His wife, Blythe, helps with the massive amounts of research his historical novels require.

Not everyone relished Brown's version of history. The Catholic Church, in particular, went to great lengths to clarify the difference between verifiable fact and imaginative license. So did many academics and journalists. Brown considers himself Christian and welcomes the debate his books have fomented, as he believes that dialogue strengthens faith and conviction. *The Da Vinci Code* was a must-read, oft-discussed novel of the early 2000s, and it hasn't lost its ability to taunt, to titillate, or to thrill.

CLOCKWISE FROM TOP: Opening pages from *The History of the Valorous and Witty-Knight Errant, Don Quixote of the Mancha* in its first English translation, published in 1620. | A portrait of the author, Miguel de Cervantes, born in 1547. | The chapter 1 opener of the first English edition.

27

DON QUIXOTE

Miguel de Cervantes · 1605

n a happy case of metafiction, the first modern novel is about novels. More precisely, *Don Quixote* (1605) demonstrates what happens when you read too much. Alonso Quixano, a rail-thin, middle-aged gentleman, loves books to the neglect of everything else in his life. One day he changes his name to Don Quixote de La Mancha, slaps on a rusty suit of armor, hops on his skinny horse, Rosinante, and sets off to have the kind of knightly adventures he's only read about. He's inspired by books to change his life, a feeling utterly familiar to bibliophiles everywhere.

On one level, it's a funny joke: reading too many romances—then the most popular type of literature in Spain, featuring honorable knights who undertake chivalric quests—drives Don Quixote insane. In his first adventure, he attacks an inn, convinced it is a castle and its prostitutes are highborn ladies. Some merchants beat him up, so he slinks back to his house. There his friends burn the majority of his library in the hopes of curing him of his romantic notions. The plan fails, as Don Quixote becomes sure that he's been the victim of evil forces that so often prevent knights from victory. For his second adventure, he enlists the practical farmer Sancho Panza as his squire, and Sancho's earthy wisdom serves as a foil to Don Quixote's wacky notions. The two meet many people and have many adventures, including attacking windmills that Don Quixote assumed were giants.

At the start of Part II, Don Quixote has achieved his dream. A novelist set down his adventures, and the resulting book is very popular, making Don Quixote and Sancho Panza famous. On their third adventure, they best another "knight," make more friends, and try to save the fair princess Dulcinea from her terrible enchantment, which forces her to take the form of a coarse peasant. They are also exploited and humiliated by those who find their delusions worthy of cruel practical jokes. Indeed, throughout the novel, Don Quixote gets battered and wounded.

The destabilization of Don Quixote's identity mirrors the destabilization of Spain and even Europe at that time. It shows how quickly people can change and become something else, just by virtue of declaring themselves so; this may be a reflection of the forced conversion of Spanish Muslims and Jews during the Spanish Inquisition in the late 15th and early 16th centuries. That era also marked a period of rapid exploration and colonization of the New World, which profoundly reshaped society. Don Quixote's shifts also point to the rise of literature; fiction, unlike nonfiction, doesn't need to adhere to any kind of verifiable truth.

Miguel de Cervantes Saavedra was born into poverty in 1547 near Madrid. He moved to Rome, then enlisted in the Spanish Navy, from which he was captured and enslaved by pirates. Five years later, he was ransomed by his family and returned to Madrid, where he began writing while working at other jobs, including tax collector. He also spent time in prison. The success of the first part of *Don Quixote* encouraged him to complete the second part in 1615. (Today, both parts are published as a single volume.) He died the following year.

Cervantes's influence has been profound: *Don Quixote* is sometimes called "the Spanish Bible," and many point to the novel as the start of modern Spanish. It gave us the word *quixotic*. *Moby-Dick* (1851), *Madame Bovary* (1856), *A Confederacy of Dunces* (1980), *The Shadow of the Wind* (2001), and other famous works borrow elements of *Don Quixote*. Cervantes inserted himself as a character in Part II, introducing a literary technique that marks the postmodern work of today. As importantly, *Don Quixote* appeals to anyone who's ever envisioned themselves as the star of a story, or who believes that words on a page create a world more real than the one we live in.

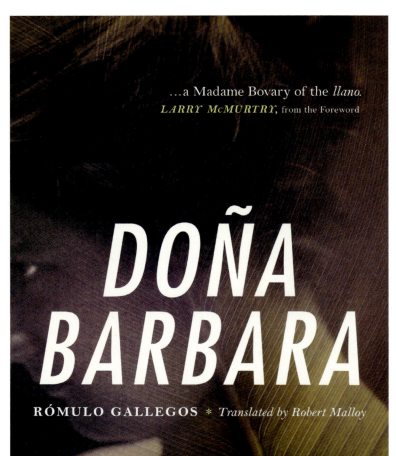

…a Madame Bovary of the *llano*.
LARRY McMURTRY, from the Foreword

DOÑA BARBARA

RÓMULO GALLEGOS * *Translated by Robert Malloy*

CLOCKWISE FROM LEFT: A paperback cover of Doña Bárbara. | Author Rómulo Gallegos, who became the first democratically elected president of Venezuela in 1947. He was ousted in a coup the following year. | President Gallegos, photographed in a meeting with US President Harry S. Truman and General Harry Vaughan.

28

DOÑA BÁRBARA

Rómulo Gallegos · 1929

Anyone who doubts the power of literature to influence politics should take a look at *Doña Bárbara*. Published in 1929, this Venezuelan novel caused such controversy that its author had to abandon his homeland and move to Spain. When he returned a few years later, he was elected to Congress, as mayor, and eventually to the presidency of Venezuela.

The discovery of oil in Venezuela in the early 20th century fundamentally and irrevocably altered almost every facet of life there, from its politics to its economics to its gender dynamics. Even as then dictator Juan Vicente Gómez sought to use the profits from the burgeoning oil industry to improve Venezuela's infrastructure and to create jobs, he ruled with viciousness and nepotism. The construction of roads enabled travel and contact among people on a much broader scale, prompting an era of patriotism that helped end regional skirmishes and violence, and, it can be argued, permitted the development of democracy.

Rómulo Gallegos wrote his grand novel while observing his rapidly changing country. Born in Caracas in 1884, he initially worked as a journalist and schoolteacher. *Doña Bárbara*'s criticism of Gómez forced Gallegos to leave Venezuela for a time. He became involved in politics upon his return in 1936, serving as minister of public education and mayor of Caracas. In 1947, Gallegos became Venezuela's first democratically elected president; he was ousted in a military coup the following year. He eventually returned to Venezuela but stayed out of politics until his death in 1969.

The novel starts with the return of Santos Luzardo, a newly minted lawyer from the city, to the rural state of Apure. Luzardo intends to sell his father's land but is surprised to learn that the estate is being run by the powerful and striking Doña Bárbara. Allegations that she might be a witch offer some insight into her reputation—she is unabashedly sexual, wielding her appetites like a weapon. Luzardo meets a man who fell under her spell but has since fallen into drunkenness, as well as Doña Bárbara's neglected daughter, Marisela. Attracted to Luzardo, Doña Bárbara promises to change her ways, but he prefers the younger, more wholesome Marisela. Rather than rescue the older woman from immorality, he opts to rescue the younger from poverty.

As contemporary scholar Maggie Hivnor notes, *Doña Bárbara*'s first readers immediately grasped the book as a "parable of how Venezuela could be saved from a corrupt and backward-thinking regime." Luzardo represents civilization while Doña Bárbara represents barbarism. Those early readers would also have seen echoes of Gómez and his regime in everything Luzardo comes to reject.

Featuring lush descriptions of the Venezuelan plains as well as its residents, the novel blends fantasy and suspense; it's often discussed as a precursor to *One Hundred Years of Solitude* (1967) and other works of magical realism. The book is all the more remarkable for its treatment of gender. The trope of the redeeming power of a good woman's love is the very definition of a cliché, with an abundance of examples as varied as *Jane Eyre* (1847) and *Fifty Shades of Grey* (2011). Here, however, it's the woman who transforms. Nevertheless, her redemption is for naught, as Luzardo resists her charms and chooses Marisela instead.

Gallegos cowrote the screenplay to the 1943 film version of the novel, shifting its lens slightly to heighten the romantic competition between Doña Bárbara and her daughter; another film came out in 1998. In addition, the novel has been made into several television series, but it received new life in 2016, when Telemundo produced *La Doña*, a telenovela based on Gallegos's book.

In recent years, Venezuela has experienced political turmoil, with attempted coups, accusations of governmental corruption, and ongoing protests and even riots. *Doña Bárbara* offers a fascinating glimpse into the extensive roots of current conflicts and crises.

Science Fiction's Supreme Masterpiece

DUNE

FRANK HERBERT

With an Afterword by Brian Herbert

29

DUNE

Frank Herbert · 1965

For many people, the future conjures images of flying cars, robotic servants, and computers imprinted on irises. In short, technology rules. Not so for Frank Herbert. When he imagined life in a time period far, far from now, his world was much more minimalist, and much more ravaged by environmental destruction. The society he pictured harked back to the medieval era, despite its outer-space setting. The novel in which he sketched out such a vision is considered one of the most important works of science fiction ever written.

Dune (1965) takes place thousands of years in the future. Humans have dispersed across the universe, inhabiting many other planets. As the novel begins, Duke Leto is getting ready to assume the governorship of Arrakis. Though it appears devoid of life, this planet boasts tons of melange, a spice drug that helps users feel better, live longer, and see the future. The duke arrives with his mistress, Jessica, whose supernatural powers intrigue the native Fremen of Arrakis. After the duke's death, their son, Paul, grows close to the people of this culture, who believe that he and his mother will transform their dry planet into a verdant paradise. In time, Paul becomes the religious and secular leader of the Fremen, and he successfully leads them in a struggle against their enemies.

The passionate environmentalism at play in the novel comes directly from Herbert's experience. As a child in Tacoma, Washington, where he was born in 1920, he watched the corrosive effects of the local smelter on the city. He saw how industrialization can do damage even as it brings progress. In the late 1950s, while working as a journalist, Herbert was assigned a story on the Oregon Dunes, which were spreading and threatening water systems and infrastructure; he never finished the piece, but he discovered enough material to create the world of Arrakis. It took another five years to complete the novel, which he dedicated to "dry-land ecologists," among others.

In addition to its conservationist themes, *Dune* explores many philosophical issues, such as the way religion might be manipulated to achieve power, the nature of inheritance, and the use of drugs to expand the mind. It's also an epic tale of adventure as well as a story about good guys versus bad guys. As a protagonist, Paul enthralls because of his depth; he's conflicted about his role and feels the burden of his fate. *Dune* won the Nebula Award and shared the Hugo Award.

Before his death in 1986 at age 65, Herbert continued the Dune saga—sometimes called the Duniverse—through five subsequent novels. Herbert's son Brian followed in his father's footsteps: he has coauthored 14 related novels, including prequels to *Dune*, and wrote a biography about his father, *Dreamer of Dune* (2003). The Duniverse novels manifest the original's concern with ecology, taking the reader deep into the past, when humans warred with computers, and into the future, with the alterations of humans into mystical, magical creatures. Indeed, *Children of Dune* (1976), which deals with the fate of Paul's offspring and his planet, was the first sci-fi hardcover bestseller.

Although the 1984 film version of *Dune* received scathing reviews upon its release, the movie, directed by David Lynch and starring Kyle MacLachlan as Paul, has become a cult classic. In 2017, director Denis Villeneuve confirmed a remake of *Dune* was in the works, promising to take that book about the future even further into the future. Recently, climate change and its resulting natural disasters and economic pressures have rendered *Dune* all the more apropos for today's readers.

MR. GREY WILL SEE YOU NOW

VALENTINE'S DAY 2015
FIFTYSHADESMOVIE.COM

Fifty Shades of Grey

E L James

#1 *New York Times* Bestseller

CLOCKWISE FROM LEFT: The cover of the first book in E. L. James's bestselling Fifty Shades series, *Fifty Shades of Grey*. | Author E. L. James at the first screening of the movie release of *Fifty Shades of Grey* in New York in 2015. | A promotional poster for the Focus Films' release of the movie.

30

FIFTY SHADES SERIES

E. L. James · 2011–present

Fifty Shades of Grey began as fan fiction inspired by Stephenie Meyer's Twilight series (2005–2008). Although E. L. James had never written a book before, she was consumed by the vampire novels and movies, and started publishing her racy version of the romantic life of Bella Swan and Edward Cullen online in 2009. Using the pen name Snowqueens Icedragon, she called her work *Master of the Universe*. That was compiled, rewritten, and published as the e-book and print-on-demand title *Fifty Shades of Grey* in 2011 by the Writer's Coffee Shop; in 2012, an imprint of Random House won the rights to publish the series. Today, James is one of the highest-grossing writers of all time, and her erotic romance novels are some of the most popular books in history.

The Fifty Shades series begins when 21-year-old Anastasia Steele (Ana) interviews 27-year-old Christian Grey, a rising titan of business, for her college newspaper. The books center on Ana's sexual awakening and the conflicts that arise from Christian's enjoyment of BDSM (bondage/discipline, dominance/submission, and sadism/masochism). While Ana is attracted to Christian, she feels alternately uncertain, curious, and anxious about his sexual predilections. Her need for the trappings of a traditional relationship, combined with his need to be dominant in every aspect of life, causes trouble between them.

The novels offer an ongoing will-they-or-won't-they-style plot, with plenty of obstacles and other potential lovers. Like any couple, Ana and Christian must navigate previous romantic partners, make choices about the future, and learn to compromise. They need to figure out the emotional, financial, and physical balance that works for them. However, what makes the Fifty Shades series different from other books in the romance genre is the particular nature of Ana and Christian's sexual life; the books are quite graphic in their descriptions of BDSM practices—and they became the first mainstream erotica bestsellers.

Erika Leonard was born in London in 1963. She graduated from the University of Kent and worked for many years in television production. She's also the happily married mother of two teenage sons. In interviews, James explains that the books were prompted by a midlife crisis and include her personal fantasies.

To date, James has released five books in the series. *Fifty Shades of Grey* (2011), *Fifty Shades Darker* (2012), and *Fifty Shades Freed* (2012) form the core trilogy; in 2015, James published *Grey: Fifty Shades of Grey as Told by Christian*, which retells the events of the first novel from his point of view, followed by *Darker: Fifty Shades Darker as Told by Christian* (2017). Another book is forthcoming. The more recent books detail Christian's troubled childhood and further explain how his BDSM proclivities allowed him to overcome his past and find success.

No one can deny the books' hold on readers: *Fifty Shades of Grey* was the fastest-selling paperback ever in the United Kingdom, and the whole series has sold more than 125 million copies around the world. James's bestselling status enabled her to exert a great amount of control over the movies based on her books. She allegedly has approval over such details as costumes and setting, as well as larger concerns like director and stars. It's working: two movies based on the series have been released, with more in production.

Some critics took umbrage with what they perceived to be a misogynistic undertone throughout the books. Christian's sexual satisfaction hinges upon his ability to dominate his female partners, known as submissives, taking away their agency and their choice. However, as the books' fans point out, Ana chooses to be involved with Christian, and he adapts some of his behaviors per her request. The series has been credited with broadening the conversation about sexuality and the wide range of possibilities for pleasure between consenting adults.

ABOVE: Jack London, writing outside in 1905. London aimed to write 1,000 words a day.

"When It Is Finished, You Are Always Surprised"

WRITERS' DAILY HABITS & RITUALS

WE ALL HAVE 24 HOURS IN A DAY, and some people use their allowance of time on earth to create masterpieces. But finding that time never comes easy, no matter who you are or how many novels you might have to your name. As J. K. Rowling once remarked, "Some people do not seem to grasp that I still have to sit down in peace and write the books, apparently believing that they pop up like mushrooms without my connivance. I must therefore guard the time allotted to writing as a Hungarian Horntail guards its firstborn egg."

Some writers wake up early to work. Toni Morrison cultivated the habit of rising before dawn, while balancing her job as an editor at Random House with raising her sons as a single parent and her literary endeavors. She found that she was "clearer-headed, more confident, and generally more intelligent in the morning." George Orwell, in contrast, wrote late into the night.

Another trick is to set a daily writing goal. That habit worked for Jack London, who aimed for 1,000 words a day, regardless of how he felt or where he was living. Mark Twain tried for a little more, usually while lying in bed, and Stephen King shoots for 10 pages a day, or about 2,000 words. "On some days those ten pages come easily," he notes in his memoir, *On Writing*. "I'm up and out and doing errands by eleven-thirty in the morning, perky as a rat in liverwurst. More frequently, as I grow older, I find myself eating lunch at my desk and finishing the day's work around one-thirty in the afternoon. Sometimes, when the words come hard, I'm still fiddling around at teatime. Either way is fine with me, but only under dire circumstances do I allow myself to shut down before I get my 2,000 words."

Charles Dickens took long walks around London to spur his creative juices. Joseph Heller liked to write in his head while riding the bus or brushing his teeth, generating ideas for the next day's pages. Ayn Rand took speed. F. Scott Fitzgerald drank and smoked—and died from alcohol-related causes at age 44.

While it's great to have isolation and privacy, as Leo Tolstoy required, some writers compose with company, either by desire or by necessity. Jane Austen would write while her mother and sister sewed nearby, switching the writing for sewing of her own when visitors arrived. Agatha Christie would plop her typewriter on any handy table.

Lewis Carroll liked to write standing up. When he gets stuck, Dan Brown goes upside down, using an inversion-therapy table to break through writer's block. Brown also keeps an hourglass on his desk and stops to do calisthenics every hour. Kurt Vonnegut said, "I do pushups and sit-ups all the time, and feel as though I am getting lean and sinewy, but maybe not." Perhaps that was due to the "several belts of Scotch and water" he'd use to calm his "twanging intellect" at the end of each day.

However the writing gets on the page, writers have to be willing to toss whatever isn't working. In a letter, Ernest Hemingway explained that he "write[s] one page of masterpiece to ninety one pages of shit. I try to put the shit in the wastebasket."

Whatever their unique habits and daily routines, all successful writers have one thing in common: they write. John Steinbeck advised to "abandon the idea that you are ever going to finish. Lose track of the 400 pages and write just one page for each day; it helps. Then when it gets finished, you are always surprised." E. B. White likewise recommended a can-do attitude: "A writer who waits for ideal conditions under which to work will die without putting a word on paper."

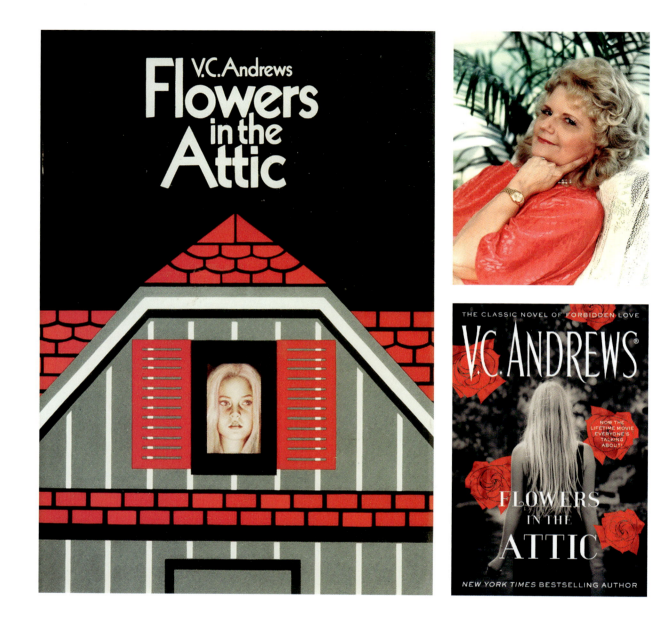

CLOCKWISE FROM LEFT: The cover of the first edition of *Flowers in the Attic*, published in 1979. | A photo of author V. C. Andrews. Andrews wrote in secret, and completed 20 short stories and 9 novels in 7 years. | An updated book cover released in 2014, to tie in with a Lifetime movie release.

31

FLOWERS IN THE ATTIC

V. C. Andrews · 1979

Our homes are our sanctuaries, where we go after a long day, where we can be most ourselves, where we shrug off our burdens and relax. There is the outside world, with its challenges and difficulties, and there is the inside world, cozy and cocooned. No home is more safe and secure than the one in which we spent our childhood, or the one where we choose to raise our family. V. C. Andrews takes these comfortable, familiar notions, and utterly upends them with her horror novel *Flowers in the Attic* (1979).

There's incest, child abuse, rape, and literal skeletons hidden by wealthy families—it's a soap opera you can read, with taboos and creepiness on every page. And readers love it.

After the death of her husband in 1957, Corrine Dollanganger returns to her ancestral family home in Virginia, along with her four children: 14-year-old Chris, 12-year-old Cathy, and 5-year-old twins Cory and Carrie. She has been estranged from her parents, Olivia and Malcolm Foxworth, for many years. When the family arrives at the big house, the four children are sent into the attic, where they'll spend the next several years being abused by their grandmother and slowly poisoned with arsenic-sprinkled doughnuts. Their grandfather cannot learn of their existence, or so they are told, in order for Corrine to receive her inheritance upon his death. Chris and Cathy try to make the time as pleasant as possible for their siblings, who become sick and stunted. Taking on parental roles while in the throes of puberty, the older siblings develop sexual and romantic feelings for each other.

Flowers in the Attic ticks every box in the gothic-literature playbook: a huge creepy house; a sense of foreboding and doom; secrets and sins that affect and afflict the innocent. It explores the ways in which repression might drive a person to do horrible things or even go insane, while demonstrating the inescapability of the past. Chris and Cathy aren't the first generation to commit incest; as we learn in subsequent books, Corrine and her husband were half-brother and -sister. Many characters endure sexual violence, including Cathy's rape by her mother's new husband. The melodrama drives the plot, shocking readers with the depth of depravity in the Dollanganger-Foxworth families. You can't look, but you can't look away either.

In selecting the name Cathy for her heroine, Andrews clearly signals her book's connection to another novel about horrors committed in the name of family: *Wuthering Heights* (1847). While Cathy and Chris truly seem to love one another, no reader could happily call *Flowers in the Attic* or its sequels a romance. That could be said for *Wuthering Heights* as well: in recollecting the love between Catherine and her adopted brother, Heathcliff, readers sometimes forget the depths of despair and violence the characters inflict upon one another.

Born Cleo Virginia Andrews in Portsmouth, Virginia, in 1923, Andrews suffered from crippling rheumatoid arthritis and endured multiple back surgeries beginning in her early teens. She spent the majority of her life in a wheelchair or on crutches. After graduating from high school, she took an art correspondence course, and eventually supported her mother with the money she made doing fashion illustrations and commercial work. She wrote on the side, in secret, completing 20 short stories and nine novels in seven years before finding success with *Flowers in the Attic*.

The Dollanganger series continues to track Cathy and Chris as they attempt to overcome their awful past, separately and together. Cathy, in particular, wants revenge on Corrine at any cost. A later book, *Garden of Shadows* (1986), helps explain the awfulness that transformed Olivia from an insecure young woman into an evangelical monster. To date, two movies have been made from *Flowers in the Attic*: one in 1987, and another in 2014. A ghostwriter handpicked by the Andrews estate after her death in 1986 carries on the tradition of sweeping, twisted tales.

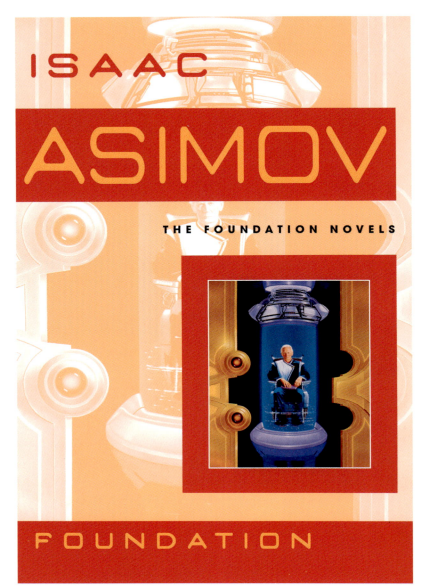

CLOCKWISE FROM LEFT: A 2004 hardcover edition dust jacket of *Foundation.* | Author Isaac Asimov, circa 1965. Asimov wrote or edited more than 500 books throughout his lifetime. | The Foundation series was first published in stories that appeared in *Astounding* magazine. Copies here are from 1942.

32

FOUNDATION SERIES

Isaac Asimov · 1951–1993

f you're trying to explain the term *polymath*, you would do well to use the example of Isaac Asimov. Over the course of his lifetime, the bespectacled, mutton-chopped figure wrote or edited more than 500 books, including both science textbooks and science fiction. As he would explain to those who asked, he managed to stay so prolific in part by jotting down "every idea [he's] ever had."

Starting in 1942, inspired by Edward Gibbon's *The History of the Decline and Fall of the Roman Empire* (1776–1789), Asimov conceived of the Galactic Empire in a series of short stories; these were later published as *Foundation* (1951), the first novel in the Foundation series. He published two more novels in rapid succession, *Foundation and Empire* (1952) and *Second Foundation* (1953), then took a 30-year break. He picked up where he left off, at the request of his publisher, with two more sequels, *Foundation's Edge* (1982) and *Foundation and Earth* (1986), and wrote two prequels, *Prelude to Foundation* (1988) and *Forward the Foundation* (1993, published posthumously) before his death in 1992. At the outset of the series, Asimov was just beginning to be noticed as a writer; by the conclusion, he was widely recognized as perhaps the greatest sci-fi writer to ever pick up a pen.

Isaac Asimov was born in 1920 in Russia. His family emigrated in 1923, to settle in New York City. His parents ran a candy store in Brooklyn. As a child, he would convince his mother and father that the pulpy sci-fi magazines he read were educational because they had "science" in their titles. Ruse aside, he loved learning. He earned a PhD in biochemistry from Columbia, taught that subject at the college level, and read widely and deeply his entire life.

Bursting with high concepts, the Foundation books trace the work of the character Hari Seldon. A brilliant thinker, Seldon invents psychohistory, a mathematical sociological model that can predict and shape the collective behavior of humans over a very, very long span of time. While Seldon cannot foresee the behavior of any one individual, his system demonstrates that the Galactic Empire is doomed to fail, at which point chaos and mayhem will descend for thousands of years, and then a second empire will rise. As he analyzes his data and its patterns, he also realizes that this terrible period could be significantly shortened via the launch of a Foundation composed of talented, capable people who will serve as the basis of the subsequent empire. Seldon forms a secret second Foundation too. Separate books cover other characters and periods, with unique plots—but in each one, math, science, and social science save the day again and again.

Readers searching for extraterrestrials, epic battles, and innovative technology might want to look elsewhere. As Nobel Prize–winning economist Paul Krugman noted in a 2012 paean to the novels, "After all, the Foundation novels aren't really about the galaxy, or even about space travel. They're about the true final frontier—understanding ourselves, and the societies we make." In particular, the books explore how close we can get to a full scientific understanding of human communities and how this effort might allow us to bend history in beneficial directions.

In 1966, the Foundation series won a special Hugo Award for Best All-Time Series, beating out J. R. R. Tolkien's Lord of the Rings (1954–1955). Of course, it might take some readers as long to get through the seven original books, plus the more recent books in the series approved by his estate, as it took Asimov to write them. It's a reading project worth the effort, though, as the Foundation books testify to an amazing mind with singular powers of creativity.

33

FRANKENSTEIN

Mary Shelley · 1818

Mary Godwin was just 16 when she ran off with poet Percy Bysshe Shelley, and just 18 when she dreamed up the world's most famous monster. In doing so, she not only launched thousands of horror stories but essentially invented science fiction as a literary genre.

Frankenstein began with a challenge. Godwin and Shelley arrived on the shores of Lake Geneva in 1816 expecting a frolicsome summer with their friend Lord Byron. Instead, it was unseasonably cold. To pass the dreary days, Byron asked everyone to come up with a ghost story. Mary longed to create a tale "which would speak to the mysterious fears of our nature, and awaken thrilling horror—one to make the reader dread to look round, to curdle the blood, and quicken the beatings of the heart." Initially, perhaps suffering from the pressure of trying to perform for her lover and his well-known friend, she got a case of writer's block.

Mary Wollstonecraft Godwin was born in London in 1797, the daughter of anarchist philosopher William Godwin and feminist philosopher Mary Wollstonecraft, who died soon after the birth. As a teen Mary Godwin would read at her mother's grave, eventually having secret meetings there with Shelley, a disciple of her father, although Shelley already had a wife and a child on the way.

According to its author, the idea for *Frankenstein* arrived in a waking dream a few days into Byron's contest, but the truth might have been far sadder. In an 1815 diary entry, Mary describes her profound grief at the sudden death of her infant daughter, and her longing to return the baby to life. At any rate, she spent a night at Byron's villa alternately dreaming and thinking about a scientist who creates a monster—and she won Byron's storytelling contest hands down.

The 1818 publication of *Frankenstein* was a ray of sunshine in Mary Shelley's otherwise-grim existence. Two more children died in infancy. A beloved sister committed suicide. Percy had multiple affairs, possibly with her stepsister. The Shelleys traveled almost constantly to avoid creditors. Mary and Percy had married in 1816, but then he drowned in 1822. The resulting unhappiness, alienation, and loneliness of widowhood inform the book, which went through a significant revision in 1831—and it's this version that we now read. At this point, too, Shelley added a preface that explains the story's genesis, an effort to correct rumors that her husband helped write it.

Captain Robert Walton encounters Victor Frankenstein in a barren, icy world. As he nurses Frankenstein back to health, he hears about the young scientist's childhood and early experiments seeking to animate dead creatures. Using corpses and slaughtered animals, he fashions a creature, but the result shocks and scares him, and he flees. A string of murders follows the scientist, who is convinced that his monster is the cause. In the mountains, Frankenstein meets the monster, who eloquently pleads for a companion to combat his isolation. The doctor agrees, then becomes increasingly horrified as the monster murders again and again, including taking the life of the doctor's fiancée. Frankenstein vows to spend the remainder of his days enacting revenge.

Aside from the three Boris Karloff movies and countless other appearances in pop culture over the past 200 years, *Frankenstein* treads some heady waters. The novel features a complex structure, stories within letters within narratives told by different people; this frame-within-a-frame arrangement was popular in the 19th century but can be challenging to follow. It's a novel of ideas, asking vast, thorny questions about science, ethics, and psychology. Who gets to play God? What is the price of knowledge? What do we owe those we usher into the world?

These questions resonate in the 21st century, when advanced technologies like stem-cell research and cloning bring us closer and closer to the possibility Shelley so compellingly imagined.

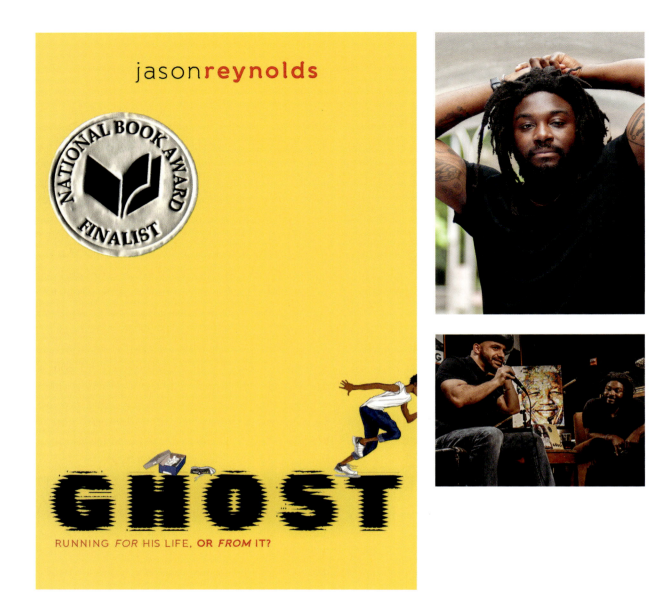

34

GHOST

Jason Reynolds · 2016

I t's a true story that would make a great novel: growing up, Jason Reynolds hated to read. He couldn't stand the books he was given in school, partly because they concerned characters who were nothing like he was—young, black, being raised by a single mom in a tough suburb outside of Washington, DC. Shortly before he turned 18, he discovered *Black Boy*, Richard Wright's 1945 memoir of an impish child who escaped the Jim Crow South to become a successful writer, and Reynolds was hooked. He went on to major in English at the University of Maryland. Now he's a bestselling, award-winning writer, publishing eight books in three years, with his first novel being made into a movie and a seven-figure deal for another four, more than making up for lost time.

Distraught at the lack of relatable protagonists in literature, Reynolds sought to create his own. He has become a middle-grade and YA super-success, particularly with so-called reluctant readers. He spends a lot of time speaking to schoolchildren, having given hundreds of talks over the past few years, chatting about "Kool-Aid and ramen noodles, Jordans and basketball, because that's what matters to them." And he promises to never, ever write boring books. Both critics and readers respond to Reynolds's approachable characters and real-world stories told in authentic voices. *Ghost* was a National Book Award finalist in 2016.

The protagonist of *Ghost* is Castle Cranshaw, an eighth grader who lives in a housing development with a single mom who's always working. He prefers the nickname Ghost, a reference to the time he took off after his drunken father shot at his mother and him. Now his dad's in jail. One day he outruns a cocky guy on his school's track team, known as the Defenders, and gets recruited by the coach, whose drug addiction destroyed his chance to run on the US Olympic team. Ghost's mom can't afford fancy running shoes, so he shoplifts a pair; the overwhelming guilt slows him down, even as he works to become the Defenders' fastest sprinter.

Running becomes the book's central metaphor: at the start of the novel Ghost runs away from his problems. However, as his coach explains, "Trouble is, you can't run away from yourself. . . . Ain't *nobody* that fast." Through the physical act of running, as well as the bonds he forms with other runners, Ghost gradually learns to speed up and even run toward his hopes and dreams. *Ghost* launched the Track series, which will continue to focus on different members of the Defenders. *Patina* (2017), the second book, tells the story of a black girl being raised by an adoptive white mother and is Reynolds's first book written from a female point of view. The third book in the series is *Sunny* (2018), about a boy with a cheerful disposition and an awful past.

At 19, Reynolds lost a friend to an execution-style killing. He writes about the subsequent pain and anger in *Long Way Down* (2017), a novel in verse about a boy looking to avenge his brother's murder: it was long-listed for the National Book Award. *The Boy in the Black Suit* (2015) tells the story of a teen who starts hanging around funeral homes after his mother dies from breast cancer and his father spins into alcoholism, and who finds solace in his grief by being around others who are grieving. *When I Was the Greatest* (2014) describes a 16-year-old with Tourette's syndrome, as a way of talking about how mental illness is, and is not, dealt with in the black community. Reynolds was born in 1983 and came of age during the AIDS and drug epidemics of the 1980s and 1990s. He points to Queen Latifah as a role model who introduced him to poetry and helped him get through a difficult childhood. His career demonstrates a passionate commitment to going far beyond familiar narratives and to crafting a wide range of books for young people from all backgrounds.

GILEAD

A NOVEL

MARILYNNE ROBINSON

AUTHOR OF *HOUSEKEEPING*

CLOCKWISE FROM LEFT: The first edition dust jacket of *Gilead*, published in 2004. | Author Marilynne Robinson hails from Idaho. She taught for 25 years at the Iowa Writers' Workshop before transitioning to professor emeritus in 2016.

35

GILEAD

Marilynne Robinson · 2004

Some novels demand to be read in great gulps; the profound beauty and spirituality of *Gilead* (2004) ask to be slowly and carefully savored.

The book opens in 1956, as Reverend John Ames writes a letter to his seven-year-old son, with the knowledge that he, as a late-in-life father, likely won't witness the boy's entrance into adulthood. So he recounts his own childhood in Gilead, a small town in Iowa. He describes how his father, a Christian pacifist, would argue passionately with his grandfather, a radical abolitionist similar to John Brown, who wore his gun while preaching at the pulpit, and who would have given away everything his family possessed in service of his beliefs. Ames discusses his entrance into the Congregationalist clergy, as well as his ongoing struggles with belief and righteousness.

Ames's first wife died giving birth to their daughter, who also died. He must cope with these losses even as the family of his best friend, Boughton, grows and grows. His envy transforms into an unyielding gratitude after the surprise arrival of Lila, an uneducated itinerant woman, into his life when he is already an old man. The passages that address his love for Lila and their son are some of the book's most potent. Ames never expected to again be a husband or a father. But having been given the opportunity to fulfill these roles, he now sees them as paramount to his identity. He is a deeply moral, deeply worthy man.

But *Gilead* offers more than a catalogue of one man's goodness and grace. Ames also writes about his feelings about the return of his namesake and godson, Boughton's wayward son. Ames watches as this man develops a special bond with Lila and grows into a second father to Ames's son. He bears witness to what his eventual absence might look like.

The novel captivated readers across the spectrum, from Barack Obama to the National Book Critics Circle, which awarded the novel its prize in 2004, to the feminist internet, which regularly posts articles about the effect of Robinson's work on its readers, devout or otherwise. The novel was awarded the 2005 Pulitzer Prize for fiction. Prior to *Gilead*, Robinson had published the well-regarded *Housekeeping*, a novel about two sisters, in 1980.

Robinson continues to revisit the world of *Gilead*. *Home* (2008) focuses on the Boughton family, taking place during much of the same time period as the earlier novel. *Lila* (2014) offers the perspective of Ames's wife, detailing her life before she met Ames. Taken together the trio offers what one critic from BuzzFeed called "religion without evangelism . . . . [T]hey wrestle, without pomposity, with what can only be described as the most important questions of life. What does it mean to be good? To forgive? To die? And what might a life of striving toward those answers look like?"

Born in Idaho in 1943, Robinson graduated from Pembroke College, at the time the women's college at Brown University, and earned a PhD from the University of Washington in 1977. After 25 years of teaching at the Iowa Writers' Workshop, she transitioned to professor emeritus in 2016, in part to focus more on writing. In addition to fiction, Robinson writes nonfiction on such subjects as Calvinism, education, American Puritanism, democracy, and environmentalism.

A recent essay for the *New York Times* offers Robinson's ruminations on how much literature teaches us. Books expand our minds, she argues, giving us access to experiences, ideas, and people vastly different from our own. One way to strive toward a life worth living, then, might be to simply start reading.

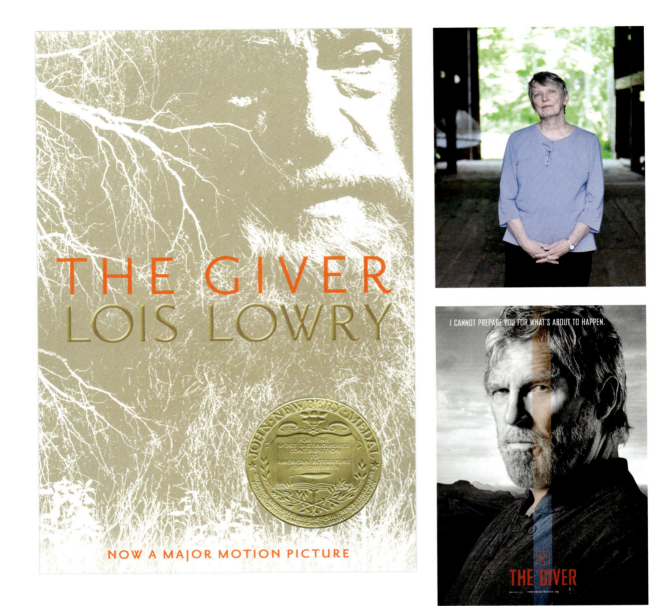

36

THE GIVER

Lois Lowry · 1993

Memory matters. The idea is central to *The Giver* (1993), the young-adult novel that won the Newbery Medal in 1994. What and how we choose to remember, to memorialize, and to pass on not only shapes us as individuals but also shapes our collective consciousness. Creating and cementing connections between people may be thought of as the broader theme of Lois Lowry's entire oeuvre, more than 40 books primarily for children and young adults.

When the novel begins, Jonas's society, known as the Community, appears to be perfect. He and his friends do fun, pleasant things. Nobody has to do the dishes, nobody goes hungry, and nobody feels pain or sadness. But, on the day he turns 12, Jonas is apprenticed as the next Receiver of Memory, and he slowly discovers "Sameness," the plan to eliminate all suffering and strife from everyone's lives. What seemed a utopia is revealed as dystopia: no one can see color, or express creativity, or experience the emotions and variety that give richness and meaning to our days.

Jonas trains with the Giver, the current repository of memory and the only person allowed to read books other than those mandated by the Community. As Jonas is introduced to new depths of knowledge and emotion, his eyes are opened to other uncomfortable truths. In his world, all infants are assigned to families rather than raised by biological parents. Jonas's father brings home a troubled baby, Gabriel, to nurture—if the baby doesn't thrive, he will be "released from the Community" and disappeared to Elsewhere. Despite warnings not to become attached, Jonas feels protective of the infant and struggles with how to reconcile his conflicting personal and societal responsibilities. Although *The Giver* ends ambiguously, the three books that follow, *Gathering Blue* (2000), *Messenger* (2004), and *Son* (2012), help clarify the fate of Jonas and Gabriel.

In the 1990s, Jeff Bridges optioned *The Giver* for a movie, after looking for a project that fit two criteria: his dad, Lloyd Bridges, could star in it, and his kids would enjoy watching. By the time the movie got made in 2014, however, his father had passed away, so Jeff wound up taking the role of the Giver himself. Meryl Streep and Taylor Swift added more star power to the cast.

Lowry was born in Honolulu in 1937 and left college to get married at age 19. She and her first husband eventually raised four children. In time she began studying at University of Southern Maine, graduating with a degree in English. She developed an interest in photography and took photos to accompany articles she submitted to publications like *Redbook* magazine. Based on the strength of her journalism, an editor asked whether she'd ever consider writing a YA book. *A Summer to Die*, based in part on the death of Lowry's older sister from cancer, was published in 1977. She also drew on her elderly father's senility to consider what life might be like without the ability to remember.

Using her books to explore demanding subjects and ideas comes naturally to Lowry. *The Giver* touches on euthanasia and depicts a boy who openly defies the authorities in his life. As a result of their challenging topics, her novels have been banned almost as frequently as they have been extolled. In a world of encroaching Sameness, *The Giver* offers readers the sweetness of rebellion.

From Page to Stage and Screen

THE BEST ADAPTATIONS

WHEN AN ADAPTATION from a novel succeeds—as those listed below do—fans get double the pleasure: the joy of reading the book coupled with the thrill of seeing beloved characters and plots enacted on-screen or onstage.

BEST MOVIES

GONE WITH THE WIND (1939)

The masterful 1939 movie *Gone with the Wind*, starring Clark Gable and Vivien Leigh, has become a cultural touchstone, outshining perhaps even the 1936 novel on which it was based. Indeed, the film's most famous line—Rhett Butler's "Frankly, my dear, I don't give a damn"—is a deviation from Margaret Mitchell's book. Hattie McDaniel became the first African American to win an Oscar for her portrayal of Mammy.

TO KILL A MOCKINGBIRD (1962)

Harper Lee loved the 1962 movie based on her 1960 novel, exclaiming, "If the integrity of a film adaptation is measured by the degree to which the novelist's intent is preserved, Mr. Foote's screenplay should be studied as a classic." Gregory Peck garnered tremendous critical praise for his portrayal of Atticus Finch, who was named the #1 movie hero of all time by the American Film Institute in 2003.

THE GODFATHER TRILOGY (1972–1990)

Directed by Francis Ford Coppola and featuring a slew of stars, *The Godfather* (1972) and *The Godfather Part II* focus on the events described in Mario Puzo's 1969 novel of the same name. The third movie came out in 1990, tracing the fate of Michael Corleone and his Italian American crime family into the 1970s and 1980s. Puzo's death in 1999 put a fourth film on hold.

THE LORD OF THE RINGS (2001–2003)

Peter Jackson's adaptation of The Lord of the Rings (1954–1955) from 2001 to 2003 proved so popular that he went on to make another three movies based on *The Hobbit* (1937). Collectively the six movies won 17 Academy Awards and have earned close to $6 billion. Amazon recently announced that it would be developing the books for the small screen.

HARRY POTTER SERIES (2001–2011)

The seven novels (1997–2007) detailing Harry Potter's coming-of-age were transformed into an incredibly successful eight movies, starring Daniel Radcliffe as the orphan boy who discovers his magical abilities and saves the world from the evil Lord Voldemort. With the involvement of J. K. Rowling, several more movies, including prequels, will be coming out over the next few years.

BEST PLAYS AND MUSICALS

MAN OF LA MANCHA (1965)

Borrowing the metafictive structure of *Don Quixote* (1605), on which it's based, *Man of La Mancha* consists of a play within a play: imprisoned during the Spanish Inquisition, Cervantes and his fellow inmates decide to dramatize a story about an insane knight. The 1965 Tony Award–winning musical has been revived a number of times on Broadway and on London's West End.

THE LION, THE WITCH AND THE WARDROBE (1989)

A staple of children's theater, *The Lion, the Witch and the Wardrobe* comes from the 1950 novel of the same name by C. S. Lewis, part of his Chronicles of Narnia series (1950–1956). As in the book, four human children discover a magical land of talking animals, wicked witches, and supernatural creatures. A version for two actors is enjoying a popular Off-Broadway run.

THE COLOR PURPLE (2004)

The Color Purple could just as easily have been slotted under best movies, so successful was the 1985 Steven Spielberg adaptation of the 1982 novel. But the beloved musical—produced by Quincy Jones and Oprah Winfrey, who also starred in the film—enjoyed an award-winning run on Broadway in the 2000s, followed by a world tour and a revival on Broadway from 2015 to 2017.

THE CURIOUS INCIDENT OF THE DOG IN THE NIGHT-TIME (2012)

Upon the play's arrival from the West End in 2014, the *New York Times* called *The Curious Incident of the Dog in the Night-Time* "one of the most fully immersive works ever to wallop Broadway." Like the 2003 source novel, the theatrical adaptation focuses on a gifted autistic teen who tries to solve a mystery in his neighborhood, but it uses a play-within-a-play to do so.

NATASHA, PIERRE & THE GREAT COMET OF 1812 (2012)

Question: How do you adapt the lengthy, discursive *War and Peace* (1869) for the stage without forcing theatergoers to spend years of their lives watching the result? Answer: you focus on the devastating affair between Anatole and Natasha, heightening it with amazing music, raucous dancing, and performers who periodically thread through the audience.

BEST TELEVISION SHOWS

LONESOME DOVE (1989)

In a nice twist of fate, Larry McMurtry wrote the novel *Lonesome Dove* (1985) after his screenplay for a film version fell through in the 1970s. The novel won the Pulitzer Prize and was made into a miniseries starring Tommy Lee Jones and Robert Duvall. The series won several Emmys and Golden Globe Awards.

PRIDE AND PREJUDICE (1995)

"It's a truth universally acknowledged that a person in want of a good project will adapt *Pride and Prejudice*— if not always to dazzling effect," wrote a critic in 2014, nodding to the frequency with which Jane Austen's 1813 novel has been adapted. Most viewers name the 1995 BBC series as their favorite, due in part to the terrific chemistry between Colin Firth as Darcy and Jennifer Ehle as Elizabeth Bennet.

GAME OF THRONES (2011–PRESENT)

HBO's series based on A Song of Ice and Fire (1996– present) by George R. R. Martin is one of the most successful shows in the history of television, airing in more than 170 countries. Individual episodes cost upward of $15 million to produce, a reflection of the show's gorgeous locations, excellent acting, epic battle scenes, and stunning, realistic CGI technology.

OUTLANDER (2014–PRESENT)

The same difficulty initially drives the *Outlander* television series on Starz as the Outlander novel series (1991– present): Will the time-traveling nurse Claire Randall stay in the 18th century or return to the 20th century? Both works become more complicated as they go on, arcing and bending in different ways, but each demonstrating a masterful hold on multiple genres.

THE HANDMAID'S TALE (2017–PRESENT)

To promote the first season of its show, Hulu hired red-cloaked handmaids to walk the streets of New York City. Starring Elisabeth Moss, *The Handmaid's Tale* became the first streaming series to win an Emmy for Outstanding Drama Series, in 2017. It updates the action of the 1985 novel to the present, making Margaret Atwood's dystopian society seem all the more real.

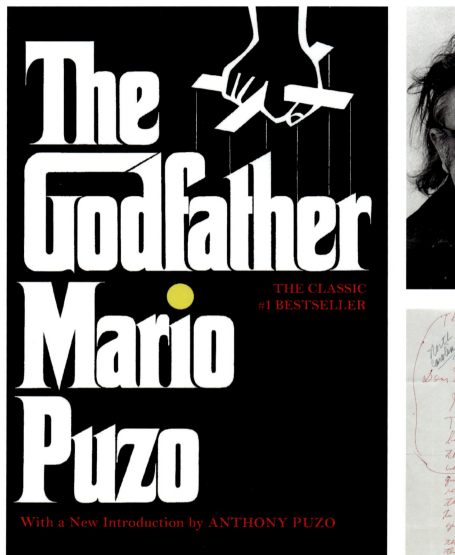

37

THE GODFATHER

Mario Puzo · 1969

The Godfather (1969) didn't start America's love affair with gangsters, but the novel and subsequent movies certainly fanned the flames of ardor. In Vito Corleone and Michael, his straitlaced son turned crime boss, readers and viewers alike found idols worth worshipping.

Born to an Italian family in Hell's Kitchen in 1920, Mario Puzo started writing stories and articles during his time in the US Army, and then worked for an array of pulp magazines in the 1950s and 1960s. A publisher encouraged him to explore the mafia as a subject, thinking it would sell well and help Puzo better support his wife and five children.

An epigraph attributed to 19th-century novelist Honoré de Balzac opens the sprawling novel about an Italian American family: "Behind every great fortune there is a crime." In the case of the Corleones, that would be *crimes*, plural. After Don Vito Corleone is shot in 1945, his sons struggle to take over the family business, sparring with one another and warring with New York's other mafia families. Despite being groomed for a life of respectability, the youngest, Michael, proves himself to be far more calculating and nefarious than his father. Settled firmly as the head of the family, he transforms into the ultimate antihero.

Puzo based his fictional characters on real people, especially the Five Families said to rule organized crime in New York. The singer Johnny Fontane, who asks the Godfather to help him get out of his studio contract (thereby inspiring the Godfather's famous declaration "I'm gonna make him an offer he can't refuse"), was said to be a thinly veiled Frank Sinatra. Puzo also looked to the historical past, basing his mafia's maneuverings on the violent power plays between dominant families during the Italian Renaissance. Even mobsters reportedly loved the book and thought Puzo must have firsthand knowledge of their world, but in fact he had none, writing instead from research and his own experience as the child of poor immigrants from Naples to give readers a vivid sense of the Italian American experience.

Expectations weren't enormously high when the eponymous movie appeared in 1972. While Puzo's emotional, bloody novel was a bestseller, Frances Ford Coppola was hardly a household name, and films about organized crime hadn't met with much success since the 1930s. The collaboration between Coppola and Puzo, however, produced two of the greatest films of American cinema. Lines wrapped around the block during *The Godfather*'s opening weekend. Book sales shot up. Together, *The Godfather* and *The Godfather II* won Best Picture at their respective Academy Awards, and Coppola and Puzo earned a pair of Oscars for Best Adapted Screenplay too.

Puzo passed away in 1999, but his characters soldier on, via new authors: *The Godfather Returns* (2004) and *The Godfather's Revenge* (2006) pick up where *The Godfather* and Puzo's sequel, *The Sicilian* (1984), end, covering the fate of the family in the 1950s and 1960s. A prequel, *The Family Corleone* (2012), describes the rise of Vito, with a focus on the impact of his son Sonny and the adopted-orphan-turned-*consigliere* Tom Hagen. Puzo's influence can still be felt across the dramatic arcs and popularity of shows like *The Sopranos*, *Breaking Bad*, and *Better Call Saul*.

In *The Godfather*, America is a land of limitless opportunity, a cutthroat meritocracy that rewards fast thinking, hard work, and the willingness to crush anyone who stands in the way. That some of this thinking or work might involve murder, exploitation, gambling, drug- and gun-running, and prostitution isn't an issue. The values at play in the novel—among them ambition, loyalty, and an unquenchable thirst for power—are distinctly American, as much a part of our culture as apple pie and baseball.

38

GONE GIRL

Gillian Flynn · 2012

The "it" novel of 2012 concerns the disappearance of "it" girl Amy Dunne on her fifth wedding anniversary. Gorgeous and charming, married to Nick, Amy appears to lead an enviable life. She lives in a nice suburban house, she's friendly with the neighbors, she's pregnant—and now she's gone.

Nick convinced Amy to leave their life in New York City and return to the struggling Missouri town where he grew up and his family still lives. When Amy disappears, suspicion falls squarely on him. Did he murder his wife? Or is something far more complicated going on? The expertly plotted novel moves back and forth in time, from Amy's diary narrating the past to Nick's search for his wife in the present. Both sections are told in the first person, a variation on the tried-and-true "he said, she said" formula that leaves readers wondering whom to believe. The novel combines elements of suspense, crime, and mystery, and is utterly unputdownable.

Intelligent, off-kilter female protagonists in troubling circumstances have become something of a specialty for Gillian Flynn. Prior to the megahit *Gone Girl* (2012), Flynn published *Sharp Objects* (2006), about a reporter who uncovers secrets in her tiny midwestern town, and *Dark Places* (2009), about a woman who tries to figure out whether her incarcerated brother actually murdered their family when she was a child. Whereas examples of dark, disturbed leading men exist throughout literature and the movies, we don't have as many female antiheroes. That's an oversight Flynn seeks to correct—since women, after all, are equally capable of sociopathy and violence.

Flynn learned about literature and movies from her professor parents, who taught reading and film, respectively, at a local community college in Kansas City, where she was born in 1971. She combined these passions into her career as a reporter and critic for *Entertainment Weekly*, working on her novels in her spare time. She also has a master's in journalism from Northwestern.

Gone Girl spent more than 100 weeks on the *New York Times* bestseller list. Flynn wrote the screenplay for the 2014 movie, produced by Reese Witherspoon and directed by David Fincher. That too was a success, captivating audiences and critics alike.

In one of the book's most-quoted passages, Amy explains what it means to be "the Cool Girl":

"Being the Cool Girl means I am a hot, brilliant, funny woman who adores football, poker, dirty jokes, and burping, who plays video games, drinks cheap beer, loves . . . sex, and jams hot dogs and hamburgers into her mouth . . . while somehow maintaining a size 2, because Cool Girls are above all hot. Hot and understanding. Cool Girls never get angry; they only smile in a chagrined, loving manner and let their men do whatever they want."

Much saltier in the novel, the full definition resonates with readers reacting to unreasonable demands placed on them by pop culture and social media. Amy's monologue—and the novel as a whole—helps give women permission to shrug off the stereotype that the fairer sex is naturally good. *Gone Girl* also captures the disillusionment experienced by the middle class at the start of the 21st century. Like Nick, Flynn herself was laid off from her magazine job, and plenty of 20- and 30-somethings heard the sound of the American dream bursting as the economy collapsed in 2008. As much as *Gone Girl* is a psychological thriller about a marriage, it's also a commentary about the failed economy, an exploration about the limits and possibilities of feminism, and a warning about the dangers of believing everything you see on TV.

39

GONE WITH THE WIND

Margaret Mitchell · 1936

A lifelong resident of Atlanta, where she was born in 1900, Margaret Mitchell was descended from soldiers in the Revolutionary and Civil Wars. She grew up hearing stories about the latter and the subsequent era of Reconstruction. As a little girl, she would ride her pony into the Georgia countryside, where veterans would point out ruined plantations as well as the destruction wrought by General William Tecumseh Sherman's 1864 March to the Sea. The Union soldiers' decimation of the South's military and civilian infrastructure would become a key plot point in Mitchell's famous novel. Mitchell was 10 before she learned—to her great surprise—that the Confederate side lost.

Working as a reporter and society columnist for the *Atlanta Journal* taught Mitchell to research and craft a story, but it was her husband who pushed her to write a novel. Exhausted from lugging books home from the library for Mitchell to read while she recuperated from an injury, her husband is alleged to have quipped, "For God's sake, Peggy, can't you write a book instead of reading thousands of them?"

Gone with the Wind (1936) opens with vain, vapid Scarlett O'Hara flitting about and flirting at a barbecue at Tara, the Georgia plantation where she lives with her family. It's 1861, just two days after the Battle of Fort Sumter launched the Civil War. She encounters the brooding Rhett Butler, who admires her fiery spirit, but her heart belongs to dandy Ashley Wilkes, who in turn is matched with his distant cousin Melanie. The sweeping historical epic traces the intertwined fates of Scarlett, Rhett, Ashley, and Melanie as the war rages, wrecking everything they hold dear.

Mitchell sought to tell a specific story about her hometown—and she succeeded beyond all expectations.

Perhaps its first readers saw parallels between the time period of the novel and the Great Depression, another instance of people experiencing extreme hardships, or perhaps they longed to escape exactly those hardships into a vanished world; whatever the reason, the novel sold like crazy. So successful was the book and Academy Award–winning 1939 film, starring Vivien Leigh and Clark Gable, that Mitchell once vowed never to write another word. She never published anything again in her lifetime. In 1949, on her way to the movies with her husband, Mitchell was hit by a car. She died five days later, at age 48.

Though the book received the National Book Award and the Pulitzer Prize, contemporary readers might be less enthusiastic. Awash in nostalgia for the antebellum South and indifferent to the real experiences and feelings of slaves, the novel is far more revealing of the stories that too many people of Mitchell's era told themselves about the country's past than it is of that past itself. People coming to the book in the 21st century are also apt to find that the celebrated passion between Scarlett and Rhett reads much more darkly than it did to its initial audiences.

Despite all that, Scarlett persists as a precursor to strong female protagonists of our own era, like Katniss Everdeen and Daenerys Targaryen. She struggles, but she survives. Mitchell saw Scarlett's perseverance in the face of adversity as the novel's true heart. Scarlett not only adapts to her circumstances, but even thrives in many ways. She becomes more resilient for all she is forced to endure, from witnessing the ruination of her beloved Tara to grieving at the death of her family to killing a Yankee soldier who threatens to assault her. How differently we might view her had she kept the name Mitchell used in the novel's initial drafts: Pansy.

40

THE GRAPES OF WRATH

John Steinbeck · 1939

n one of the most iconic images of the Great Depression, a woman furrows her brow and stares into the distance. Lines carve the map of her face into counties and cities. One hand claws her cheek, one hand cradles a filthy infant. Two other children turn their faces away from the camera and burrow against her. She was 32, an itinerant farmhand surviving on birds she managed to kill, doing whatever she had to do to care for her seven children. Dorothea Lange shot the picture, which she named *Migrant Mother*, in 1936, three years before John Steinbeck published *The Grapes of Wrath*. He might as well have been describing the black-and-white photo.

Like Lange, Steinbeck wanted to portray the truth of the Great Depression. His fictional family, along with thousands of others, set off for California. The Joads desert their Oklahoma farm, which is collapsing under the dual weight of depression and drought, and succumb to the spell of an ad promising fruit-picking jobs. Grampa and Granma Joad die during the arduous journey west. Two of the Joad sons disappear, one leaving behind a pregnant wife. Even as the remaining Joads meet people who warn that the situation is as awful in California as everywhere else, including a man whose children starved to death as he watched helplessly, the family pushes forward. Once in California, they move from one migrant camp to another, encountering suffering and violence. Ma Joad holds everyone together as best she can. She is the Migrant Mother, removed from Lange's frame and confronting challenges with courage.

In 1962, Steinbeck received the Nobel Prize for Literature, praised by the selection committee for his social realism. He based *The Grapes of Wrath* on a series of articles he wrote for the *San Francisco News* in 1936 about the joys and sadness in the lives of migrant workers in California. The book won the Pulitzer Prize and the National Book Award. John Ford earned an Academy Award for the 1940 movie, which very quickly became as beloved as the novel. Both Eleanor Roosevelt and President Franklin Delano Roosevelt talked publicly about their great respect for the book, particularly as they stumped for policies meant to pull Americans out of the Depression's lingering effects.

Born in Salinas, California, in 1902, Steinbeck frequently explored his home state in writing: *Tortilla Flat* (1935) concerns a group of homeless men in Monterey at the end of World War I. *Of Mice and Men* (1937) describes the friendship between two itinerant ranch hands, and is based on Steinbeck's experiences working on farms. When he criticized the California agriculture industry, he did so having witnessed firsthand the crushing effects of its stratified system, exploited by those who wished to keep wealth and power. He died in 1968 and was buried, in accordance with his wishes, in the family plot in Salinas.

Steinbeck goes to great lengths to demonstrate that the true source of the Joads' trouble is not the economy or the environment. Rather, it's other people. The primary theme of the book may very well be the idea that we are one another's worst enemies. He describes the history of California, in which settlers essentially stole land, and he repeatedly shows how self-interest erodes familial and societal bonds. At the same time, however, he demonstrates how acts of kindness, both big and small, have an uplifting effect, which in turn furthers more acts of kindness. Man may pass inhumanity on to man, but he is equally capable of passing on benevolence and selflessness. There is a choice; terrible circumstances may throw it into relief, but there is always a choice.

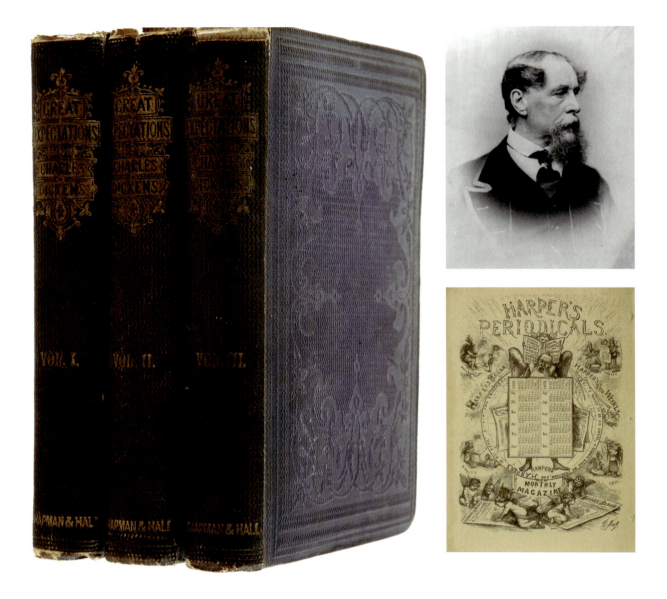

41

GREAT EXPECTATIONS

Charles Dickens · 1861

Across 15 novels, Charles Dickens created thousands of characters. Few, however, are as memorable as *Great Expectations*' Miss Havisham. She stops time at the exact moment her fiancé abandoned her at the altar. She ceases to wind the clocks. As the years go by, the wedding dress she wears becomes increasingly ragged, she loses a shoe, and the cake, party favors, and even her house decay and disintegrate around her. Readers could write the recluse off as crazy if she weren't so heartbreaking, or if she didn't provide a clue into how to read *Great Expectations*: her name—*Hav[e] is sham*—conveys the novel's main message that the pursuit of wealth will end in folly.

The most significant chronicler of Victorian England, Dickens became an outspoken advocate for socioeconomic reform, and movingly portrayed children forced to grow up too fast, from the thieving street urchins in *Oliver Twist* (1838) to the deformed doll maker in *Our Mutual Friend* (1865).

Pip, whose social and moral development propels *Great Expectations*, fits into that category as well. Orphaned and residing with his detestable older sister, the seven-year-old boy meets an escaped convict who begs for his help; though Pip tries to assist him, the man is recaptured and sent to a penal colony in Australia. This brief, strange encounter proves to be the fulcrum of Pip's life, yet he won't discover how—or grasp the full dimensions of the tragedy into which he has been thrust—until years later. In the interval he falls in love with Miss Havisham's adopted daughter, Estella, a captivating girl groomed to avenge Miss Havisham's own broken heart, and he tries to climb the slippery class ladder. His struggles to escape his bleak origins without losing himself form the backbone of this psychologically complex novel.

Although *Great Expectations* has few literal parallels with Dickens's life, a strong line of emotional autobiography runs through it. Born in 1812 in southeast England, Charles Dickens left school at age 12 after his father was imprisoned for failure to pay debts. While the rest of the family joined him in jail, Dickens was sent to paste labels on bottles in a factory, difficult physical labor he not only detested but which profoundly influenced his writing and personal beliefs. Like Pip, Dickens felt abandoned in childhood and found that sudden financial success as a young man left him torn between his social expectations and his familial obligations. Dickens wrote *Great Expectations* in a dark, difficult period. He had recently separated from his wife of 22 years while he pursued the actress Ellen Ternan; one of his 10 children had racked up gambling debts, and another had recently married a man Dickens detested. His anxieties about money, relationships, and personal character take vivid form in the novel's characters and plot.

Great Expectations came out serially in the magazine *All the Year Round* beginning in 1860 and was published as a complete text the following year. There were cliffhangers galore to keep readers interested as they waited for the next installment, and the novel's cast had memorable verbal and physical characteristics so that readers could keep everyone straight. The serial format made the book's intricate structure all the more remarkable: nearly every major character and plot point has a double.

Great Expectations ends twice, as well. In the first ending Dickens wrote, Pip and Estella meet again later in life but don't marry. Dickens's friend and fellow novelist Edward Bulwer-Lytton found that too depressing a conclusion. So Dickens rewrote the final paragraphs before it went to press, giving readers the ending that many of them want. Nevertheless, the book's famously indirect last line leaves open multiple interpretations. Like the psychological and social problems probed by the novel as a whole, the final words allow no easy resolution.

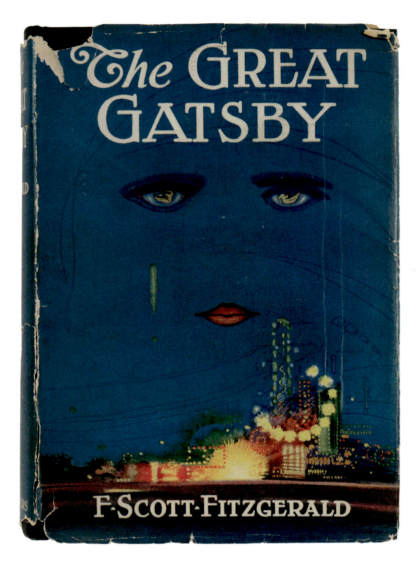

42

THE GREAT GATSBY

F. Scott Fitzgerald · 1925

Long considered to be one of the best American novels of the 20th century, *The Great Gatsby* (1925) may very well be *the* best. This short novel offers the definitive portrait of the Roaring Twenties while exploring the dangers of the American dream.

Named for his famous cousin, who penned "The Star-Spangled Banner," Francis Scott Key Fitzgerald published his first story at age 13. Despite a lackluster academic career, he entered Princeton in 1913 but left to enroll in the army. While stationed in Alabama, he met the wild, fiery Zelda Sayre. She refused to marry him until he could support the lavish lifestyle she craved, a feat he was able to accomplish with the success of his first novel, *This Side of Paradise* (1920), a semiautobiographical account of a freshman at Princeton, published when its author was just 23.

Fitzgerald would continue mining his circumstances for material. He based aspects of *The Great Gatsby*, his third novel, on the nouveau riche with whom he and Zelda hobnobbed in New York City, on Long Island, and abroad. Bouncing from yacht to nightclub to hotel, they danced, drank bootleg liquor, and epitomized the excesses of the Jazz Age. Fitzgerald based the character of Daisy Buchanan on his wife, a young, fashionable flapper later diagnosed with schizophrenia.

The homage wasn't wholly favorable. In the summer of 1922, Jay Gatsby arrives in the fictional West Egg, a village on Long Island. Wealthy and enigmatic, he throws magnificent parties to which he invites his neighbor, Nick Carraway, the book's everyman narrator. Nick discovers that Gatsby is possessed by an obsessive reverence for the two-dimensional Daisy, Nick's cousin and Gatsby's first love back when he was known as James Gatz. For the remainder of the summer, Nick helps as Gatsby tries to win back Daisy.

In *The Great Gatsby*, wealth corrupts absolutely. Daisy is married to the well-heeled, boorish Tom Buchanan, who detests Gatsby and his "new money." Gatsby's parties are meant to impress Daisy, but they draw vacuous uppercrusters who care only about having fun. Ideals gone, disgusted with the shallowness of everyone around him, Nick ultimately moves back to his midwestern hometown.

Fitzgerald's own excesses caught up to him, and he died of alcohol-related diseases at age 44 in 1940, believing himself to be a failure. In his obituary, the *New York Times* called *The Great Gatsby* an "ironic tale of life on Long Island [published] at a time when gin was the national drink and sex the national obsession." But the novel is no mere slice of a bygone age. Fitzgerald's pointed criticism of a society with too much money and too little soul speaks across the decades and looks set to continue doing so, as surveys place *The Great Gatsby* as one of the 10 most frequently taught books in American high schools. For many people, its key images—the green light on Daisy's dock, the billboard eyes of Dr. T. J. Eckleburg—are the quintessential examples of literary symbolism, and the book's oft-quoted ending has been described as "the best closing lines in American fiction."

The novel's elasticity and deep resonance have led to it being adapted into several movies, including one starring Robert Redford in 1974 and another featuring Leonardo DiCaprio in 2013, as well as plays, television shows, and at least one ballet. Its plot has also been refashioned in novels like *Great* (2014), a YA book featuring a same-sex love story, and *No One Is Coming to Save Us* (2017), about failure and heartache in a contemporary African American community. Few novels have had such rich afterlives, or have spoken so powerfully to so many readers about the elusive promises of America.

Libraries to Long For

FIRST EDITIONS AND OUTSTANDING COLLECTIONS

BOOKS ARE PRECIOUS OBJECTS, filled as they are with someone else's thoughts, hopes, and fears. Some particularly valuable books sell for the price of a small car, while others could purchase the entire dealership. If you don't have the cash, however, there's always the library, which costs nothing—assuming you return checked-out titles by the due date, that is.

The next time you go poking around an elderly relative's attic or garage, keep an eye out for books—you just might find a fortune. Only 250 copies of the first edition of *Wuthering Heights* (1847) were printed; people lucky enough to have one can expect to sell it for more than $200,000. A first edition of *Atlas Shrugged* (1957) went for $8,500 in 2016, while *Great Expectations* (1861) fetched $25,000 that same year.

Unsatisfied with the quality of the first printing of *Alice's Adventures in Wonderland* (1865), illustrator John Tenniel asked that the title be reprinted, making those first copies extremely rare—and pricey (into the seven figures). Copies of a 1932 edition signed by Alice Liddell, on whom Lewis Carroll likely based his fictional protagonist, range from a somewhat more accessible $3,500 to $7,000.

Not surprisingly, the most expensive editions tend to have some historic or cultural significance in addition to literary merit. In 2007, J. K. Rowling auctioned off a handwritten, bejeweled edition of *The Tales of Beedle the Bard*, the book bestowed to Hermione Granger by Albus Dumbledore and which helps Harry Potter vanquish Lord Voldemort in the final book of the *Harry Potter* series (1997–2007). Amazon.com purchased the book for almost $4 million, with proceeds going to Rowling's charity for institutionalized children.

If your checks don't have room for that many zeros, try heading to a library—such as the Library of Congress. Founded in 1800, it's considered to be the national library of the United States and contains almost 840 miles of bookshelves, many of them stocked with rare and valuable editions. Among the artifacts held—and made available either online or in its Washington, DC, location—are a Gutenberg Bible (~1455) and *The Bay Psalm Book* (1640), the first book printed in North America, along with first editions of numerous classics, including *The Adventures of Tom Sawyer* (1876) and *Little Women* (1868–1869). The New York Public Library, meanwhile, holds approximately 53 million titles, encompassing the first edition of *The Pilgrim's Progress* (1678), the first four folios of Shakespeare, and curiosities like Charlotte Brontë's writing desk, a lock of Mary Shelley's hair, and a letter opener that Charles Dickens had made from the paw of his favorite cat. Its main branch in Midtown boasts a gorgeous reading room open to anyone and everyone.

Universities also house astonishing collections. The Harry Ransom Center at the University of Texas at Austin, for example, offers curious readers access to such holdings as an early manuscript of *The Canterbury Tales* (1387), true-crime reference books used by Sir Arthur Conan Doyle when writing his Sherlock Holmes stories, a journal kept by John Steinbeck in preparation for writing *The Grapes of Wrath* (1939), and several versions of *Another Country* (1962) by James Baldwin.

As one of the wealthiest people on the planet, Bill Gates doesn't need to go to a library to see treasures; an avid reader and book collector, he brings the treasures to himself. He paid more than $30 million for *The Codex Leicester*, a 16th-century notebook full of sketches and ideas kept by Leonardo da Vinci. He and his wife also love *The Great Gatsby* (1925), especially this line, which is painted on the ceiling of his

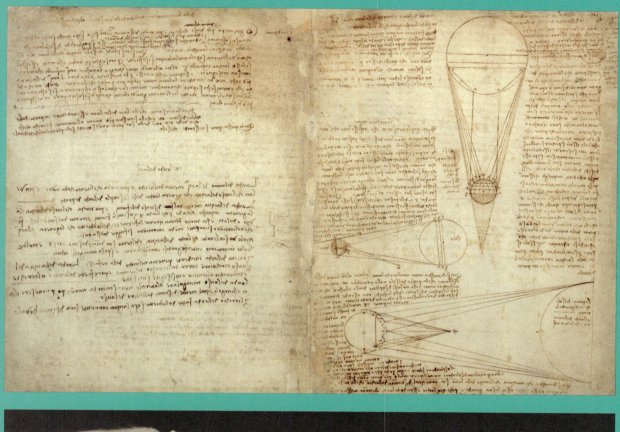

home library: "He had come a long way to this blue lawn, and his dream must have seemed so close that he could hardly fail to grasp it."

Another celebrity bibliophile, Oprah Winfrey, has the singular power to transform a book into a bestseller. Her eponymous book club selected 70 titles throughout the 15-year run of her talk show, from *One Hundred Years of Solitude* (1967) in 2004 to *The Pillars of the Earth* (1989) in 2007 to *Great Expectations* (1861) in 2010. Oprah's personal collection contains a range of fiction and nonfiction: *To Kill a Mockingbird* (1960) signed by Harper Lee, as well as everything written by Zora Neale Hurston. "I'm not a book snob," she said in an interview about her love of books. "First editions are great, but so are all books. If you're starting your own library, all that matters is that you start with what you love."

ABOVE, TOP TO BOTTOM: Bill Gates is a dedicated reader and book collector. Among his treasures is *The Codex of Leicester*, the notebook that Leonardo da Vinci kept of his sketches and ideas, valued at $30 million. | The New York Public Library has a vast collection that includes quirky artifacts, like this letter opener, which Charles Dickens had made from the paw of his cat.

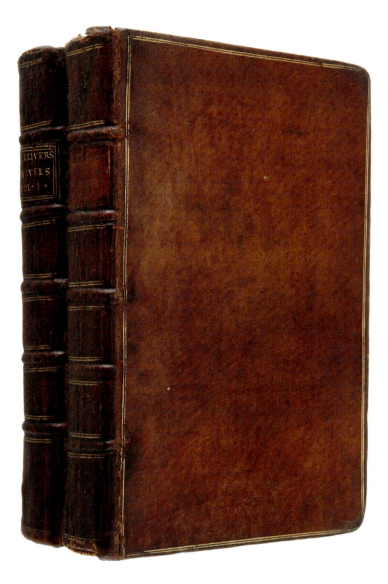

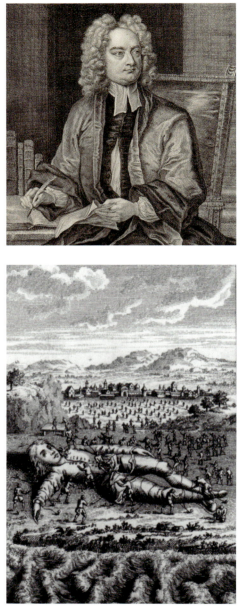

CLOCKWISE FROM LEFT: Volumes from one of the first printings of *Gulliver's Travels*, published in 1726. | An 1875 portrait of author Jonathan Swift, entitled "Dear Swift from Garvis." Swift was a poet, pamphleteer, and cleric, who combined his political activism with his writing. | An engraved illustration accompanied each of the four volumes of *Swift, Voyages de Gulliver*, printed in Paris in 1795.

43

GULLIVER'S TRAVELS

Jonathan Swift · 1726

The true title of the novel we know as *Gulliver's Travels* is *Travels into Several Remote Nations of the World, in Four Parts, by Lemuel Gulliver, First a Surgeon, and Then a Captain of Several Ships*, a tip-off about the world we're about to enter. Its author, Jonathan Swift, was an acknowledged master of satire by the time the book came out in 1726.

A poet, a pamphleteer, and a cleric, Swift was also a founding member of the Scriblerus Club, kind of like an Algonquin Round Table for 18th-century British writers; his friend Alexander Pope also belonged. Born in Dublin in 1667, Swift left Ireland for England as a result of political troubles, but political troubles would, in time, send him back to his homeland. He earned a master's from Oxford, as well as a doctor of divinity from Trinity College, and was ordained in the Church of Ireland.

In the early 1700s, Swift began publishing in earnest while becoming increasingly politically active. He used his writing to lambast the English and further Irish causes during a time of great economic disparity and a rising sense of patriotism. *A Modest Proposal* (1729), for example, lays out a careful argument for one way the poor might solve their problems of overcrowding and famine: Swift facetiously suggests they sell their babies as food to the rich.

Gulliver's Travels is a unique mix of absurdity and criticism, revealed through the journeys of the main character, Lemuel Gulliver, a married surgeon who seeks fortune abroad. In Part I, after a storm in the South Seas, he awakes to find himself held captive by a race of people just six inches tall. He meets the emperor of Lilliput, who asks his gigantic new friend to help the Lilliputians defeat the people of Blefuscu. The two kingdoms are fighting over the ridiculous question of whether eggs should be broken on their small or big ends. He eventually goes back to England, then lands on an island of giants in Part II. Everything is bigger in Brobdingnag, including the insects who sometimes perch on his food, so he's not unhappy when an eagle plucks him up and takes him away.

In Part III, Gulliver's ship is attacked by pirates. He's saved by the Laputans, who inhabit floating islands. These people worship music, technology, and mathematics above all else, but never seem to use their knowledge in any sort of practical way. In Part IV, Gulliver arrives on an island populated by the Yahoos, a humanlike race who serve the Houyhnhnms, horses who value reason and thought. Gulliver enjoys his time here, having interesting conversations and soaking up the culture, until the Houyhnhnms glimpse his torso and discover his similarities to the Yahoos.

Throughout his adventures, Gulliver bears witness to different modes of oppression. Some groups dominate using their sheer size and brute force, while others rely on their more powerful intellect. The common thread, of course, is oppression itself. The power held by one race or group comes at the expense of another. Neither Gulliver nor his readers witness people working together or even using their knowledge and intellectual pursuits in the service of civilization.

For all its comedy, much of which relies on bodily functions, the work as a whole paints a fairly grim picture of human nature. Gulliver's misadventures grow increasingly worse, until his crew mutinies against him in Part IV. By the end of the novel, Gulliver can't stand to be near humans, preferring instead the company of his horses.

The book may be interpreted as sci-fi, philosophy, satire, and travelogue. In addition to these multiple interpretations, *Gulliver's Travels* lends itself to multiple adaptations. To date, it's been transformed into a short silent film by pioneer Georges Méliès, a Disney cartoon, an Indian live-action children's movie, and a surrealist feature-length film that critiques communist Czechoslovakia. All in all, it has earned its place in literary history as an inspired, imaginative combination of entertainment and social analysis.

44

THE HANDMAID'S TALE

Margaret Atwood · 1985

Every year, betting bookmakers take odds on possibilities for the Nobel Prize for Literature, and every year, Margaret Atwood seems to rank among the favorites. While she hasn't yet won that prize, it seems to be the only one she hasn't won; her long list of accolades includes the Arthur C. Clarke Award, the Man Booker Prize, and Chevalier dans l'Ordre des Arts et des Lettres, as well as honorary degrees from Harvard and Oxford. Over the arc of an incredibly prolific career, which began with her first book of poetry, *Double Persephone* (1961), she has written some of the most defining books of our time—from the ecological crisis portrayed in the MaddAddam trilogy (2003–2013) to the feminist classic *The Edible Woman* (1969) to the frightening dystopia explored in *The Handmaid's Tale* (1985).

Offred narrates the novel; we never learn her real name, but we very quickly come to understand the repressive society in which she now lives. Through flashbacks she describes her life with her partner, Luke, and their daughter, in the time before a patriarchal, theocratic dictatorship took over and transformed part of the United States into the Republic of Gilead. Repressive edicts based on the Bible mean women can't read or work, raise their own children, or develop friendships. If they are fertile, they are forced into sexual servitude as Handmaids for the barren upper class. They no longer have names ("Offred" means "of Fred," the name of the Commander with whom the narrator lives and must copulate, in the hopes that she will bear him a child).

One of Atwood's many achievements in the book is resisting the urge to paint only in blacks and whites. Instead, she gives readers plausible, fully realized characters. Offred is not fully a saint, the Commander not fully a sinner. No great victory of good over evil occurs at the climax, and the fates of the characters can only be speculated upon, as the novel itself does in the head-spinning "Historical Notes" that follow Offred's story as a kind of epilogue. *The Handmaid's Tale* thus eludes simplistic interpretations—Atwood does not reassure us with easy lessons but instead compels us to look upon our own messy society in a cracked mirror.

The Handmaid's Tale was Atwood's first book of speculative fiction; since then she's become a dominant figure of the genre. The scope of her work also encompasses children's stories, poetry, essays, and nonfiction. Regardless of the format, her writing touches on themes such as the perils of ideology, the need for environmental conservation, and the complex effects of sexual politics. She often explores intersectional feminism, a philosophy that holds that a woman's multiple identities—her class, race, religion, and beyond—overlap and influence her experience of the world and the world's treatment of her. Canada's most famous writer, Atwood was born in 1939 in Ottawa, and lives in Toronto with her husband, writer Graeme Gibson.

In 2017, a television series based on *The Handmaid's Tale* was the first streaming series to win an Emmy for Outstanding Drama Series. The immensely popular show differed from the book in a few key ways—namely in updating the action to today (characters use smartphones, for example), portraying the fate of Luke, and having Offred get pregnant. Previously, the book had been turned into a movie (1990) from a screenplay written by Harold Pinter, starring Natasha Richardson and Faye Dunaway. With an enormous fan base on social media, and through her novels and nonfiction, Atwood continues to command our attention as she ruminates on—and, some might say, predicts—our future.

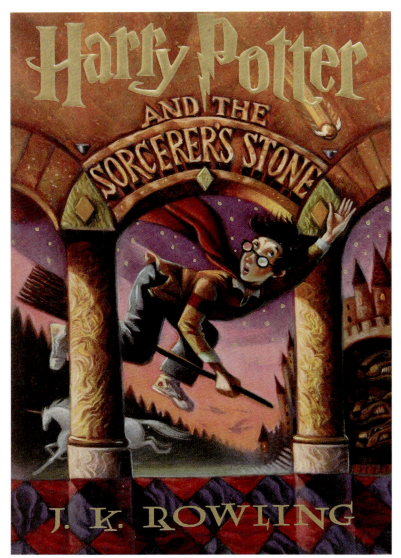

45

HARRY POTTER SERIES

J. K. Rowling · 1997–2007

The next time you're stuck on a bus or similarly inconvenienced by transportation, remember this: J. K. Rowling used four hours on a delayed train to London to conceive of one of the most indelible characters in the entire literary canon—a bespectacled orphan boy, with messy black hair, green eyes, and a scar shaped like a lightning bolt on his forehead, named Harry Potter.

As Rowling recalled later, she didn't have a pen, so she just sat and thought about the life of this boy who "simply fell into my head." She started writing that night. Over the next five years, she finished the manuscript, outlined the rest of the book series, secured an agent, and found a publisher. In 1997, *Harry Potter and the Philosopher's Stone* was released, thereby kicking off the bestselling book series of all time, with some 500 million copies sold. (In America, the first volume was retitled *Harry Potter and the Sorcerer's Stone.*)

On his 11th birthday, Harry Potter is surprised to learn he's been granted admission to the Hogwarts School of Witchcraft and Wizardry on account of his heretofore-unknown magical abilities. Less happily, he discovers he's destined to do battle with Lord Voldemort, "the most dangerous Dark wizard of all time," who seeks to establish the dominance of wizards and witches over nonmagical people, or muggles. At Hogwarts, Harry develops intense friendships with the clever Hermione Granger and the likable Ron Weasley, and he is mentored and protected by the wise and honorable headmaster, Albus Dumbledore. He grows increasingly comfortable with his power as well as his destiny.

The series offers a master class in meticulous plotting, such that its final climax is foreshadowed in various ways throughout. The books grow longer and more complex as the characters grow older and Rowling builds out her fictional universe. Inventive details abound: All first-years at Hogwarts, for example, must wear the Sorting Hat, which reads their thoughts and determines which house they'll be in. A scatterbrained character is given a "Remembrall"

that changes color when its owner forgets something. This rich context is seamlessly woven into a story about an orphan who finds friends, defeats his mortal enemy, and becomes a man. Anyone who believes that this series is strictly for kids hasn't been hit by its magic.

The publication of the seventh and final book in 2007 was a worldwide cultural phenomenon. Bookstores opened at midnight on publication day for *Harry Potter and the Deathly Hallows*, throwing parties and encouraging fans to dress up as favorite characters. Copies flew off the shelves faster than an owl carrying an important parcel, at a rate of more than 95 sold per second in the United States in the first 24 hours. Nowadays, Rowling periodically offers social-media updates about the characters. And under the pen name Robert Galbraith, she is currently writing a series of well-regarded mysteries for adults.

Joanne Rowling was born in 1965 in Gloucestershire, England. She studied French at the University of Exeter, then worked a variety of jobs, including researcher at Amnesty International and English teacher in Portugal. But she always longed to be a writer, composing her first story at age six and first novel at age seven. Her mother died the same year Rowling began writing Harry Potter, and a sense of grief and loss pervades the books, as Harry must come to terms with the absence of his own parents.

Eight movies based on the books were released between 2001 and 2011. In 2016, the prequel *Fantastic Beasts and Where to Find Them*, with a script written by Rowling, was released, and more are in development. *Harry Potter and the Cursed Child*, an award-winning play about an adult Harry, based on a story by Rowling, premiered on London's West End, with a Broadway debut in the works. The books have also inspired theme parks and studio tours around the globe.

A contemporary classic, the Harry Potter series demonstrates tremendous skill and creativity—and it introduced a generation of readers to the bewitching world of literature.

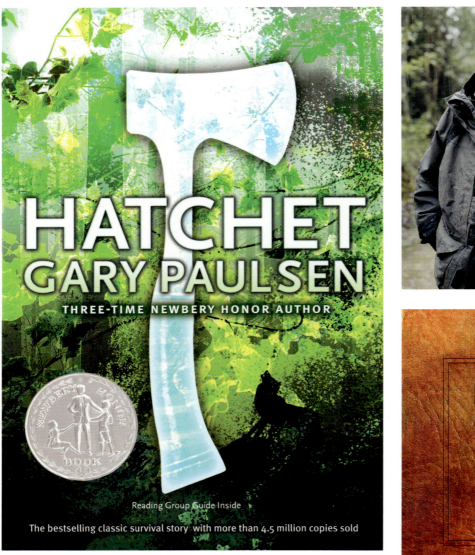

46

HATCHET SERIES

Gary Paulsen · 1987–2003

Man versus nature" is a fundamental literary motif. From the adventure tale *Robinson Crusoe* (1719) to the television series *Lost*, the classic YA novel *Lord of the Flies* (1954) to the bestselling memoir *Wild* (2012), the confrontation between individuals and unforgiving environments makes for extremely popular entertainment. *Hatchet* (1987) and the four books that follow feature a young boy forced to persevere on his own, and their dramatic storytelling have earned them a place within this storied tradition.

In the first novel of the series, a plane carrying 13-year-old Brian Robeson crashes in a lake somewhere in the Canadian wilderness. Before he left his New York City home for a visit with his father in the north woods, his mother gave Brian a hatchet. Stranded hundreds of miles from civilization, Brian must learn to live in challenging conditions, using that gift and whatever he can fashion from nature itself. Over the course of several solitary weeks, he deals with pests like mosquitoes and skunk as well as more serious threats like wolves and bears, figures out how to hunt and fish, and becomes an adept outdoorsman. After a tornado shifts the wreckage's position in the lake, he manages to retrieve various items from the plane, including an emergency transmitter. A bush pilot hears the distress call, and Brian is saved.

Brian goes back to nature in the subsequent books: *The River* (1991), *Brian's Winter* (1996), *Brian's Return* (1999), and *Brian's Hunt* (2003). The five novels are sometimes referred to collectively as Brian's Saga—an apt title given the adversities he must endure. He spends 54 days alone in the Yukon in the first book, must help transport a dying government psychologist downriver to safety in the second, copes with the isolation and extremities of winter in the third, experiences the difficulties of being a regular high-school student in the fourth, and befriends a stray dog and makes the decision to essentially abandon civilization in the fifth.

While Brian's circumstances are unusual, his struggles, in many ways, are not. Young people often feel isolated and alone, and they seek to discover themselves, separate from their parents, institutions like church or school, and society. Paulsen takes universal coming-of-age experiences and combines them with gripping stories of adventure. He also explores deep-seated American cultural beliefs, like the unbreakable bond that forms between a boy and his dog, or the stifling effects of civilization compared to the freedom of nature. Through hard work and stubborn drive, Brian survives. He teaches himself what he needs to know. He's even a model of positive thinking, because if he falls prey to despair, he will literally die. In order to survive, he must never stop believing in himself and his capabilities.

Like Brian, Gary Paulsen learned to exist on his own at a young age. He was born in Minneapolis, in 1939, but at age 14 left home to escape his alcoholic parents. After jobs as varied as television writer and missile tester, he wrote his first book, a series of funny essays about the weapons industry, in 1966. Since then, Paulsen has published more than 200 books, completing a new novel or novella every few months, mostly for young adults. In honor of his contributions to children's literature, Paulsen has received three Newbery Awards, including one for *Hatchet* in 1988. The Hatchet series has been praised for its ability to persuade reluctant readers to give books a try, and for its transfixing depiction of how one boy transforms into a man.

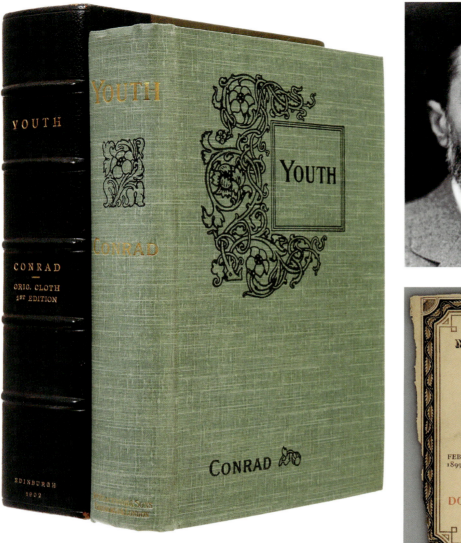

CLOCKWISE FROM LEFT: *Heart of Darkness* first appeared in book form in this English edition, entitled *Youth: A Narrative and Two Other Stories*, published in 1902. | Joseph Conrad wrote about his experiences as a sailor on the Congo River in the novella that would become *Heart of Darkness*. | The novella was originally published in three parts in *Blackwood's Magazine.* Part 1 of 3 appeared in this volume, released February 1899.

47

HEART OF DARKNESS

Joseph Conrad · 1899

n 1890, Polish sailor Józef Teodor Konrad Korzeniowski journeyed up the Congo River as a steamboat captain. He witnessed the terrible greed and horrific cruelty of Belgian imperial rule and thoughtfully transcribed his impressions into a diary. Disgusted by his experiences, he resigned his post and returned to England. Nine years later, after anglicizing his pen name to Joseph Conrad, he published a novella based on his time in Africa.

Heart of Darkness (1899) begins as Charles Marlow waits for a ship to be readied. To pass the time with his new crew, he tells a tale of a previous journey as captain of a riverboat steamer in Africa. He describes his youthful fascination with "a mighty big river . . . resembling an immense snake uncoiled, with its head in the sea, its body at rest curving afar over a vast country, and its tail lost in the depths of the land." In the recounting, as young Marlow travels to this river to assume his post, he hears about Kurtz, who runs a very successful ivory-trading post in the interior.

Marlow endures a series of setbacks and delays. His steamboat is badly damaged under mysterious circumstances. Conflicting reports of Kurtz continue to swirl. The steamboat finally fixed, Marlow journeys to Kurtz's Inner Station. He meets a man who praises Kurtz's intellect and influence, but Marlow suspects that Kurtz has gone insane—a belief that gains credence when Marlow encounters the man at last.

As Marlow moves in physical space, heading deeper inland, he simultaneously moves in inner space, learning more about himself. He tells the story as a flashback, and what he now knows informs his retelling. The journey to find Kurtz is complicated, and Marlow hears increasingly bizarre rumors about what's happening upriver.

Even as the novella reviles imperialism, it has been criticized for promoting stereotypes about Africa as a "dark continent." The Africans who appear in *Heart of Darkness* are enfeebled, dead, or dying. They are neither individualized nor personalized. Instead, as portrayed by Conrad, Africans are a monolithic group in a primitive place. Racist as Conrad's views may be, he nevertheless offers a harsh critique of the European exploitation of Africa in the name of development and growth.

Heart of Darkness received new life when it served as the basis for Francis Ford Coppola's 1979 movie *Apocalypse Now*, a searing indictment of US involvement in Vietnam. This film offers some of the most impressive scenes in cinematic history, from a helicopter attack on a village scored to Wagner's "Ride of the Valkyries" to the emergence of a mud-covered Martin Sheen from the steaming water on his way to assassinate Kurtz, played so memorably by Marlon Brando.

Like his narrator, Marlow, Conrad loved the sea. He left Poland, where he was born in 1857, as an adolescent to become a merchant marine. In time, he joined British ships, learning English in the process. As much as he wanted to be a writer, he felt conflicted about giving up his seafaring life and settling in Britain at age 36. But his 19-year naval career gave him plenty of material. *Lord Jim* (1900), for example, describes the aftermath of a passenger ship that gets abandoned by its captain and crew; it's also narrated by Marlow.

In his later years, Conrad published more overtly political novels, including *The Secret Agent* (1907) and *Under Western Eyes* (1911). An undercurrent of cynicism runs through these works, reflecting Conrad's disillusionment with revolutionary movements and their ability to alleviate suffering. Nevertheless, as in *Heart of Darkness*, he cautions against the dangers of man. We are one another's worst enemies.

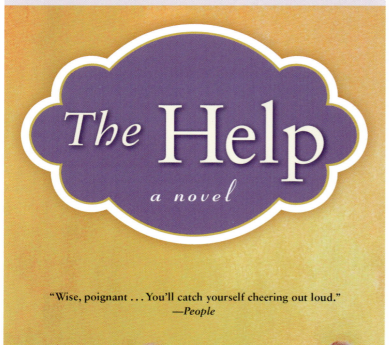

#1 NEW YORK TIMES BESTSELLER
OVER 11 MILLION COPIES SOLD

The Help
a novel

"Wise, poignant . . . You'll catch yourself cheering out loud."
—*People*

KATHRYN STOCKETT

CLOCKWISE FROM LEFT: The book cover for *The Help*, originally published in 2009. | Author Kathryn Stockett photographed at the premiere of Dreamworks' movie release of *The Help* in 2011. Stockett drew inspiration for her story from the African American maid who helped raise her. | Actress Octavia Spencer in 2012, accepting her award for Best Supporting Actress for her role in the movie adaptation of *The Help*.

48

THE HELP

Kathryn Stockett · 2009

One of the most well-known, most widely read books about the American South in recent years, *The Help* (2009) focuses on a group of African American women who work in white households during the 1960s in Jackson, Mississippi. The book highlights the variety of tensions at play in employee-employer relationships and the domestic sphere in the pre–civil rights era.

Kathryn Stockett began writing *The Help* on September 12, 2001. She was living in New York City at the time, working in marketing and magazine publishing. In the aftermath of 9/11, she wasn't able to get in touch with her family in Mississippi to let them know she was OK; her sadness and homesickness spurred a creative burst inspired by the African American maid who helped raise her. That woman's voice eventually became the character of Aibileen, one of *The Help*'s three narrators. For the next five years, Stockett received roughly 60 rejections from literary agents. Ultimately, however, the book found an agent and a publisher, and debuted on the *New York Times* bestseller list. The *Huffington Post* called it "the must-read choice of every book club in the country."

Coping with the recent loss of her son, the normally reticent Aibileen Clark finds her stoicism starting to crack. Her friend Minny Jackson often speaks her mind, but, as the longtime maid of one particular family, she knows some things are best kept quiet. The novel's third voice comes from Eugenia "Skeeter" Phelan, a young white woman newly graduated from college. To her mother's chagrin, she'd rather be a journalist than a wife. She becomes obsessed with discovering the fate of Constantine, who worked for her family when Skeeter was a child. She decides to write about the world of maids, to tell their side of the story, despite the dangers. Together, Aibileen, Minny, and Skeeter uncover cruelty and even crime.

Stockett was born in 1969 in Jackson, Mississippi. As she got older, she realized that the family maid she loved, who so helped her in the aftermath of her parents' divorce and served, to some degree, as a surrogate mother, was almost a complete mystery. "I never once wondered what she was thinking," the white Stockett told an interviewer. This lacuna forms a cornerstone of *The Help*: during the era described in the novel, African American maids often stayed with white employers for years, becoming almost a part of the family. And yet these women frequently experienced such humiliations as being forbidden to use the same bathrooms as the families they lived with and their guests and forbidden from eating at the same table. "The help" were relegated to a distinct underclass, especially in the time of the "separate but equal" doctrine.

Film director Tate Taylor grew up with Stockett in Jackson, where they went to the same preschool and became best friends, and he encouraged her as she drafted and redrafted her debut. As soon as he read her unpublished manuscript, he knew he wanted to direct it. He did so in 2011, and Octavia Spencer, who starred as Minny Jackson, won a Best Supporting Actress award. The film was also nominated for Best Picture, among other Academy Awards, becoming almost as popular as the novel on which it was based.

Trying to convince her New York editor to support her project, in the novel Skeeter evokes Mammy from *Gone with the Wind* (1936): "[E]veryone knows how we white people feel, the glorified Mammy figure who dedicates her whole life to a white family. Margaret Mitchell covered that. But no one ever asked Mammy how she felt about it." By revealing what goes on inside the home, Skeeter—and Stockett—want to empower those who often get shunted to the side, in literature and in reality.

Predictive Text

TECHNOLOGY AND THE REAL, IMAGINED WORLD OF BOOKS

ALTHOUGH WRITERS rely first and foremost on their imaginations to populate the universes they create, some seem to have a crystal ball tucked alongside their computers or typewriters, especially when it comes to technology. Authors of fantasy, sci-fi, and speculative fiction, in particular, conceived of many tools and machines we rely on today, including credit cards, nuclear power, mood-enhancing drugs, radar, tablets, and earbuds. It feels almost as if these writers wrote the very world we live in into existence.

In *The Hitchhiker's Guide to the Galaxy* (1979), to take one example, the so-called Babel fish lets users instantly understand whatever language they hear. Contemporary readers might see in this invention a fictive analogue to any one of a number of translation apps available for download on their smartphone. The novel's narrator calls it "probably the oddest thing in the Universe," but anyone who's ever tried to order food or get directions in a foreign land would likely disagree.

Over the course of his long career, Isaac Asimov undertook many roles: professor of biochemistry, bestselling sci-fi writer, international vice president of Mensa, spokesperson for Radio Shack. Asimov was leery, at first, about appearing in ads for the company, but he allegedly had a change of heart after getting some one-on-one help using its new personal computer and word-processing software. Eventually he said that the TRS-80 model echoed technology he'd dreamed up as part of his *Foundation* series (1951–1993). His short stories and novels also predicted microwaves, automated coffee machines, and self-driving cars.

In some cases, people look to fiction for inspiration. An Italian neurosurgeon is currently trying to undertake the world's first full-body transplant on a human, using *Frankenstein* (1818) as a muse. Along with launching modern science fiction as a genre, that novel posited important questions about proper motivation and methods for scientific inquiry, questions that form the core of the contemporary philosophy of bioethics. Despite the fact that the plot of *The Martian* (2011) kicks off after NASA makes a mistake and leaves behind an astronaut, the US space program hasn't shied away from its connection to the novel and related movie directed by Ridley Scott. Along with explaining the relative merits and possibilities of technologies predicted by author Andy Weir, NASA often relies on the popularity of the story to shore up support for its goal of sending astronauts to the Red Planet in 2030. And with a nod to *Jurassic Park* (1990), "some paleontologists are exploring another way to revive dinosaur traits, by reverse-engineering birds to look more like their dinosaur ancestors," according to a 2015 article in *National Geographic*. Lucky for us, however, DNA from fossils older than about seven million years doesn't last long enough to yield useful specimens, making dino cells too old to clone.

Like science fiction, dystopian novels seem to have a knack for knowing what's to come. In its portrayal of an authoritarian society, *Nineteen Eighty-Four* (1949) described computer screens that could watch your every move, as well as other means of mass surveillance that are likely familiar to 21st-century readers. *Ready Player One* (2011) may feel prescient to anyone who would rather play video games—which are getting increasingly immersive—than hang out in real life. Sales of *The Handmaid's Tale* (1985) shot up in 2017, in part because of perceived, and unnerving, parallels between the theocratic totalitarian regime portrayed in the novel (and the affiliated Emmy Award–winning television

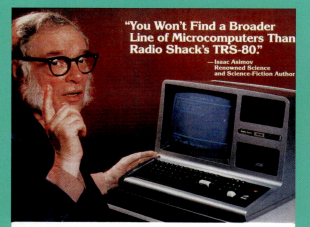

series) and the actions of some governments around the world. In an interview, Margaret Atwood cautioned people about making too much of her prognostic powers: "I did not predict the future because you can't really predict the future. There isn't any 'the future.' There are many possible futures, but we don't know which one we're going to have. We can guess. We can speculate. But we cannot really predict." That said, novelists like Atwood can help show us where not to go, what not to invent, how not to be.

ABOVE, LEFT TO RIGHT: Author Isaac Asimov became a spokesperson for technology retailer Radio Shack after getting a tutorial on word-processing software. Here he appears in a Radio Shack print ad in 1980 for the TRS-80. | Protesters dressed as handmaids from *The Handmaid's Tale* began appearing in protests in 2017. The group pictured here is at the capitol in Austin, Texas.

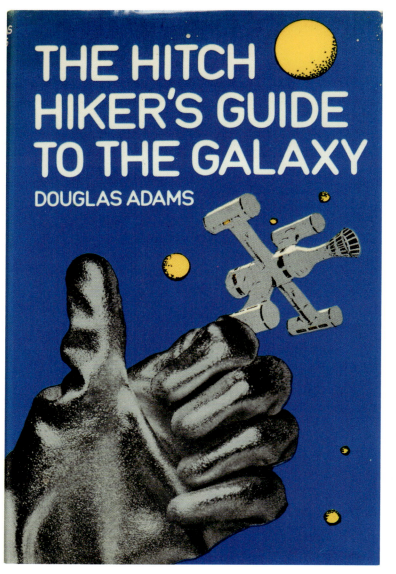

49

THE HITCHHIKER'S GUIDE TO THE GALAXY

Douglas Adams · 1979

"Don't panic." This excellent advice from *The Hitchhiker's Guide to the Galaxy* (1979) resonates with readers. We'll likely never lack for reasons to feel anxious about the states of our lives or the state of the world, whether we live on Earth or Magrathea, now or decades in the future, but, as this novel proves, humor and escapism in literature make for excellent coping tools.

Arthur Dent—an average Joe in the West Country of England—learns of the imminent end of the world when his friend Ford Prefect comes to save him. As an alien race known as the Vogons arrives to smash Earth to smithereens, Arthur and Ford sneak onto a Vogon ship and embark on a series of absurd adventures. Ford, as it turns out, is actually an alien writer who landed on Earth to research the planet for an encyclopedic reference book called *The Hitchhiker's Guide to the Galaxy*. The friends get sent into space, where they meet a depressed robot and a woman traveling with the president of the galaxy. In addition to both discovering Earth's origin story and battling for Arthur's brain, they learn the answer to the Ultimate Question of Life, the Universe, and Everything. Oh, and there are superintelligent, pandimensional mice.

The Hitchhiker's Guide to the Galaxy is a sci-fi novel filled with comedy, and it stands out for its mash-up of these two genres. Jokes abound. The Vogons force Ford and Arthur to listen to their poetry as a form of torture. The president of the galaxy rides around in a ship known as the *Heart of Gold*. Arthur is satisfied enough with zooming about, looking for the meaning of life, but what he'd really like is a nice cup of tea. Perhaps the biggest gag of them all, however, is "42"—the answer produced by supercomputer Deep Thought after 7.5 million years of calculating. The trouble is that no one knows the question, which is partly the point. In our quest for answers, we sometimes forget that the question matters as well; we can't get so fixated on results that we forget about method, or so obsessed with the destination that we forget about the journey.

Douglas Adams created the story as part of a radio play for the BBC in 1978. But he'd had the idea much earlier, while traveling around Europe. One night, before passing out in a field in Innsbruck, Austria, he stared at the stars and thought that someone should write a travel guide for the whole universe. Then, as he recalled, "I fell asleep and forgot about it for six years." Despite writing and acting in some episodes of *Monty Python's Flying Circus*, Adams's career as a sketch writer for television and radio had stalled by the late 1970s when he revisited the concept. Following the radio program and release of the novel the following year, the story became a 1981 BBC television series and a 2005 film, along with comic-book adaptations and computer games. Adams also expanded on his original vision, publishing four subsequent novels about the galaxy as he envisioned it, as well as other novels and screenplays.

Every year on May 25, Adams's fans around the world carry towels. "Towel Day" began in 2001, just two weeks after Adams died at age 49. *The Hitchhiker's Guide to the Galaxy* recommends carrying a towel with you at all times—to use as a blanket, a sail, a cover-up, a flag, or a weapon. And "of course [you can] dry yourself off with it if it still seems to be clean enough." To keep your towel with you shows that you're ready for anything. As Adams and his novels imply, in times of great strife (i.e., always), sometimes all you can do is grab your towel and laugh.

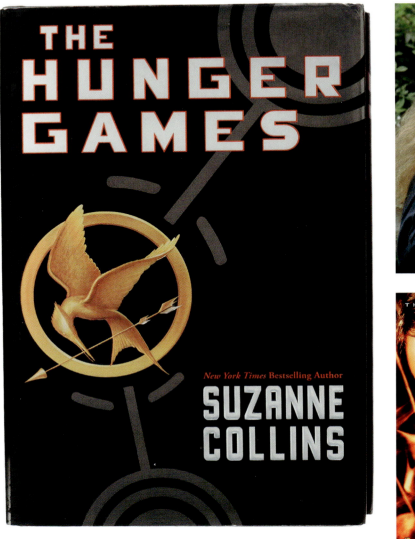

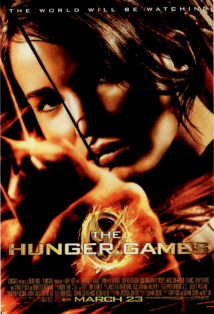

CLOCKWISE FROM TOP LEFT: First edition of *The Hunger Games* (2008), the first book in the Hunger Games trilogy. | Author Suzanne Collins. She generally shies away from media interviews, citing the books' critique of the media. | The successful book series spurred a successful movie series, starring Jennifer Lawrence as Katniss Everdeen. Lions Gate created this promotional poster for *The Hunger Games* 2012 movie release.

50

THE HUNGER GAMES TRILOGY

Suzanne Collins · 2008–2010

Set in the fictional country of Panem, the Hunger Games trilogy traces the fate of Katniss Everdeen as she does what she needs to do to survive in a futuristic dystopian universe. Every year, 12 boys and 12 girls—one of each from Panem's 12 districts—are sent as tributes to the wealthy, corrupt Capitol to compete in a televised fight to the death. This is the world of the Hunger Games, and it's intense.

As the young-adult series begins, 16-year-old Katniss lives in the poorest, least populated district in Panem. When her sister, Primrose, known as Prim, gets randomly selected to fight, Katniss volunteers to go in her stead. A talented hunter and archer, Katniss uses her survival skills and her wits to outfox her fellow tributes and outsmart the rules of the Hunger Games. She is forced to adhere to the "kill or be killed" philosophy of her society, but nevertheless manages to develop strong relationships with other participants, including a gentle young competitor named Rue as well as her fellow District 12 tribute, Peeta Mellark. They are trained, coiffed, and costumed in order to be rendered fit for competition and television.

Witnessing other people's misery as a form of entertainment has a long history in human culture. Suzanne Collins's books update the Greek myth of Theseus and the Minotaur. In that tale, after defeating Athens in war, Crete decided to enact a particularly painful punishment. Every few years, Athenians were required to send 14 young adults. These souls were thrown into a labyrinth, home to a half-man, half-bull monster. Theseus volunteered to go, then used brainpower and brawn to defeat the Minotaur. Another inspiration for *The Hunger Games* (2008) came from the gladiatorial combat of the Roman Empire. Collins also uses the books to critique the modern-day phenomenon of reality shows, which often spotlight participants' suffering and humiliations. For example, Peeta reveals a long-standing crush on Katniss during the Games, partly as a way of generating sympathy and heightening his storyline for Capitol viewers—a strategic move, as the audience can provide assistance to tributes. Popularity has life-or-death consequences.

The subsequent books, *Catching Fire* (2009) and *Mockingjay* (2010), track the repercussions of Katniss's upending of the Hunger Games, which forms the climax of the first novel. The trilogy earned comparisons to the chilly politics of *Nineteen Eighty-Four* (1949), the ingenious plotting of the Harry Potter books (1997–2007), and the fully imagined fantasy world of The Chronicles of Narnia (1950–1956). Collins makes Katniss a complicated protagonist. Moody and guarded, she's never entirely likable, and that's part of her appeal; the authenticity of her feelings for Peeta remains questionable, even through her honest first-person narration. Despite their violence and grim outlook, the books keep their contemporary YA audience in mind; they are pointed and descriptive without being gratuitous. Readers were hooked, rocketing the trilogy to one of the most popular series of all time, and the four films made from the books were all blockbusters.

Collins largely refuses to give interviews, pointing to the Hunger Games novels, with their damning critique of the media, to explain why. She was born in 1962 in Hartford, Connecticut, the daughter of a US Air Force pilot who served in Korea and Vietnam. She drew on her dad's stories of deprivation and persistence to create her books. Before writing novels, she wrote for children's television shows.

Many aspects of Panem are, thankfully, far from our own world. Collins's purpose, though, isn't to show us as we are, but rather to show us as we could be—both the depths to which we might sink as a society and the heights to which we might rise in resistance.

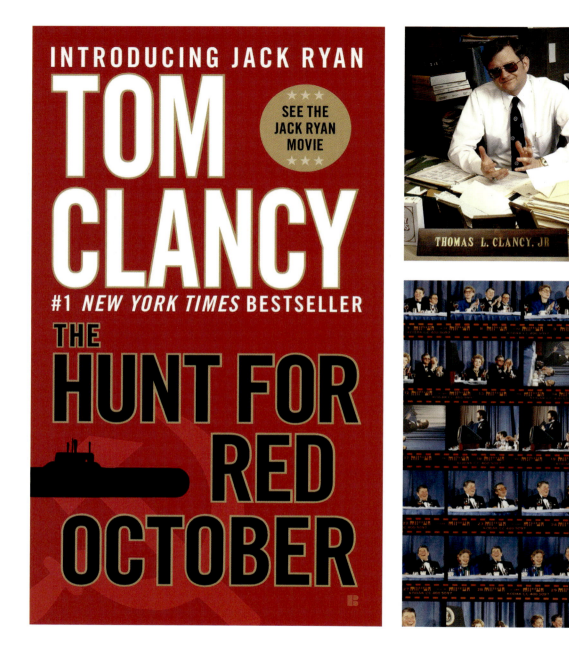

CLOCKWISE FROM LEFT: Cover for *The Hunt for Red October*, first published in 1984. | Author Tom Clancy, pictured at his desk in 1985, wrote at night and on the weekends, spending his days running an insurance agency. | Clancy pictured with President Ronald Reagan. The president loved *The Hunt for Red October* so much that he invited the author and his wife to the White House.

51

THE HUNT FOR RED OCTOBER

Tom Clancy · 1984

The *Hunt for Red October* (1984) launched the Jack Ryan military-thriller series—as well as the career of debut author Tom Clancy. Before his bestselling novel, Clancy's literary output consisted of exactly one letter to the editor and a short article about a missile.

Stealthily slicing through water, the experimental Russian nuclear submarine *Red October* uses a pioneering propulsion system. Curiosity piqued, CIA analyst Jack Ryan begins to investigate. What he doesn't yet know is that the submarine's captain, Marko Aleksandrovich Ramius, intends to defect to the United States, and has already killed at least one member of his crew to ensure the success of his plan.

It's the height of the Cold War. When Ryan figures out what's really happening on board the sub, he must convince his superiors of Ramius's integrity, protect the vessel and its crew from the Russians, who don't want to lose the technology on board, and basically prevent a conflict that could lead to World War III. As Clancy continued the series, Ryan's brave efforts on behalf of the defectors enable him to bargain with the KGB and to earn accolades and respect at the CIA. Eventually Ryan, an ex-marine with a strict conscience, rises to the highest level of government service: president of the United States.

The combination of fast-paced drama and intricate technical details attracted a slew of readers, including Ronald Reagan, who loved the book enough to invite its author and his wife to the White House. He called it a "perfect yarn," a compliment that helped shoot the novel up the bestseller lists. Clancy was also questioned by then Secretary of the Navy John Lehman, who wondered, "'Who the hell cleared it?'"

The answer, surprisingly, was *no one*: despite his seemingly insider knowledge, Clancy never served in the military. He took ROTC classes as a student at Loyola College, but poor eyesight prevented him from joining the armed forces. After graduating with a degree in English in 1969, he worked in insurance, eventually taking over an agency founded by his wife's grandfather; he wrote at night and on weekends. He didn't even visit a nuclear submarine until he was almost finished with the manuscript for *The Hunt for Red October*. He just had a strong interest in the military and intelligence communities and an unmatched ability to relate their intricacies in an accessible way.

His first novel was inspired by a couple of real-life incidents. In 1961, a Soviet naval officer aimed his ship to Sweden, where he defected. Another Soviet officer mutinied in 1975. In that case, however, his actions weren't motivated by a love of the West or desire to leave the USSR. Rather, he wanted his homeland to become even more socialist.

Jack Ryan's world is one in which the United States faces dire threats both foreign and domestic, threats that can be met only by the rectitude and ingenuity of individual Americans. Born in Baltimore in 1947, Clancy closely observed the changing political landscape of the late 20th century, from America's involvement in Vietnam to the dissolution of the Soviet Union. He often dedicated his books, which also included nonfiction accounts of history and biography, to notable American conservatives like Reagan.

To date, Dr. John Patrick "Jack" Ryan Sr., has appeared in 24 Clancy novels and has been portrayed by Harrison Ford, Chris Pine, John Krasinski, and Alec Baldwin, among others, on the big screen, on television, and in video games. Ryan's son—who shares his dad's name, sense of ethics, and unshakable patriotism—carries on the family legacy, featuring in a number of novels that depict the post-9/11 world. Clancy passed away in 2013, but thanks to authors like Mark Greaney and Grant Blackwood, who took up Clancy's mantle, his characters continue to find new life.

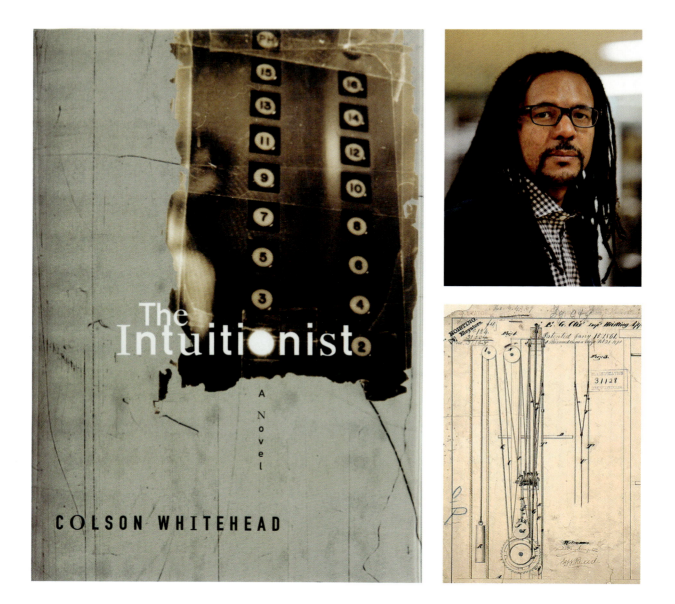

52

THE INTUITIONIST

Colson Whitehead · 1999

Colson Whitehead counts among his influences *The Twilight Zone*, the Misfits, Stephen King and like-minded masters of horror, and comic books—maybe not exactly what you'd expect from a novelist who has garnered a Pulitzer Prize, a MacArthur Fellowship (also known as a "genius grant"), a National Book Award, a Whiting Award, and a Guggenheim Fellowship.

Reviewers hailed the arrival of a great new talent when *The Intuitionist* was published in 1999. The speculative, noir-ish novel about machinations in the world of elevator inspection received almost universal praise, with one critic noting that Whitehead's debut marked him for the upper floors of the literary establishment. Punny as that may be, said critic wound up being dead right.

The Intuitionist reads like a hard-boiled detective novel. Described as "the first colored woman in the Department of Elevator Inspectors," Lila Mae Watson adheres to the "Intuitionist" method of using instinct and perception to assess the state of the machine. She has a perfect safety record. The other school of elevator inspection, practiced by the "Empiricists," relies on instruments to diagnose problems and check systems. When an elevator she recently examined crashes, Lila Mae needs to figure out who set her up—and why.

So she sets off into the unseemly underbelly of a city very similar to Dashiell Hammett's or Mickey Spillane's New York, one that demands ever-taller buildings in order to function. What she uncovers threatens to destroy her very sense of self. Whitehead stops the novel from tipping over into a parody of pulp fiction through the sheer power of his language. He handles sentences with a facility and deftness most writers can only dream of, and his word choice practically shoots off the page and sends firecrackers around your brain. He's a master of the alliterative phrase.

Born in 1969 and raised in Manhattan, Whitehead concentrated in English at Harvard, graduating in 1991. He was reviewing TV shows for the alt-weekly *Village Voice* when he began working on *The Intuitionist*. The first novel he wrote, loosely based on child actor Gary Coleman, was rejected by 25 publishers.

Whitehead strives to make each book different from the others. *John Henry Days* (2001) reimagines the classic American tale of man versus machine; the autobiographical *Sag Harbor* (2009) depicts coming-of-age in the black middle class during the 1980s; *Zone One* (2011) focuses on a postapocalyptic world of zombies. *The Colossus of New York* (2003) is a series of impressionistic essays about his hometown, while *The Noble Hustle* (2014), a memoir, twines high-stakes poker with Whitehead's midlife depression.

In 2016, Whitehead returned to the intersection of identity and technology with *The Underground Railroad*. This prizewinning novel follows Cora, a 16-year-old slave who boards the underground railroad—a real, physical train, complete with stations, tunnels, and conductors. When Oprah picked it for her book club, she launched it onto the bestseller list before it had even arrived in stores. Whereas *The Intuitionist* uses the elevator as a metaphor to explore the ways in which race distorts our perception of the world, *The Underground Railroad* renders the metaphoric literal.

The author is also funny. When Barack Obama was elected president in 2008, Whitehead called it a victory for "Skinny Black Guys" in a *New York Times* op-ed. His Twitter feed is full of wit and sarcasm, such as this gem: "Computer? Notebook? I engrave all my first drafts in stone tablets. Just get it down, you know? I can edit later." As long as he gets his words out there, not one of us can complain.

invisible man

ralph ellison

53

INVISIBLE MAN

Ralph Ellison · 1952

The nameless narrator of *Invisible Man* lives in a basement amid 1,369 lightbulbs, which he keeps simultaneously illuminated. He seeks to record key moments of his life and to explain his present circumstances: "I am an invisible man," he writes. "No, I am not a spook like those who haunted Edgar Allan Poe; nor am I one of your Hollywood-movie ectoplasms. I am a man of substance, of flesh and bone, fiber and liquids—and I might even be said to possess a mind. I am invisible, understand, simply because people refuse to see me."

One of the most important novels of the 20th century, Ralph Ellison's *Invisible Man* directly addresses the alienating effects of racism. It also describes significant aspects of African American history, such as the long-lasting legacy of slavery, the Great Migration, and segregation, which was still legal when the novel was published in 1952.

What has transformed the protagonist into an invisible man? In short, a lifetime of coping with violence, both physical and psychic, and of prejudice, both overt and subtle. The narrator recounts episode after episode of discrimination, betrayal, and cruelty, starting with his adolescence in the South. As a teen, he receives a scholarship to a prestigious black university. But in order to utilize it, he's forced by the white town elders to compete in a vicious battle royal against other blindfolded black boys.

He gets expelled from college after inadvertently taking a white trustee into the old slave quarters. The college president gives him several letters of recommendation, which turn out to betray the narrator with false accounts of dishonesty. He settles in 1930s-era Harlem, falls into what he believes to be a multiracial brotherhood trying to change the world, and rediscovers his love of making speeches. He survives an explosion at the paint factory where he works but is unwillingly given shock therapy. He manages to avoid being embroiled in a white woman's rape fantasy. Finally, he goes into hiding when a black nationalist threatens to lynch him.

Named for Ralph Waldo Emerson, Ralph Waldo Ellison was born in Oklahoma in 1913. He worked a series of odd jobs as a child and teenager, including dental assistant, shoe-shine boy, and waiter, to help support his family. At age 20 he entered Tuskegee Institute, an all-black university in Alabama, because its orchestra needed his skills as a trumpet player. Although he studied music, Ellison also read widely and deeply. He left before graduating, moving to New York City in 1936.

There, Ellison encountered some of the major figures of the Harlem Renaissance, like Langston Hughes and Richard Wright. With their encouragement, Ellison began writing, focusing on book reviews, articles, and short stories. He worked on *Invisible Man* for five years, largely supported by his wife.

His narrator listens to "(What Did I Do to Be So) Black and Blue" and other songs by Louis Armstrong at full volume, and Ellison's love of jazz directly informs his prose. Like a song, the novel shifts in tone, style, and genre, but everything forms a unifying whole, in this case a searing portrait of American society. Scholars speculate that the success of *Invisible Man* stifled Ellison's creativity; even though he released two books of essays, he spent the next 40 years working on a second novel and left behind roughly 1,600 pages upon his death in 1994.

In 2003, a sculpture was erected in New York's Riverside Park and dedicated to Ellison, who had long lived nearby. It features the shape of a man cut out of a huge sheet of bronze. He is invisible, but he is nevertheless striding, head held high, into the future.

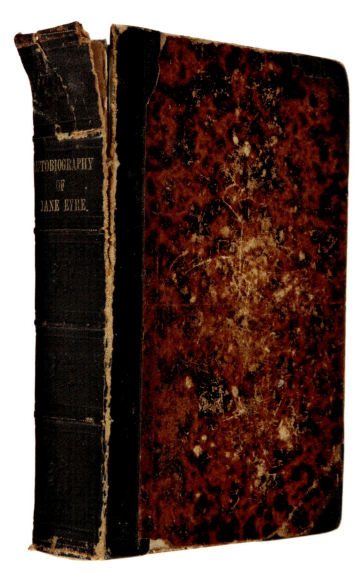

54

JANE EYRE

Charlotte Brontë · 1847

Consider the dinner-table conversation that must have transpired at the Brontë house in rural Yorkshire. Patriarch Patrick Brontë, an Irish clergyman, wrote poetry and tutored his son, Branwell, at home. Branwell and his sisters, Anne, Charlotte, and Emily, constructed full-on imaginary worlds with names like Gondal and Angria, and published their own magazines, featuring their stories, plays, criticism, poetry, and histories. Within a few decades, the sisters would professionally publish *Poems by Currer, Ellis, and Acton Bell* (1846), followed in 1847 by three now-classic novels: *Agnes Grey* by Anne; *Wuthering Heights* by Emily; and *Jane Eyre* by Charlotte. For one household to have produced three novelists is extraordinary enough; for those novelists to still be read and beloved a century and a half later is something else entirely.

Jane Eyre follows its titular protagonist from her early childhood as a mistreated orphan living with a vile aunt to her first real friendship (and further mistreatment) at school to her first job, as a governess at Thornfield Hall. In that lonely, brooding mansion she encounters the equally lonely and brooding Edward Rochester, an enigmatic and domineering older man whose ward Jane teaches. As Jane finds herself pulled toward Edward, strange things begin to befall the residents of the house, until Jane learns the terrible secret within it and must decide whether to follow her heart or her conscience.

Charlotte Brontë was born in Yorkshire in 1816. She began writing *Jane Eyre* while helping her father recover from eye surgery (in the days before anesthesia), and blindness plays a significant role in the resulting novel. She also reimagined her own experiences as an ill-treated boarding-school student—two of her sisters died as a result of the poor conditions at the school—and as a governess. The pseudonymously published novel stirred controversy over its "unfeminine" depiction of passionate feelings and biting social observations, and it engendered considerable speculation about the real name of its author. Two more novels followed, *Shirley* in 1849 and *Villette* in 1853, by which time the now-identified Brontë had become a literary celebrity, albeit a reclusive and reluctant one. She married one of her father's curates in 1854, and died unexpectedly in 1855, likely from pregnancy-related complications.

A bildungsroman, *Jane Eyre* portrays its eponymous protagonist in various states of suffering. Yet Jane stays strong and perseveres—thanks to books. We meet her first as a 10-year-old, secluded with a text from the awful family she lives with. Reading provides a wellspring from which Jane dips in moments of great difficulty. In constructing her novel, Brontë incorporates elements from literary genres that were popular in the Victorian era, including gothic literature and romance. Jane encounters gloom, ghosts, and the possibility of a life-changing romantic love.

What has resonated through the years since the novel's publication is the voice of Jane herself. Through her first-person narration, she often addresses us directly, either by using "you" or the word *reader*, and she lets us into her private concerns, worries, and struggles to figure out who she is and what she wants. In fact, many scholars point to this novel as pivotal to the construction of our modern concept of selfhood, in which the individual, with all its idiosyncrasies, reigns supreme. In perhaps the book's most central conflict, Jane must decide whether she wants to pursue the safety and security of marriage, which means subjugating the self, or pursue independence, which means forgoing a deep emotional attachment to another. She has to assess her own conscience, even if her choice may run counter to commonly held Victorian assumptions about gender. Her careful consideration and contemplation make *Jane Eyre* all the more remarkable and Jane Eyre all the more relatable.

"What's the Use of a Book Without Pictures?"

THE IMPACT OF ILLUSTRATORS

ILLUSTRATORS CAN MAKE—or break—a book. As contemporary illustrator and author Posy Simmonds remarks, "There's lots of choice, whether to interpret, decorate, contradict. It can add to or detract from the writing." In the best instances of illustrated texts, the pictures and writing blend seamlessly, a marriage of two compatible mates who contribute their own unique capabilities and sensibilities.

As Alice idly watches her older sister reading, she summarizes the opinion of many readers: "'And what is the use of a book,' thought Alice, 'without pictures or conversation?'" Her creator, Lewis Carroll, concurred, and initially sought to decorate *Alice's Adventures in Wonderland* (1865) with his own illustrations. However, it was eventually agreed that the book needed a professional's touch. Enter illustrator John Tenniel, known for his political cartoons done in a dark, grotesque style. All told, Tenniel drew more than 90 illustrations for *Alice* and its sequel, *Through the Looking-Glass, and What Alice Found There* (1871). Initially, many found the line drawings, particularly of lovely Alice with her big eyes and rosebud lips, to be even more captivating than Carroll's words.

Certainly artwork was seen as a crucial component of bookmaking throughout the 19th century. Charles Dickens originally published his novels as serials in magazines. He believed illustrations to be indispensable to his audience's reading experience, so he worked closely with artists to ensure that their work matched his creative vision. In fact, a publisher originally approached Dickens to write a novel—his first—based on illustrations drawn by Robert Seymour, then a very successful artist (some scholars believe that the idea for the book even came from Seymour). *The Posthumous Papers of the Pickwick Club* came out in 1836, but the collaboration proved so taxing that the troubled Seymour killed himself.

Dickens was right: the best illustrations fundamentally determine our reading experience. As we open the first edition of *Charlotte's Web* (1952), for example, the concerned Fern with a messy ponytail on the cover, drawn by Garth Williams, becomes the Fern inside our head. Antoine de Saint-Exupéry both wrote and illustrated *The Little Prince* (1943); his depiction of the funny little titular character as a blond boy with a flamboyant scarf counterbalances some of the book's serious philosophical inquiries. J. R. R. Tolkien used a pen to do more than write stories, drafting maps and illustrations for *The Hobbit* (1937) and *The Lord of the Rings* (1954–1955). Kurt Vonnegut likewise loved to doodle, and his drawings—including an American flag and an asterisk-shaped anus—accompanied such novels as *Breakfast of Champions* (1973).

Today the author-as-illustrator trend continues unabated, as evidenced by the popularity of graphic novels. Art Spiegelman's *Maus* (1991) portrays Jews as mice and Nazis as cats in its consideration of the lasting effects of the Holocaust. As the first graphic novel to win a Pulitzer Prize, *Maus* helped elevate this genre in literary circles. Modern hits like *Persepolis* (2000), *Fun Home* (2006), and *The Best We Could Do* (2017) continue the theme of blending words and drawings to deal with difficult, often autobiographical subject matter, and they appeal to readers of all ages.

Books marketed to children and young adults often feature extraordinary illustrations. Mary GrandPré was tasked with bringing Harry Potter to life, and her designs grace not only the covers of the original American editions of the Harry Potter

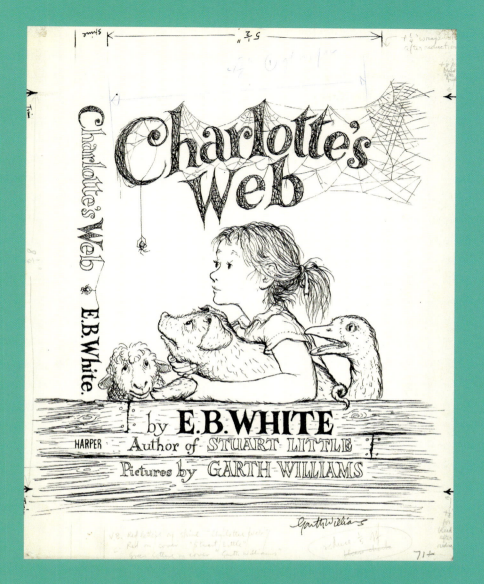

books but also their chapters. Her work on the series garnered GrandPré many accolades, appeared on the cover of *Time* magazine, and helped smooth the transition for early or reluctant readers into chapter books. In recognition of the novels' ongoing popularity, as well as the changing technologies in which to read them, Amazon released a stunning electronic edition for the Kindle, in which Jim Kay's illustrations move across the screen—ensuring that future generations will fall in love with the series. A picture might be worth 1,000 words, but the worth of a book with pictures just might be incalculable.

ABOVE: The original book cover illustration by Garth Montgomery Williams for E. B. White's *Charlotte's Web*. Williams's illustrations set the scene for young readers in this iconic classic.

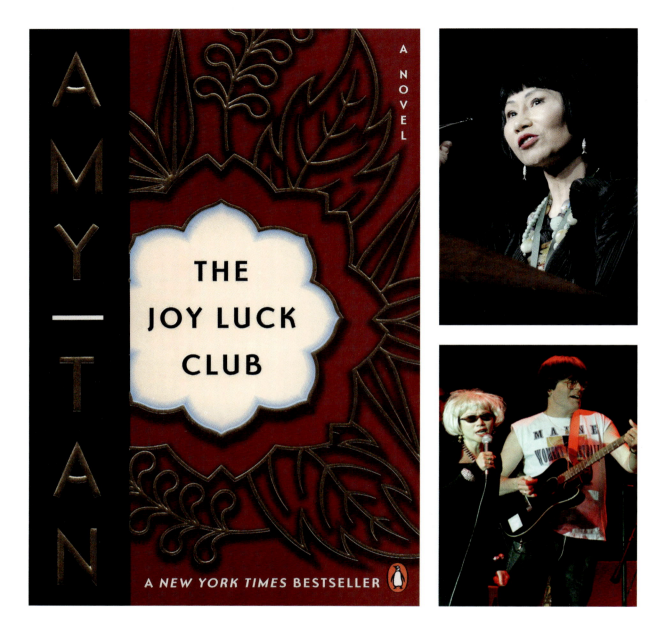

55

THE JOY LUCK CLUB

Amy Tan · 1989

As a teenager, Amy Tan discovered her mother's previous life: not only had Daisy Tan been married before, but she left three children behind in Shanghai when she fled the Communists and immigrated to the United States in 1949. Tan traveled with her mother to meet her half sisters in 1987, when she was 35, and drew on her mother's life story to draft *The Joy Luck Club* (1989), her debut novel.

The interlocking stories that make up Tan's book focus on four pairs of Chinese mothers—members of the Joy Luck Club—and their Chinese American daughters. This range of characters allows Tan to focus on different aspects of the immigrant and first-generation experiences. In the stories narrated by the mothers, readers understand how painful histories in China led to the women's childrearing philosophies in the United States. From a mother who cuts off a piece of her arm to make medicine for her own sick mother to another who is betrothed at a young age and becomes an indentured servant to her husband's family, these women lived lives vastly different from their daughters'. Yet despite often-domineering attitudes, the mothers truly want their daughters to be healthy, happy, and successful.

When Suyuan dies suddenly, members of the Joy Luck Club invite her daughter, June Woo, to take Suyuan's place. The Joy Luck Club plays mahjong once a week, and its members are one another's oldest friends. Through the games, June starts to see her mother as an idiosyncratic person; appreciating one's mother as an individual beyond her maternal identities is an important stop along the road to adulthood, for June and for us. From her mother's friends, June hears about Suyuan's twin girls, now grown, back in China. By the end of the novel, June, like Amy Tan herself, travels to China to meet this side of her family.

Daughters in the novel wrestle with the burden of their parents' expectations. One must act as an interpreter between her Chinese mother and white American father, while another abandons her talent for chess because she can't stomach her mother's compliments or criticisms. The mothers want their daughters to assimilate and fit in but are frustrated when the daughters can't understand Chinese or don't recognize the significance of a tradition. Nevertheless, the novel shows the women of both generations coming together, as opposed to drifting apart, in a depiction of the resilience of the mother-daughter bond even when stretched across cultures.

Tan was born in 1952 in California to Chinese immigrants. Defying her mother's wishes, she left a religious college and earned undergraduate and graduate degrees in English and linguistics from San Jose State University. Later she began a corporate-communications business, drafting such materials as "Telecommunications and You" for IBM. She wrote fiction in her spare time.

Subsequent books like *The Kitchen God's Wife* (1991) and *The Bonesetter's Daughter* (2001) continue to explore the relationships between mothers and daughters, but Tan's first novel remains her most successful. *The Joy Luck Club* was a finalist for both the National Book Award and the National Book Critics Circle Award. A film adaptation, which Tan cowrote, was released in 1993. With the novel's bestseller status, Tan was often pushed to act as a spokesperson for Asian American literature, a role she struggled with, as she sees her work not as representative of Asian American experience but rather of human experience. "Placing on writers the responsibility to represent a culture is an onerous burden," she explained in an interview around the publication of her third novel. "Even when you write in a specific context, you still tap into that subtext of emotions that we all feel about love and hope, and mothers and obligations and responsibilities."

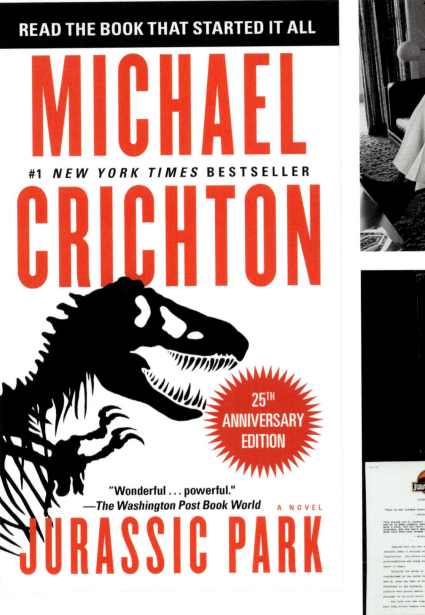

READ THE BOOK THAT STARTED IT ALL

MICHAEL

#1 *NEW YORK TIMES* BESTSELLER

CRICHTON

25TH ANNIVERSARY EDITION

"Wonderful . . . powerful."
—*The Washington Post Book World*

A NOVEL

JURASSIC PARK

CLOCKWISE FROM LEFT: The 25th-anniversary edition cover for *Jurassic Park*. The book was first published in 1990. | Michael Crichton, photographed at home, relaxing on his couch. *Jurassic Park* was his 17th novel. | The book was adapted for the screen for 1993's *Jurassic Park*. A press kit released by Universal included production notes.

56

JURASSIC PARK

Michael Crichton · 1990

Many literary works begin when their authors take an accepted orthodoxy and flip it on its side. The most fruitful—and fun—of these tap into our innate curiosity. Over his long career as a writer and director, Michael Crichton thought up some of the best and most compelling twists on reality. In *Jurassic Park* (1990), he began with the fact that nonavian dinosaurs went extinct some 65 million years ago, and then he explored what might happen if we brought them back.

Crichton's 17th novel begins in 1989, when paleontologist Dr. Alan Grant is asked to investigate a series of strange animal attacks in Costa Rica. He and Ellie Sattler, one of his graduate students, travel to Isla Nublar, where they discover that John Hammond and InGen, his corporation, are preparing to open a theme park with genetically engineered dinosaurs as the star attraction. Along with mathematician Ian Malcolm (a specialist in chaos theory), Hammond's grandkids, a lawyer, and some other park staff, Grant and Sattler are treated to a tour that starts to go desperately, dangerously awry right in front of the *Tyrannosaurus rex* enclosure. Before the Costa Rican national guard arrives to destroy the island, several people will be dead, and the door for the sequel left wide open.

Jurassic Park laments the hubris of humans who misunderstand the potential for havoc they hold in their hands. Dennis Nedry, a computer programmer, shuts down the security system in order to steal dino embryos that he plans to sell to another corporation, and this action sets off a chain reaction of pandemonium. Because the park was designed to be run remotely, no one is on hand to physically close the gates when they are inadvertently unlocked, proving the danger of overreliance on technology. Hammond's entire project depends on the assumption that humans can master nature, but even though the park scientists created only females, the dinosaurs have been breeding—life always eludes our efforts to control it.

Or, as Jeff Goldblum famously quipped in the role of Ian Malcolm in the film version, "Life, uh, finds a way."

John Michael Crichton was born in 1942 in Chicago, and started writing while an undergraduate at Harvard. He switched to writing thrillers using a pseudonym to earn money while attending Harvard Medical School; he won an Edgar Award for best novel before graduating in 1969. Crichton candidly acknowledged his literary forebears: he looked to *The War of the Worlds* (1898) when writing *The Andromeda Strain* (1969), for example, and tipped his keyboard to Arthur Conan Doyle, whose novel *The Lost World* (1912) also features the unlikely survival of prehistoric creatures, by borrowing its title for his 1995 sequel to *Jurassic Park*. Crichton had the science chops to back up the imaginative ones. He knew the "hard stuff," as his editor, Robert Gottlieb, would say. Fans were shocked when Crichton died unexpectedly in 2008 at age 66.

The universe of *Jurassic Park* had legs, as well as tails, heads, and really sharp claws. After the success of the novel came the megasuccess of the Steven Spielberg–directed film in 1993. Spielberg knew he had a hit: he optioned the book even before its 1990 publication, with Crichton signing on to write the screenplay, and the movie went on to earn more than $1 billion. Three more movie sequels came out in 1997, 2001, and 2015, with a fourth due in theaters in 2018. Crichton's characters and plots also serve as the basis for rides at Universal theme parks, as well as video games.

In the years since Crichton published *Jurassic Park*, genetic engineering technology has advanced such that private companies regularly duplicate livestock and pets with little fanfare or media interest. But like its predecessor *Frankenstein* (1818), which also concerns a murderous monster who owes its existence to science, *Jurassic Park* offers well-founded concerns about bioethics. In their respective works, Mary Shelley and Michael Crichton urge us to never stop considering the moral implications of unbridled scientific inquiry.

57

LEFT BEHIND SERIES

Tim LaHaye and Jerry B. Jenkins · 1995–2007

The 16 books that make up the Left Behind series begin after the Rapture has instantly transported believers from the Earth to Heaven and focus on various characters who remain as they make sense of the new world, also known as End Times. According to the Christian belief system espoused by the authors, a period called the Tribulation, full of nightmares, discord, pain, famine, and other horrors, will occur in the aftermath of the Rapture. Many people will die during the apocalypse, but there will still be an opportunity for redemption. A Second Coming of Jesus will take place, ending the darkness and ushering in paradise for those who choose faith.

Left Behind (1995), the first book of the series, describes the struggle for those left behind not only to figure out what happened to their loved ones, but to cope in a changed world. A core group of American survivors—including pilot Rayford Steele; his daughter, Chloe; journalist Buck Williams; and assistant pastor Bruce Barnes—band together to form the Tribulation Force. Over subsequent novels, the Tribulation Force combats the powerful, elite Global Community, a sort of postapocalyptic United Nations headed by Nicolae Carpathia. In time, it's revealed that Carpathia is actually the Antichrist.

Timothy Francis LaHaye was born in 1926 in Detroit, Michigan. An evangelical minister as well as a writer, he published more than 75 books before his death in 2016, but he is best known for the Left Behind series he created with Jerry B. Jenkins. LaHaye came up with the idea for the novels while traveling: one day he watched a married pilot flirting with an unmarried flight attendant, and wondered what would happen if the Rapture occurred at that very moment. Jerry Bruce Jenkins was born in 1949 in Kalamazoo, Michigan; he handled the writing, working from LaHaye's notes and edits. A long-standing interest in Christian eschatology, or the study of "last things," as well as a deep belief in dispensational premillennialism, which

claims that the Second Coming is imminent, linked the men; this shared sensibility drives the Left Behind series.

Just because the books borrow liberally from the Book of Revelation doesn't mean they aren't page-turners. This portion of the New Testament lays out the apocalyptic predictions of John, a first-century-CE Jewish Christian whose identity remains uncertain. It's a very dark text, focused on an epic, violent battle between Christ and the Antichrist at Armageddon. LaHaye—who argued that institutions as diverse as the NAACP and the US State Department are part of a conspiracy to destroy morality in America—encourages a reading of the Book of Revelation as literal truth. When the Rapture comes, a certain strain of Christians will be saved, and everyone else will be tortured and tormented.

Some have called the Left Behind series "a revenge fantasy, in which right-wing Christians win out over the rational, scientific, modern, post-Enlightenment world," but readers were enraptured by the books. The Left Behind series has sold 80 million copies, making it one of the bestselling Christian fiction series in history. In fact, an obituary for LaHaye estimated that the books spent almost as long on the *New York Times* bestseller list—about 300 weeks—as the Tribulation is supposed to last. To date, a few movies have been made based on the series, some featuring Kirk Cameron, a well-known child actor who grew up to become a popular force in American evangelicalism.

For the faithful, part of the pleasure of the series comes from seeing the Book of Revelation turned into a narrative with characters, scenes, and plots. As LaHaye realized when he conceived his series, people learn lots from nonfiction, but they especially love stories. No doubt another aspect of the books' popularity may be explained by the driving good-versus-evil scenario. Enemies can't get much worse than the Antichrist, so the stakes feel particularly high, the tale especially riveting.

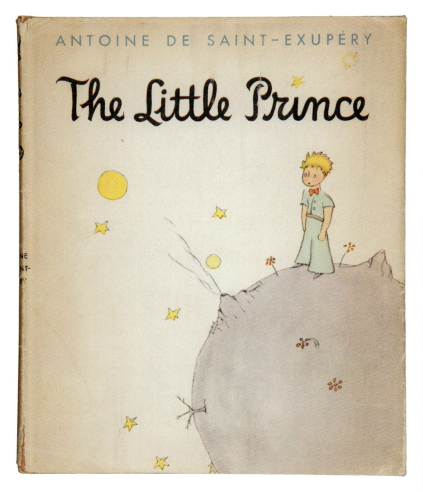

58

THE LITTLE PRINCE

Antoine de Saint-Exupéry · 1943

Practically every page of *The Little Prince* (1943) tenders an aphorism. "It is only with the heart that one can see rightly; what is essential is invisible to the eye," writes Antoine de Saint-Exupéry, in what is arguably the book's most famous line. Elsewhere the little prince neatly sums up one of the novel's primary points: "All grown-ups were once children . . . but only few of them remember it." This slim classic, with its charming, iconic watercolor illustrations, seeks to detail the pleasant perplexity of being young in order to combat some of the existential crises that come with growing old.

Stranded in the Sahara when his airplane breaks down, the novel's narrator is befriended by an odd young boy with blond hair and a gold scarf. The narrator names him "the little prince." The boy grew up on an asteroid, where he spent his days tending a single rose. In time he felt stifled by the rose's vanity and seemingly bottomless need, so he went off to explore the universe. Thus far, he says, he has met just a few people on various planets, including a drunk who drinks to forget he's a drunk and a businessperson who wants only to acquire more money. From a railroad operator, he learns that only children take the time to look out the window; adults are too busy rushing from one place to another. A fox on Earth teaches him about friendship. The little prince and his observations make a profound impression on the narrator—and the reader.

Inseparable from *The Little Prince* is the life of its author and illustrator. Born to a poor but aristocratic family in Lyon, France, in 1900, Antoine de Saint-Exupéry lost a beloved brother to rheumatic fever as a teenager. He may have based the capricious character of the rose on his wife, Consuelo, with whom he had a somewhat rocky marriage.

Like his unnamed narrator, Saint-Exupéry's plane crashed in the desert, leaving him stranded for a time with nothing but the sand, the stars, and his thoughts to keep him company. Saint-Exupéry left his native France during World War II, after the Nazis took over; he wrote and illustrated his book while living in exile in the United States. A sense of rootlessness and deep sadness haunt the book.

Saint-Exupéry found himself while flying. An indifferent student, he went into the army, transferred to the air force, and became a commercial pilot, mostly flying postal runs. While in the air, Saint-Exupéry sometimes daydreamed or even read. His wistfulness aside, he patented several aircraft aids in the 1930s. Fittingly, he died in flight. Speculation about Saint-Exupéry's death in 1944 almost overshadowed his accomplishments in life. The discovery of his bracelet in 1998 and the remains of his airplane in 2003 renewed debate about whether he was shot down by the Luftwaffe or committed suicide after being publicly accused of supporting the Vichy French government.

Many readers see the little prince as the narrator's inner child come to life. Certainly the book makes the case that children lose not only their innocence but also their capacity for appreciating the world as they mature. Everyone the little prince meets has ceased to marvel at the wonders around them. At the same time, however, the little prince has lessons to learn. He realizes how cruelly he has treated the rose, and, in another well-known line, he recognizes his responsibilities to the flower: "You become responsible, forever, for what you have tamed." To fully exist, then, we must ground our search for beauty with the more earthbound concerns of how we treat one another. The book offers readers the chance to ruminate on all they have to admire and appreciate in their lives.

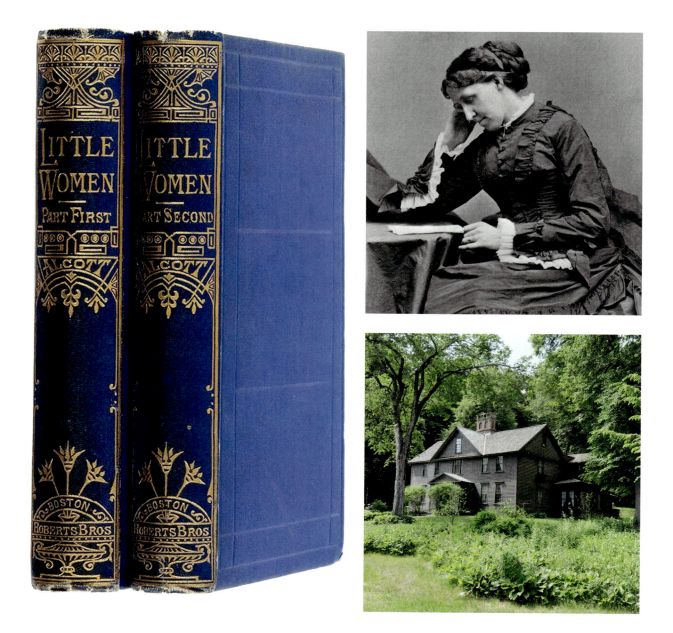

59

LITTLE WOMEN

Louisa May Alcott · 1868–1869

Asked to name their favorite literary character from childhood, many women will respond with nary a pause or hesitation: Jo March. For a little girl with a literary bent, smart, tomboyish Jo was a revelation. She'd rather run than curtsy, write than cook, live independently than marry. She defies gender norms, at least for a while. She feels modern.

When an editor inquired whether Louisa May Alcott wanted to write a book expressly for girls, she initially said no. Alcott was a fast writer who often cranked out pseudonymous pulp novels for money. But she wasn't interested in creating a story about a group of young women. However, she relented when the editor promised to publish a manuscript of her father's if she submitted one too. She finished *Little Women* (1868–1869) in about 10 weeks of furious work. While most of her other fiction and nonfiction has disappeared into the mists of the past, *Little Women* evidences plenty of staying power.

Set in 19th-century New England, the novel focuses on the March family, specifically its four daughters: Meg (16), Jo (15), Beth (13), and Amy (12). They live with their beloved mother, Marmee, while their father serves as a chaplain in the Civil War. Having each received a copy of the religious novel *The Pilgrim's Progress* (1678) one Christmas, they decide to embody its Christian values through circumstances that range from good-natured fun to tragedy, including competing for boys' attention, falling in love, getting married, coping with terminal illness, and choosing between a conventional life of domesticity and fulfilling one's artistic dreams. They grow up, and virtue and decency guide their days.

In many ways, the fates of the four sisters represent the options available to women at the time. The eldest, Meg, marries first, and starts a family immediately. The youngest, blonde-haired and blue-eyed Amy, is valued for her beauty, and she becomes a lady of society. Religious Beth stays at home, keeps house, and dies young. At first, Jo forgoes marriage in pursuit of her dream of becoming a writer. While she eventually lets that aspiration wither and marries Professor Friedrich Bhaer, they develop an equitable partnership based on mutual respect. Alcott herself never married.

Louisa May Alcott was born in what is now Philadelphia in 1832, but her family soon moved to Boston, where her father associated with transcendentalists like Henry David Thoreau and Ralph Waldo Emerson. Amos Alcott was an influential educator and thinker, but the family was nonetheless very poor. From a young age Louisa worked, writing on the side. She achieved some success with a series of shorts about working in a Union hospital in 1863, but *Little Women* made her famous. So famous, in fact, that devotees would make pilgrimages to her house in Concord, which has since been turned into a museum.

Even as she wrote it, she derided the book as "moral pap." *Little Women* abounds with homilies espousing the value of hard work and the joy of putting family first. The girls make do with very little. Alcott couldn't deny the book's life-changing success, and she wrote two sequels: *Little Men* (1871) and *Jo's Boys* (1886). She died in 1888 at age 55.

After a few silent adaptations, George Cukor directed a 1933 film version, with Katharine Hepburn as Jo. Elizabeth Taylor took the role of Amy in the 1949 remake, while Winona Ryder was Jo in the 1994 update. A 21st-century version is currently in the works. Perhaps every generation needs to find its take on *Little Women*. Today, of course, girls have options Alcott never could have imagined, but her work continues to normalize the wish of every little woman who's longed to be more than "wife" or "mother."

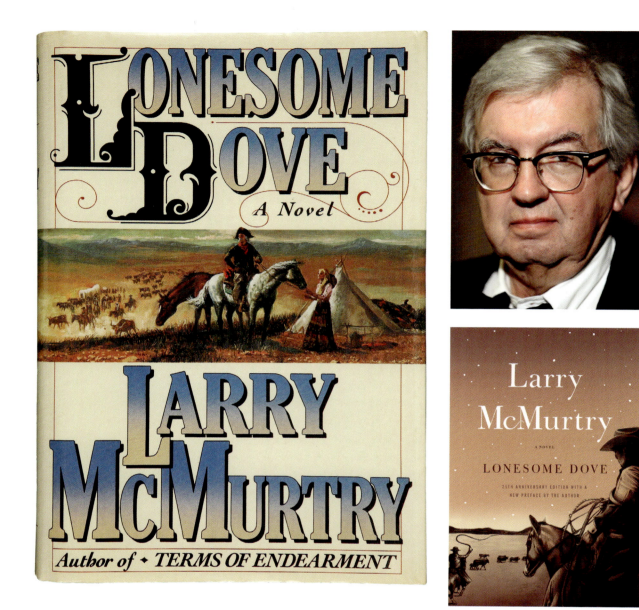

60

LONESOME DOVE

Larry McMurtry · 1985

A journalist once described *Lonesome Dove* (1985) as "the *War and Peace* of cattle-drive novels." Larry McMurtry offered a different take on his Pulitzer Prize–winning novel, referring to it as "*Gone with the Wind* of the West." The comparisons hold: all three novels offer expansive looks at societies in transition, depicting colorful, compelling characters caught up in the bloody progress of history.

Initially McMurtry conceived of the story of Texas Rangers in *Lonesome Dove* as a movie. After John Wayne passed on the project, James Stewart, who had been attached to play a role, dropped out, and production plans fizzled. So McMurtry bought back the screenplay from the studio that owned it, and transformed *Lonesome Dove* into a novel. It was such a success that CBS decided to make a miniseries featuring Robert Duvall and Tommy Lee Jones in 1989; that too was a critical and commercial darling.

Gone for more than 10 years, former Texas Ranger Jake Spoon returns to the tiny Texas town of Lonesome Dove, where he reunites with his friends Captain Woodrow F. Call and Captain Augustus "Gus" McCrae. After retiring from the Rangers, Call and McCrae now oversee the Hat Creek Cattle Company and Livery Emporium, living a peaceful life. Jake, however, is on the run after accidentally killing a sheriff's brother, and he convinces McCrae, Call, and some other men to go to Montana, where they intend to create the area's first cattle ranch. Soon the Hat Creek boys, Jake, his prostitute-lover Lorena, and the sheriff and his crew are winding through the dangerous landscape.

The novel takes place in the 1870s, a time when the West was a place of boundless freedom but also of vicious lawlessness. Very slowly states began to join the Union, completing the dream of manifest destiny and stretching America from sea to sea. Settlers, with the approval and encouragement of the federal government, claimed territory from Native American inhabitants, causing chaos, mass murder, and increasingly desperate, violent retaliation. Hunters slaughtered vast herds of buffalo. Farmers started, quite literally, to put down roots. Robbers roamed, looking for wealth and prey, and vigilantes dispensed their form of justice. All of these actual events inform the ambitious, sinuous plot of *Lonesome Dove*, as McMurtry seeks to strip away glorifying myths and show readers how the West was really won.

He knows the region's truths as well as its legends deep in his bones. Larry McMurtry was born in 1936 to a family of ranchers outside of Archer City, Texas. He grew up hearing stories but discovered books after a cousin left behind a bunch and McMurtry cracked one open. After living elsewhere around the United States, including in California while a Stegner Fellow at Stanford University, McMurtry returned to Archer City in the 1980s and opened a large used bookstore in the town. In addition to books he writes screenplays, a genre in which he's also garnered significant accolades. He cowrote the Academy Award–winning *The Last Picture Show* (1971), based on his 1966 semiautobiographical novel of the same name, and won an Oscar for his screenplay for *Brokeback Mountain* (2005).

McMurtry continued to visit the world of Lonesome Dove, Texas, after the publication of the original novel, with three more works following the exploits of Call, McCrae, McCrae's true love Clara, Comanche war chief Buffalo Hump, a bandit known as Blue Duck, and other memorable characters. He's set many of his 30-odd novels in the West, from Houston to an imagined version of Archer City to the Great Plains. The region's pull seems inescapable, for him and for us.

If You Like . . .

WHAT'S YOUR NEXT READ?

LOOKING FOR your next great read? Our chart enables you to quickly and easily find similar titles. If you like one, read the next and the next and the next, then try another category.

IF YOU LIKE THESE EPIC FANTASY TITLES...

The Chronicles of Narnia

Foundation

A Game of Thrones

Lord of the Rings

The Wheel of Time

TRY THESE CATEGORIES:
Intense Quests, Alternate Worlds

IF YOU LIKE THESE MAN VS. NATURE TITLES...

The Call of the Wild

The Clan of the Cave Bear

Hatchet

The Martian

Moby-Dick

TRY THESE CATEGORIES:
Dystopia, Thrills & Chills

IF YOU LIKE THESE STRONG FEMALE PROTAGONIST TITLES...

Gone with the Wind

The Help

The Hunger Games

Jane Eyre

Their Eyes Were Watching God

TRY THESE CATEGORIES:
Urban Life, Families in Turmoil

IF YOU LIKE THESE SATIRE TITLES...

A Confederacy of Dunces

Catch-22

Gulliver's Travels

The Intuitionist

The Sirens of Titan

TRY THESE CATEGORIES:
Epic Fantasy, Alternate Worlds

IF YOU LIKE THESE INTENSE QUEST TITLES...

The Alchemist

The Count of Monte Cristo

Don Quixote

Heart of Darkness

Siddhartha

TRY THESE CATEGORIES:
Thrills & Chills, Urban Life

IF YOU LIKE THESE SCIENCE GONE AWRY TITLES...

Dune

Frankenstein

Jurassic Park

Ready Player One

Watchers

TRY THESE CATEGORIES:
Man vs. Nature, Satire

IF YOU LIKE THESE CHRISTIAN THEME TITLES...

The Left Behind series

Mind Invaders

The Pilgrim's Progress

The Shack

This Present Darkness

TRY THESE CATEGORIES:
Science Gone Awry, Intense Quests

IF YOU LIKE THESE DYSTOPIA TITLES...

Atlas Shrugged

The Handmaid's Tale

Nineteen Eighty-Four

The Stand

Swan Song

TRY THESE CATEGORIES:
Epic Fantasy; History, Revisited

IF YOU LIKE THESE PSYCHOLOGY TITLES...

Crime and Punishment

Gone Girl

Invisible Man

The Picture of Dorian Gray

The Sun Also Rises

TRY THESE CATEGORIES:
Growing Up, Families in Turmoil

IF YOU LIKE THESE HISTORY, REVISITED TITLES...

The Book Thief

Lonesome Dove

Memoirs of a Geisha

The Pillars of the Earth

War and Peace

TRY THESE CATEGORIES:
Satire, Kids' Books with Grown-Up Themes

IF YOU LIKE THESE MOTHERS & DAUGHTERS, FATHERS & SONS TITLES...

Beloved

Bless Me, Ultima

Gilead

The Godfather

The Joy Luck Club

TRY THESE CATEGORIES:
Families in Turmoil, Oooo La La

IF YOU LIKE THESE THRILLS & CHILLS TITLES...

Alex Cross Mysteries

And Then There Were None

The Curious Incident of the Dog in the Night-Time

The Da Vinci Code

The Hunt for Red October

TRY THESE CATEGORIES:
Christian Themes, Man vs. Nature

IF YOU LIKE THESE GROWING UP TITLES...

A Prayer for Owen Meany

The Adventures of Tom Sawyer

Anne of Green Gables

Great Expectations

Little Women

TRY THESE CATEGORIES:
Oooo La La; Mothers & Daughters, Fathers & Sons

IF YOU LIKE THESE KIDS' BOOKS WITH GROWN-UP THEMES TITLES...

Charlotte's Web

Ghost

To Kill a Mockingbird

The Little Prince

Where the Red Fern Grows

TRY THESE CATEGORIES:
Teen Troubles, Families in Turmoil

IF YOU LIKE THESE TEEN TROUBLES TITLES...

A Separate Peace

The Catcher in the Rye

Looking for Alaska

The Lovely Bones

The Outsiders

TRY THESE CATEGORIES:
Growing Up, Strong Female Protagonists

IF YOU LIKE THESE ALTERNATE WORLDS TITLES...

Alice in Wonderland

Harry Potter

Outlander

The Giver

The Hitchhiker's Guide to the Galaxy

TRY THESE CATEGORIES:
Science Gone Awry, Thrills & Chills

IF YOU LIKE THESE OOOO LA LA TITLES...

Fifty Shades of Grey

The Notebook

Pride and Prejudice

Rebecca

Twilight Saga

TRY THESE CATEGORIES:
Strong Female Protagonists, Dystopia

IF YOU LIKE THESE FAMILIES IN TURMOIL TITLES...

The Brief Wondrous Life of Oscar Wao

The Color Purple

Flowers in the Attic

One Hundred Years of Solitude

Wuthering Heights

TRY THESE CATEGORIES:
Mothers & Daughters, Fathers & Sons; Social Strife

IF YOU LIKE THESE URBAN LIFE TITLES...

A Tree Grows in Brooklyn

Americanah

The Coldest Winter Ever

Tales of the City

White Teeth

TRY THESE CATEGORIES:
Growing Up, Teen Troubles

IF YOU LIKE THESE SOCIAL STRIFE TITLES...

Another Country

Doña Bárbara

The Grapes of Wrath

The Great Gatsby

Things Fall Apart

TRY THESE CATEGORIES:
History, Revisited; Growing Up

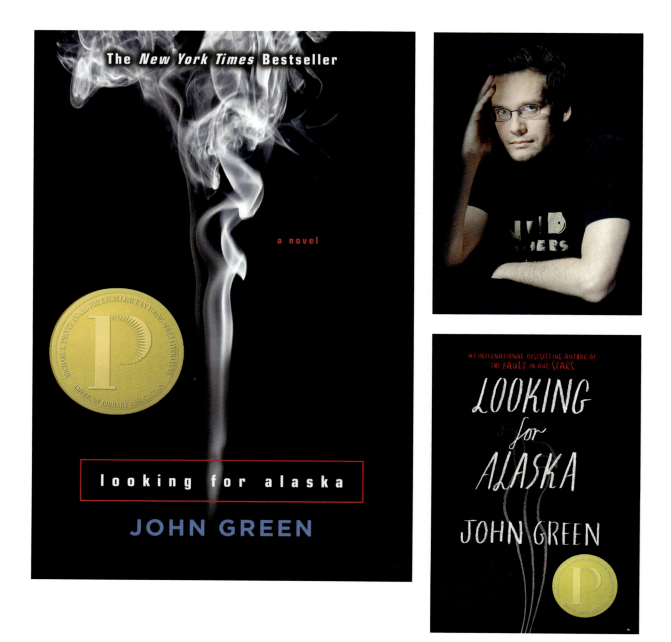

The *New York Times* Bestseller

a novel

looking for alaska

JOHN GREEN

#1 INTERNATIONAL BESTSELLING AUTHOR OF
THE *FAULT IN OUR STARS*

LOOKING
for
ALASKA
JOHN GREEN

CLOCKWISE FROM LEFT: A paperback cover of *Looking for Alaska*, first published in 2005. | Author John Green, photographed in *The Hollywood Reporter* in 2004. Green is often called "the teen whisperer" for his deep understanding of teenagers and their experiences. | The 10th-anniversary edition cover of the book.

61

LOOKING FOR ALASKA

John Green · 2005

He's called "the teen whisperer." The label reflects the YA author's deep, almost preternatural understanding of adolescence—its pain, its excitement, its over-the-top emotions and energy. John Green might be a married middle-aged man with children, but he appears to have a direct pipeline into the worries and wonders of young adulthood. And it all started with *Looking for Alaska* (2005).

Told in the first person by a high-school junior named Miles Halter, Green's debut novel focuses on the before and after of a life-changing event. Chapter titles keep track of the time, beginning with "One Hundred Thirty-Six Days Before" and concluding with "One Hundred Thirty-Six Days After." Miles arrives at Culver Creek Preparatory High School looking to make some changes. He meets Chip, Takumi, and the gorgeous, temperamental, free-spirited Alaska. These new friends nickname him Pudge, encourage him to cut loose, and teach him the school's main rule: don't be a tattletale. They play pranks, they have fun, they bond over their deepest, funniest, wildest moments. In short, they become close as only teens can be—until one moment turns everything upside down.

Looking for Alaska bursts with beautiful lines and metaphors: "[I]f people were rain," Miles thinks about Alaska, "I was drizzle and she was a hurricane." Later he compares the passing of a loved one to losing a pair of glasses and then being told that, since glasses no longer exist in the world, he would just have to make do. Miles starts school hoping to find what he calls his "Great Perhaps," the last words of poet François Rabelais. He seeks out and quotes people's dying words in an attempt to discern the life that came before. Yet Miles wants to find mystery and magic now, in life, rather than in death. It's a sad twist that he finds both mystery and magic in death too.

Green was born in Indianapolis, Indiana, in 1977, grew up in Orlando, Florida, and attended boarding school in Birmingham, Alabama, much as his protagonist Miles does. In Birmingham Green knew a student who died, but, as he repeatedly stresses, *Looking for Alaska* isn't a roman à clef. In honor of the book's 10th anniversary, a special edition was released with early drafts and ephemera. Since the success of his first novel, Green has released several other bestsellers, including the megahit *The Fault in Our Stars* (2012), a love story about two teens with cancer. His books often feature smart-alecky characters who experience profound anguish on their journey to adulthood.

With its prep-school setting and tragic loss, *Looking for Alaska* has been compared to *A Separate Peace* (1959). Miles's voice sometimes reminds readers of Holden Caulfield's in *The Catcher in the Rye* (1951), another novel about a young person concerned about what's to come. The stakes in books like these feel great because they are: it is as teens that we start to seriously consider how lives take shape, when we begin to understand the importance of not only asking questions about what might make our days meaningful but striving to answer them.

Despite the parallels with earlier writers, Green exists in a world of his own creation, much of it online: entire sections of the internet are devoted to people displaying tattoos of lines from his novels, and Green is widely considered to be peerless in his mastery of social media as a means of connecting with readers. In 2007, Green and his brother, Hank, began communicating with one another via videos, a process known as vlogging, and their shared YouTube channel has millions of subscribers. Green's fans call themselves "nerdfighters," a positive term meant to show their pleasure in being interested in stuff that others might find dorky. One of their catchphrases is "Don't forget to be awesome." Green unquestionably takes that advice to heart.

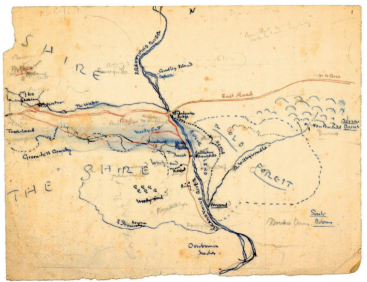

CLOCKWISE FROM TOP: The first complete American editions of the Lord of the Rings trilogy, originally published from 1954 to 1955. | Photographed here in 1982, J. R. R. Tolkien was a writer and a specialist in medieval literature, which inspired his novels. | An early map of the Shire, drawn by Tolkien, shows Frodo, Sam, and Pippin's travels in blue. Edits and other notes are written in pencil.

62

THE LORD OF THE RINGS SERIES

J. R. R. Tolkien · 1954–1955

Bored one day while grading student exams, an Oxford professor of Anglo-Saxon jotted *In a hole in the ground there lived a hobbit* on someone's paper. That idle scrawl became the first line of *The Hobbit* (1937), which introduced readers to the race of halflings known as hobbits, with their love of fireworks and food. When the book became a bestseller, its publisher asked its author, J. R. R. Tolkien, to write a sequel. He did, and more than a decade later published three volumes: *The Fellowship of the Ring, The Two Towers,* and *The Return of the King.* Collectively known as The Lord of the Rings (1954–1955), the works fundamentally altered the genre of fantasy.

Long before the beginning of *The Hobbit,* Sauron, the Dark Lord, created the One Ring. This ring would enable its wearer to rule over all the inhabitants of Middle-earth, among them elves, humans, and dwarves. Defeated in battle, Sauron lost his physical form, and the ring wound up in the hands of Bilbo Baggins, a lovable hobbit who gifts it to his ward, Frodo Baggins, as The Lord of the Rings begins. With the help of the wise wizard Gandalf the Grey, Frodo discovers the ring's menacing purpose, and the improbable hero and various friends and companions set off to destroy it via the fire of Mount Doom in Mordor.

The series is an astonishing accomplishment. Its descriptions feel like transcriptions, so vivid are the details of Middle-earth, from its geography to its multiple languages to its diverse inhabitants. Then there are the complicated lineages and histories spread over the ages, much of which Tolkien included not in the novel's proper text but in lengthy appendices.

John Ronald Reuel Tolkien was born in 1892 to British parents in what is now South Africa. When he was four his family moved to England, where he was home-schooled by his mother and raised a Roman Catholic. Even as a child he showed admirable facility with languages, inventing several fictional tongues—some of which he would continue to work on for decades—and eventually becoming a scholar of Old and Middle English, among other dialects. He worked for a time at the Oxford English Dictionary, where he handled words beginning with the letter *w.* Years later he entered the OED pantheon once again, as the creator of such gems as *mithril* (a beautiful, hard metal) and *orcish* (resembling a foul, nasty orc).

Power corrupts, goes the saying, and absolute power corrupts absolutely. The ring, as a symbol of unchecked power, causes anyone who wears it to become evil. In some cases, just being near the ring is tempting enough to bring about a personality alteration. Almost everyone who comes into contact with the ring changes: the human Black Riders become the zombielike Ringwraiths, nice Sméagol becomes the murderous Gollum, and the noble warrior Boromir decides he'd rather hang on to the ring and go after Sauron than destroy the ring (which would also destroy Sauron). Even Frodo feels the ring's corrosive effects by the end of the novel. Far better to stay at home and gobble up your second breakfast.

Peter Jackson adapted Tolkien's books for the big screen, releasing six movies between 2001 and 2014. All told, the movies earned almost $6 billion and won 17 Academy Awards. Amazon recently announced that it would be developing the books for the small screen.

The Lord of the Rings offers unambiguous heroes and antiheroes in the form of such characters as Legolas, Aragorn, and the Witch-king of Angmar. Many scholars and readers trace a Christian through line in Tolkien's work, a reflection of his religiosity in life. Nevertheless, Tolkien denied any symbolic implications, saying to his publisher, "[The Lord of the Rings] is not 'about' anything but itself. Certainly it has no allegorical intentions, general, particular, or topical, moral, religious, or political." However they interpret the books, readers have developed a deep affection for Middle-earth, a place where heroes still walk, even if their strides are short and their feet are hairy.

THE

LOVELY

BONES

A novel

ALICE SEBOLD

In the tunnel where I was raped, a tunnel that was once an underground entry to an amphitheater, a place where actors burst forth from underneath the seats of a crowd, a girl had been murdered and dismembered. I was told this story by the police. In comparison, they said, I was

LUCKY

ALICE SEBOLD
The NEW YORK TIMES Bestselling Author of THE LOVELY BONES

CLOCKWISE FROM LEFT: First edition cover of *The Lovely Bones*, from 2002. | Author Alice Sebold, photographed in New York City. *The Lovely Bones* was her debut novel, which was wildly successful. | In her memoir, *Lucky*, Sebold writes about being assaulted and raped coming home from a party in college. The title was inspired by a police officer, who told Sebold she was lucky to be alive.

63

THE LOVELY BONES

Alice Sebold · 2002

I n Alice Sebold's 2002 novel, there are two meanings to the title. One emphasizes the connections among people—we are held up by things we cannot see, and they link us to life and those we love. A second, more literal, meaning concerns real bones: the physical remains of the narrator, a 14-year-old girl in heaven, who was abducted, raped, and murdered by a neighbor in 1973.

Despite the dark subject matter, Sebold's fiction debut is an uplifting story. Susie Salmon might be dead, but she nevertheless revels in the joys of life. Readers learn what happened to her at the hands of Mr. Harvey in the first chapter. The rest of the book focuses on Susie's family and friends as they cope with her death. While some withdraw and drift away, others seek answers and closure. Susie occasionally comes to visit. In one particularly supernatural scene, Susie inhabits her best friend's body in order to share an intimate moment with the boy she loved before her death. The novel also describes Susie's growing acceptance of her new state, which includes meeting Harvey's other victims.

Sebold knows about the way light does and does not follow darkness. *Lucky* (1999), her memoir, details an attack she survived at age 18. Walking home from a party as a college freshman, she was brutally assaulted and raped. The title comes from a comment made by a police officer, who said that a young woman had previously been murdered and dismembered in the same spot, and that Sebold was lucky to be alive. Police were not able to identify her attacker until Sebold recognized him on the street a few months later. During the trial, a court official called her "the best rape witness [he'd] ever seen on the stand." The rapist was convicted and sent to prison.

In the aftermath, Sebold returned to Syracuse University, studying writing with Raymond Carver, and graduated with a degree in English. Then came a rocky period of drifting, drug use, and alienation. She later earned an MFA from the University of California, Irvine, in 1998, where she started working on a fictionalized account of a young rape victim. She stopped that work to concentrate on her memoir, which was published to little fanfare. A second novel, *The Almost Moon*, about an artist who suffocates her agoraphobic, severely senile mother with a towel, was published in 2007. But it didn't reach nearly the heights of reader adoration as *The Lonely Bones*. Then again, not many novels could. Sebold's debut may very well be the most successful debut novel since *Gone with the Wind* appeared in 1936, with bookstores calling Sebold's publisher directly to beg for more copies to be printed and shipped. Peter Jackson adapted *The Lovely Bones* for the big screen in 2009.

The unusual focus of the novel—few stories about a murder reveal all the relevant details, including the perpetrator, at the outset—allows Sebold to go beyond the questions typical of crime novels. Instead of asking who did it or why, Sebold is interested in what happens to people when they lose someone they love, in how an extraordinarily horrible event affects ordinary lives. Carefully avoiding cheap sentimentality or easy moralizing, Sebold presents her story plainly and sympathetically, and the blessing with which the novel ends is as moving as it is munificent: "I wish you all a long and happy life."

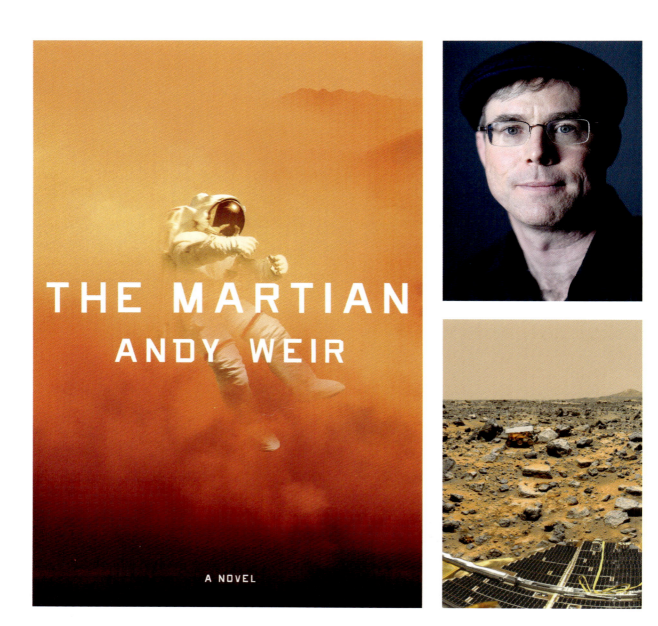

CLOCKWISE FROM LEFT: The hardcover of *The Martian*, printed in 2014. | Andy Weir, photographed at the Toronto International Film Festival in 2015. His novel was adapted for the film that came out that year, directed by Ridley Scott and starring Matt Damon. | *The Martian* chronicles botanist Mark Watney's survival as he's stranded alone on Mars. This is a view of the Martian landscape from NASA's Pathfinder mission.

64

THE MARTIAN

Andy Weir · 2011, self-published as e-book; 2014

For researchers and engineers, science fiction sometimes proves tricky to read. In creating their worlds, writers often take liberties with facts, stretching the limits of possibility and aggravating those who might know better. Having experienced this frustration himself, Andy Weir sought to be as accurate as possible in his first novel. "I was writing for this core group of extremely technical, science-minded dorks like me," he said later. "I'm one of those guys that'll nitpick every little physics problem in a movie." As a result, *The Martian* (2011) is full of precise details and legitimate resolutions to issues that someone might face on the Red Planet—so much so that a special edition of this adventure thriller is being used in schools to teach physics and chemistry.

A vicious sandstorm overtakes a group of astronauts stationed on Mars in 2035. Presumed dead, botanist Mark Watney gets left behind as the rest of the crew heads back to Earth. Once he recovers consciousness, Watney determines what he needs to do in order to survive in their base, known as the Hab. He writes about his experiences and discoveries in a logbook, and these entries constitute much of the novel. Back on Earth, a NASA team searches images to see whether anything from the mission is salvageable and discovers that Watney is alive. The novel alternates between the NASA team generating and executing a plan to bring Watney home and Watney's life on Mars.

Alone in a harsh land, Watney endures. *The Martian* thus sits squarely in the adventure genre, alongside other contemporary man-versus-nature stories such as *Into the Wild* (1996), *The Perfect Storm* (1997), and the Hatchet series (1987–2003). Watney uses creativity, persistence, technical training and knowledge, and plain old common sense to stay alive, and his passages provide readers with extensive details of his solutions for problems like how to generate water for irrigation and what to do with an excess of explosive hydrogen. He doesn't give up or wallow, making him a quietly heroic, if decidedly pragmatic, figure.

Moreover, Watney is not afraid to express his fear. To cope with his loneliness, he plays his colleague's disco music, which lends the book a moment of levity. Nevertheless, he yearns for human contact. He figures out how to adapt a rover and takes it on a 3,200-kilometer trip to secure an old probe that contains communication technology. Back at the Hab, he fixes it and manages to email NASA. Overjoyed as he is to be back in touch with others, he occasionally chafes at the micromanagement that ensues, a not-so-subtle nod to the often-stifling effect of bureaucracy on vision and inventiveness.

The only son of a particle physicist and an electronics engineer, Weir seemed destined for a career in the sciences. He began programming at age 15, and eventually helped code the video game *Warcraft II*. On his website, he would publish writing for fun and for free, including "The Egg," a popular short story about reincarnation and divinity, as well as *The Martian*. He self-published it via Amazon when fans began requesting alternate file formats. From there, it got picked up by a traditional publisher in 2014 and optioned for a movie.

Ridley Scott directed Matt Damon as Watney in the 2015 film, one of the highest-grossing movies of the year. Like the book, the movie praises scientific endeavor and inquiry, showing the great accomplishments that are possible when people work diligently, creatively, and rationally. NASA has capitalized on the success of the book and the movie to renew interest and funding in its space program. If all goes according to plan, NASA intends to send humans to Mars in the 2030s. It's a long journey, and *The Martian* will make the ideal read.

CLOCKWISE FROM LEFT: Cover of *Memoirs of a Geisha*, first published in 1997. | Author Arthur Golden, photographed in 2005 at the movie premiere of *Memoirs of a Geisha*. Golden was inspired to write the book while living in Japan, after meeting someone whose mother had been a geisha. | Two geisha, photographed in Kyoto in 1929.

65

MEMOIRS OF A GEISHA

Arthur Golden · 1997

Arthur Golden lends his bestselling novel the gravitas of nonfiction by beginning with a translator's note. As the fictional Japanese-history professor Jakob Haarhuis recounts, he traveled to Kyoto as a young boy and was captivated by geisha. Decades later, as an adult, he is overjoyed to have the opportunity to tell the story of the famous Sayuri Nitta, the book readers now hold in their hands. The artifice works, and *Memoirs of a Geisha* (1997) reads like lived history.

It took Golden two complete drafts before deciding to write his debut novel in the first person. Roughly 15 years earlier, while living in Japan, he met someone whose mother had been a geisha. He was fascinated by her story. Golden specialized in Japanese art as an undergraduate at Harvard and Japanese history as a graduate student at Columbia. Not only did he return to his studies to write his novel, but he also interviewed a former geisha in order to lend the world of Sayuri such verisimilitude.

Sayuri Nitta's real name is Chiyo Sakamoto. In *Memoirs of a Geisha*, readers learn of her humble beginnings as the beautiful, gray-eyed daughter of a poor fisherman, and of her sale to a Kyoto *okiya* (geisha house) at the age of nine in 1929. Renamed Sayuri, she receives extensive training to become a geisha. In time, she falls in love with Chairman Ken Iwamura, but she encounters many obstacles before getting the happy ending she dreams of several years later. For example, to increase Sayuri's worth as a geisha in the Kyoto community, her mentor, Mameha, essentially auctions off Sayuri's virginity, and Sayuri agrees to serve as another man's mistress in exchange for patronage.

Memoirs of a Geisha peels back a curtain to reveal the world of geisha culture. The Japanese word *geisha* loosely translates as "artist," a reflection of the artistry—and artifice—required for the role. Women are compelled to tamp down their true identities to take on the character of consummate entertainer, musician, dancer, and companion, with elaborate hair, makeup, and dress. Sometimes a geisha would perform sexual acts, but not always. She would, however, need to compete with others in her field to ensure that the wealthiest or best man supported her, rather than a rival. The novel seeks to probe beneath outward appearances to the cutthroat inner workings and maneuverings of a strict hierarchical society.

On the one hand, Sayuri's world offers an extremely limited role for women. Geisha cater to men's desires and embody male fantasies. In this sense, they are not independent thinkers or doers. The men they entertain return home to other wives and mothers of their children. On the other hand, being a geisha saves Sayuri from alternate unhappy fates, such as the poverty of her childhood and life as a maid. Her less attractive sister, sold at the same time as Sayuri, was forced into prostitution, although she later escapes and runs off with her lover. Characters in the novel who leave the geisha house for whatever reason fall into drunkenness and homelessness. Within the confines of geisha culture, Sayuri learns how to wield her feminine power for her great gain, and thus to some extent she controls her destiny.

Born in 1956, Arthur Sulzberger Golden grew up in Tennessee, where his mother ran the *Chattanooga Times*. She was a granddaughter of Adolph S. Ochs, who bought the *New York Times* in 1896, and Golden's extended family continues to own and control the paper. An Academy Award–winning movie based on Golden's book came out in 2005. Geisha culture began to wane after World War II, although there has been a renewed interest in geisha life as part of Japanese tourism, and there is a growing sense that geisha constitute an important part of the country's tradition and culture. *Memoirs of a Geisha* offers an excellent entry.

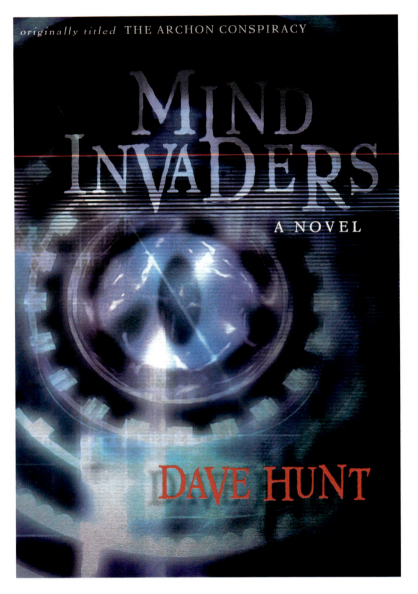

originally titled THE ARCHON CONSPIRACY

MIND INVADERS

A NOVEL

DAVE HUNT

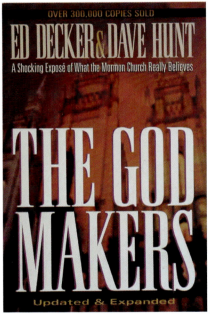

OVER 300,000 COPIES SOLD

ED DECKER & DAVE HUNT

A Shocking Exposé of What the Mormon Church Really Believes

THE GOD MAKERS

Updated & Expanded

CLOCKWISE FROM LEFT: A paperback cover of *Mind Invaders*. This edition was first published in 2007. | Author David Hunt signs books for readers at an event. Hunt preached and published his books through Berean Call, a ministry he formed with T. A. McMahon. | *The God Makers*, written by Dave Hunt and Ed Decker, looks at the Mormon Church.

66

MIND INVADERS

Dave Hunt · 1989

Originally titled *The Archon Conspiracy*, *Mind Invaders* (1989) is an action-packed story about psychic power, Christianity, and the cold war.

Ken Inman reaches out to shadowy forces for a living. A computer genius, he's thrilled to make contact with the alien Archons, who promise to give Ken a mind-expanding gift. The Archons claim to promote harmony and come in peace. But when the CIA and the Russians get involved, seeking to harness the Archons' psychic power for the gain of their respective governments, violence and war loom. Carla Bertelli is a journalist trying to uncover the true story of the intelligence community's plans as well as to solve the mystery of the Archons. Although she loves Ken, his newfound fundamentalist Christianity troubles her and causes conflict in their relationship. While she sees the Archons as benevolent angels, Ken deems them to be hellish demons. It's a race against time, with the fate of humanity hanging in the balance.

Before his death in 2013, Dave Hunt was well known as a Christian thinker and bestselling author. He wrote numerous Christian apologetics, seeking to defend his view of religion against a world he saw as increasingly hostile to faith. Hunt held to the literal truth of the Bible, and he vigorously attacked not only scientific consensus but also Catholicism and Mormonism, among other religious traditions, for deviating from what he believed was the correct understanding of the world and divine will.

David Charles Haddon Hunt was born in 1926 in California, earned a degree in mathematics from UCLA, and married his college sweetheart. Before turning full-time to his ministry, he worked as a CPA. In 1992, Hunt and T. A. McMahon founded the Berean Call, a ministry through which he preached and disseminated Christian books, videos, newsletters, and other materials. With McMahon, he cowrote several works of nonfiction, including *The Seduction of Christianity* (1985), meant to help people return Christianity to what the authors perceived to be its original teachings as outlined in the Bible. They sought to remove what they saw as the dangerous influences of mysticism and holistic approaches, and tried to give their followers tools with which to defend their beliefs from those who might otherwise cast doubt.

Hunt's novel serves in some ways as an allegory, and he sought to evangelize through his fiction. He believed that much of modern life, with its emphasis on psychology and ecumenism, made it difficult for people to live their religious convictions. The modern world offers no end to distraction and concerns that might vie for space in one's mind. On a very literal level, *Mind Invaders* functions as a reminder that what seems like a benevolent force may in fact be extremely destructive, and the novel urges readers to heed its calls for caution.

As C. S. Lewis, another Christian theologian, once wrote, "For me, reason is the natural organ of truth; but imagination is the organ of meaning. Imagination, producing new metaphors or revivifying old, is not the cause of truth, but its condition." *Mind Invaders* might be viewed through a similar lens: while there are those readers who might believe that the Archons exist, others will see in Ken and Carla analogues to their own struggles to maintain their faith in the face of doubt—whether from loved ones, from strangers, or even from within.

Boring, Strange, and Just Not Good

SOMETIMES THE MOST LOVED BOOKS DON'T GET ANY LOVE

IT'S EASIER THAN EVER to offer a scathing review—just have a look at the comments on Amazon for such works as *The Sun Also Rises* ("boring, boring, and more boring"), *The Call of the Wild* ("The worst book ever. Who cares about dogs in the Yukon?"), and *One Hundred Years of Solitude* ("This books [sic] should be banned for 100 years.") Cringeworthy as such appraisals may be, the worst reviews come from experts—journalists, professional book critics, and other writers.

Wuthering Heights famously shocked readers upon its publication in 1847, with contemporary critics calling it "strange" and advising that the text be burned. One reviewer thought it amplified the missteps and faults of *Jane Eyre* (1847) "a thousand fold," a succinct way of swiping at both novels in one go. But the author of an 1848 review went still further: "How a human being could have attempted such a book as the present without committing suicide before he had finished a dozen chapters, is a mystery. It is a compound of vulgar depravity and unnatural horrors."

Emily Brontë's novel isn't the only now-canonical text to be roundly panned initially. "It repels the reader," wrote one journalist about *Moby-Dick* (1851), while another explained that "the idea of a connected and collected story has obviously visited and abandoned its writer again and again in the course of composition." *The Great Gatsby* (1925) was termed "absurd" and F. Scott Fitzgerald deserving of a "good shaking."

The *New York Times* reviewed *The Catcher in the Rye* not once but twice when it debuted in 1951. Entitled "Aw, the World's a Crumby Place," the first review consisted of an extremely awkward attempt to throw shade at the novel using the book's own distinctive style. The result points to the singular accomplishment of J. D. Salinger in creating such a unique voice in Holden Caulfield—using words like *crumby* and *phony* in a natural way is harder than it looks. The next day, the newspaper ran a second review, which praised the text in all its profanity and slanginess.

Writers may offer the harshest feedback of all. Take Mark Twain's evaluation of Jane Austen: "I often want to criticize Jane Austen, but her books madden me so that I can't conceal my frenzy from the reader; and therefore I have to stop every time I begin. Every time I read *Pride and Prejudice*, I want to dig her up and hit her over the skull with her own shin-bone." However, Twain got a comeuppance from William Faulkner, who called Twain a "hack."

Sometimes the sheer popularity of a book or a writer seems to increase criticism or derision. Scholar Harold Bloom hates the Harry Potter series, for example. A critical assessment of the Left Behind series (1995–2007) was titled "When Truth Gets Left Behind," while *The Shack* (2007), by William P. Young, was deemed "a load of crap." And occasionally even readers come in for a licking, as in this review of *The Da Vinci Code*: "Certainly, the novel's success can be attributed to those who read Nostradamus and believe that the smoke from the blazing twin towers formed the face of the devil or Osama bin Laden."

Salman Rushdie unabashedly expressed his scorn for *Fifty Shades of Grey* (2011): "I've never read anything so badly written that got published. It made *Twilight* look like *War and Peace*." Subpar prose or not, E. L. James is obviously onto something with her works of erotic fiction, some of the bestselling books in history. Indeed, haters might hate, loudly and passionately. But every book ever published was launched into the world in the hope that someone, somewhere, would love it enough to read it and, these days, maybe leave a nice comment.

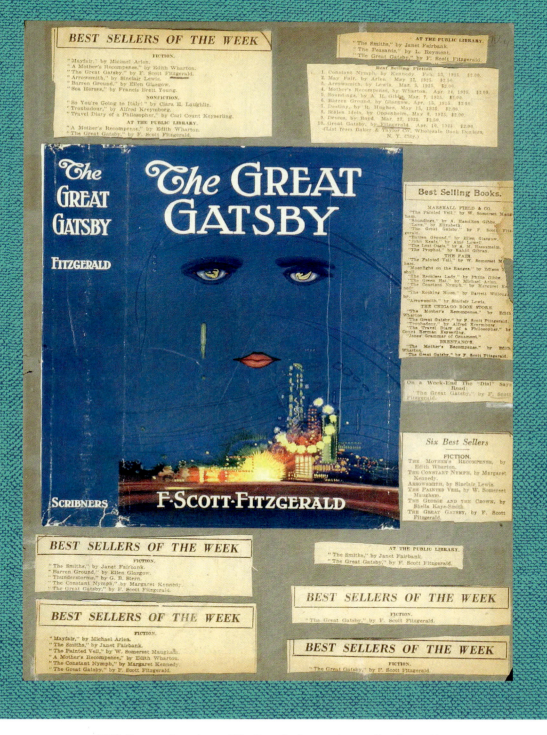

ABOVE: Some early reviews of *The Great Gatsby* weren't so stellar. One critic called it "absurd," and said its author needed a "good shaking."

CLOCKWISE FROM LEFT: The first US edition of *Moby-Dick*, published in 1851. | Author Herman Melville at about age 66. Melville left his rich, New York City upbringing and shipped out to sea at age 19. His adventures would provide inspiration for much of his writing. | Melville published *Moby-Dick* (also known as *The Whale*) with Harper and Brothers. This is their original publishing agreement.

67

MOBY-DICK

Herman Melville · 1851

"Call me Ishmael." Is there a more famous opening line in literature? This simple sentence begins a novel that's anything but. Although *Moby-Dick* (1851) is usually shelved in the literature section, the book transcends classification. It's simultaneously a psychological study, an exegesis of the Bible, a work of philosophy, an allegorical treatise, a cautionary tale about the dangers of revenge and ambition, an epic prose poem, and a textbook on 19th-century whaling.

Melancholic and misanthropic, Ishmael decides to give whaling a try. He meets the tattooed Queequeg, and together they sign on to the *Pequod.* Although they encounter other members of the crew, including the thoughtful, courageous Starbuck (yup, that's where the coffee behemoth got its name), they don't see or hear from the mysterious captain. When he finally appears, Ahab makes a riveting impression—stomping around on a fake leg made from the jaw of a sperm whale and swearing to find and kill Moby Dick, the huge white creature who maimed him.

The ship sails, lots of other whales are caught and butchered, and a cabin boy goes insane. Ahab hails every passing vessel for news of his mortal enemy. Terrible omens abound. After Queequeg gets sick, the ship's carpenter makes him a coffin, which becomes the boat's life preserver. Somewhere near the equator, about a year after leaving shore, Ahab espies Moby Dick, and a harrowing, days-long battle begins, dragging both man and beast down into the dark depths.

Herman Melville first shipped out to sea at age 19—a far cry from the opulent New York City life into which he was born in 1819. He was descended from what passed as American royalty at the time, with two Revolutionary War heroes on either side. After a brief return to land, at age 21 he joined a whaling voyage, traveling around South America and across the Pacific Ocean. He jumped ship in the South Seas and took up with a group of cannibals in the Marquesas Islands, an adventure that inspired his first book, *Typee: A Peep at Polynesian Life* (1846). This combination of novel and travelogue was by far his most popular work during his lifetime.

Moby-Dick, on the other hand, foundered. The novel received reviews ranging from the negative to the baffled, with critics attacking Ahab's long speeches, the mixture of genres, and the extremely complex themes and use of symbols. His publisher reissued Melville's books upon his death in 1891, leading to a popular and scholarly revival around the centennial of his birth. Nowadays, no one would argue about the book's centrality in the literary canon; as English novelist D. H. Lawrence said, *Moby-Dick* is "one of the strangest and most wonderful books in the world. . . . It moves awe in the soul."

An actual animal attack inspired the novel: in 1820, a sperm whale destroyed the whale ship *Essex.* (Nathan Philbrick wrote the history of the *Essex* in the National Book Award–winning *In the Heart of the Sea* [2000]; a decade later, he published a book of literary criticism/advocacy: *Why Read Moby-Dick?* [2011].) Melville's Ahab is a monomaniac who sees his cetacean nemesis as the embodiment of evil and is quite possibly the most single-minded lunatic ever described on paper. While it might be interesting to consider the book in light of contemporary environmentalism, the text isn't an anti-whaling screed by any account. By the time *Moby-Dick* was published, whaling was on the wane, a victim of its own success.

Melville continued writing after *Moby-Dick* but never again attained his earlier heights of fame. He embarked on an unsuccessful lecture tour, an attempt to earn some money for his growing family, and eventually took a job as a customs inspector in New York. He died in 1891.

In 2010, paleontologists discovered the fossil of a whale with teeth so ferocious, it probably hunted other whales; they named it *Leviathan melvillei.*

CLOCKWISE FROM LEFT: The Signet Classic edition of *Nineteen Eighty-Four*, from 1950. | Author George Orwell, the pen name of Eric Arthur Blair, was influenced by Jack London, his literary hero. | *Nineteen Eighty-Four* was adapted for the big screen. This poster is for a 1956 movie.

68

NINETEEN EIGHTY-FOUR

George Orwell · 1949

We may be decades past the date at which George Orwell published his book and predicted society's demise, yet we are no doubt living in a world he would recognize: one in which we are bombarded with slogans and truncated speech, surrounded by machines capable of recording our every move, plied with easy access to intoxicants and pornography. It's impossible to deny the eerie foresight of *Nineteen Eighty-Four* (1949).

Eric Arthur Blair was born in 1903 in India but moved to England with his mother and sisters a year later. Although he earned scholarships to excellent boarding schools, he never felt as if he fit in, and he abandoned the prospect of college to become a police officer in Burma. He never quite fit in there, either, as he detested being asked to enforce policies and politics he didn't believe in against a disadvantaged population. By 1927, beset by health problems that would continue to trouble him for the rest of his life, he set out in earnest to become a writer.

Influenced by his literary hero Jack London, Blair went undercover in the poorer parts of London and Paris. The pieces he wrote formed the core of *Down and Out in Paris and London* (1933), his first full-length published work. He also lived with coal miners and served in the Loyalist militia during the Spanish Civil War. These experiences gave Blair a lifelong hatred of totalitarianism and cemented his determination to wield his words in the service of his antifascist politics. Using the pen name George Orwell, he wrote essays, poems, literary criticism, memoirs, short stories, and novels, including the ever-popular allegory *Animal Farm* (1945). In *Nineteen Eighty-Four*, published a year before he died, Orwell managed to calibrate his key themes with developed characters

and a well-paced plot. Dystopian as it may be, the novel transcends its dire warnings and makes for a great read.

Winston Smith spends his days rewriting articles and altering photographs at the Ministry of Truth. Like everyone else in Airstrip One, formerly known as Great Britain, he is assaulted with propaganda—including reminders that "war is peace" and "ignorance is strength"—and he has ready access to distracting vices. Curious about the "true past," he finds an old blank diary in a junk store. Crammed into the one corner of his apartment that isn't viewable by the telescreen, through which the enigmatic Big Brother and his government monitor and send messages to its citizens, Winston begins to write. He describes his attraction to Julia, a member of the Junior Anti-Sex League whom he suspects is an informant for the ruling party.

Even as Winston undertakes his first subversive act of literary exploration, he predicts his end: the Thought Police will uncover his thoughtcrime, and he will be severely punished. Still, the feel of pen on paper, and the freedom to express what he thinks, compel him to continue. In a powerful scene, Winston wonders to what extent an authoritarian regime might manipulate facts. Could citizens be convinced that two plus two equals five?

Big Brother, *Thought Police*, *unperson*, *thoughtcrime*, *bellyfeel*, *Newspeak*, *doublethink*, equations that don't add up—the terms and themes in *Nineteen Eighty-Four* continue to offer us a meaningful way to discuss the rights and responsibilities of governments around the globe. When people talk about "outing lies" and "winning the war on truth," they're speaking a language and describing a political outlook Orwell would no doubt recognize.

69

THE NOTEBOOK

Nicholas Sparks · 1996

The Notebook (1996) is a romance novel with an especially romantic origin: twenty-eight-year-old Nicholas Sparks was inspired to write the novel after getting to know his wife's grandparents, who were married for more than sixty years. From there, the story becomes even more improbable: a literary agent pulled the manuscript out of the slush pile. Despite having been an agent for only about six months, and despite never having sold a novel, she negotiated a $1 million advance for the first-time author. The Notebook then spent months on the bestseller list, was made into a beloved movie, and launched the career of one of the most popular romance novelists working today. Talk about a fairy tale.

As the novel begins, an older man reads to an older woman suffering from Alzheimer's disease. He rustles the pages of a notebook and tells the story of a young man named Noah Calhoun, recently graduated from high school, as he falls in love with a young woman named Allison (Allie) Nelson, vacationing with her family in his tiny North Carolina town. At the end of the summer, she leaves New Bern to return to her life in the city, and her family forces her to break off the relationship. Noah writes her a letter a day for a year, none of which gets answered. Eventually he leaves to join the service. When World War II ends, he comes back to New Bern and makes over a farmhouse, modeled on Allie's dream house, and his renovation project generates some newspaper coverage. Fourteen years after they last spoke, Allie sees the article and returns to Noah for two glorious days—after which she must decide whether to stay or go back to her fiancé, Lon Hammond Jr.

Even as The Notebook details the love affair between Noah and Allie, it enthralls as a mystery. Readers start to see that the elderly woman is Allie but don't know whether the man reading to her is Noah or Lon. The elderly Allie can't remember which man her younger self selected: the poor, dreamy Noah, who works with his hands, or Lon, a lawyer with a bright future and stable bank account. But she adores the tale being told, and falls under its spell with every recounting. The man who reads to Allie clearly loves her, and thus Sparks adds another dimension to his romance by contrasting the intense, fiery passion of young love with the richer, deeper bond that forms after decades of marriage.

Ryan Gosling starred as Noah and Rachel McAdams as Allie in the 2004 film adaptation, which was well regarded. More than 10 movies have been made from Sparks's subsequent novels, collectively grossing close to $1 billion. Sparks wrote The Wedding (2003) as a kind of sequel to The Notebook, and he hasn't ruled out the possibility of revisiting the characters in another novel. The success of the book enabled Sparks to devote himself full-time to writing. He was born in 1965, in Omaha, Nebraska, and started writing fiction while an undergraduate at the University of Notre Dame. He wrote two other manuscripts before selling The Notebook, and has published almost a book a year since it came out.

Sparks attributes the long-lasting appeal of The Notebook to its simplicity and its wholesomeness. The language is direct and unvarnished, the love scenes sensual rather than graphic. As a romance novel, it offers readers both hope and wish fulfillment, but it also wants to encourage us to see true love everywhere. Behind every tender gesture—from teens embracing in a doorway to seniors holding one another as they walk along the sidewalk—lies a story worth hearing.

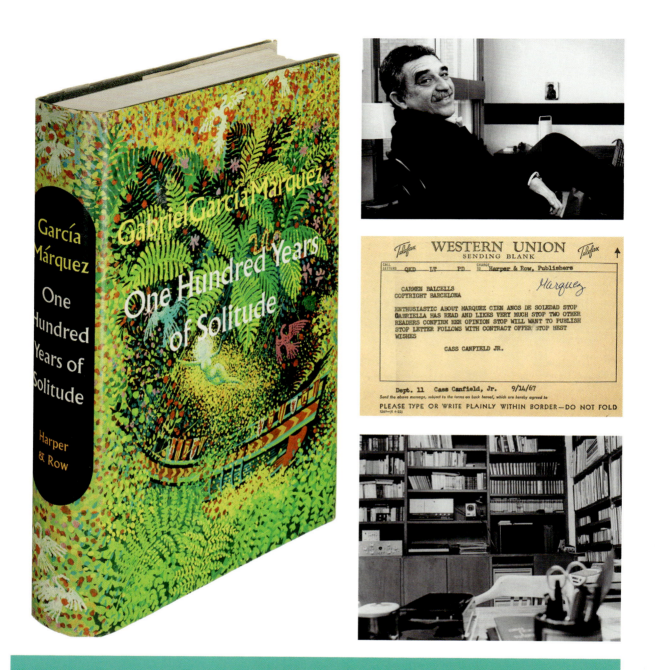

CLOCKWISE FROM LEFT: A 1970 first US edition printing of *One Hundred Years of Solitude*, which was originally published in 1967. | Author Gabriel García Márquez, known by friends and family as Gabo, says the idea for *One Hundred Years of Solitude* came to him fully formed, as he and his family set out on vacation. | A telegram from Harper editor Cass Canfield to Gabo's agent, Carmen Balcells, says emphatically that Harper wants to publish the first US translation of the novel. | Gabo's office in his home in Mexico City.

70

ONE HUNDRED YEARS OF SOLITUDE

Gabriel García Márquez · 1967

A man stands before a firing squad. In the last seconds of his life, his mind flashes to the moment he first saw ice.

The very best novels always give readers clues about how they should be read, but perhaps none so clearly telegraphs its desire to capture the subjective experience of time as *One Hundred Years of Solitude* (1967). From the opening pages of this sprawling epic, in which Colonel Aureliano Buendía returns to a childhood afternoon as he prepares to die, readers can recognize that they too will move back, forth, and sideways through the long story of a big family in a tiny Latin American village.

José Arcadio Buendía and his wife, Úrsula Iguarán, settle near a river, after José dreams of founding a city made of mirrors. The novel proceeds to portray subsequent generations of their descendants, as they fall in love (sometimes with one another), make terrible mistakes, go mad, wrestle with what it means to be alone, but also learn to dance, feel joy, and delight in sensual pleasures. As if to further emphasize the inescapability of the past, characters often share first names. The storytelling intentionally echoes the Bible in scope, style, and thematic richness.

Intertwined with the fate of the Buendías is that of the fictional city Macondo. It grows from an isolated, somewhat Edenic settlement to a thriving city to the would-be capital of a "banana republic." However, much as the family cannot avoid the repetitions of history, Macondo can't escape the very real fate that befell much of Latin America as indigenous populations were wiped out or enslaved, as foreign imperialists arrived, and as civil war ensued.

Gabriel García Márquez is an exemplar of magical realism, which treats fanciful situations as if they were true. Examples of this literary style abound in *One Hundred Years*

of Solitude: a girl grows so beautiful and stays so innocent that she ascends into heaven, along with some bedsheets she happened to be folding. At another point in the novel, it rains "for four years, eleven months, and two days." And, at the very end, as the last Buendía dies, the area itself is decimated by a hurricane, and nothing remains.

One of 16 children, Gabriel García Márquez was born in Aracataca, a small town in Colombia, in 1927. He was raised mostly by his maternal grandparents. In later years, he would claim that hardly a day passed when he didn't wake up having dreamed of being back in their big house, and for some two decades he envisioned writing a novel that would honor his family's tales.

Affectionately known as Gabo, he'd published a few novels and worked as a reporter for many years before *One Hundred Years of Solitude* arrived, fully formed, in his imagination. García Márquez would later tell interviewers he was driving with his family to go on vacation when he felt compelled to turn the car around and return to his study to start writing. Eighteen months and 30,000 cigarettes later, the novel was finished.

Alas, Gabo and his wife were so poor by then that they could only afford to send half the manuscript to the publisher. The scrimping wouldn't last for long. Upon the novel's publication in English, the *New York Times Book Review* noted that the novel "should be required reading for the entire human race." It proved so popular that García Márquez moved his family to Spain for a while to escape his fame. He received the Nobel Prize in Literature in 1982 and left behind a significant body of work in multiple genres when he died in 2014. In a career of extraordinary depth and range, *One Hundred Years of Solitude* stands out for its inventiveness and richness.

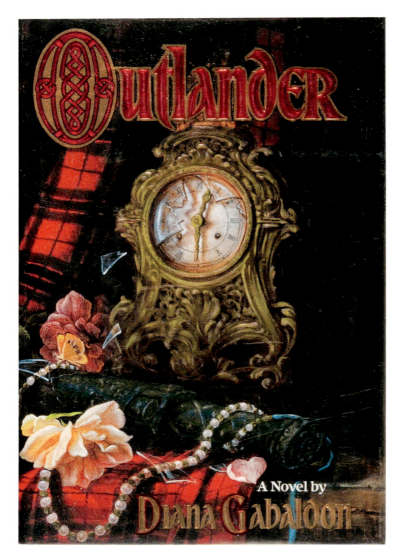

71

OUTLANDER SERIES

Diana Gabaldon · 1991–present

One way to sum up the inventive, genre-bending Outlander series would be as follows: the course of true love never does run smooth, especially when time travel is involved. But the novels go far beyond romance, incorporating historical fact, science fiction, and epic family drama.

In *Outlander* (1991), the first of eight books, independent, practical Claire Randall takes a second honeymoon to Scotland in 1946 with her husband, Frank Randall, a history professor. She faints while picking flowers and wakes up some 200 years in the past, where she encounters Frank's ancestors as well as Jamie Fraser, a handsome, educated landowner. Trained as a nurse, Claire raises deep suspicion among 18th-century Scots, some of whom see her as a witch because of her medical knowledge. She must also navigate different perceptions of femininity within the two eras she straddles, as well as her love for Frank in the 1940s and her love for Jamie in the 1740s.

The novels and several linked novellas integrate true historic events, and Claire, of course, is cursed with often knowing how things turn out. The settings range from England to the American colonies to the Scottish Highlands to Jamaica, in time periods from the 1940s to the 1960s to the 1750s and 1760s. Through Claire's eyes, the past's familiar tales of violence, bloodshed, and power dynamics take on a new sheen.

Born in Arizona in 1952, Diana Gabaldon wrote a lot academically, as a student—she earned a PhD in behavioral ecology—and during her lengthy career as a science professor at Arizona State University. In 1988 she set out to write a novel, fulfilling a lifelong dream. She grew frustrated when her main character kept making sarcastic remarks wholly out of keeping with the historical setting Gabaldon was describing. When she saw an episode of *Doctor Who* that featured time travel, she realized how she could marry setting, character, and plot.

Gabaldon plans to end the Outlander series with book 10. Like her friend George R. R. Martin, she must contend with furthering her imaginative world even as her characters take on new life in another medium. Parts of the series have been transformed into a graphic novel and a musical, but the sexy, popular television series, which premiered on Starz in 2014, introduced the books to legions of new fans. (In fact, *Outlander* the book zoomed to the top of the *New York Times* bestseller list again after the series premiere, 23 years after it was published.) Viewers and critics revel in the series' steadfast refusal to sit squarely in any one genre; instead, like the books on which it's based, it encompasses wartime drama, time travel, fantasy, historical drama, and romance.

Gabaldon divides her characters into three types: "mushrooms," who seem to come out of nowhere and take over the scene; "onions," who develop layers and complexities as Gabaldon writes about them; and "hard nuts," who appear as a result of a plot device, and whom she must work to crack open. At the core of the books are Claire and Jamie, who must overcome an unusual amount of hurdles in order to continue their romance, including Jamie's rape at the hands of the evil Jonathan "Black Jack" Randall, and Claire's need to ensure that Frank's ancestors live on, thereby guaranteeing that Frank himself will be born. Through Frank, Gabaldon can explore eternal concerns about marriage and long-term relationships. Everyone changes, of course, even if one doesn't get to travel through time. The challenge lies in changing in such a way that you stay true to yourself and to those you love.

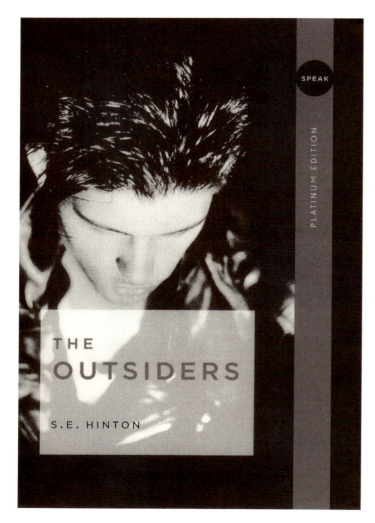

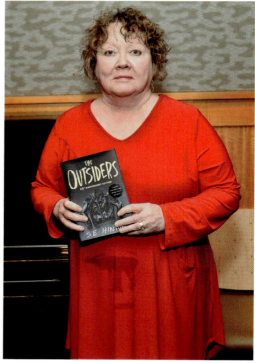

72

THE OUTSIDERS

S. E. Hinton · 1967

S. E. Hinton began writing *The Outsiders* (1967) at age 15, while still in high school. In fact, she flunked creative writing that year. She was 17 and a freshman at the University of Tulsa when the book was published. Very few authors can lay claim to helping invent a literary genre, let alone doing so before voting age.

Before Hinton's book about bad boys in Oklahoma, there were books for adults and there were books for children. Dissatisfied with the portrayal of teenagers in literature, Hinton began writing a story loosely based on rival gangs at her high school. They drink, smoke, fight, and die, largely in a world without adult supervision—a stark contrast to the typical books of the time, in which, as Hinton has noted, "Mary Jane Goes to the Prom and Tommy Hits a Home Run." That Hinton's debut deals directly with complicated themes and issues helps explain its lasting popularity. *The Outsiders* portrays alienation, aimlessness, poverty, and violence. Today's YA books, with their fearless confrontation of such subjects as racism, homophobia, and suicide, owe a deep debt to *The Outsiders*.

Susie Hinton, as she is known, still lives in Tulsa, Oklahoma, where she was born in 1948. Her publisher suggested she abbreviate her given name, Susan Eloise, which wouldn't be the last time a new author felt that masculinizing her name and using initials would welcome more readers. She signed the contract for *The Outsiders* on the day she graduated high school, and the contract for her next novel, *That Was Then, This Is Now* (1971), on the day she married her high-school sweetheart, four years later. Since then, she has written other novels for young adults, as well as books for children and adults, but she largely remains out of the public eye. She did, however, go on a book tour in honor of the 50th anniversary of *The Outsiders* in 2017.

The Outsiders takes place in 1965, over two weeks in the life of 14-year-old Ponyboy Curtis. Ponyboy belongs to the Greasers, along with many other teens from the proverbial wrong side of the tracks in Tulsa. They battle with a bunch of rich kids called the Socs (short for "Socials"). When a Soc dies during a fight, the Greasers disappear into hiding. Ponyboy and his best friend, Johnny, hole up in an abandoned church, where Pony reads *Gone with the Wind* and recites "Nothing Gold Can Stay," by Robert Frost. With tensions escalating between the gangs, Johnny decides to turn himself in to the police; as they leave, the church catches on fire, trapping several children who have wandered inside. Although they are declared heroes for saving the kids, Ponyboy and Johnny still have to face the consequences of the Soc's death—and meet the Socs in a final showdown.

Ponyboy serves as the book's introspective narrator. Like the other Greasers, Ponyboy is an outsider, and bitterly feels the economic gulf that separates the poor kids from the rich ones. The loyalty between members helps them form a close-knit family. As he discovers through both his love of literature and his friendship with Cherry Valance, a Soc girl, people can transcend their backgrounds. In fact, identities can be superficial—an individual will always prove more complex than his or her group.

The 1983 movie based on Hinton's book furthered the careers of several actors, among them Rob Lowe, Matt Dillon, Diane Lane, and Tom Cruise. Director Frances Ford Coppola found Hinton's fictional world so captivating that he filmed Hinton's sequel at the same time, writing the screenplay for the latter with Hinton while working on the former; *Rumble Fish* was released in 1983. *The Outsiders'* most famous line—"Stay gold, Ponyboy"—has taken on a life of its own: half a century after the novel's publication, "Stay gold" can be spotted on sweaters, pillows, and even bodies in the form of tattoos, a sign of the lasting resonance of this plaintive, futile plea for the fleeting innocence of youth.

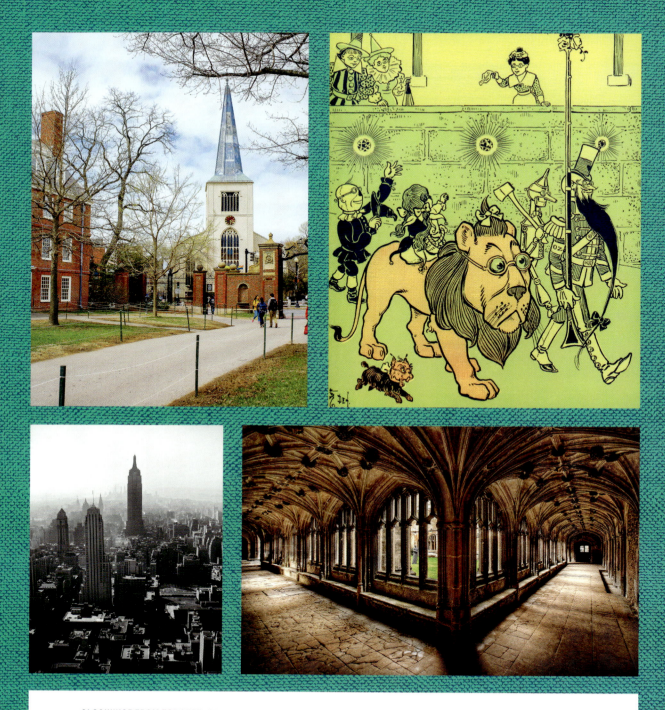

CLOCKWISE FROM TOP LEFT: Harvard Square in Boston, which became part of the Republic of Gilead in *The Handmaid's Tale*. | Art by W. W. Denslow showing *The Wonderful Wizard of Oz*, created by L. Frank Baum. | The cloisters at Lacock Abbey gave a real-life setting for the film location for Hogwarts in the movie *Harry Potter and the Chamber of Secrets*. | An aerial view of 1940s New York City, the setting for any number of literary tales.

A Sense of Place

SENSATIONAL SETTINGS

NO DOUBT fiction takes you places. Some novels are set in real cities, which means you may be able to walk the same streets beloved characters walked, eat in the same places, or see the same sights. Other novels, however, describe cities and countries that exist solely in the writer's imagination—only to then enter ours.

ARRAKIS: What seems like a desiccated wasteland actually holds a tremendous amount of treasure. Arrakis is a desert planet, but it is here that the incredibly valuable "melange" is found, in Frank Herbert's 1965 sci-fi classic *Dune* (the novel takes its title from another name for Arrakis). Melange heightens people's perceptions, enabling some to see the future, and helps those who consume it to live better and longer. No wonder everyone wants it.

CELESTIAL CITY: After making their way through such places as Difficulty Hill, the Valley of Humiliation, and the Village of Morality, the main characters in *The Pilgrim's Progress* (1678) at last reach the magnificent Celestial City. As befits a Christian allegory such as this one by John Bunyan, the Celestial City stands in for heaven, where the streets are paved with gold and the king— also known as God—lives. It's a magical, glorious place.

EMERALD CITY: To get to the Emerald City, you need to follow road of yellow brick, which begins in the land of the Munchkins, according to *The Wonderful Wizard of Oz* (1900). You may or may not choose to sing "We're off to see the wizard, the wonderful wizard of Oz," just like Judy Garland in the 1939 movie. L. Frank Baum likely based his fictional city on the structures and street lamps he saw at the 1893 World's Fair, which he visited while living in Chicago.

GOTHAM CITY: Legend has it that Washington Irving gave New York City the nickname "Gotham" in the early 19th century. At any rate, the safe, clean New York of the 21st century bears little resemblance to the dark, dirty town portrayed by DC Comics, where criminals run rampant and only a superhero or two can save the day. Gotham is within driving distance of Metropolis, enabling Batman and Superman to team up as an unstoppable duo.

HOGWARTS SCHOOL OF WITCHCRAFT AND WIZARDRY: Located somewhere in Scotland, the Hogwarts School of Witchcraft and Wizardry teaches magic to qualified students between the ages of 11 and 18, according to J. K. Rowling's Harry Potter series (1997–2007). If you go, take the train at Platform 9¾ from King's Cross in London, then prepare to contend with all kinds of supernatural creatures, learn the rules of Quidditch, and attend classes like Potions and Defense Against the Dark Arts.

LILLIPUT: A little fed up with regular life, Lemuel Gulliver sets off to have some adventures, landing first in Lilliput, ruled by a race of people just six inches tall. The Lilliputians are in a fight with the inhabitants of Blefuscu over the right way to break an egg. Jonathan Swift's satirical *Gulliver's Travels* (1726) gave us several memorable imaginary places, including Brobding-nag, where everything is huge, and the Land of the Houyhnhnms, home to a race of reason-loving horses.

MACONDO: So closely aligned are the fates of the Buendía family and the city of Macondo that an apocalyptic storm destroys both at the end of *One Hundred Years of Solitude* (1967). Family patriarch José Arcadio Buendía founds the Latin American city, which grows and prospers only to fall prey to colonialism and imperialism. Gabriel García Márquez may have had his own birthplace of Aracataca, Colombia, in mind as he wrote.

MIDDLE-EARTH: Among the creatures who inhabit Middle-earth are elves, orcs, dragons, wizards, trolls, eagles, Valar (angelic beings), hobbits, and humans, living in areas like the terrible Mordor and the quaint, quiet Shire. J. R. R. Tolkien created multiple maps of this universe—as well as attendant languages and histories—to show how his characters complete the quests so aptly described in *The Hobbit* (1937) and The Lord of the Rings (1954–1955).

MIDDLEMARCH: With *Middlemarch: A Study of Provincial Life* (1871–1872), George Eliot sought to write a novel that would help its readers be better people—as lofty a goal as an author may aspire to. Through her careful depic-tions of the interior lives of characters who inhabit this English town circa 1830, itself as painstakingly described as any person in the book, Eliot wishes to instill compassion and cultivate empathy in all who decide to visit.

NARNIA: Over the course of seven fantasy novels collectively called The Chronicles of Narnia (1950–1956), C. S. Lewis developed a detailed imaginative world full of talking beasts and horrid witches, heroic beings and curious children. He later claimed that the genesis of these works and Narnia stemmed, at least in part, from a picture he saw at age 16 of a faun carrying parcels and an umbrella through a snow-covered forest. The human children get there by entering a wardrobe.

REPUBLIC OF GILEAD: Careful readers of *The Handmaid's Tale* (1985) may notice remarkable resemblances between the Republic of Gilead and Cambridge, Massachusetts, such as descriptions of Harvard University and the city's stately brick manses. Of course, the republic of the dystopian novel is a theocratic military dictatorship run by Christian

ABOVE, FROM LEFT TO RIGHT: A building in the Colombian village of Aracataca, hometown of Gabriel García Márquez. | Bilbo Baggins's Hobbiton home, brought to life on the film set for *Lord of the Rings* in Matamata, New Zealand.

fundamentalists who control every aspect of women's lives, so the similarities may be only on the surface.

TARA: Scarlett O'Hara will seemingly do anything to protect Tara, her childhood home. Margaret Mitchell based the house and its extensive grounds, represented so memorably in *Gone with the Wind* (1936), on antebellum plantations she would explore while growing up in rural Georgia. Some readers see Tara as an embodiment of Scarlett's spirit—battered but never broken, shattered but never stamped out, wrecked but resilient.

WESTEROS: We have HBO to thank for gorgeous renderings of Westeros, home to the Seven Kingdoms, whose throne is at stake throughout the epic series. Its lands include the icy, snowy North; the huge, magical Wall; and the tropical, fertile South. For even more descriptions, we can turn to the ongoing fantasy series by George R. R. Martin, *A Song of Ice and Fire* (1996–present). Not since Middle-earth have we been treated to a universe so abundantly detailed.

WONDERLAND: When Alice follows the white rabbit, she arrives in a world where a drink makes her shrink, a cake makes her grow, and a queen wants to cut off her head. Her sense of logic no longer applies, and her attempts to impose order are met with mockery and derision. Lewis Carroll's book, *Alice's Adventures in Wonderland* (1865), demonstrates what it feels like to be young, when entering adulthood appears to require passage into a new land.

YOKNAPATAWPHA COUNTY: Inspired by actual places in Mississippi, Yoknapatawpha County served as the basis for several novels by William Faulkner, each of which probed the damaged psyches of Southern families, ravaged by poverty, alcoholism, incest, slavery, and the Civil War. With *Absalom, Absalom!* (1936), Faulkner included a hand-drawn map of the county, enabling readers to envision the area as he did and showing how the places, and their related pain, intersect and overlap.

ABOVE, FROM LEFT TO RIGHT: The caterpillar gives Alice advice in *Alice's Adventures in Wonderland*, printed in a 1891 lithograph. | *Middlemarch*, illustrated by Patty Townsend, Lilian Russell, and G. G. Kilburne for George Eliot.

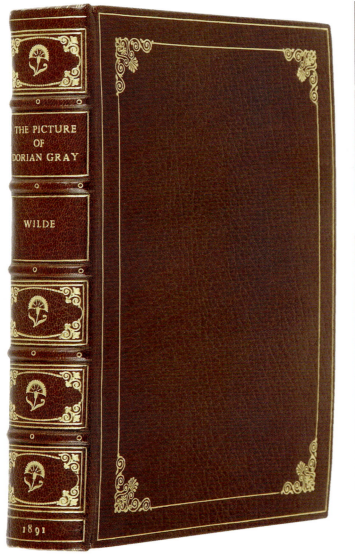

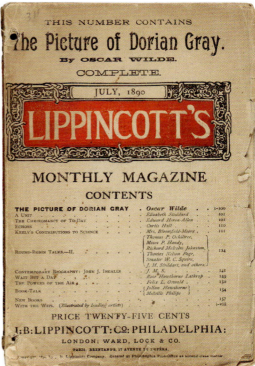

CLOCKWISE FROM LEFT: A first book edition of *The Picture of Dorian Gray*, printed in 1891. | Oscar Wilde, photographed by Napoleon Sarony circa 1882. Wilde was famous for his plays, such as *A Woman of No Importance* (1893) and *The Importance of Being Earnest*, but *The Picture of Dorian Gray* has entered the literary canon. | The novel was published in *Lippincott's Monthly Magazine* in 1890. It was the first printing of the complete novel.

73

THE PICTURE OF DORIAN GRAY

Oscar Wilde · 1890

Oscar Wilde would have been the toast of Twitter. Throughout his life, he produced a seemingly unending supply of one-liners and aphorisms on nearly every subject: "True friends stab you in the front." "Anyone who lives within their means suffers from a lack of imagination." "In this world there are only two tragedies in life. One is not getting what one wants, and the other is getting it." Funny even as he lay dying, friendless and penniless, in 1900, he reportedly exclaimed on his deathbed, "This wallpaper and I are fighting a duel to the death. Either it goes or I do." But his one and only novel, *The Picture of Dorian Gray* (1890), is a deadly serious treatment of virtue, sin, and the contrast between one's outer appearance and inner desires.

As the short book begins, artist Basil Hallward confides in his friend Lord Henry Wotton. Basil worries that his recent painting of the gorgeous Dorian Gray perhaps reveals too much about his feelings toward the subject. Lord Henry meets Dorian, affecting him with a speech about the emphasis society places on shallow characteristics like youth and attractiveness, which fade. This criticism cuts Dorian, and he begins to detest his portrait, knowing that it will stay lovely as he grows old and ugly. He wishes, more than anything, to remain young and handsome so that he may continue to indulge his vices. The portrait begins to reflect Dorian's increasingly horrible behavior—his likeness sometimes grimaces, it starts to decay and become grotesque, and it ultimately reflects the hate Dorian holds in his soul.

When *The Picture of Dorian Gray* appeared, the British press wasn't shy in its criticism. The novel was deemed "vulgar" and "unclean." Wilde's editor reacted by removing passages that too strongly implied homosexual feelings; in effect, the novel went from rated R to rated PG-13. In 2011, Harvard University Press released a definitive edition of the novel, restoring its cut pages and allowing contemporary readers to experience the work as Wilde envisioned it. The book is now considered part of the literary canon because of its scintillating prose, examination of moral dilemmas in art and philosophy, and riveting take on a Faustian bargain.

The son of a successful doctor and his Irish nationalist–poet wife, Oscar Fingal O'Flahertie Wills Wilde was born in Dublin in 1854. Educated at Trinity College and Oxford, he married in 1884, had two sons almost immediately, and socialized with a literary crowd in London, including W. B. Yeats. He gained fame through his clever, comedic plays, including *A Woman of No Importance* (1893), *An Ideal Husband* (1895), and *The Importance of Being Earnest* (1895), but he also published poetry, journalism, short stories, and essays. In addition, he was, by all accounts, a lot of fun to be around, as witty in person as on the page.

During the writing of *The Picture of Dorian Gray*, Wilde began a romantic relationship with Lord Alfred Douglas, the nature of which Douglas's father publicly denounced. Wilde sued for libel, and not only lost but was himself charged with sodomy and other indecent acts in 1895. He served two years of hard labor—the maximum sentence—falling into poverty and despair upon his release. Wilde died a few years later, abandoned, in exile, and alone. In 2017, when the United Kingdom decriminalized homosexuality, Wilde received an official pardon.

Wherever we live, whomever we are, we are bombarded with stunning images, often encouraging us to pursue pleasure at all costs. Even though we know on some level that every ad gets manipulated with Photoshop, or that people take thousands of photos to get that one perfect shot for Instagram, we long to be like what we see and to possess whatever it is we want. Yet when that longing starts to become overwhelming, we need only open *The Picture of Dorian Gray* to be reminded of the dangers of narcissism and hedonism.

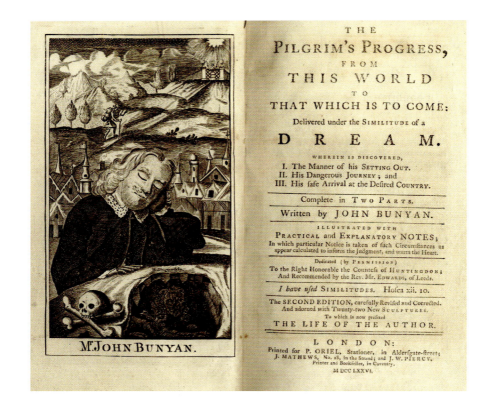

Imaged by Heritage Auctions, HA.com

CLOCKWISE FROM TOP: The title page of the 1776 edition of *The Pilgrim's Progress*, printed in London. | An engraving of John Bunyan, printed in the 19th century. Buyan was known as "Bishop Bunyan," and was a powerful Puritan preacher. | A commemorative illustrated edition of *The Pilgrim's Progress* was printed in 1877. | Bunyan is buried in Bunhill Fields cemetery, in Islington, London. A sculpture of a pilgrim is detailed on his memorial.

74

THE PILGRIM'S PROGRESS

John Bunyan · 1678

The Pilgrim's Progress (1678) is a clear-cut allegory about Christianity, meant to help weary souls find the strength to soldier on and stay the course to deliverance. For centuries, readers have turned to the text for inspiration and solace.

Born in England in 1628, John Bunyan was expected to follow his father into the tinker trade but joined the English Civil War instead, fighting in the Parliamentary army for three years. After his marriage in the late 1640s, his wife encouraged him to read the Bible and go to church. Eventually he became a powerful Puritan preacher, nicknamed "Bishop Bunyan," as a result of the crowds who would come to hear him. The restoration of the monarchy in 1660 curtailed deviations from the doctrine and practices of the Church of England, and Bunyan was imprisoned, along with like-minded individuals with whom he debated and discussed his ideas. He started The Pilgrim's Progress during his 12 years in jail, and after his release he continued writing that work and many others before his death in 1688.

From its very first lines, The Pilgrim's Progress reveals its intent to instruct. The text opens with "The Author's Apology for His Book," a poem in rhyme about the book's origin and goals. As Bunyan explains, his "Scribble" came quickly, so much did he have to say about individuals on their "way to Glory." The rest of the novel, told in prose, concerns a dream the narrator had about a man named Christian. Evangelist, a spiritual guide, tells Christian to leave the City of Destruction and seek salvation in the Celestial City. Christian tries to convince his family to come too, but they initially refuse.

Part I tracks Christian's adventures, while Part II focuses on the journey his wife and four sons take to find their husband and father in the Celestial City. The pilgrims stop at places like the Slough of Despond, the Doubting Castle, and the town of Vanity, where they meet people named Hopeful, Old Honest, and Great-heart. The book shouts, rather than whispers, its message: life is full of trials and tribulations, but adhering to the tenets of Christianity offers a guarantee about what's to come.

Readers not only heard Bunyan's call but heeded it. During the 17th and 18th centuries the novel was extremely popular and influential. People admired its frank style, as well as its rejection of the idea of an intermediary between a believer and the divine. The novel also criticizes the stratified system of economics in which the rich get richer and the poor get nothing. Whereas material wealth rises and falls, spiritual wealth remains steadfast within those blessed enough to possess it, and, The Pilgrim's Progress tells us, spiritual wealth can be acquired by anyone.

Outlining a strict moral code, Bunyan's novel helped shape Christian teachings and interpretations in the years to come. The character of Christian suffers throughout his journey, but the suffering has a purpose, and he receives the reward he seeks at the novel's end. Suffering begets progress. Indeed, the March sisters use the book as a self-help guide to life in Little Women (1868–1869), and an epigraph from Bunyan's novel kicks off Louisa May Alcott's. Today the book is widely used by missionaries because of its imaginative dramatization of the Bible's edicts concerning faith and redemption. But America was, to some extent, founded and shaped by Puritans—and The Pilgrim's Progress offers an excellent window into their worldview.

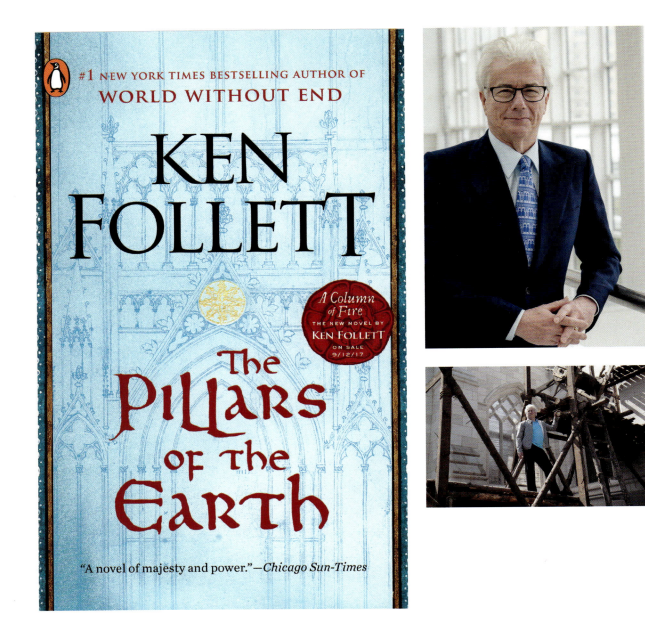

75

THE PILLARS OF THE EARTH

Ken Follett · 1989

Everywhere you go in Europe, you're bound to bump into a cathedral. Most people, as Ken Follett likes to point out, spend just an hour or two roaming around these religious edifices, checking out the nave and the altar, considering how flying buttresses work, maybe watching the light come in through the stained glass. Follett, in contrast, likes to spend several days engrossing himself in a cathedral's architecture and absorbing its atmosphere. With *The Pillars of the Earth* (1989), he sought to offer readers the same immersive effect.

Fans of Follett were a little stunned when he turned from spy thrillers to historical fiction. "I was known as a thriller writer," Follett said later. "Clowns should not try to play Hamlet; pop stars should not write symphonies." But *The Pillars of the Earth* wound up jump-starting a new series for the popular author, and readers now gobble up his writing on medieval architecture and society as much as on counterintelligence and international espionage, subjects of two of his previous bestsellers. Follett himself was excited to transform his lifelong interest in cathedrals into an epic tale of adventure, war, romance, religion, and politics.

The Pillars of the Earth takes place during the Anarchy, as clergy and nobles vie for the throne left empty after King Henry I's death in 12th-century England. Distraught after the loss of his wife, Tom Builder abandons his infant son and meets up with an outlaw named Ellen and her son, Jack. Eventually a prior named Philip hires Tom to construct a new cathedral in Kingsbridge. Getting the structure built will require the cooperation of local landowning families, including the spirited, determined Lady Aliena, the clergy, and the monarchy, with conflicting motivations and equally intense aspirations.

Since a cathedral typically took generations to go from conception to execution, Follett dives deep into the lives of his characters, showing how every aspect of the building affected their village, their fortunes, and their fates. He demonstrates the tremendous number of decisions that went into the design and construction, and shows how seemingly little labors served to make the building rise to prominence. When Oprah Winfrey picked *The Pillars of the Earth* for her book club in 2007, she provided a six-part reading guide, so detailed is the novel's plot. Follett kept everything and everyone straight with a thorough outline.

Ken Follett was born in 1949 in Cardiff, Wales. He had his first big hit with *Eye of the Needle* (1978), followed by several more. A decade later, he broadened his writing style with *The Pillars of the Earth*, and these days he continues to navigate multiple genres, having published *World Without End* (2008) and *A Column of Fire* (2017), sequels to *The Pillars of the Earth*, as well as stand-alone thrillers. Currently he's working on a series of novels that will use the fates of five interconnected families to explore 20th-century history.

The Pillars of the Earth was turned into an eight-hour miniseries, starring Donald Sutherland and Eddie Redmayne, in 2011. Follett also worked with artist Petra Röhr-Rouendaal to produce images of the cathedral at Kingsbridge in various stages of completion. The result is glorious.

"Nobody who reads it ever looks at a church or a cathedral the same," said Oprah. While Kingsbridge and its cathedral are imaginary, Follett did base the latter in part on actual edifices in England. As a work of historical fiction, *The Pillars of the Earth* strives to show how individuals were affected by significant events and, in some cases, even set them into motion. Kingsbridge's rise in prosperity echoes similar trajectories of cities during the Middle Ages, as do the tussles within and between the Church and the Crown. But the novel isn't a dry series of facts wrapped around a bunch of characters—instead, it's a compulsively readable saga about fascinating people undertaking a fascinating project.

CLOCKWISE FROM LEFT: First trade edition printing of *A Prayer for Owen Meany*, published in 1989. | Author John Irving published his first novel at age 26, and has since published 14 other novels. | A bookplate signed by the author accompanied a first edition.

76

A PRAYER FOR OWEN MEANY

John Irving · 1989

While not a religious man, John Irving is an imaginative one, so he set about pondering what, if anything, might transform him into a person of faith. He wrote an answer of sorts in the form of a novel, his seventh: *A Prayer for Owen Meany* (1989).

The book explores doubt, religious belief, fate, late 20th-century American history, social justice, and friendship. As an adult, narrator John Wheelwright looks back on his life, reflecting on the events of his childhood, his friendship with Owen Meany in a small New Hampshire town during the 1950s and 1960s, and the awakening of his faith. After Owen accidentally kills John's mother with a foul ball during a Little League game, Owen becomes convinced that he is an instrument of God.

Unusually small, with a bizarre voice denoted by all capitals in the text, Owen thinks he can change the world. In some ways, of course, he does: he cuts off John's trigger finger with a diamond saw, for example, when John asks for help avoiding the Vietnam War. He swears that divine intervention will assist John in discovering the identity of his biological father—and it does, sort of. In exchange for Owen helping the dyslexic John with schoolwork, John helps Owen dunk a basketball by lifting him over his head, a move they call "The Shot"; this maneuver saves the lives of a group of Vietnamese children many years later.

Owen grew up in a quarry, and exposure to its dust from an early age offers a rational explanation for his delusions. Nevertheless, his father tells John that Owen's was a virgin birth, just like Jesus's. Mr. Meany also shows John a gravestone Owen made when he was 11, on which is inscribed the correct date of his death. The novel's critiques of organized religion put Owen's spirituality into high relief, as Irving shows readers how people find their own paths to the divine.

Irving's extensive cast of characters and comedic sensibility earn him comparisons to Charles Dickens; both novelists write big—and bighearted—books that often explore people on the outskirts of mainstream society. Their novels demonstrate care and concern for the marginalized without crossing over into sentimentality. He published his first novel, *Setting Free the Bears* (1968), at age 26, and won the National Book Award for *The World According to Garp* (1978). To date, he has published 15 novels, along with nonfiction, essays, and screenplays.

Born John Wallace Blunt Jr. in 1942 in New Hampshire, Irving never knew his biological father, who died in a heroic mission during World War II. He adopted the surname of his stepfather, who taught at Phillips Exeter Academy. As an Exeter student, Irving suffered from dyslexia, an untreated condition that didn't dampen his love of reading. He competed as a wrestler for 20 years and coached the sport into his 40s. *Owen Meany* makes many references to the American obsession with sports, and Irving seeks to explore the ways in which our focus on seemingly unimportant events like football games may detract from our focus on important events like the Iran-Contra affair.

Rumors swirled upon the 1998 release of the movie *Simon Birch*, loosely based on *A Prayer for Owen Meany*, that Irving demanded his name be removed from the film. The truth, however, is that Irving didn't want the book's fans to be disappointed by differences between the two works. The movie borrows the book's beginning and key relationships but then moves into an equally compelling story about two outcasts who find comfort and companionship in one another.

A Prayer for Owen Meany earned readers' love because it blends Irving's trademark quirkiness with pointed philosophical queries. Its supernatural elements feel relevant to the story, rather than contrived, and the plot neatly folds in on itself. Regardless of whether we know an oddball like Owen, each of us has wondered to what extent fate touches our lives.

CLOCKWISE FROM TOP: A first edition printing of *Pride and Prejudice*, published in 1813. | An illustration by Hugh Thomson, entitled "The entreaties of several," accompanied the "Peacock" edition of the book—a cover decorated with prideful peacocks—published by George Allen in 1894. | A portrait of Jane Austen, circa 1790. Only her immediate family knew that Austen wrote her novels; she published anonymously because of her role as an upper-class woman.

77

PRIDE AND PREJUDICE

Jane Austen · 1813

That Jane Austen's *Pride and Prejudice* (1813) has endured over the past 200 years is something of an understatement. T-shirts that proclaim "Team Darcy." A 12-foot fiberglass statue of Colin Firth, depicting the scene from the 1995 BBC miniseries in which he emerges as Darcy, soaking wet and very buff, to the surprise of Jennifer Ehle's Elizabeth. Packaged pilgrimages to Bath, complete with visits to key homes and churches. *Bride and Prejudice* (2004), a Bollywood version. The novels *Bridget Jones's Diary* (1996), which turns Elizabeth Bennet into a bumbling yet lovable single gal in London, and *Eligible* (2016), which moves the plot into 21st-century Cincinnati and drops a reality show into the mix. *Pride and Prejudice and Zombies* (2009), an elaborate parody featuring the undead, which was later made into a movie.

Born in 1775 near the southern coast of England, Austen grew up in a literary family, the daughter of a minister. At age 20, she fell in love with a young man whose family rejected the match on account of her low income; around this time she also began writing novels, including one called *First Impressions*. When it failed to find a publisher, she focused on *Sense and Sensibility*, which came out to much fanfare in 1811. This success gave her the confidence to return to her earlier efforts, and the novel we now know as *Pride and Prejudice* was published two years later. Of her six novels, *Pride and Prejudice* inspires the most fervent adoration.

No one except her immediate family knew Austen had authored the novels. Mindful of her role as an upper-class woman in the late 1700s and early 1800s, she published her work anonymously. After her death in 1817 at age 41, her brother revealed her identity. But what really seemed to drive Austen's popularity was bibliotherapy, or the practice of reading certain texts for their healing benefits. Soldiers carried Austen into the trenches of World War I, and her work was prescribed as an antidote to the horrors of World War II as well. At the time of its publication, the novel gave an entertaining peek into parlors, serving as a mirror for the pleasures and pressures of Regency society. The details of dresses, dinners, and dances provide a window into life for a certain class during that specific era. Readers continue to return to the beloved characters and their domestic dramas for reassurance and diversion, swept up in Austen's prose.

With five unmarried daughters, the Bennet family greets the arrival of an eligible bachelor to the neighborhood with great delight. Charles Bingley falls hard for Jane Bennet, but his friend Fitzwilliam Darcy feels less keen toward Jane's sister Elizabeth. As Jane and Mr. Bingley court, Elizabeth and Darcy both come together and clash. Meanwhile, the insufferable Mr. Collins proposes to Elizabeth—a match she rejects, even though Collins stands to inherit the Bennet property (the law of entailment stipulates that the property must pass to a male heir). Her best friend, Charlotte, marries Collins instead, because, as she explains, she's getting older and must consider her financial future. Lydia, the youngest and most boy-crazy Bennet girl, runs off with a soldier, forcing Darcy into some shady dealings and Elizabeth into some soul searching.

Pride and Prejudice can be viewed through many lenses: at its core, it's a comedy of manners about a girl who rejects a man, discovers her grave error, and lives happily ever after. It skewers society in Regency England, which saw marriage as a means of cementing wealth and consolidating power; marrying for love would have been unconventional. It offers a pointed critique of a class system that overly values a woman's reputation, and shows how swiftly one's reputation could unravel. And then there's the writing, with a sharpness that sparkles even as it cuts to the quick. From its famous first line—"It is a truth universally acknowledged, that a single man in possession of a good fortune, must be in want of a wife"—this novel offers sly barbs and sarcastic asides. To open its pages is to fall through time, to smile, to smirk, and, perhaps, to join Team Darcy.

CLOCKWISE FROM LEFT: The hardcover design for *Ready Player One*, published in 2011. | Author Ernest Cline, photographed at a Comic-Con party in 2015. Cline turned to novel writing after tiring of screenwriting. | A trade paperback cover design of *Ready Player One*.

78

READY PLAYER ONE

Ernest Cline · 2011

The titular character of *Ready Player One* (2011) is Wade Watts, an orphan with fierce gaming skills. It's 2044, and Wade lives with his aunt in an environmentally damaged world where global warming has wreaked havoc, causing economic disaster and social collapse. To escape this dystopia, people play OASIS, an elaborate virtual-reality (VR) game, whenever they can. When billionaire James Halliday, who created OASIS, dies, he bequeaths his fortune to the first person who can solve a series of riddles and trivia based on 1980s pop culture and embedded in his VR world, and the game is quite literally on.

Video-game designers sometimes leave "Easter eggs" in their work, hidden graphics or puzzles that act as a kind of signature, like a graffiti tag on the street. If you know where to look and can interpret the Easter eggs correctly, your experience is enhanced. As a gunter (slang for "egg hunter"), Wade knows where to look. He leaves his house in the stacks, a tower of mobile homes, and heads to an abandoned van, where he slaps on the required haptic technology and transforms into Parzival, his alter ego. He joins forces with four other gamers, becoming a group known as the High Five.

Hundreds of pop culture references litter the sci-fi book, themselves a type of Easter egg. If you've never watched an episode of *Family Ties*, can't name a single character from a John Hughes movie, or don't know the music of Def Leppard, then you might skim over these various mentions. Although collaging references and in-the-know allusions has a long literary history, Cline's debut novel promotes these subtexts into much of the main text. The name-dropping and references also speak to the rise of "nerd culture" in contemporary life, where knowing the origin story of every Marvel superhero, for instance, is considered cool, not geeky.

Ernest Cline was born in Ohio in 1972. He grew up to become a spoken-word-poetry champion and amateur screenwriter; his screenplay about Star Wars über-fans generated enormous buzz but took nearly a decade to finally become the 2009 movie *Fanboys*. Growing exasperated with screenwriting, Cline turned to novels. At a tech-support call center where he worked, he witnessed employees playing multiple games simultaneously; for many, the world on the screen seemed more real than the world around them. Cline's favorite game, *Black Tiger*, features prominently in *Ready Player One*.

In the novel, almost all human interaction takes place as a series of 1s and 0s, where people no longer know each other in the flesh but rather only as stylized avatars. High Five member Art3mis appears strong, gorgeous, and female on the screen, but she might really be a chunky middle-aged man in real life. Technology becomes a screen between people and the world. However, *Ready Player One*'s virtual reality enables authentic emotional connections, and its plot tugs on the reader's heartstrings in a way reminiscent of the 1985 underdog adventure classic *The Goonies*, a film that is explicitly referenced.

Tipping his hat to the universe he so aptly describes, Cline concealed a URL as an Easter egg inside *Ready Player One*, which led to three increasingly difficult video-game challenges. The first reader to solve the mystery won a 1981 DeLorean DMC-12, a cool car with doors that open like wings, featured in Back to the Future movies.

Andy Weir, author of *The Martian* (2011), was so taken with *Ready Player One* that he wrote a fan-fiction prequel, "Lacero." It's now considered a major part of the fictional universe. Steven Spielberg directed the movie version of the novel, slated for release in 2018. Reading a book or watching a movie about gamers runs the risk of being far less exciting than anything you could do on the screen. Your fingers might itch with impatience to get back to scrolling and tapping, your eyes might dart around looking for GIFs and pixelated characters. But Cline's book speaks to the pleasures of letting the game unfold entirely in your head.

By Design

COMPELLING COVERS

GREAT BOOK COVERS are as varied as great books themselves, but each one seduces you through a seemingly magical combination of color, type, and image. The most influential cover designs have become nearly as iconic as the novels themselves.

If you've been in a bookstore in the past 30 years, you've no doubt seen a cover designed by Chip Kidd. One of the most talented and best-known art directors working in publishing today, Kidd has created covers for authors as diverse as Donna Tartt, Ernest Hemingway, and Haruki Murakami. Regardless of the writer or the type of work, he asks himself one question as he begins: "What do the stories look like?" The cover acts like a face, he explained in a TED talk, "giv[ing] form to content." When tasked with giving a face to Michael Crichton's *Jurassic Park* (1990), Kidd headed to the American Museum of Natural History, where he bought a book of drawings of dinosaurs in various poses. His resulting effort—a black tyrannosaur skeleton in midroar—became so linked to the story that it was used not only to advertise the movie adaptation but within the movie itself, and it went on to grace countless pieces of tie-in merchandise.

F. Scott Fitzgerald saw Francis Cugat's cover design for *The Great Gatsby* (1925) before he'd completed the novel. So taken was he with the weeping, figurative face rising above a gaudy cityscape that he decided to play up the images of eyes in the text itself. Stephenie Meyer felt that the cover of *Breaking Dawn* (2008), featuring a stately white queen on a chessboard, perfectly embodies the "metaphor for Bella's progression throughout the entire [Twilight] saga. She began as the weakest (at least physically, when compared to vampires and werewolves) player on the board: the pawn. She ended

as the strongest: the queen." Not every author felt satisfied with his or her book cover, however. Upon seeing the 1965 paperback edition of *The Hobbit* (1937), J. R. R. Tolkien wrote to his publisher, "I therefore will not enter into a debate about taste," instead pointing out that "I do not understand how anybody who had read the tale (I hope you are one) could think such a picture would please the author."

Other iconic covers include a line drawing of a carousel horse in orange, designed by E. Michael Mitchell, for the first edition of *The Catcher in the Rye* (1951) and an unassuming, semiabstract tree adorning *To Kill a Mockingbird* (1960), conceived of by Shirley Smith. S. Neil Fujita's use of weighty lettering and an eerie outline of a marionette on a black background for *The Godfather* (1969) subsequently informed the visual tone of the Godfather movies. And then there are the psychedelic, almost lurid designs fashioned by Richard Powers to illustrate such sci-fi and fantasy classics as *Pebble in the Sky* (1950) by Isaac Asimov and *The Sirens of Titan* (1959) by Kurt Vonnegut.

While designers may develop a signature style, not many can be said to have a style named for them. But such is the case with Paul Bacon, who, over the course of a long career, produced covers for approximately 6,500 books. His signature style, which included a conceptual image, a few colors, and pronounced hand-drawn lettering, is known in the publishing industry as the "Big Book Look." For a particularly well-known version of the Big Book Look, check out the cover of *Catch-22* (1961), on which a jaunty red soldier boogies against a jagged blue background.

More recently, design trends have taken into account the need for covers to be flexible and beautiful across media, from physical book to

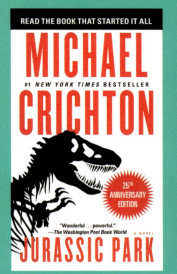

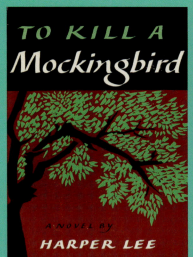

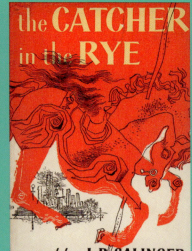

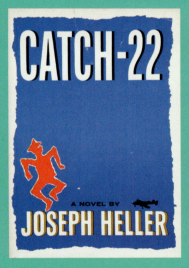

electronic editions. Contemporary jackets tend to be bold and minimalist, with a bright palette, prominent type, and a tiny image, if any; the eye-popping red-and-yellow cover of *Ready Player One* (2011) is one notable example. Shepard Fairey looked to the past as he reimagined the cover for a reissue of *Nineteen Eighty-Four* (1949), co-opting Soviet imagery and even nodding to *The Great Gatsby*'s eyes with a single unblinking orb. Another designer would have taken a different tack—but as long as the design hooks the reader and honors the author, it just might work.

JUDGING BY THEIR COVERS: Chip Kidd created the striking cover for *Jurassic Park*, with the classic image repeated in this 25th-anniversary edition; *To Kill a Mockingbird*'s classic 1960 tree cover was conceived by Shirley Smith; E. Michael Mitchell created the classic drawing on the cover of *The Catcher in the Rye*; the 1961 cover of *Catch-22* is an example of the Big Book Look; the 2011 cover for *Ready Player One* (2011) is a bold, type-based design.

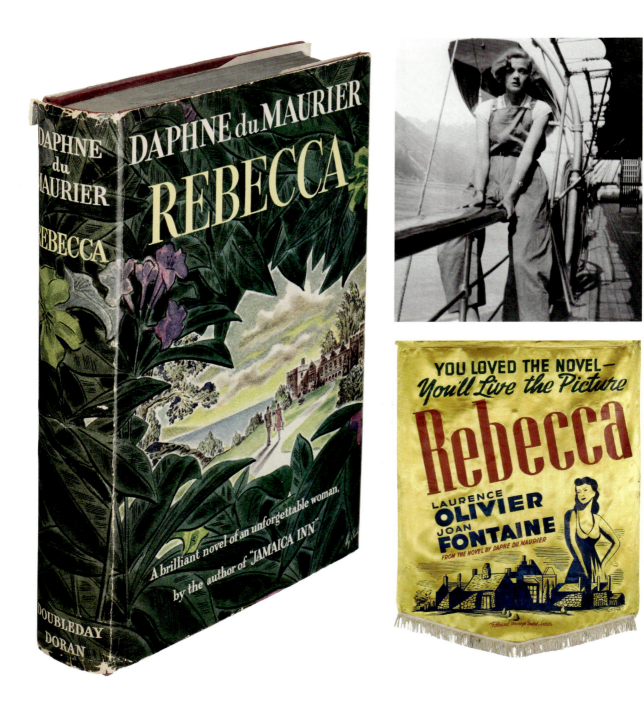

CLOCKWISE FROM LEFT: A first US edition of *Rebecca*, originally published in 1938. | Author Daphne du Maurier called her novel a "study in jealousy." | Alfred Hitchcock adapted the novel for his 1940 movie, advertised here in a silk banner.

79

REBECCA

Daphne du Maurier · 1938

Readers of *Rebecca* (1938) can't help but close the thriller with at least two questions: Was Manderley based on a real place? And what was the state of Dame Daphne du Maurier's marriage?

The answer to the first question is yes. Born in London in 1907 to a literary and intellectual family—her grandfather created the creepy character Svengali in his 1894 novel *Trilby* and coined the medical term "bedside manner"—du Maurier visited Milton Hall in Cambridgeshire during the First World War, when the grand country house was used as an auxiliary hospital. For Manderley, she mentally moved aspects of that house to the grounds of Menabilly, a large, old property in Cornwall where du Maurier lived for many years. She adored that house so much that she would sometimes kiss it. Manderley proved to be one of the most evocative and memorable settings in literature.

When the unnamed narrator of *Rebecca* meets Maximilian (Maxim) de Winter in Monte Carlo, she falls hard and fast for the rich and charismatic widower. Upon their marriage, Maxim brings her back to Manderley, his huge family estate in southern England. There she meets Mrs. Danvers, a malicious housekeeper with an obsessive devotion to the first Mrs. de Winter, Rebecca, who died in a boating accident the year before. Mrs. Danvers proceeds to undermine the narrator's self-confidence, her marriage, and at times even her psyche. When Mrs. Danvers convinces the narrator to wear a dress of Rebecca's to a costume ball, the narrator learns the truth about Rebecca's death.

As for the second question, the book may have been influenced by the author's marriage. In later years, du Maurier referred to her novel as a "study in jealousy," and she admitted that she based the second Mrs. de Winter's intensity of feelings on her own. Du Maurier's husband, the distinguished British army lieutenant-general Frederick "Boy" Browning, had been engaged prior to their courtship in the early 1930s; this previous partner eventually killed herself. Du Maurier discovered love letters from the woman, signed with a big swooping R (the first letter of her last name). Although both du Maurier and Browning had affairs, they raised three children and stayed married until Browning's death in 1965. Du Maurier died in 1989 at age 81.

Since its publication some eight decades ago, *Rebecca* has never been out of print. Its influence is wider than readers might realize; during World War II, the Germans attempted to use the novel as the basis of a code, but some technology was captured before the code could be employed. It has made numerous appearances in popular culture, from a 1972 episode of *The Carol Burnett Show* to Stephen King's *Bag of Bones* (1998) to the *Twilight*-fanfic-erotica sequel *Fifty Shades Darker* (2012).

Rebecca's most famous adaptation, however, was the 1940 film of the same name by Alfred Hitchcock, starring Laurence Olivier. Hitchcock played up the novel's gothic elements and heightened its psychological edge. The second Mrs. de Winter doesn't have a name in the movie, either, although she was called Daphne during the shoot. In 1963, Hitchcock adapted another du Maurier story for the screen, again keeping the author's original title, "The Birds."

Aside from its exploration of jealousy, the novel questions the inescapability of the past. The narrator opens the book by reflecting on what happened: "Last night I dreamt I went to Manderley again." In its exploration of haunting former wives, *Rebecca* owes a debt to *Jane Eyre* (1847). Although the book doesn't have any supernatural elements, a ghost nevertheless haunts its pages, much as she haunts the house. The ghost is unknowable—she exists in one form for Mrs. Danvers, who worshipped her; in another form for Maxim, who perhaps knew her best; and for the second Mrs. de Winter, Rebecca is someone else entirely. The ghosts that haunt us most, however, may very well be the selves we once were.

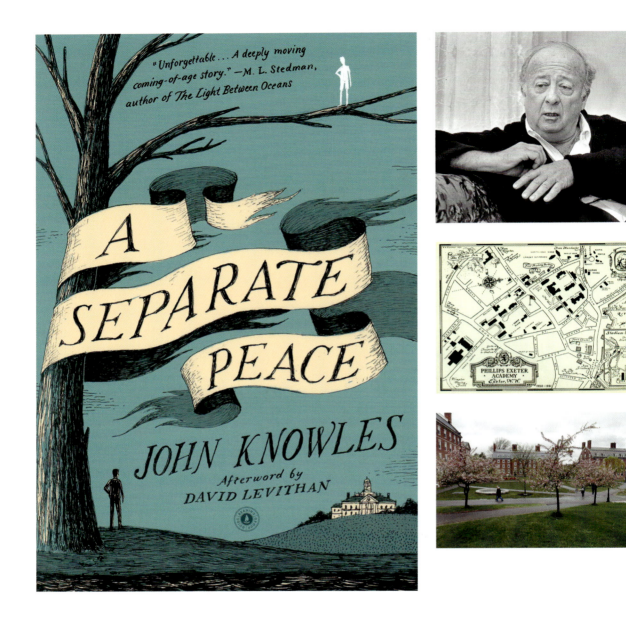

80

A SEPARATE PEACE

John Knowles · 1959

John Knowles was born in 1926 and raised in West Virginia, but he fell in love with New England as a student at Phillips Exeter Academy, which he entered at age 15. In later years he would praise the elite boarding school for lifting him out of the South, helping him get into Yale, teaching him to study, and catalyzing his bestselling debut, thereby launching his writing career. Throughout his life, he candidly acknowledged the many ways in which he based *A Separate Peace* (1959), his first and most successful novel, on his experiences at Exeter in the 1940s.

As the novel opens, 30-something Gene Forrester returns to the fictional Devon, a decade and a half after graduation. Being back at his prep school stirs up recollections of his roommate, Phineas, with whom he became close, if competitive, friends. The solitary, introverted Gene envies Finny his physical gifts, while believing, incorrectly, that Finny envies Gene's intellectual ones and therefore attempts to distract Gene from his schoolwork. On the day Gene learns that he's been wrong about Finny, who truly wants Gene to thrive, the boys head to a favorite tree to jump into a river. Standing together on a branch, Gene wobbles, causing Finny to fall and badly break a leg. He recovers, and everyone considers what happened to be an accident, but Gene feels profoundly guilty upon learning that Finny will never again be able to play sports.

The truth is that Gene shook the branch on purpose. When he tries to confess, Finny shrugs him off, in part because Devon, like the rest of the country, has become consumed with World War II. Classmates leave school to join the war effort. One friend enlists, only to go AWOL, deeply shaken by what he's seen and perhaps driven insane. The novel shows how distant wars can touch even seemingly idyllic places, and it emphasizes internal conflict as a form of violence. Gene must struggle to cope with the consequences of his actions and reconcile who he thought he was with who he actually is.

Knowles wrote *A Separate Peace* in the mornings before heading to his day job at a travel magazine. The novel's popularity enabled him to quit and write full-time. It received the inaugural William Faulkner Foundation Award for notable first novel, and was nominated for a National Book Award. He cowrote the screenplay for the 1972 eponymous movie. He also revisited Devon in fiction, publishing *Phineas: Six Stories* (1968) and *Peace Breaks Out* (1981), a sequel, along with other works of fiction and nonfiction, before his death in 2001.

Like his protagonists, who create the Super Suicide Society of the Summer Session, Knowles formed a secret society with his classmates. New members were required to jump from a tall tree into a river, just as Finny and Gene do. Knowles based key characters on fellow students, including Gore Vidal, who inspired the novel's Brinker Hadley, an older student who is as moral and conventional as Finny is spirited and charismatic. Finny was said to resemble a classmate who later went on to compete in the Olympics, which Finny dreamed of doing. Knowles claimed too that he put a little of himself in the boys, even Gene, but stressed that his school years were a time of camaraderie and closeness, not resentment and revenge.

Few friendships feel as intense as those formed during adolescence, and *A Separate Peace* captures that headiness and passion. It's shocking to grow up and discover just how fine a line sometimes exists between love and hate, between our closest friends and worst enemies, between our worst enemies and ourselves.

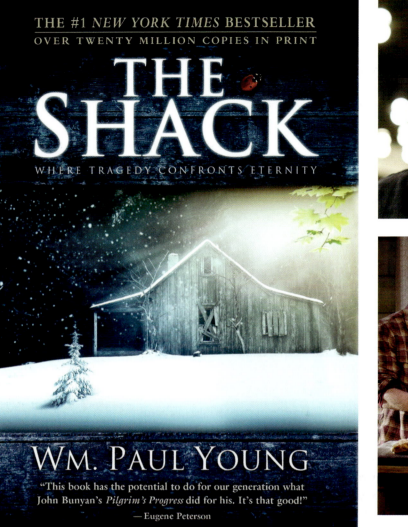

81

THE SHACK

f God called, would you answer? If God sent you a summons, would you accept it? Mourning the murder of his daughter, Mack Phillips receives an enigmatic invitation to meet God in a place known only as "the shack." He goes.

There he learns that God the Father is actually a kindly African American woman who goes by "Papa." This interpretation of God angered readers who subscribed to an image of God as an elderly, bearded white man with a fiery temper, but Phillips's depiction resonated with others looking for a multicultural interpretation of divinity. To date, *The Shack* (2007) has sold 20 million copies. Academy Award–winner Octavia Spencer plays God in the 2017 film version of *The Shack*, which also stars Tim McGraw.

Before the blockbuster Christian thriller begins, Mackenzie Allen Phillips (known as Mack) took three of his children on a camping trip in Oregon. While Mack rescued two from drowning, his youngest, Missy, was captured by a serial killer. Four years later, Mack receives a note, purportedly from Papa—the name Mack and his wife use for God—instructing Mack to go to the shack where Missy is thought to have been murdered. At first the shack resembles the horrible, falling-down structure where his daughter may have spent her last hours. But then it transforms into an incredible place inhabited by God, Jesus, and the Holy Spirit.

As Mack discovers during his weekend at the shack, Papa is unstinting and generous, sympathetic and caring. She urges him to forgive his daughter's killer, yet Mack must also learn to forgive Papa, who let the murder happen. He speaks at length to Sophia, the embodiment of Papa's wisdom. Jesus is a Middle Eastern carpenter, and together he and Mack walk across water. The Holy Spirit manifests as Sarayu, an Asian woman. She catches Mack's tears, then pours them over Missy's grave. As flowers bloom, Mack begins to understand how suffering might finally have a broader, bigger purpose, one that could enhance and enrich a person's life.

Young wrote *The Shack* while commuting among his three jobs. He envisioned it as a Christmas present for his six kids, a way of sharing his outlook and belief system, as well as a means of giving them something for the holidays when he couldn't afford anything else. The self-published novel garnered so much word-of-mouth praise that a publisher came calling in 2008. The shack, as Young has explained, is a metaphor for the place people construct inside themselves to put shame, suffering, and pain. Secrets inhabit the shack, as does addiction. Young has been candid about the ways his own experiences, including sexual abuse and adultery, shaped his novel.

William Paul Young was born in Canada in 1955 but moved to New Guinea as an infant with his missionary parents. He graduated from Warner Pacific College, married his wife, Kim, and worked a variety of jobs in a range of industries, some of which involved corporate communications and other types of business writing. On the side he wrote short stories, songs, and poetry. He printed the first 15 copies of *The Shack* at a local Office Depot. Since the book's incredible success, Young has published two more novels, *Cross Roads* (2012) and *Eve* (2015), along with a nonfiction book entitled *Lies We Believe About God* (2017).

The Shack deals with how to cope with an almost-unimaginable horror—the loss of a child. But the novel functions less as a handbook for working through grief, and more as a guide to spirituality. It offers an alternative to prescriptive dogma and features the warm, loving embrace of a God who covers her children in grace.

CLOCKWISE FROM LEFT: The Bantam Books paperback edition of *Siddhartha*, originally published in 1922. | Author Hermann Hesse was celebrated for years in Germany before his novels garnered attention in the United States in the 1960s. | Prince Siddhartha (563–400 BCE) became Gautama Buddha, and his teachings made the foundation of Buddhism.

82

SIDDHARTHA

Hermann Hesse · 1922

Hermann Hesse won the 1946 Nobel Prize in Literature. In making its selection, the committee recognized "his inspired writings which, while growing in boldness and penetration, exemplify the classical humanitarian ideals and high qualities of style." Widely revered in Germany, his novels came to prominence in the United States in the 1960s; with its emphasis on an individual, idiosyncratic, and independent route to spiritual enlightenment, *Siddhartha* (1922) enabled generations to turn on, tune in, and find their own truth.

As a child in a missionary family, Hesse seemed destined to follow a pious path. Born in 1877 in the Black Forest region of Germany, he was close to his grandfather, who had proselytized in India and helped translate the Bible into Malayalam, the official language of Kerala. Even as he stoked his grandson's religious faith, this grandfather encouraged Hesse to develop a cosmopolitan outlook that would influence his writing. In his youth Hesse began to suffer from depression and attempted suicide on at least one occasion, after which he was institutionalized. He began working in a bookstore that specialized in theology, and started reading carefully and thoroughly.

Siddhartha, Hesse's ninth novel, describes the spiritual journey of a well-liked young Brahmin named Siddhartha in India around 625 BCE. He spends his days romping about with his best friend, Govinda. Yet he feels as if something is missing. Siddhartha and Govinda meet a group of Samanas, who renounce physical desire in their quest for enlightenment, and they decide to join these ascetics. Depriving himself of clothes and food helps for a while, but eventually Siddhartha's emptiness returns. He and his friend set off to find Gautama the Buddha, who, they're given to understand, recently reached Nirvana. While Govinda senses a kinship and decides to stay with the Buddha, Siddhartha decides to go the opposite route and devote himself to the pleasures of the flesh.

The earthly realm bears fruit: Siddhartha falls in love with a courtesan named Kamala and becomes wealthy. He develops a fondness for gambling. In a now-familiar pattern, however, Siddhartha once again grows ill at ease. As he tries to commit suicide by drowning, he hears the river gurgling "om." He decides to apprentice himself to a ferryman named Vasudeva. Although Vasudeva's life seems simple—he spends his days listening to and watching the river—he seems utterly at home in himself. At last, Siddhartha discovers peace and the boundless unity at work in the world.

Siddhartha's journey to transcendence takes the form of a quest. Unlike Arthur's knights, who seek the Holy Grail, or Odysseus, who longs to return home, Siddhartha searches for inner peace. While Govinda finds what he needs as a follower of the Buddha, Siddhartha discovers his Nirvana only when he forges his own way. It's a radical notion, as Siddhartha basically rejects sanctioned intermediaries and established dogma. By the end, Govinda comes to Siddhartha as a pupil does to a teacher, seeking to understand his old friend's doctrine.

Following *Siddhartha*, Hesse wrote two autobiographical novels. Then, in 1927, he published *Steppenwolf*. Like *Siddhartha*, *Steppenwolf* features a protagonist in spiritual crisis. Drawing on Hesse's life as well as psychoanalytic techniques, *Steppenwolf* is a dark study of a dark soul split between his immoral urges and his desire for respectability. These two novels remain widely read in the years since Hesse's death in 1962, in effect showing two sides of the same existential coin. As thinking beings, we are both cursed and blessed—cursed because we constantly perceive the ways we fail; blessed because we are capable of continuing to strive for redemption.

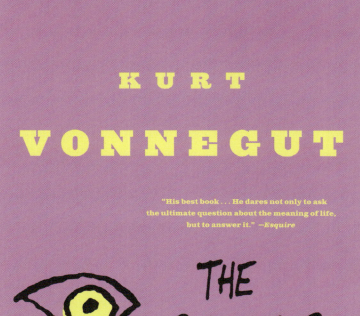

KURT VONNEGUT

"His best book . . . He dares not only to ask the ultimate question about the meaning of life, but to answer it." —*Esquire*

THE SIRENS OF TITAN

A NOVEL

CLOCKWISE FROM TOP: A paperback edition cover of *The Sirens of Titan*, from 1998. | Kurt Vonnegut, photographed circa 1970, smokes a cigarette, probably his favorite Pall Malls. | Vonnegut in his office, sitting at his typewriter. The author weaved philosophy with silly absurdism.

83

THE SIRENS OF TITAN

Kurt Vonnegut · 1959

While it's tempting to look down on a sci-fi story about Martian invaders told in a flat style across short paragraphs, Kurt Vonnegut's second novel, *The Sirens of Titan* (1959), is a sophisticated work of philosophical literature. As absurd and seemingly silly as it might be, it is also an intellectual extravaganza.

In *The Sirens of Titan*, Vonnegut posits a question he would wrestle with through many other novels and short stories: To what extent do we have free will, and to what extent are we at the mercy of fate? The wealthiest man in the United States, Malachi Constant, gains a fortune through what he believes to be divine favor, but which may actually be random luck. He encounters another rich man, Winston Niles Rumfoord, who may or may not hold Malachi's destiny in his hands. Rumfoord is stuck in a time warp that enables him to see the past and predict the future. He intends to wage war with a Martian army against Earth in order to introduce his new religion, which posits that God is indifferent to humankind. Salo, a robot from a planet called Tralfamadore, convinces Constant that Rumfoord, along with everyone else, is being manipulated by forces they can't see. In fact, human history's sole purpose has been to help the Tralfamadorians get the part Salo needs to fix his spaceship.

The plot gets even more complicated from there, but essentially it tracks the characters as they search for meaning in what could be a meaningless universe. As with an onion, readers can keep pulling back layers, possibly tearing up as they do. If nothing matters, how might one live? But for all its pessimism and nihilism, the novel ultimately offers love as a solution.

Along with philosophy, the novel serves up a healthy portion of satire. Vonnegut constantly turned a sharp eye on the society in which he lived. In *The Sirens of Titan*, as well as other works, he lambasts the unequal distribution of wealth. Unpleasant people get rich, while deserving people stay poor.

Biographers sometimes theorize that Vonnegut developed his sense of humor in response to decidedly unfunny events, as a laugh-so-you-don't-cry coping mechanism. He was born into an affluent family in Indianapolis, Indiana, in 1922, but the money evaporated during the Great Depression. In 1944, his mother committed suicide. A few months later, he was captured during the Battle of the Bulge, along with thousands of other American soldiers, and was a prisoner of war in Dresden. He survived the intense Allied firebombing of that city in 1945 by hiding in a meat locker inside a slaughterhouse, an experience he would revisit in *Slaughterhouse-Five* (1969). Around the time he was working on *The Sirens of Titan*, he and his wife, Jane, took in three nephews after his sister and her husband died, adding to their family of three biological children.

Success took a while, but it found Vonnegut eventually. The novel was nominated for a Hugo Award in 1960, and the author received a Guggenheim Fellowship in 1967. Douglas Adams, another master of the absurdist school of science fiction, cited Vonnegut as an influence, as did Joseph Heller and John Irving. Vonnegut died in 2007 at age 84. The Grateful Dead's Jerry Garcia purchased movie rights to *The Sirens of Titan* in 1983, but nothing came of the option. A television series based on the book is currently in development.

Though we may not be—or even know how to pronounce—Tralfamadorians, we can see in the adventures of Vonnegut's characters our own cosmic struggles. *The Sirens of Titan* is complex and a little confusing, much like our existence is complex and a little confusing. The novel both mines our world for ideas and mimics our world in experience.

84

A SONG OF ICE AND FIRE SERIES

George R. R. Martin · 1996–present

Winter is coming." Along with launching a thousand memes, the motto of House Stark has been used to describe everything from meteorological events to presidential elections. It originated in the novel *A Game of Thrones* (1996), the first in an epic, and immensely popular, fantasy series that tracks the battle for the Iron Throne and dominion over the Seven Kingdoms of Westeros.

As a series of five novels thus far, A Song of Ice and Fire ranks with The Lord of the Rings (1954–1955) and The Wheel of Time (1990–2013). All three series offer vast, thoroughly realized imaginary universes full of charismatic characters, interesting settings, and supernatural elements. The novels—*A Game of Thrones*, *A Clash of Kings* (1999), *A Storm of Swords* (2000), *A Feast for Crows* (2005), *A Dance with Dragons* (2011), *The Winds of Winter* (forthcoming)—pose moral dilemmas, depict worlds in the throes of great change, and introduce a range of individuals to root for or despise. Unlike its predecessors, however, George R. R. Martin's work features more sex and more politics. Indeed, Martin's books have such complicated plots that he often consults with the person in charge of maintaining the internet's largest forum devoted to A Song of Ice and Fire just to make sure he's keeping everything straight.

Martin cites conflicts like the Hundred Years' War and Wars of the Roses in England as inspiration. His books detail the fates of several noble families. As they fight among themselves and with one another with notable vehemence and viciousness, a second battle rages: the 8,000-year-old Wall is all that stands between the Seven Kingdoms and an undead army bent on destruction. Meanwhile, across the Narrow Sea, a young woman named Daenerys Targaryen amasses people and harnesses her dragons to prepare a devastating attack on Westeros for the Iron Throne.

Born in 1948 in New Jersey and christened George Raymond Martin, he adopted the middle name "Richard" when he was confirmed at age 13. Martin earned a bachelor's and a master's in journalism from Northwestern, then taught at the college level and ran chess tournaments while writing on the side. The death of a friend caused him to turn to writing full-time in the late 1970s. As he published short stories and novels in the 1980s, he also worked on television shows like *Beauty and the Beast*. In the early 1990s, he began penning the series that would become A Song of Ice and Fire.

Many people refer to the novels by the title of the first volume, which is the name HBO chose when it debuted its adaptation in 2011: *Game of Thrones*. The lush TV recreation of Martin's fiction quickly became one of the most watched series in history. For various reasons, the show departs from the books, but Martin has been heavily involved in the HBO production from the beginning. A slow writer by his own admission, Martin has promised that he will finish the sixth novel even as HBO plans to end the television series after season eight, and as he consults on HBO's forthcoming multiple prequel spin-offs.

Fans mention point-of-view characters like Daenerys, Arya Stark, and Cersei Lannister when discussing the series' treatment of gender roles. Strong female protagonists and secondary characters appear throughout the novels, and several significant plotlines demonstrate an arc from waiflike girl to formidable warrior-like woman. However, the series has also been accused of misogyny, as many of these same women undergo some form of sexual violence. Martin responds to such criticism by citing the past: "My novels are epic fantasy, but they are inspired by and grounded in history. Rape and sexual violence have been a part of every war ever fought. . . . To omit them from a narrative centered on war and power would have been fundamentally false and dishonest, and would have undermined one of the themes of the books: that the true horrors of human history derive not from orcs and Dark Lords, but from ourselves."

"It's a beautiful thing, the destruction of words. ~~It can~~ [it can be got rid of as well] It isn't
only the synonyms; there are also the antonyms. After all, what justification
is there for any word which is simply the opposite of some other
word? A word contains its opposite in itself. Take good, for instance.
If you have a word like good, what need is there for a word like bad?
Ungood will do just as well - better, in fact, because it's an exact
opposite, which the other is not. ~~And~~ Or again, if you want a stronger
version of good, what sense is there in having a whole string of
vague useless words like excellent and splendid and all the rest of
them? Plusgood covers the meaning; or doubleplus good if you want
something stronger still. ~~In the end~~ the whole range of words comes
down to this: good, plusgood, doubleplusgood; ungood, plusungood,
doubleplusungood. Only six words - in reality, only one word. Don't ~~You~~ see
the beauty of that, (Winston?) It was Big Brother's idea originally, of course,"

Of course we use these forms already, but in the ~~old~~ ~~the~~ final [version] of Newspeak
there'll ~~this~~ ~~will~~ be nothing else. In the end

The comparative suffixes are — ~~nla~~ nya, compar; -nta superl.
In a few cases — probably where what now appears as the adjectival stem
really contains an old suffix as bara 'good' = ba+ra — this is irregular.
Thus mora 'dark' moranya darker moranta darkest.
    bara 'good' {baranya better {baranta best.
              {banya   {banta

-nta is not merely augmentative. For augmentative suffix see below.
This strictly comparative and requires no article.

ABOVE, TOP TO BOTTOM: A copy of the original typed manuscript for *Nineteen Eighty-Four*, with Orwell's notes. The novel coined terms like *Big Brother* and doublethink. | J. R. R. Tolkien kept careful notes to keep track of his Elvish language, something he'd started creating as a child.

In a Manner of Speaking

NEOLOGISMS, PORTMANTEAUX, AND NEW LANGUAGES

LANGUAGES EVOLVE, bending and changing with the times, and through the efforts of those who know them best. Writers can set new species loose in the linguistic environment by giving us idioms and sayings that capture ideas and feelings better than any of our previous options. And in some cases, writers create entirely new verbal kingdoms as a way of rendering their fictional worlds a little more real and a little more readable.

THE CHEESIEST SNARK

Novelists have a long history of lending words to English and the culture at large. One of the most noteworthy such writers was George Orwell. In *Nineteen Eighty-Four* (1949), Orwell fashioned such neologisms as *Thought Police, thoughtcrime, Newspeak, doublethink,* and *Big Brother*—words that routinely pepper political discourse, particularly with regard to totalitarian and authoritarian policies.

We worry about eating *Frankenfood,* a catchall term for genetically modified food, that combines *Frankenstein* and food—and reminds us that, in the 1818 novel by Mary Shelley, it's the doctor who's named Frankenstein, not the monster, as is commonly believed.

When talking about *snark,* we might *chortle*—two portmanteaux (words created by combining two separate words) coined by Lewis Carroll: the first marrying "snake" and "shark," and the second "chuckle" and "snort." The word *yahoo* arrived in Jonathan Swift's *Gulliver's Travels* (1726), where it describes a race of ignoble humans enslaved by horses. J. D. Salinger popularized the phrase *screw up*; Stephen King gave us *pie-hole,* slang for "mouth"; and Charles Dickens invented *cheesiness, rampage, butter-fingers,* and *flummox,* among others. We have Dr. Seuss to thank for *nerd,* and John Green and his fans for *nerdfighter* (a positive appellation celebrating those who love all things geeky).

These days the phrase *catch-22* has become a routine way of describing the experience of facing a problem that prevents its own solution. But the term got its start in the novel of the same name published by Joseph Heller in 1961. In that satirical work, Heller's pilots can get out of flying missions if they are found to be insane—yet asking for a medical evaluation demonstrates their capacity for rational thought and ability to worry about themselves, two hallmarks of sanity. Things that puzzle us or strike us as impractical to the point of ridiculous may be termed *quixotic,* which comes from *Don Quixote* (1605), a novel about a man who has trouble separating reality from literature. Anything nightmarish and off-kilter could be called Kafkaesque.

Science fiction offers a treasure trove of jargon that has made its way into everyday—and even scientific—usage. H. G. Wells developed the concept of a *time machine* in his 1895 novel by the same name, as well as *parallel universe* in a later work. Isaac Asimov created a bunch, including *microcomputer* and *robotics. Bot* arrived later, in a 1969 novel by Richard C. Meredith called *We All Died at Breakaway Station.* William Gibson invented the word *cyberspace* in his 1982 short story "Burning Chrome."

J. R. R. TOLKIEN, LEXICOGRAPHER

As a professor of English language and literature at Oxford University, J. R. R. Tolkien spent his days thinking about vocabulary and grammar. But these

ABOVE: A portrait of William Shakespeare, circa 1610. Shakespeare
coined countless new terms, such as *assassination* and *bedazzled*.

thoughts began much earlier, when, as a child, he first started constructing an Elvish language he called Quenya, a project he would work on throughout his life. In novels like *The Hobbit* (1937) and The Lord of the Rings (1954–1955), Tolkien drew on his academic training and lexicographic hobby, incorporating roots from Old English, Middle English, Latin, Greek, Finnish, and Welsh into the tongues of Middle-earth; in fact, he saw these fully formed yet imaginary languages as central to his mythmaking and literary efforts. Tolkien's son Christopher later published many of his father's linguistic guides and detailed etymologies, as well as maps, drawings, notes, and scenes, in the 12-volume *History of Middle-earth* (1983–1996).

In the late 1960s, the venerable *Oxford English Dictionary (OED)*—considered the definitive guide to English and featuring some 218,632 words—decided to include the word *hobbit* among its pages. While at Oxford, the *OED*'s editor in charge of the word had studied under Tolkien, so he wrote to his former professor for feedback on the proposed definition. Tolkien's subsequent response forms the core of the current version: "In the tales of J. R. R. Tolkien (1892–1973): one of an imaginary people, a small variety of the human race, that gave themselves this name (meaning 'hole-dweller') but were called by others *halflings*, since they were half the height of normal men." Other words derived from or revived by Tolkien that now appear in the *OED* include *orc* and *mathom*. Written by three *OED* editors, *The Ring of Words* (2006) explores the mutually beneficial relationship between Tolkien and the *OED*, with a focus on the author as "a word user and word creator."

ATHCHOMAR CHOMAKEA, OR GREETINGS TO YOU ALL

Linguist David J. Peterson may not be a household name, but his work extends far into pop culture. In 2017 he taught a course at the University of California, Berkeley, based on Dothraki, a language he created for the HBO series *Game of Thrones*. Peterson used bits of vocabulary found throughout A Song of Ice and Fire (1996–present), the fantasy novels by George R. R. Martin on which the show is based, to create the language of the powerful nomadic warriors. In inventing the language, Peterson often drops in references to his family and friends. For example, *jolinat* means "to cook," an homage to his mother-in-law, Jolyn, and her culinary skill. If you're not in California, don't worry: you can learn High Valyrian, another language from Martin's series, via the website Duolingo.

Probably no writer in history more fundamentally altered English as we know it than William Shakespeare. Additions to the language attributed to him include *assassination*, *new-fangled*, *bedazzled*, and even *puking*. Like Tolkien, Shakespeare took a magpie approach, appropriating in some cases, inventing in others, bedazzling, whatever words he could. He recognized that language is inherently, utterly mutable, and literally lives in the recitation of a word by one person to another. Words survive if they meet our communicative needs, and must adapt or go extinct if they don't. So, for all we know, our children or children's children may very well someday wish each other "Asshekhqoyi vezhvena" and "Man aur."

85

THE STAND

Stephen King · 1978

Long popular with readers, in recent years Stephen King has been openly embraced by critics and other members of the literary establishment. He won the Medal for Distinguished Contribution to American Letters from the National Book Foundation in 2003, and in 2016 was recognized by the Library of Congress for his lifelong commitment to promoting literacy; his fiction has graced the pages of the *New Yorker* and *Tin House*. The master of horror is stepping out from the shadows of genre.

Born in Portland, Maine, in 1947, King grew up with a single mother and started writing stories at a young age, including novelizations of movies he'd seen (which he'd then sell to classmates for a quarter). He published his first story in 1965, a few years before he graduated from the University of Maine.

In 1999, King was almost killed by a van while walking along back roads near his house. He chronicled the experience in *On Writing* (2000), his celebrated book about the craft. He noted how much his wife, Tabitha, recognized his need to be creative as he recuperated. It wasn't the first time she'd played a crucial role: she fished out some crumpled-up pages from the trash can, smoothed them out, and encouraged King to keep working on the novel that would become the horror classic *Carrie* (1974). They have three children, two of whom are also writers.

If there's such a thing as the opposite of writer's block, a journalist once quipped, King suffers from it. He's the author of 54 novels and six nonfiction books, which are estimated to have sold more than 350 million copies all told. Many of his works, including *The Stand*, have been made into movies or television series. Indeed, his legions of readers relish his fiction in part for its cinematic qualities—King can reveal the essentials about a character in just a single scene.

With *The Stand*, his most ambitious stand-alone novel, King set out to create an enormous world on par with that of the Lord of the Rings (1954–1955). He explained when asked about his inspiration: "Only instead of a hobbit, my hero was a Texan named Stu Redman, and instead of a Dark Lord, my villain was a ruthless drifter and supernatural madman named Randall Flagg. The land of Mordor ('where the shadows lie,' according to Tolkien) was played by Las Vegas." Fearful that no one would buy or read such a long book, King's editors made substantive cuts to the 1978 manuscript. In 1990, King restored that material, and *The Stand: The Complete & Uncut Edition* is now the official edition.

In the opening chapters of this modern-day dystopian epic, some 99.4 percent of the world's population dies following the accidental release of a biological superweapon. The few survivors begin having prophetic dreams and gravitating to two polar-opposite leaders: Abagail Freemantle, also known as Mother Abagail, a 108-year-old black woman in Nebraska, and the malevolent Flagg. Freemantle and her followers establish a Free Zone in Boulder, while Flagg opts for Vegas. The novel's title refers to the showdown between good and evil, between those who embrace community and those who embrace self-indulgence, between those who see the ruined world as an opportunity to build a better society and those who seek to dominate, exploit, and destroy.

As compelling as this moral confrontation may be, the power of *The Stand* comes from King's fascinating descriptions of social collapse, his unmatched ability to conjure shuddering terror in readers—Larry Underwood's journey on foot through the pitch-black, corpse-filled Lincoln Tunnel has become a touchstone of modern horror—and the instantly relatable men and women he follows in their struggle to find meaning in a chaotic, broken world.

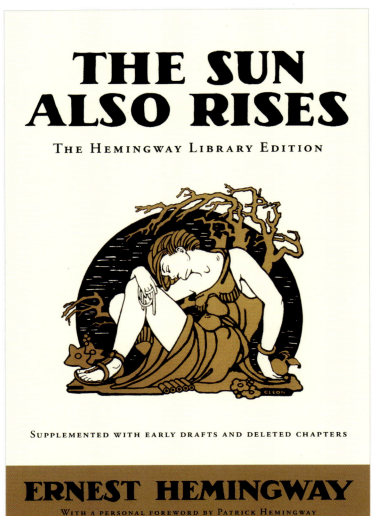

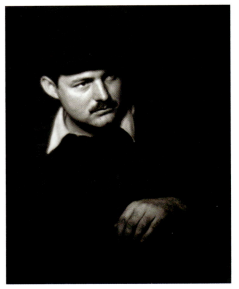

86

THE SUN ALSO RISES

Ernest Hemingway · 1926

For someone well known for his simple prose, Ernest Hemingway was a complicated guy. He went fishing with a machine gun so he could shoot at the sharks that might otherwise bother his catch. He was a quintessential man's man who loved a dry, extremely cold martini. He adored cats. He won the Nobel Prize in 1954, and killed himself in 1961. He cherished his friends, but used their disaffections and affairs to inspire *The Sun Also Rises* (1926).

Hemingway's first novel grew out of his time in Paris, where he palled around with artists and writers like Pablo Picasso, Ezra Pound, John Dos Passos, and Gertrude Stein. It was Stein who coined the term *the lost generation*, as a way of describing the young people like themselves adrift in feelings of alienation and disorientation in the aftermath of World War I. Hemingway so liked the phrase that he used it as an epigraph to the book, attributing it to his friend.

The plot can be summed up in a single sentence: an intertwined group of British and American expats heads to Spain to watch some bullfights. Jake Barnes, who narrates the book, fought in World War I but now works as a journalist in Paris. He and his friend Robert Cohn run into the beautiful, promiscuous Lady Brett Ashley, who nursed Jake during the war after he received a mysterious injury that likely left him impotent. Although they care for one another, Brett makes it clear that she needs physicality and therefore can't commit to him. Cohn develops feelings for Brett, which disturbs her fiancé, Mike. Everyone meets up in Pamplona for the fiesta and bullfighting, and Brett becomes enamored of a gifted young matador.

What saves the book from being merely a gossipy roman à clef is first and foremost the revolutionary prose. It's hard to imagine a time before Hemingway, so ingrained are his spare, unadorned sentences in American literature. He did away with flowery descriptions and the long, winding sentences of the 19th century, and ushered novels into modernity with quick jabs and punchy paragraphs. The style that launched a million imitators began right here. In its 1926 review of the book, the *New York Times* called it "a truly gripping story, told in a lean, hard, athletic narrative prose that puts more literary English to shame."

Hemingway started to develop his distinctive understated style as a journalist. Born in 1899 in a Chicago suburb, he left home after high school to drive an ambulance on the Italian Front, where he was wounded. Back in the States, he took a job writing for the *Toronto Star* and reported on war-torn areas as a foreign correspondent. By the early 1920s, he was living in Paris with his first wife and young son, socializing, and writing all the while. After the enormous success of *The Sun Also Rises*, Hemingway continued writing short stories, nonfiction, travelogues, and novels. He traveled to and lived in many parts of the world, from Havana to Key West to Ketchum, Idaho, where he committed suicide at age 61.

The Sun Also Rises deals with heady themes, among them changing gender expectations. In Brett, Hemingway portrayed a sexually liberated woman, independent and unafraid to ask for what she wants. Jake, in contrast, embodies a man who has been neutered by the war, both physically, on account of his wound, and spiritually. World War I rendered the stereotype of the brave soldier useless, as survival in the trenches depended more on random luck than skill. Outwardly Jake, Brett, and the others appear to enjoy a carefree existence of fishing, road trips, and bed hopping, but inwardly they despair and long for a life of greater meaning. If only they knew how much their tale would alter the course of fiction in the 20th century and beyond.

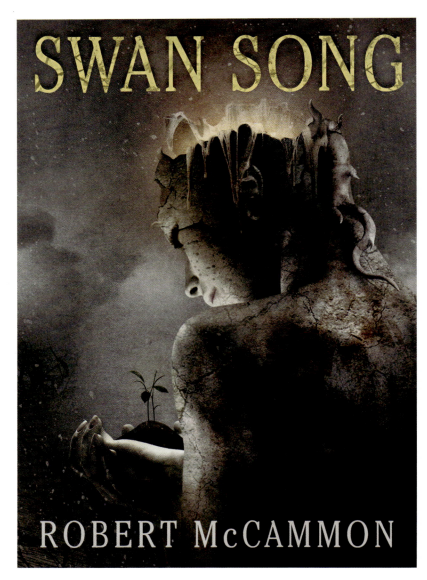

"I guess you could say my stories are about
what characters do when faced with the
crisis of their life—The Wall—faced with it,
they can either go up, or down..."

CLOCKWISE FROM LEFT: A 2017 hardcover of *Swan Song* from Subterranean Press.
The book was first published in 1987. | Author Robert R. McCammon lives and writes
in Birmingham, Alabama. | The author page in the first printing of *Swan Song*.

87

SWAN SONG

Robert R. McCammon · 1987

Consider the title *Swan Song*. The phrase, as it's commonly used, implies a bittersweet last effort, an encore or final act, already tinted with nostalgia. In the 1987 horror novel by Robert R. McCammon, the phrase takes on an entirely different meaning, seeing as how it describes the few who remain after a nuclear war has decimated humankind.

But, as readers discover, Swan is also the nickname of nine-year-old Sue Wanda Prescott, a girl with special powers of rejuvenation. Swan meets Josh, a wrestler on his way to a match, who protects her. She learns of a prophecy in which she's fated to meet the devil. Meanwhile, in a destroyed New York, Sister Creep finds a glass ring encrusted with jewels, which has magical properties, and encounters "the man with the scarlet eye," one of the book's primary villains. Another is Vietnam vet Colonel James "Jimbo" Macklin, who has amassed an "Army of Excellence," with the intention of killing disfigured survivors and getting revenge on the Russians who launched the nuclear weapons.

When readers speak about great horror writers of the late 20th century, the names Dean Koontz, Stephen King, and Robert R. McCammon roll out in one breath. Given its postapocalyptic setting, lengthy cast of characters, and their quest to start anew, *Swan Song* covers much of the same territory as King's novel *The Stand* (1978), which also focuses on the collapse of society and its aftermath. McCammon's book, however, is edgier, almost hallucinatory at times, and much more interested in how individual actions bring about calamity and chaos. After a furious period of writing horror from the late 1970s through the early 1990s, McCammon turned to historical fiction, creating a series of books that feature detective Matthew Corbett, an 18th-century "professional problem solver" in New York. He also writes stand-alone books set in the present day.

McCammon continues to live in Birmingham, Alabama, where he was born in 1952 and grew up. His books often take the Deep South as their setting, and McCammon, deeply influenced by the civil rights movement, often takes race as a theme. He has spoken about witnessing fear and violence during crucial moments in the struggle for racial equality; even more importantly, the politics of his childhood helped give him the sense that society could be altered, for the better or for the worse. He was influenced as well by a supposedly haunted house next door to his childhood home, with some of his earliest ghost stories imagining what went on inside.

Much of *Swan Song* describes the vicious encounters between survivors as they struggle to meet their basic needs. Like the *Walking Dead* television series or Cormac McCarthy's *The Road* (2006), *Swan Song* highlights the fragility of the norms that hold civilization back from anarchy. As portrayed in these and similar dystopian works, without the benefit of society, many people would quickly and maybe eagerly transform into violent predators, with no compunction about terrorizing others. Holding on to one's humanity might prove even more difficult than navigating the physical hardships of a ruined land.

With the release of previously classified documents in recent years, we have been able to see just how close the United States and the Soviet Union came to mutual destruction in the 1980s. From our vantage point in a post-Communist world, fighting a much different enemy as part of the war on terror, it can be difficult to recall the precipitous power balance of the Cold War. *Swan Song* serves as a reminder of the past and a warning about the future. After all, weapons continue to get more devastating, and more widespread. If we're not careful, this could be us.

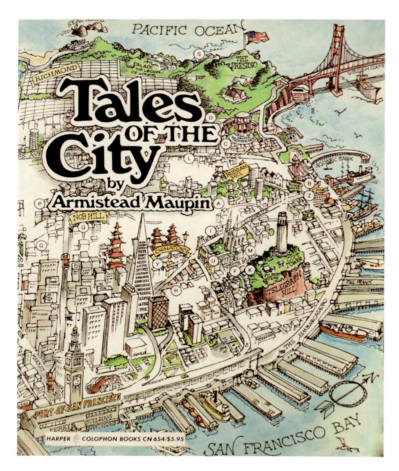

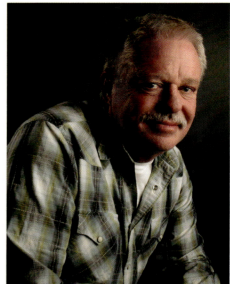

88

TALES OF THE CITY SERIES

Armistead Maupin · 1978–2014

Books can give us permission to be who we truly are. As we read about others who represent furtive parts of ourselves, we begin to understand the possibilities for our lives and to consider a way forward. If we're lucky, this process occurs when we're children, enabling us to reach adulthood with an identity rooted in comfort and confidence. But even if we discover books like those in the Tales of the City series—with its glorious celebration of diversity—late in life, they still have much to teach about walking one's particular path with pride.

Armistead Maupin created Tales of the City as a serial for Bay Area newspapers in 1974. The first book appeared in 1978 and immediately altered the landscape of LGBTQ literature. Midwesterner Mary Ann Singleton impulsively decides, while vacationing in San Francisco, to start a new life there. She moves into the fictional Barbary Lane, where she gets to know her colorful neighbors, like Mouse and Mona. Their free-spiritedness and confident sexuality expand Mary Ann's horizons. She shrugs off her naïveté and embraces urbanity, in all its messiness and splendor.

Over nine books, Maupin traces the lives of a multitude of gay and straight characters as they fall in love, have sex, uncover secrets, build friendships, and create families in the 1970s and beyond. He does an excellent job of normalizing difference. Praising the series' exuberance, the *New York Times* once likened the experience of reading the interconnected books to "dipping into an inexhaustible bag of M&Ms, with no risk of sugar overload." The series is chock-full of period-specific details, giving the prose a newsy immediacy and serving, now that some time has passed, as a firsthand record of the decades in which queer culture entered the American mainstream. It became the basis for an acclaimed series on PBS in 1993.

Born Armistead Jones Maupin, Jr., in 1944 in Washington, DC, Maupin studied journalism at the University of North Carolina, where he led the charge to establish a memorial to Thomas Wolfe, and served in the Vietnam War. He moved to San Francisco to work for the Associated Press bureau there. Maupin came out as gay around the time he began writing his Tales. His novels celebrate the freedom that comes with being happy in one's skin. They also have autobiographical elements. *Further Tales of the City* (1982), describes, in veiled terms, Maupin's affair with Rock Hudson. *Babycakes* (1984), the fourth novel in the series, addresses the AIDS crisis, one of the first works of fiction to do so directly. Maupin has always sought to be as honest as possible in the series, confronting difficult or potentially inflammatory issues with candor and humor.

With *Sure of You* (1989), Maupin attempted to end the series. That sixth novel covers the 1980s, a much different time politically and socially than the 1970s, when Mary Ann arrived: she's preparing to decamp for New York, while Barbary Lane's landlady, Anna, thinks she might sell the property and settle permanently in Greece. However, there were other books to come. With the ninth book, *The Days of Anna Madrigal* (2014), Maupin concluded the series once again. Now in her 90s, Anna Madrigal, the transgender landlady of Barbary Lane, looks back on her long life and many tenants. Perhaps Maupin ended Tales because he wants to focus on other work, or perhaps he wants to let the forthcoming Netflix series stand on its own. Or maybe he plans to surprise readers with still another book, another take on the city he loves and the people who make it marvelous. We can only hope.

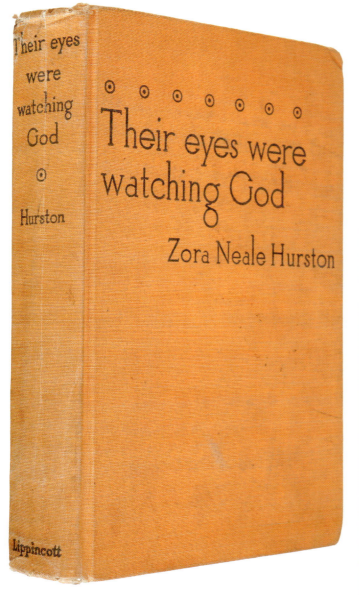

89

THEIR EYES WERE WATCHING GOD

Zora Neale Hurston · 1937

Writers die two deaths: they pass away, as everyone does. But they die a second time when their work stops being read. Author Alice Walker gave Zora Neale Hurston a new life, some fifteen years after Hurston died in poverty and obscurity in 1960. Today, Hurston is a touchstone, having influenced new generations of writers, and her posthumous honors include conferences and awards in her name. Her voice continues to be heard; her words continue to exist.

The fifth of eight children, Hurston was born to a preacher and his schoolteacher wife in 1891 in Alabama. A few years later, the family moved to Eatonville, Florida, one of the first all-black towns in the United States. Her father eventually became mayor. After concentrating on writing at Howard University, Hurston landed in New York, where she was a part of the Harlem Renaissance, befriending writers such as Langston Hughes and Countee Cullen. Along with founding a magazine and writing plays that landed on Broadway, she began studying with Franz Boas, sometimes called "the Father of American Anthropology." While in Haiti to research its folk culture and voodoo, she wrote *Their Eyes Were Watching God* (1937).

Charismatic Janie Crawford returns to Eatonville in the early 20th century. While the town's women gossip and its men gawk, Pheoby Watson welcomes her friend and learns of Janie's life since leaving for Jacksonville with her much-younger paramour, Tea Cake. The novel then switches to flashback. Raised by her grandmother, a former slave named Nanny, Janie was forced to marry Logan, who treats her poorly. She leaves, then marries the scheming Jody, who takes her to Eatonville. He becomes a wealthy landowner and mayor. Ambitious, he treats Janie as if he owns her. Upon Jody's death, she meets the flirtatious Tea Cake, with whom she falls in love; they marry and move to the Everglades. Tea Cake, infected with rabies after a dog bite, goes insane, and Janie is forced to make an awful choice.

Their Eyes Were Watching God puts gender front and center. Janie's interaction with men drives the novel's plot, from her first kiss and sexual awakening as a young girl, which propels Nanny to marry her off to Logan, to her final act of mercy with Tea Cake and subsequent trial with an all-male, all-white jury. Janie refuses to settle in the way Nanny—whose rape produced Janie's mother—wants her to. She holds out for genuine love but doesn't find it until she meets Tea Cake, when she's in her forties. Both Logan and Jody wish Janie would fulfill a stereotypical role of wife, subjugating her desires to those of her husbands'. Even Tea Cake, who gives Janie some leeway to develop her own identity, still whips her.

Drawing on her academic training as an anthropologist, Hurston wrote in the vernacular forms of speech she grew up hearing; this approach helps give her characters distinct identities. She mixes those voices with a more traditional, dispassionate narrative one. While Jody literally attempts to prevent Janie from speaking, it is Janie's voice we hear telling the story of her hardships and ultimate empowerment.

Hurston's own story has become the stuff of literary legend. In the 1940s and 1950s, she had such trouble getting her writing published that she began working as a maid. The 1960s witnessed a great shift in literary trends, elevating works that had a distinct political slant, so Hurston's output fell further into obscurity. In 1973, Alice Walker discovered Hurston's grave in Florida, with her name spelled incorrectly. She paid for a new headstone, including the epitaph "A Genius of the South," and wrote an essay for *Ms.* magazine about the experience as well as the significance of Hurston's legacy. Walker's "In Search of Zora Neale Hurston" rebooted Hurston's career, and *Their Eyes Were Watching God* breathes on.

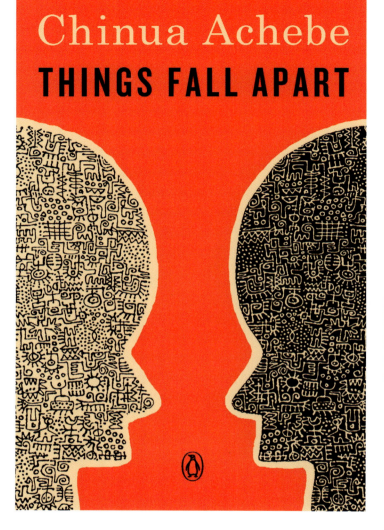

90

THINGS FALL APART

Chinua Achebe · 1958

Things fall apart," writes William Butler Yeats in his 1919 poem "The Second Coming." The verse continues, "[T]he centre cannot hold; / Mere anarchy is loosed upon the world, / The blood-dimmed tide is loosed, and everywhere / The ceremony of innocence is drowned." With its forceful imagery of chaos and destruction, the poem makes a fitting source of inspiration for *Things Fall Apart* (1958), a powerfully influential novel about the effects of colonialism in Africa, and perhaps the continent's most important literary work of the 20th century.

As *Things Fall Apart* begins, Okonkwo lives in an 1890s-era Nigerian village, where he earns respect and renown as a wrestler, then prospers as a farmer. He embodies many masculine ideals, in contrast to his eldest son, Nwoye, who strikes Okonkwo as shiftless. Ikemefuna, a prisoner from a neighboring village, lives with Okonkwo and grows close to the family, but Okonkwo doesn't hesitate to slay him when the time comes to carry out Ikemefuna's death sentence. After accidentally killing someone else, Okonkwo and his family are forced to move to the village of Mbanta. Here, missionaries are spreading religion, colonizers are imposing a different government, and the community is starting to pull apart.

The novel dramatizes several conflicts. Okonkwo represents indigenous beliefs and rituals, and much of the book concerns the manner in which Okonkwo fulfills or breaks accepted societal norms. He largely subscribes to the rules of his clan, even if that means violence and exile. Nwoye, in contrast, feels troubled by some of these behaviors, such as the society's sanctioned murder of infants, and he abandons the faith of his ancestors to join the Christians. The gentle missionary Mr. Brown builds a school and a hospital, helping to usher in modernity, but his replacement, Reverend Smith, encourages divisiveness and foments trouble within the clan. Things cannot stay the same, given the external pressures coming to bear on the indigenous culture, but they cannot change in exactly the way the hubristic foreigners wish them to, either.

Albert Chinụalụmọgụ Achebe was born in 1930 in Ogidi, a town in southeastern Nigeria, where he was exposed to Igbo oral traditions as well as his parents' Protestant faith. Over the course of his career, he wrote four other novels, one memoir, and various books for children, and in 2007 he won a Man Booker Prize for lifetime achievement. In 1975, Achebe published an impassioned analysis of *Heart of Darkness* (1899), in which he called Joseph Conrad a "bloody racist," fundamentally altering the reception of that work. Achebe taught at various universities in the United States, and died in 2013. In a plot straight out of fiction, Nigerian American novelist Chimamanda Ngozi Adichie was raised in a house once inhabited by Achebe on the University of Nigeria's campus. She, like many other writers in Africa and the African diaspora, considers Achebe to be an enormous source of inspiration.

Somewhat controversially, Achebe opted to write *Things Fall Apart*, his debut novel, in English rather than Igbo, in part because it was the colonizer's language. Making one's message heard means speaking, or writing, so that your audience can understand you. But he incorporated many Igbo words into his text, a nod to the depth and richness of Igbo storytelling and language, as well as his story's geographic setting and characters' heritage. At the same time, the spread of English throughout Nigeria gave Nigerians a shared language across clans and cultures, so Achebe's use of English enabled the colonized to read the work as well, thereby expanding the novel's readership. And read it has been, widely taught and greatly admired throughout the world.

Monday Morning
25th Oct: 1852.

My Dear Hawthorne —

If you thought
it worth while to write the story of Agatha,
and should you be engaged upon it; then
I have a little idea touching it, which
however trifling, may not be entirely out
of place. Perhaps, tho', the idea has
occurred to yourself. — The probable
facility with which Robinson first leaves
his wife & then takes another, may, possibly,
be ascribed to the peculiarly latitudinarian
notions, which most sailors have of all
tender obligations of that sort. In his previous
sailor life Robinson had found a wife (for
a night) in every port. The sense of the
obligation of the marriage-vow to Agatha
had little weight with him at first. It
was only when some years of life ashore

Mothers, Lovers, and BFFs

RELATIONSHIPS AMONG WRITERS

IN CONTRAST TO THE MYTH of the lonely artist toiling away in a bare garret, writers are just as social as the rest of the human race. They need friends, lovers, parents, siblings, and neighbors, both for companionship and to serve as sounding boards and spurs to greater accomplishments than could be achieved alone. Here are just a few of the many relationships writers have relied on.

THE FAMILY THAT COMPOSES TOGETHER

Being a part of a literary family no doubt gives some writers a head start when it comes to creative endeavors. As children, the Brontës—sisters Charlotte, Emily, and Anne, and brother Branwell—created fictional worlds, which they wrote about in their self-published literary magazines. Later, as adults, the three women jointly published a book of poetry, *Poems by Currer, Ellis, and Acton Bell* (1846), and Charlotte and Emily separately published the canonical novels *Jane Eyre* (1847) and *Wuthering Heights* (1847).

Prizewinning poet and novelist Nick Laird sometimes claims he set Zadie Smith on her path to stardom when he accepted her short story for inclusion in an anthology he was working on while both were students at Cambridge University. Nowadays the pair is married with children. Stephen King also married a fellow writer he met while an undergraduate, and has joked that he fell for her in large part because she owned a typewriter. Of their three children, two have followed in their parents' footsteps and published novels. In addition, for about 20 years King periodically played in a band called the Rock Bottom Remainders with other writers, including Dave Barry and Amy Tan.

WITH FRIENDS LIKE THESE

Ernest Hemingway drew on the experiences, ennui, and anomie of his expat friends, a group Gertrude Stein dubbed "the lost generation," to write *The Sun Also Rises* (1926), with F. Scott Fitzgerald offering suggestions and edits. After a while, their friendship went south, culminating in a likely fictionalized scene in the memoir *A Moveable Feast* (1964), in which Hemingway tries to reassure his former friend and mentor about his genitals by telling him to compare them to statues at the Louvre. Let's hope the relationship stays better between pals George R. R. Martin and Diana Gabaldon, who share the unusual experience of writing an ongoing series of novels even as their imaginative universes get tweaked and altered for the popular television shows *Game of Thrones* and *Outlander*.

Dandy Truman Capote became best friends with tomboyish Harper Lee when they lived next door to one another as young children in the small town of Monroeville, Alabama. As Capote would remark during an interview some years later, the two of them often felt like "apart people." Lee allegedly based the character of Dill, Scout's best friend in *To Kill a Mockingbird* (1960), on Capote. She traveled with him to do research for his true-crime masterpiece *In Cold Blood* (1966), a contribution he recognized via that book's acknowledgments. Nevertheless, she felt her assistance merited more gratitude, and their friendship suffered

LITERARY FAST FRIENDS: Harper Lee and Truman Capote, photographed in New York City in 1976; the Inklings were an informal writing group that met for 16 years at Oxford University, and had such esteemed members as C. S. Lewis and J. R. R. Tolkien.

from jealousy and competitiveness. Childhood friends Kathryn Stockett and Tate Taylor, meanwhile, have managed to maintain their closeness into maturity. They met in nursery school in Jackson, Mississippi, and when they grew up Taylor directed the film version of his chum's megasuccessful book *The Help* (2009).

American literary titans Herman Melville and Nathaniel Hawthorne didn't meet until adulthood, but they did so in suitably dramatic fashion, on a mountain during a thunderstorm—they were coincidentally living just a few miles apart from one another in western Massachusetts in 1850 and joined a hike and picnic organized by mutual acquaintances. Their bond grew so rapidly that Melville dedicated *Moby-Dick* to Hawthorne the next year. Later in the 19th century, another set of icons became neighbors when Mark Twain settled in Hartford, Connecticut, right next door to Harriet Beecher Stowe, whose antislavery novel *Uncle Tom's Cabin* (1852) had made her one of the most famous writers of the period. The two would often visit one another across their adjoining lawns, and it was here that Twain wrote *The Adventures of Tom Sawyer* (1876) and *Adventures of Huckleberry Finn* (1884). *Little Women* (1868–1869) author Louisa May Alcott not only also had a famous writer as a close neighbor—Ralph Waldo Emerson, whose library she regularly raided when growing up—but her schoolteacher was Henry David Thoreau, who by then had moved back into town from Walden Pond, the site made famous by his *Walden: or, Life in the Woods* (1854).

AT SCHOOL AND AT WORK

Schools have brought together numerous writers. C. S. Lewis and J. R. R. Tolkien were introduced at a faculty meeting at Oxford, and although Lewis noted in his diary that day that Tolkien "needs a smack or so," the two grew to be friends as well as collaborators in the effort to get fantasy literature taken seriously. As a young girl, Chimamanda Ngozi Adichie moved into a house on the University of Nigeria's campus recently vacated by Chinua Achebe, and she has emphasized the importance of the elder Nigerian writer on her development. Bret Easton Ellis and Donna Tartt had an even more direct university connection, as they were two of only three students in a writing seminar at Bennington College in the early 1980s, where they each began the debut novels that would make them famous: *Less Than Zero* (1985) and *The Secret History* (1992), respectively. Kurt Vonnegut and John Irving likewise shared a classroom, with the former teaching the latter at the Iowa Writers' Workshop in the 1960s. When Vonnegut died in 2007, Irving reminisced, "The only criticism he ever made of my writing was making fun of my fondness for semicolons, which Kurt never liked very much. He called semicolons 'transvestite hermaphrodites.'" Vonnegut helped Irving see how a writer might be "both funny and kind," even while describing humanity's worst impulses.

Then-editor Toni Morrison met James Baldwin when she tried to sign him to a book deal. That didn't work out, but the two became friends, and on Baldwin's death, Morrison wrote a reminiscence that eloquently captures the power of close relationships among writers: "I discover that in your company it is myself I know. . . . You gave me a language to dwell in, a gift so perfect it seems my own invention. I have been thinking your spoken and written thoughts for so long I believed they were mine."

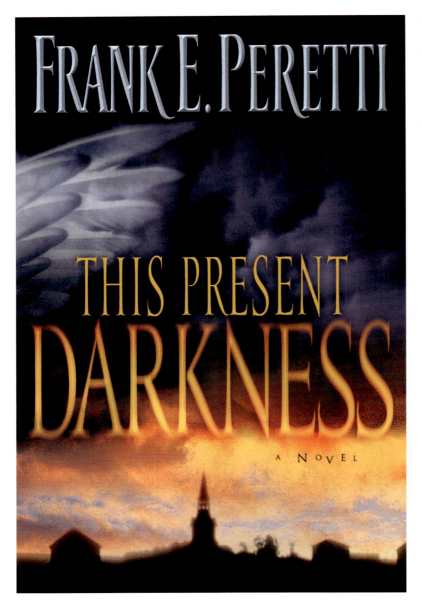

91

THIS PRESENT DARKNESS

Frank E. Peretti · 1986

Many of the first printed texts were religious works. Fiction—with its emphasis on storyline, character development, and description—became a natural medium for exploring religious themes, with early novels like *The Pilgrim's Progress* (1678) giving readers a great dose of story with a healthy dollop of message. Frank E. Peretti continues the tradition of marrying spiritual belief with literary techniques in *This Present Darkness* (1986), his first novel for adults.

This Present Darkness exposes the intrigue and evil at play in the small town of Ashton. Editor in chief Marshall Hogan gets curious when one of his star reporters is arrested on trumped-up charges. The town police chief dodges Marshall's inquiries, further piquing Marshall's nosiness and eventually leading to his arrest. Born-again pastor Hank Busche also begins to notice strange doings among his congregation. When Hank's investigation goes too deep, he is falsely imprisoned on rape charges. He meets Marshall in jail, and the two share their experiences and join forces against the New Age threat trying to capture the souls of the town. While Marshall and Hank develop and execute their plan, the story moves more deeply into the supernatural, and we are introduced to angels and demons who are constantly battling for humanity. Even though we have a good sense of which side will win, the novel nevertheless reads like a traditional thriller.

Peretti takes his title and his epigraph from the New Testament's Epistle to the Ephesians: "For we do not wrestle against flesh and blood, but against the rulers, against the authorities, against the cosmic powers over this present darkness, against the spiritual forces of evil in the heavenly places." To believers, the immutability of these words sweep over Peretti's novel and into the present day. The novel bolsters those who might otherwise feel beaten down by a lack of faith or confrontations with nonbelievers—one of the many reasons it's one of the bestselling works of Christian fiction of all time. A sequel, *Piercing the Darkness*, came out in 1989.

When Peretti is credited with reinventing Christian fiction, as he often is, people point to this book as Exhibit One. *This Present Darkness* is a page-turner. It offers plenty of descriptive passages of evil, exorcisms, and wretches. Demons are deformed and horrible, angels graceful and gorgeous. The stakes feel significant as humans fight on Earth and the celestial creatures simultaneously do combat in their dominion. The book's main characters go from ordinary to extraordinary, forced by circumstances to fight a terrible fight. The novel turns the comforting platitude that the antidote to darkness is prayer into a tale of supernatural heroism.

Childhood hardship helped shape Peretti's worldview. In the memoir *The Wounded Spirit* (2000), he writes movingly of growing up with a deformity as the result of a sickness in infancy. His experiences with tormentors not only prompted a crusade to stamp out bullying, but it also helped fuel a lifelong interest in monsters. Peretti was born in Canada in 1951, then moved to the United States. His novels, including several books for kids, have sold 12 million copies.

Peretti points to a conversation he believes he had with God as a major motivation for his writing: "The Lord said, 'Frank, I want you to be a builder. I want you to build the body of Christ. Build them up, give them what they need to live their lives. Give them what they need to face these other things that they're confronting.'" For its fans, *This Present Darkness* more than fulfills this mission.

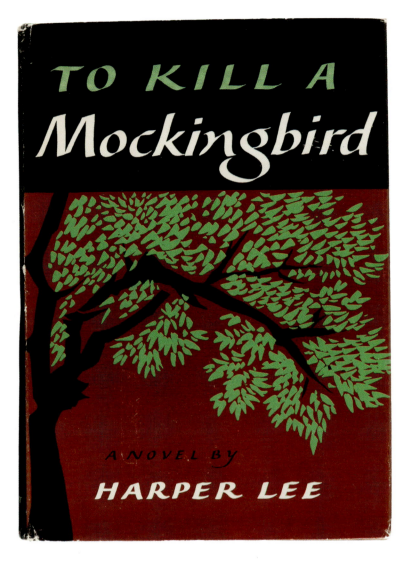

92

TO KILL A MOCKINGBIRD

Harper Lee · 1960

Harper Lee's *To Kill a Mockingbird* (1960) may be America's best-loved book, and Atticus Finch may be America's best-loved fictional hero. Although the novel tells hard truths about American society, Atticus offers an antidote to despair. If we were all a little more like him, the world would be a much better place.

Five-year-old Jean Louise "Scout" Finch and her brother, Jem, live with their father, Atticus, a widower and small-town lawyer in fictional Maycomb County, Alabama, during the Great Depression. Scout and Jem befriend a neighborhood newcomer named Dill, and the three become obsessed with the creepy house on the corner and its agoraphobic inhabitant, Boo Radley. Atticus, meanwhile, has agreed to defend a black man accused of raping a white woman, risking ostracism and even violent retribution from many of his fellow citizens.

To Kill a Mockingbird won the Pulitzer Prize in 1961 and has sold 40 million copies. The novel's film adaptation came out in 1962 to immediate success. Gregory Peck won an Academy Award for his masterful portrayal of Atticus, and Lee grew so close to the actor and his family that a child was eventually named after her. Peck's Atticus was named the #1 movie hero of all time by the American Film Institute in 2003.

Lee stayed out of the spotlight even as her novel grew in fame and popularity. She continued to live in her birthplace of Monroeville, Alabama, with her sister. Shortly before Lee's death in 2016 at age 89, she published *Go Set a Watchman* (2015). Considered a sequel of sorts to *To Kill a Mockingbird*, the novel was actually written first and finished in 1957. It focuses on some of the same characters and concerns. Her editor, however, persuaded Lee to concentrate on the original draft's flashbacks concerning a young Scout. For Christmas, Lee's friends gave her a year's worth of wages,

which allowed her to quit her job taking reservations for an airline and focus on writing full-time. *To Kill a Mockingbird* was the result, a book that has given so much to so many. In a 2006 poll, British librarians named the novel the #1 book everyone should read, ahead of the Bible.

Born Nelle Harper Lee in 1926, Lee initially seemed destined for a career in the law. Her father, a model for Atticus, practiced, as did a sister. But after a summer spent studying at Oxford, Lee quit law school and moved to New York to begin writing in earnest. She drew on her youth as inspiration in other ways as well: Dill is based on her childhood best friend, Truman Capote, with whom she stayed close into adulthood, even helping to research his masterpiece of true crime, *In Cold Blood* (1966). Lee may also have had in mind the fates of the Scottsboro Boys, nine African American teens who were falsely accused of raping two white women and harshly sentenced by all-white juries, despite exculpating evidence, in the 1930s.

As a bildungsroman, the novel centers on Scout's loss of innocence. She witnesses hatred, racism, and intolerance; she learns the importance of decency and probity, characteristics which sometimes require immense courage to display. In short, she starts to grow up. But the novel also addresses racial injustice and inequality, pointing out lessons society still needs to learn. Segregation, whether in law or just in fact, existed in many parts of the United States when the novel came out; the Greensboro Woolworth sit-in to protest segregation was ongoing the summer that Lee's novel was published. In subsequent years, critics have pointed to Lee's flat descriptions of black characters as evidence of the insidiousness of racial prejudice. Nevertheless, the book offers an appealing kind of moral code, a belief that doing right, no matter how hard or dangerous, is always worth it.

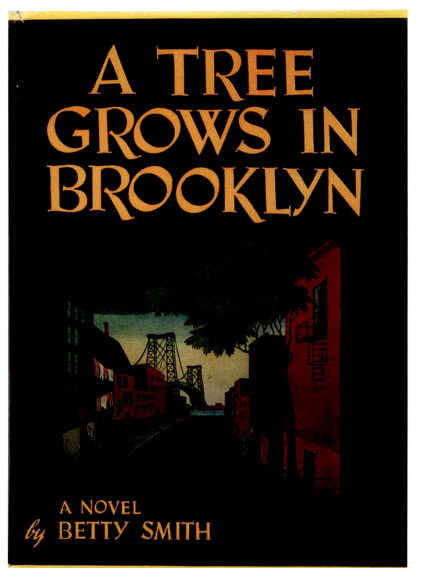

CLOCKWISE FROM LEFT: Cover art for *A Tree Grows in Brooklyn*, published in 1943. | Betty Smith, shortly after her debut novel was published. Smith grew up in Brooklyn, before moving to Michigan with her first husband. She attended classes while he went to law school. | A crowd of young women gather around to read *A Tree Grows in Brooklyn*, circa 1940.

93

A TREE GROWS IN BROOKLYN

Betty Smith · 1943

Lovers of Betty Smith's *A Tree Grows in Brooklyn* (1943) might not recognize the Williamsburg of today, replete as it is with high-rises, hipsters, and gourmet coffee shops. The vast changes to this neighborhood, and to New York City as a whole, make the coming-of-age classic all the more treasured, as it preserves a vanished past. Smith's novel informs our perceptions about urban life in early 20th-century America. While it depicts a bygone era, its themes of the loss of innocence, the rewards of hard work, and the importance of tenacity are timeless.

The novel is divided into five books, each of which covers a different period in the life of key characters. Book 1 opens in 1912. Francie Nolan, the 11-year-old daughter of Irish and Austrian immigrants, reads widely and deeply in order to escape her impoverished home life. She has a younger brother known as Neeley. Book 2 traces the meeting and marriage of Johnny and Katie, Francie's parents, in 1900. Johnny dies from alcohol-related disease in Book 3, but the industrious Katie manages to keep the family afloat, even as she gives birth to her third child. She also kills a pedophile who attacks Francie shortly before the girl's 14th birthday.

Too poor to send both children to high school, Katie pays for her favorite, Neeley, to attend; Francie gets a job in a factory. In Book 4 she meets various people who encourage her educational pursuits, including a young man with whom she may eventually develop a romantic relationship. In the final book, Katie prepares to marry a rich politician, a wonderful change in circumstance that enables her to leave the tenement forever. Now almost 17, Francie says goodbye as well, as she makes plans to enter the University of Michigan.

Like her protagonist, Smith grew up in Brooklyn, where she was born Elisabeth Wehner in 1896, the daughter of first-generation German Americans. After raising her daughters, she enrolled at the University of Michigan despite not having a high-school diploma, while her first husband attended law school there. Around this time she began writing plays; she won the Avery Hopwood Award in playwriting as an undergrad, went on to study drama at Yale, and earned many other dramatist awards, including Rockefeller and Dramatists Guild Fellowships. Although she published more novels before her death in 1972, none displays the staying power of *A Tree Grows in Brooklyn*. Its critical and commercial success enabled her to write for the *New York Times*, among other publications, and she proudly embraced her lifelong status as a champion of Brooklyn, even as she made her home in North Carolina.

First-time director Elia Kazan made the movie version in 1945, further cementing the story's image of Brooklyn in the public eye. His Academy Award–nominated film was followed by a musical adaptation in 1951.

From her tenement window, Francie observes a so-called tree of heaven growing in the air shaft. It rises out of the cement, and despite a lack of water and sunlight, it thrives. Not even a fire can destroy it; not even an ax can kill it. The people of Francie's neighborhood suffer crushing poverty, working menial jobs and barely staying afloat, but they too persist. In some cases, as with Francie, they do more than simply get by—they blossom. Francie's Brooklyn has died out, but the city continues to maintain its trees of heaven. Imported from China in the 1780s, Frederick Law Olmsted planted the hardy *Ailanthus altissima* throughout Central Park in the 1850s, and its seeds spread throughout the five boroughs and beyond. Similarly, immigrants continue to represent a significant portion of New York's population, putting down roots and dreaming their version of the American dream.

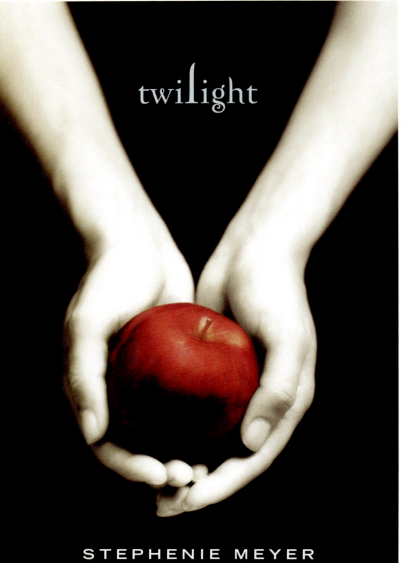

twilight

STEPHENIE MEYER
THE INTERNATIONAL BESTSELLER

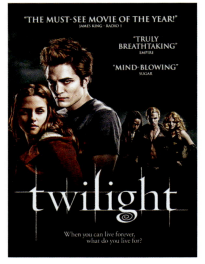

"THE MUST-SEE MOVIE OF THE YEAR!"
JAMES KING · RADIO 1

"TRULY
BREATHTAKING"
EMPIRE

"MIND-BLOWING"
SUGAR

twilight

When you can live forever,
what do you live for?

CLOCKWISE FROM LEFT: *Twilight* (2005), the first book in the Twilight saga. | Author Stephenie Meyer's strong religious beliefs are woven into the fantasy love triangle between Bella, Edward, and Jacob. | *Twilight* the movie was released in 2008, and made mega stars of actors Kristen Stewart (playing Bella) and Robert Pattinson (playing Edward Cullen).

94

TWILIGHT SERIES

Stephenie Meyer · 2005–2008

Over the course of the Twilight series, Bella Swan transforms from an inexperienced girl to a powerful woman capable of making choices that will fundamentally alter the trajectory of her life. The four novels have sold 120 million copies and have been translated into more than 35 languages. Readers far beyond the initially intended young-adult audience have been hypnotized by Stephenie Meyer's paranormal romances.

As *Twilight* (2005) begins, 17-year-old Bella moves from sunny Arizona to Forks, a rainy town in Washington State. She meets and falls in love with Edward Cullen, a 104-year-old vampire who attends her high school, can read people's minds, and saves Bella's life on multiple occasions. After uncovering Edward's secret, Bella wants to become a vampire to ensure that she and Edward can stay together forever. But Edward's deep distaste for his own immortality complicates their relationship.

New Moon (2006) seeks to answer the question *What if your true love abandons you?* Edward has left Forks in an effort to protect Bella. She's heartbroken. Believing her to have committed suicide, Edward instigates a conflict with the Volturi, a sort of vampire royalty who police other vampires. In *Eclipse* (2007), Bella struggles with her complex feelings for both Edward and Jacob, a werewolf, even as the trio prepares to fight an army of newly formed vampires that's been terrorizing Seattle. The last book in the series from Bella's point of view is *Breaking Dawn* (2008). Newly married to Edward, Bella discovers she's pregnant with a half-human, half-vampire child. During her life-threatening labor, Edward transforms her into a vampire. In her new state, she's capable of contending with the Volturi, which forces a truce between the factions.

The idea for *Twilight* came to Meyer in a dream. Within a few months she'd written a first draft for fun, with no intention of seeking publication. However, her sister convinced Meyer to send the novel to agents, where it was discovered in the slush pile. Born in Hartford in 1973, Meyer graduated from Brigham Young University with a degree in English, and married her childhood sweetheart at age 20. They have three sons.

A member of the Church of Jesus Christ of Latter-day Saints, Meyer holds religious views that inform many of her novels' main themes and interactions. In fact, some readers see the books as an allegory about the founding of Mormonism. Her characters struggle to overcome temptation; for example, Edward desires Bella's blood, but at the same time he wants to maintain her purity. Bella is inextricably drawn to Edward even though he commits some atrocious acts, an embodiment of the fate-versus-free-will debate.

Meyer has continued to revisit the Twilight world after the completion of the series in 2008. She published a novella about the life of a new vampire, *The Short Second Life of Bree Tanner* (2010), as well as a 10th-anniversary "dual edition" of *Twilight* that included *Life and Death* (2015), a retelling of the first novel that switches the genders of the protagonists. She has also published books for adults, including *The Host* (2008).

The first Twilight movie came out in 2008, followed by another four based on the books. All were hits at the box office. Meyer served as an executive producer on later films, leading her to form her own film-production company. The books also inspired another blockbuster book series: *Fifty Shades of Grey* (2011) by E. L. James, which began as Twilight fan fiction.

While the Twilight novels have been criticized on both literary and political grounds, Meyer imaginatively dramatizes the intensity of emotion so characteristic of late adolescence, a time when first love feels like the greatest love and the stakes of every decision seem unbearably large.

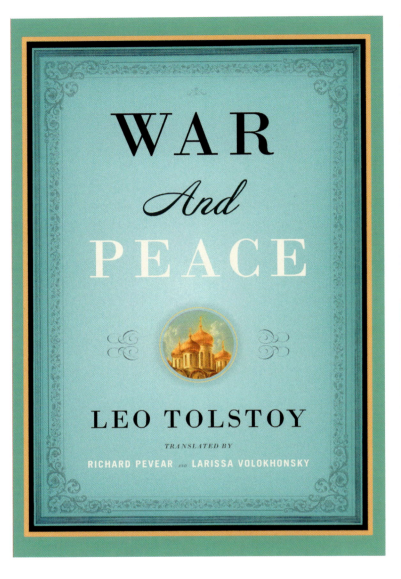

WAR AND PEACE

A HISTORICAL NOVEL

BY
COUNT LÉON TOLSTOÏ

TRANSLATED INTO FRENCH
BY A RUSSIAN LADY

AND

FROM THE FRENCH BY CLARA BELL

BEFORE TILSIT
1805—1807
TWO VOLUMES—VOL. I.

REVISED AND CORRECTED IN THE UNITED STATES

NEW YORK
WILLIAM S. GOTTSBERGER, PUBLISHER
11 MURRAY STREET
1887

CLOCKWISE FROM TOP: A 2007 hardcover edition of *War and Peace*, published by Knopf. | The title page of the first US edition. In one poll of writers, *War and Peace* ranked third among all books written. | Leo Tolstoy, pictured circa 1910, wrote early works of fiction. After a spiritual awakening at age 50, he focused on nonfiction. | The title page of an 1887 edition of the book, "translated into French by a Russian Lady."

95

WAR AND PEACE

Leo Tolstoy · 1869

Few novels are as massive in scope and spirit as the Russian classic *War and Peace* (1869). As the abstraction of the title suggests, the book is not merely about a particular war and particular peace, but about war and peace as states of life and forces in the progression of history. It's also about the revelatory power of true love, the confrontation between grand ambition and harsh reality, and the desperate search for significance. There are epic battle scenes, happy marriages, joyful births, tragic deaths, and lengthy historical and philosophical discussions. Leo Tolstoy's masterpiece stands as a major accomplishment in the history of literature.

The novel opens at a fancy ball, a beginning Tolstoy rewrote 15 times to ensure the perfect *mise-en-scène*. Here, readers meet some of the novel's primary aristocratic characters, including the lovely and charming Natasha Rostova; the chunky, affable Pierre Bezukhov, illegitimate son of a count; and Andrei Bolkonsky, a practical, rational, and patriotic aristocrat. It's 1805, and residents of Saint Petersburg are just beginning to hear about Napoleon's conquering of the west. By the time the novel ends, seven years later, the Russians have defeated the French in a rout that turns the tide of the Napoleonic Wars—and readers have encountered almost 600 characters in all, some wholly fictional, some actual figures from history. *War and Peace* works like a camera swooping into a close-up on a small moment, then pulling back to reveal a broad swath of action.

On the surface, *War and Peace* is a novel about the French invasion of Russia and its effect on the aristocracy. Going a little deeper, the novel explores how to make one's life meaningful. History, after all, is the story of those who make it as well as those who live through it. For example,

as Andrei lies wounded at the Battle of Austerlitz, a momentous and crucial confrontation, he stares into the sky and grasps that he possesses the ability to help himself be happy, a small victory for an individual amid the carnage.

In 1828, Count Leo Nikolayevich Tolstoy was born into a storied, landowning Russian family. Many of his early works focus on a wealthy youth's political awakening with regard to serfdom. After *Anna Karenina* (1877), he shifted into nonfiction, largely as a result of a spiritual awakening he experienced at age 50. Tolstoy developed his own radical Christian belief system and became increasingly anarchist, arguing that to live in a truly Christian society would necessitate an overthrow of the government. His theories concerning nonviolence influenced later leaders like Mahatma Gandhi, Martin Luther King Jr., and Nelson Mandela. In 1910, at age 82, Tolstoy left his family and prosperity behind to embark on a pilgrimage; he died a few weeks later at a train station.

A *Time* poll of 125 writers picked *War and Peace* as the third-best book of any type ever written; Tolstoy also took the top spot, with *Anna Karenina*. It's no surprise that a work this rich has been adapted for the stage and screen on multiple occasions. Audrey Hepburn and Henry Fonda starred in a 1956 film. In 1966 and 1967, a Russian version was released in an effort to foster patriotism; it took the same length of time to make the movie as it did for Tolstoy to write the novel—six years. A 15-hour miniseries debuted on BBC in 1972, followed by a shorter version in 2016. Josh Groban starred on Broadway as Pierre Bezukhov in *Natasha, Pierre & The Great Comet of 1812*, a musical based on a short segment of the novel; it was nominated for 12 Tony Awards. Nevertheless, nothing compares to the novel, which is, as one critic noted, like reading "life itself."

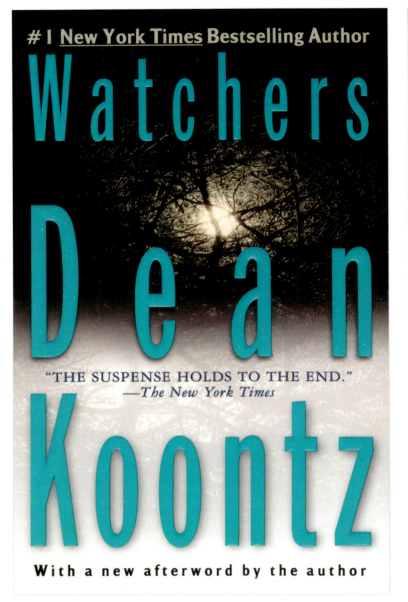

#1 New York Times Bestselling Author

Watchers
Dean
Koontz

"THE SUSPENSE HOLDS TO THE END."
—*The New York Times*

With a new afterword by the author

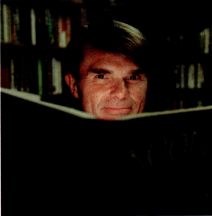

CLOCKWISE FROM LEFT: Front cover art for *Watchers*, first published in 1987. | Dean Koontz has sold 450 million copies of his work. | A letter from Koontz to a fan named Jim, sent in April 1989.

96

WATCHERS

Dean Koontz · 1987

Everyone we know will die. This hard truth drives *Watchers* (1987), much as it drives Travis Cornell, the protagonist of Dean Koontz's suspenseful, supernatural thriller. Having this knowledge doesn't make it easier to accept, of course, or lessen the grief that comes when we lose a loved one. As a former Delta Force operative, Travis must also cope with having directly caused death, grief, and despair.

One day while hiking in a canyon near his house, 36-year-old Travis stumbles across two creatures, one of whom appears to be stalking and trying to kill the other. The victim, a golden retriever, befriends Travis, who takes the dog home and names him Einstein after he discovers the stray dog's tremendous intelligence. The other creature, known as the Outsider, with the deformed body of a baboon and ferocious jaws, slinks off. Later, Travis and Einstein together rescue Nora Devon from a sexual predator. Nora is a 30-year-old recluse with terrible self-esteem, but her relationships with Travis and Einstein help her experience the world in a new way.

The tight plot also includes an assassin, hired by an unknown entity to wipe out the scientists who worked in the top-secret lab where Einstein and the Outsider were created. But while tracking his prey, the assassin decides to try to kidnap and ransom Einstein. The Outsider wants to get rid of Einstein as well, a case of sibling rivalry gone terribly, terribly wrong.

Born in 1945 in Pennsylvania, Koontz grew up in an abusive household, with an alcoholic gambler for a father. As a senior at Shippensburg State College (now Shippensburg University), he won a fiction contest sponsored by *Atlantic Monthly*. In college he met his now-wife, Gerda, and converted from Protestantism to Catholicism, in part because the religion offers both morality and mystery. A few years after college, Gerda made an offer to support the family while Koontz built up his writing career; by the end of that period, she had quit her job to run the business of her husband's creative empire. To date, he's sold 450 million copies of such novels as *Lightning* (1988), *Intensity* (1995), and *Odd Thomas* (2003), the first in a series of books about a short-order cook who can communicate with the dead.

Watchers and its genetically enhanced creatures call to mind another work about a dangerous monster born in the name of science: *Frankenstein*. Like Mary Shelley's 1818 novel, Koontz's work explores two sides of scientific endeavor: on the one hand, Einstein is dazzlingly smart and loyal, a superior model of canine. He represents beneficial progress like penicillin, the birth-control pill, and countless other life-changing inventions. On the other hand, the same lab that created Einstein also unleashed the rampaging Outsider, a reminder of the dark side of progress. After all, scientists are responsible for destructive technologies like nuclear weapons and napalm too. These starkly contrasting potential applications of scientific inquiry raise important questions about the relationship between morality and the pursuit of knowledge.

Koontz's book also explores a less heady but no less powerful subject: the proverbial bond between man and his best friend, even if the best friend in this case happens to be a cross between Lassie and E.T., as one early review described Einstein. Travis meets Einstein at a very depressed time in his life, and their friendship becomes a source of joy and light, even as they must avoid being killed or kidnapped. Nora too discovers the redeeming power of connection. Amid the page-turning scenes, this thriller manages to highlight the fact that the fleetingness of our relationships, whether with animals or fellow humans, makes them all the sweeter. We need to hold close those closest to us while we can.

"There Are Better Ways to Starve to Death"

WRITERS ON WRITING

THESE QUOTES about writing express a range of attitudes and advice, from the specific to the general, from the purpose of art to the trouble with adverbs. They might make you chuckle or squirm, or they might make you put fingers to keyboard to see what happens.

ON WRITING

I do not over-intellectualize the production process. I try to keep it simple: Tell the damned story.
—Tom Clancy

The road to hell is paved with adverbs.
—Stephen King

Good fiction is made of what is real, and reality is difficult to come by.
—Ralph Ellison

Write to please just one person. If you open a window and make love to the world, so to speak, your story will get pneumonia.
—Kurt Vonnegut

Writing is not an exercise in excision, it's a journey into sound.
—E. B. White

A work that aspires, however humbly, to the condition of art should carry its justification in every line. And art itself may be defined as a single-minded attempt to render the highest kind of justice to the visible universe, by bringing to light the truth, manifold and one, underlying its every aspect.
—Joseph Conrad

Talent is insignificant. I know a lot of talented ruins. Beyond talent lie all the usual words: discipline, love, luck, but most of all, endurance.
—James Baldwin

Any novel is hopeful in that it presupposes a reader. It is, actually, a hopeful act just to write anything, really, because you're assuming that someone will be around to [read] it.
—Margaret Atwood

Write what you know: your own interests, feelings, beliefs, friends, family and even pets will be your raw materials when you start writing. Develop a fondness for solitude if you can, because writing is one of the loneliest professions in the world!
—J. K. Rowling

ON BEING A WRITER

Don't romanticise your "vocation." You can either write good sentences or you can't. There is no "writer's life-style." All that matters is what you leave on the page.
—Zadie Smith

Writing a book is a horrible, exhausting struggle, like a long bout of some painful illness. One would never undertake such a thing if one were not driven on by some demon whom one can neither resist nor understand.
—George Orwell

If there is a magic in story writing, and I am convinced there is, no one has ever been able to reduce it to a recipe that can be passed from one person to another. The formula seems to lie solely in the aching urge of the writer to convey something he feels important to the reader. If the writer has that urge, he may sometimes but by no means always find the way to do it.

—John Steinbeck

Write without pay until somebody offers pay; if nobody offers within three years, sawing wood is what you were intended for.

—Mark Twain

As a writer you should not judge. You should understand.

—Ernest Hemingway

If [writers] have any role at all, I think it's the role of optimism, not blind or stupid optimism, but the kind which is meaningful, one that is rather close to that notion of the world which is not perfect, but which can be improved. In other words, we don't just sit and hope that things will work out; we have a role to play to make that come about. That seems to me to be the reason for the existence of the writer.

—Chinua Achebe

If you're going to be a writer you have to be one of the great ones. . . . After all, there are better ways to starve to death.

—Gabriel García Márquez

I know how to write forever. I don't think I could have happily stayed here in the world if I did not have a way of thinking about it, which is what writing is for me.

—Toni Morrison

If my doctor told me I had only six months to live, I wouldn't brood. I'd type a little faster.

—Isaac Asimov

ABOVE: James Baldwin writing notes to himself in his New York apartment, photographed in 1951. He said that endurance was one of the most important qualities in a writer.

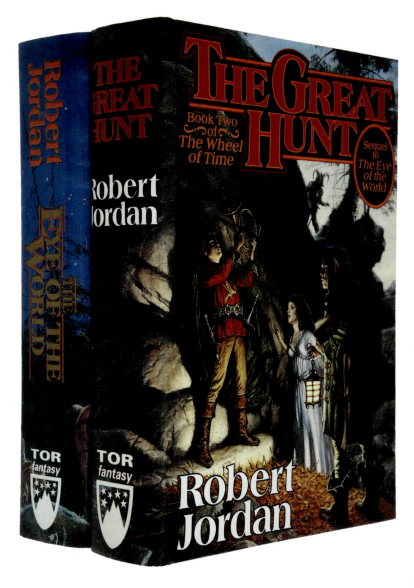

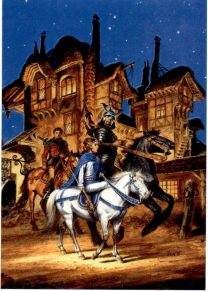

CLOCKWISE FROM LEFT: *The Great Hunt*, the second book in The Wheel of Time series, was published in 1990 by Tor. | Author Robert Jordan completed 11 books in the series before his death in 2007. Brandon Sanderson picked up the series, following Jordan's comprehensive notes, and wrote the volumes 12–14. | Art from a preview booklet for *Eye of the World*.

97

THE WHEEL OF TIME SERIES

Robert Jordan and Brandon Sanderson · 1990–2013

There's something so satisfying about falling into the first book of a fantasy series, knowing that the reading experience will continue through thousands of pages, stretch across multiple volumes, and feature hundreds of characters maneuvering through intricate plots. Robert Jordan understood this particular literary pleasure, as fans have noted, and announced his intentions to go both deep and broad in the opening lines of his novel *The Eye of the World* (1990): "The Wheel of Time turns, and Ages come and pass, leaving memories that become legend. Legend fades to myth, and even myth is long forgotten when the Age that gave it birth comes again. . . . There are neither beginnings nor endings to the turning of the Wheel of Time." It's the kind of series that makes you want to clear your calendar and hunker down.

From this beginning unspools an ornately textured universe. The overarching plot of the books concerns various attempts to destroy the Dark One, the archenemy of the Creator. The Creator fashioned the cosmos and the Wheel of Time, which has seven spokes representing different ages of history. Divided into male and female halves, the so-called One Power turns the Wheel. At one point, the Wheel created the Dragon, an amazing force of Light. The Dark One eventually gets neutralized, destroying civilization in the process. But a prophecy predicts that the Dark One will escape—and only the Dragon Reborn can prevent evil from taking over. The novels detail the journeys and experiences of a group of young people with various talents and abilities, one of whom may be the Dragon Reborn.

In creating his mythology, Jordan collaged various religions and folkloric traditions. The bending, circular nature of time nods to concepts in Hinduism, while the series' emphasis on duality harks back to Judeo-Christian tradition and the common cultural archetype of good versus evil. The books also play with time in the sense that the setting seems to both echo our past and predict our future. Like A Song of Ice and Fire (1996–present), another similarly impressive fantasy series, the books don't hew to any historical timeline but their own.

When Jordan died in 2007, he left behind comprehensive notes concerning what he imagined would be the final volume of the series. Fantasy writer Brandon Sanderson accepted the challenge of shaping those notes into a cohesive story. He transformed what was supposed to be the 12th volume into three more novels, bringing the total number of Wheel of Time books to 14. Sanderson was selected in part for a eulogy he wrote upon Jordan's premature death, in which he described the importance of Jordan's work in Sanderson's youth, meaningfully summarizing the feelings of millions of readers.

James Oliver Rigney Jr. adopted the pen name Robert Jordan while working on a series of fantasy novels based on the character of Conan the Barbarian in the 1980s. He was born in 1948, grew up in Charleston, South Carolina, and served multiple tours as a helicopter gunner during the Vietnam War. Jordan's wife, Harriet McDougal, was an influential editor in the world of fantasy and science fiction, working on books like *Ender's Game* (1985) as well as her husband's Wheel of Time series. McDougal will serve as a producer on the upcoming television series based on the books.

In its massive scope and intricate detail, the Wheel of Time series offers something for every reader: elaborate mythologies, controversial depictions of gender roles, ferocious magical battles. Characters drawn from all walks of life lend Jordan's civilization a verisimilitude, even as they have jobs like Truthspeaker and Empress. And the Chosen One appealingly toggles between accepting his destiny and rebelling against it. Fate and free will, larger-than-life battles, ecstasy, agony, victory, defeat. All of it, and more, is right here.

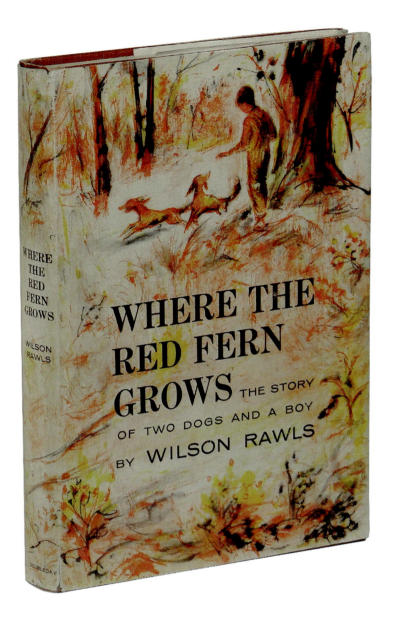

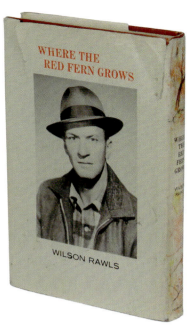

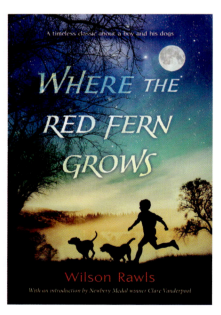

CLOCKWISE FROM LEFT: The first edition jacket for *Where the Red Fern Grows*, published in 1961. | The back of the same jacket, featuring a photo of author Wilson Rawls. | A 2016 paperback cover from Yearling.

98

WHERE THE RED FERN GROWS

Wilson Rawls · 1961

Few readers forget where they were when they finished *Where the Red Fern Grows* (1961), so moving is the book's climax. The quintessential tale of a boy and his two dogs is a coming-of-age classic, widely taught and firmly fixed in the hearts of millions of readers.

Woodrow Wilson Rawls was open about his novel's many autobiographical elements. He was born in 1913 and grew up poor in rural Oklahoma, where he loved to roam and explore with his dog. In the absence of any local schools, Rawls's mother taught him to read and write. When he stumbled upon *The Call of the Wild* (1903) as a child, Rawls fantasized about writing his own dog-and-boy story, but his parents couldn't afford to buy paper or pencils. The Great Depression forced his family out of Oklahoma and into the west, and they settled in New Mexico after their car broke down there. Rawls left home as an adolescent to earn money. He started writing while working in construction throughout the Americas, but he was embarrassed by his grammatical and punctuation errors. On the eve of his wedding, he burned his manuscripts, so ashamed was he of his failure to get anything published. When his wife discovered what he'd done, she encouraged him to rewrite the lost novels. *Where the Red Fern Grows* took three weeks.

Growing up in the Ozark Mountains, 10-year-old Billy really wants a dog. With no extra money to spare in his family, he must toil and save. Some two years later, he is delighted when he finally picks up his two coonhound pups, walking the long way into town. That night, while bedding down in a cave, they hear a mountain lion roar. The dogs sound back. Billy names them Old Dan and Little Ann. He starts training the dogs to catch raccoons, and they become skilled hunters and Billy's constant loyal companions. But he also sees the dogs' protective, even violent natures.

The book extols delayed gratification, responsibility, and hard work. Simply wanting the dogs doesn't mean Billy will get them; he needs to find and perform odd jobs, set the money aside, and travel to pick them up. Receiving the dogs after such a long wait makes their arrival all the more precious—the adult Billy narrates the novel, and his understanding of the pleasures of anticipation lends this lesson its weight. Young Billy completely dedicates himself to his dogs and their training, showing how much he appreciates the fruits of his efforts and how willing he is to continue working hard to achieve the results he wants. Rawls underscores the importance of perseverance, a particular American characteristic he witnessed as a child in the Depression, when giving up simply wasn't an option.

Perhaps more significant than its emphasis on tenacity, *Where the Red Fern Grows* features a fair amount of death. Troublemaker Rubin Pritchard, a neighbor just two years older than Billy, falls on his own ax after trying to attack Billy's dogs. While Billy is deeply affected by the death, Rubin's family betrays little emotion upon learning about the accident. As adults living hard lives themselves, they understand the fact of mortality in a way that Billy does not. The graphic nature of Rubin's end prepares readers for the death of the dogs. Shocking as it may be to anyone who expected a happy ending, the dogs' demise helps ground the book in realism. Like *Old Yeller* (1956), it's a weeper of a classic—an exemplar of the dog-dies genre that inspired Gordon Korman's contemporary middle-grade novel *No More Dead Dogs* (2000). Nature is dangerous, these books remind us, and we are all heading toward an inescapable fate.

Rawls narrated the 1974 movie, drawing on speaking skills he'd honed over the years in schools. He published just one more novel, *Summer of Monkeys* (1976), before his death in 1984. But he motivated thousands of kids with stories about his childhood, emphasizing how he himself persevered in his goal of becoming a writer despite little formal education, and encouraging his listeners to follow their dreams. His simple, plainspoken style, in person and on the page, inculcates timeless, essential values.

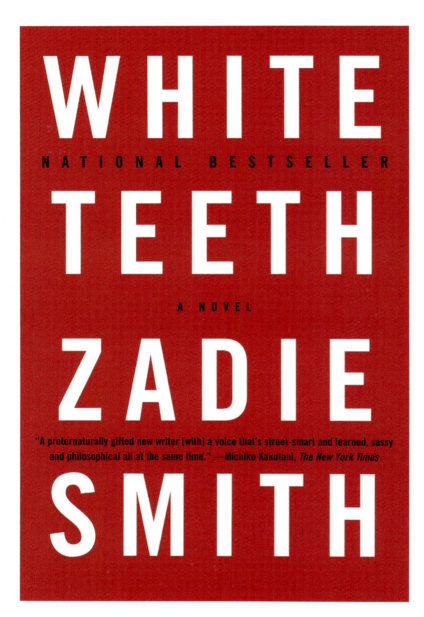

WHITE

NATIONAL BESTSELLER

TEETH

A NOVEL

ZADIE

"A preternaturally gifted new writer [with] a voice that's street-smart and learned, sassy and philosophical all at the same time." —Michiko Kakutani, *The New York Times*

SMITH

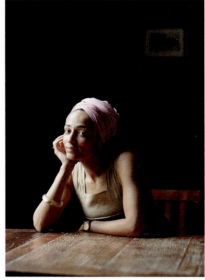

CLOCKWISE FROM LEFT: A 2001 paperback cover of *White Teeth.* | Author Zadie Smith. *White Teeth* was her debut novel, and an immediate bestseller. | Smith photographed in 2014, speaking at a panel during the New Yorker Festival. Smith currently teaches writing at New York University.

99

WHITE TEETH

Zadie Smith · 2000

London still teems with possibility, much as it did when William Shakespeare strode the boards at the Globe, Charles Dickens walked its streets, Arthur Conan Doyle uncovered its mysteries, and Virginia Woolf described its postwar denizens. For English writers, London sometimes seems like Mount Everest, the peak they must scale to reach great heights. To tell the story of her London, Zadie Smith created the Joneses and the Iqbals, two very different families who come to represent the city's manifold multicultural threads.

Archie Jones and Samad Iqbal met in the army during World War II. Decades later, they live near one another in northwest London, Jones with his much younger Jamaican wife, Clara, and their smart daughter, Irie, and Samad with his arranged wife, Alsana, and their twin boys, Magid and Millat. The friendship between the run-of-the-mill Englishman and the immigrant from Bangladesh acts as the fulcrum around which *White Teeth* maneuvers.

White Teeth (2000) launched Smith's career as a comic novelist as well as her role as a spokesperson for multiethnic, multiracial Britain. Alsana sews clothes for a popular S&M shop, while Samad worries that his frequent masturbation undermines his religious values. Their son Millat joins an Islamist fundamentalist group that goes by the acronym KEVIN (Keepers of the Eternal and Victorious Islamic Nation). It's supposed to be funny, and it is. But behind the jokes burst razor-sharp ideas. The characters of Archie and Samad allow Smith to explore the intersections of racial and economic prejudice. Archie works for a paper-folding company, pretty satisfied with his lot; Samad works as a waiter, and rages against how far his family has fallen from its once-lofty heights. Smith is also concerned with the impact of immigration on subsequent generations: Samad sends one son to Bangladesh to become a devout Muslim, yet he returns having lost his faith. His other son goes from

being a womanizer to a radical. And as a biracial woman, Irie straddles two worlds—the England of her dad and the Jamaica of her mom—though she feels that she fits into neither. As Irie, Magid, and Millat all come into the orbit of geneticist Marcus Chalfen, they find themselves asking how much control they really have over their lives.

Smith's novel is all the more remarkable considering that she began writing it while earning an undergraduate degree at Cambridge. The book became an immediate bestseller and won such honors as the Guardian First Book Award, Whitbread Award for First Novel, and Commonwealth Writers' Prize for Best First Book. The author was born in London in 1975 to a Jamaican mother and a white British father. She changed her name from Sadie to Zadie as a teen, influenced by Zora Neale Hurston, and was the first person in her family to go to college. Now she teaches creative writing at New York University. Recently Smith has become known as an essayist as well as a novelist, publishing on topics as varied as British comedians, Brooklyn rappers, and novelists from all over, in the *New York Review of Books*, the *New Yorker*, and elsewhere; some of these essays are collected in *Changing My Mind: Occasional Essays* (2009) and *Feel Free* (2018).

Critic James Wood invented the term *hysterical realism* to describe Smith's debut and similar novels that combine social realism, stylized prose full of pyrotechnics and digressions, and elaborate, twisty plots. Addressing his critique, Smith noted that "writers do not write what they want, they write what they can." In the years since the astonishing *White Teeth* kicked off, she's retold *Howards End* (1910), by E. M. Forster, as *On Beauty* (2005); juxtaposed different types of prose to describe urban life in *NW* (2012); and addressed friendship in an allegedly postracial world in *Swing Time* (2016). It's our great fortune that there is so much in her, and so much left to come.

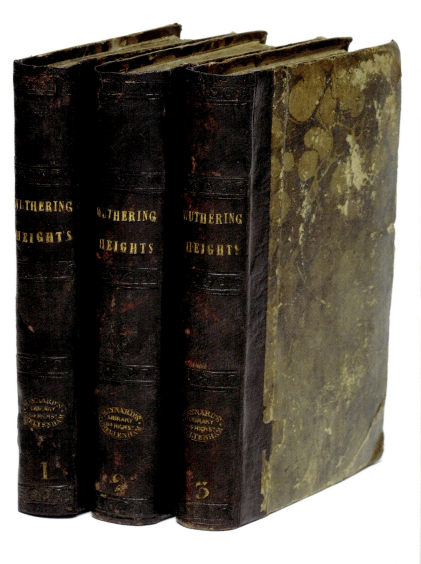

100

WUTHERING HEIGHTS

Emily Brontë · 1847

We have Charlotte Brontë to thank for our conception of Emily Brontë. After Charlotte's success with *Jane Eyre* (1847), she wrote a preface to an edition of her sister's novel, *Wuthering Heights* (1847). In it, Charlotte explains that the novel "was hewn in a wild workshop, with simple tools, out of homely materials . . . wrought with a rude chisel, and from no model but the vision of [the artist's] meditations." There begins our image of the author, too shy to speak to anyone but her family, yet in possession of an incredible imagination, capable of creating a work of astonishing feeling and yawning depravity.

Born to an Irish clergyman in 1818 in Yorkshire, Emily grew up writing poems, plays, and stories about countries in the imaginary Glass Town Federation with her brother Branwell and sisters Charlotte and Anne, both of whom became celebrated novelists as well. As teens, they collected their literary efforts in a series of self-published magazines. Emily briefly attended boarding school, but she and Charlotte were removed due to the school's harsh and horrid conditions (two other Brontë sisters grew ill at the school and died). As an adult, she taught for a short time and studied with Charlotte in Brussels, but mostly she stayed on the moors where she grew up and where she set *Wuthering Heights*. She died of tuberculosis in 1848, a year after the book was published, at age 30.

As the novel begins, Mr. Lockwood rents Thrushcross Grange in the lonely Yorkshire landscape. Puzzled and bored by his surroundings, Lockwood asks his housekeeper, Nelly Dean, to tell him about the inscrutable Heathcliff, his landlord and neighbor in nearby Wuthering Heights. She describes the entangled destinies of the Lintons and the Earnshaws, explaining how Heathcliff arrived, how he and Catherine Earnshaw fell in love, and how they became involved with Edgar and Isabella Linton, who lived at Thrushcross Grange, to the detriment of all.

Right away *Wuthering Heights* makes clear the problem of interpretation. Lockwood recounts stories that he hears from Nelly, who is often recollecting events that happened decades before, or paraphrasing conversations that she couldn't have been privy to. Nelly interprets as she goes, and Lockwood consistently and comically misreads Heathcliff and Cathy, Catherine's daughter and Heathcliff's daughter-in-law. These frames within frames leave the reader on shaky ground: everyone in this novel is an unreliable narrator, and despite the small number of characters and confined setting, the story becomes, as Charlotte said, "knotty as a root of heath."

The welter of confusion that *Wuthering Heights* sows is reflected in its reception. Its first reviewers were baffled, marveling at its power but struck mute when trying to explain what the book is ultimately about; one critic recommended it be burned, while another described it as "one of the greatest novels in the language." Often thought of as a sweeping romance, in reality it presents a truly discomforting vision of love, showing it to be an obsessive, violent passion that drives individuals to wholly subsume themselves in one another. Over the course of the novel, the love plot gives way to a revenge plot that threatens to drag everyone in the story toward inexorable doom. Infamously, William Wyler's 1939 film version, with Laurence Olivier as Heathcliff, simply omits that problematic part of the book.

Charlotte fostered the image of her sister as an untrained savant in part because *Wuthering Heights* is utterly unlike anything that came before. In his 1948 book *The Great Tradition*, the eminent critic F. R. Leavis admitted that he could say nothing about *Wuthering Heights* because it seems to be completely outside of any literary tradition. Even today it stands alone in literature, a solitary crag rearing up from the windswept moors.

How to Read a Literary Text

UNLESS THE SPINE SAYS *Agatha Christie*, in most instances reading a novel isn't about unlocking or uncovering a mystery planted by an author, nor is there a single message waiting to be deciphered. Instead, literature yields many diverse interpretations, depending on the attitudes, backgrounds, and understanding of its readers. Asking questions helps deepen the reading experience, offering the chance to engage with a literary text on multiple levels, as well as heightening your intellectual and imaginative involvement with what's on the page.

What is the point of view? Who tells the story? Is the narrator reliable or unreliable?
The Coldest Winter Ever (1999) employs the first-person point of view; the person telling the story, also known as the narrator, uses "I" and is directly involved in the events depicted. In the books comprising A Song of Ice and Fire (1996–present), by contrast, George R. R. Martin shifts point of view so that readers often see the same event from multiple perspectives.

What is the setting of the novel? What kind of world is being portrayed?
Doña Bárbara (1929) takes place in rural Venezuela, a world so recognizable to its initial readers that the author had to go into exile to protect himself from retaliation from the government. *The Adventures of Tom Sawyer* (1876) transpires in a lightly fictionalized version of Mark Twain's hometown of Hannibal, Missouri, while the action portrayed in the Wheel of Time books (1990–2013) happens in an entirely imagined setting.

What's the order of events? How is the work structured? Why is the story told in the order that it is?
War and Peace (1869) begins as members of Saint Petersburg's high society start to hear rumblings about Napoleon's march through Europe, and it ends shortly after the Russian rout of the French invasion.

In between, Leo Tolstoy detours into philosophical ruminations inspired by the events being narrated. *Invisible Man* (1952), *A Separate Peace* (1959), and *Beloved* (1987) rely on flashbacks to drive their plots, suggesting the importance of history and the personal past to the present.

When does the action take place? Over what time period? In what era? Now, the past, the very very past? The future?
The Clan of the Cave Bear (1980) takes place thousands of years ago, when Cro-Magnons and Neanderthals walked the earth. The nine novels that form the Tales of the City series (1978–2014) move roughly contemporarily, from the 1970s, when the first book was published, into the 2010s, when the final book came out. Isaac Asimov imagined a very distant future in the Foundation series (1951–1993): its Galactic Empire resets the calendar to 1 GE in 12,500 CE.

What kind of language is used? Descriptive? Straightforward? Plainspoken? Lofty?
The Brief Wondrous Life of Oscar Wao (2007) jumbles English and Spanish, high and low diction, and references to erudite literature and comic books—sometimes in the same paragraph or even sentence. Nicholas Sparks attributes the success of *The Notebook* (1996) in part to its use of simple

and chaste language, while George Orwell invented several words—among them *minipax*, *sexcrime*, and *unperson*—to describe life in the totalitarian society of *Nineteen Eighty-Four* (1949).

What's the pace of the novel? Fast? Slow? Does it take place over a day, a month, a decade?
The Curious Incident of the Dog in the Night-Time (2003) begins when narrator Christopher finds the body of his neighbor's dog, murdered with a pitchfork. As Christopher learns the truth about what happened to Wellington the poodle, he also starts to learn the truth about what happened to his mother, whom he believes to be dead. The novel offers a neat symmetry between Christopher's external and emotional discoveries over roughly the course of a school year.

What form does the work take?
As an epistolary novel, *The Color Purple* (1982) consists of letters written by an uneducated woman named Celie to her sister Nettie and to God. *Gilead* (2004) also takes the form of a letter, in this case a discursive, diary-like account written by an elderly father to his young son. *Wuthering Heights* (1847) folds in on itself, as a series of stories, retellings, and interpretations by narrators with varying degrees of unreliability.

What are the key ideas or themes?
The Hunger Games (2008) directly censures a voyeuristic culture in which reality shows traffic in the humiliation and pain of their participants. *The Alchemist* (1988) urges readers to follow their dreams. *The Little Prince* (1943) proffers life lessons on every page. Christian novels like *This Present Darkness* (1986), *Swan Song* (1987), and *Mind Invaders* (1989) promote religious messages, such as the power of prayer or a belief in an omnipotent divinity.

What are the recurring images or symbols?
Eyes—and the related action of watching—appear throughout *The Great Gatsby* (1925). Narrator Nick Carraway observes the behavior of Jay Gatsby and Daisy Buchanan, among others. Gatsby gazes at the green light at the end of Daisy's dock, itself a symbol of his hopes and regrets. On a fateful journey to New York City, the characters pass a billboard featuring the bespectacled eyes of Doctor T. J. Eckleburg—a creepy advertisement that literally looms. The white whale known as Moby Dick in the 1851 novel may be the most famous, and mutable, of all literary symbols, sometimes said to stand in for death, nature, and even God.

Put yourself in the shoes of the main character. What would you do differently? How would you feel if you were put into the same situation?
The Martian (2011) opens as astronaut Mark Watney realizes he's alone on Mars, his fellow NASA crewmembers having returned to Earth, as horrifying a fate as one could imagine. The book then presents a sequence of problems that Watney must solve, leading readers to ask themselves what solutions they would or wouldn't select. In *Great Expectations* (1861), Pip is repeatedly confronted with difficult choices, and readers continue to debate whether he makes the correct decisions in those challenging situations.

What drives the main character? What does he or she want? What obstacles stand in the way?
A strong sense of right and wrong motivates such heroes as Jack Ryan and Alex Cross, in novels by

Tom Clancy and James Patterson, respectively, as they seek to preserve justice and order. In The Lord of the Rings (1954–1955), Frodo Baggins wants to destroy the One Ring, which simultaneously attracts and wounds everyone in its presence, but his quest to throw it into the fires of Mount Doom is thwarted by an array of enemies, including Gollum and followers of Sauron.

How well do the characters understand the situation they're in? What do readers know that characters don't?

The characters in the Left Behind series (1995–2007) have literally been left behind, as the truly faithful went to heaven during the Rapture, a fate that those remaining strive to comprehend. Over the 16 novels, their faith is severely tested, and they gradually discover that the Antichrist walks among them. A recent trend in publishing has been the popularity of YA fiction with adult readers, who, from their more mature vantage points, may take a more even-keeled approach to the dramatic heartache and headaches of teen life.

What is the primary conflict of the story?

Sometimes the primary conflict might be external, such as the epic battle between Harry Potter and Lord Voldemort, or the escalating tension and ensuing violence between gangs in The Outsiders (1967). Other times the conflict is internal, such as whether Buck will choose to heed "the call of the wild" in Jack London's novel by the same name, or whether Raskolnikov should turn himself in for his terrible deeds in Crime and Punishment (1866).

What other books did this book remind you of?

In their warnings about the dangers of unethical scientific inquiry, Watchers (1987) and Jurassic Park (1990) put contemporary spins on Frankenstein (1818). The Fifty Shades of Grey novels (2011–present) got their start as fan fiction written by E. L. James, after she fell under the spell of the Twilight saga (2005–2008) by Stephenie Meyer. Pretty much any novel featuring an antsy, irreverent teen takes us straight back to The Catcher in the Rye (1951).

If you could ask the author one question, what would it be?

Some novels end conclusively: we know, for instance, that Don Quixote loses his illusions about the permeability between fiction and reality, returning sadly to sanity, and that Alice dreamed her adventures in Wonderland. Other books, however, leave us hungry for more information. What kind of adult does Tony, from Bless Me, Ultima (1972), become? What happens to Nick and Amy after Gone Girl (2012) ends? Do they make it, or continue to mess with one another?

How do the characters change? What do they learn?

Siddhartha (1922) carefully tracks the changes of Siddhartha, as he seeks spiritual solace in various places and through various intermediaries. Ultimately, he finds that true peace comes from developing a connection to the natural world. After his extensive travels, however, Gulliver returns home despairing and despondent. In The Joy Luck Club (1989), a daughter uncovers the hidden life of her mother, which creates a new sense of cultural ties and deepens familial bonds.

What's the title of the work, and why does it matter? How does it set up your expectations before you begin reading? How does your understanding of the title change after you've finished?
In the thriller *Rebecca* (1938), the second Mrs. de Winter eventually ferrets out what happened to the first, the Rebecca of the title. Her obsession to find out the truth drives the book's plot. However, the titular character never appears in the novel itself—she's dead before the main action begins—and, although we're told that the narrator has a "lovely and unusual" first name, we never learn it.

What strikes you about the names used for characters and places in the novel? What kind of information or insight do you get from these labels?
Probably no book so clearly telegraphs its message via the names of its characters and places as *The Pilgrim's Progress* (1678). In this religious allegory about spiritual awakening, Christian, the protagonist, travels up Difficulty Hill, across the Valley of Humiliation, and through the Delectable Mountains, meeting people with names like Old Honest, Contrite, and Standfast, on his way to the Celestial City.

How does the era of the book's composition play into the novel?
Although *To Kill a Mockingbird* (1960) is set during the 1930s, Harper Lee wrote it in the 1950s, as the civil rights movement became increasingly organized and impactful in the United States; this contemporary context looms over the events of the novel. *One Hundred Years of Solitude* (1967), written during a period of rapid political and social change in many parts of Latin America, explores the phenomenon of historical change in the region through its portrayal of the fictional Buendía family and Macondo, the town the family founds.

Would you want to be friends with the protagonist? Or is the protagonist unlikable? If so, why?
Stephen King is a master of putting everyman characters in extreme circumstances, and *The Stand* (1978) is no exception. Confronted with the atrocities of a postapocalyptic world, smart, unassuming Stuart Redman transforms into a leader and voice of reason. *Jane Eyre* (1847) offers an entirely different narrative, but the novel's first-person point of view allows readers to sympathize with the struggles of the eponymous protagonist.

APPENDICES

THE GREAT AMERICAN READ: 100 BOOKS

BY RELEASE YEAR

1605 *Don Quixote* by Miguel de Cervantes

1678 *The Pilgrim's Progress* by John Bunyan

1726 *Gulliver's Travels* by Jonathan Swift

1813 *Pride and Prejudice* by Jane Austen

1818 *Frankenstein* by Mary Shelley

1844–1846 *The Count of Monte Cristo* by Alexandre Dumas

1847 *Jane Eyre* by Charlotte Brontë

1847 *Wuthering Heights* by Emily Brontë

1951 *Moby-Dick* by Herman Melville

1861 *Great Expectations* by Charles Dickens

1865 *Alice's Adventures in Wonderland* by Lewis Carroll

1866 *Crime and Punishment* by Fyodor Dostoyevsky

1868 *Little Women* by Louisa May Alcott

1869 *War and Peace* by Leo Tolstoy

1876 *The Adventures of Tom Sawyer* by Mark Twain

1890 *The Picture of Dorian Gray* by Oscar Wilde

1899 *Heart of Darkness* by Joseph Conrad

1903 *The Call of the Wild* by Jack London

1908 *Anne of Green Gables* by L. M. Montgomery

1922 *Siddhartha* by Hermann Hesse

1925 *The Great Gatsby* by F. Scott Fitzgerald

1926 *The Sun Also Rises* by Ernest Hemingway

1929 *Doña Bárbara* by Rómulo Gallegos

1936 *Gone with The Wind* by Margaret Mitchell

1937 *Their Eyes Were Watching God* by Zora Neale Hurston

1938 *Rebecca* by Daphne du Maurier

1939 *And Then There Were None* by Agatha Christie

1939 *The Grapes of Wrath* by John Steinbeck

1943 *The Little Prince* by Antoine de Saint-Exupéry

1943 *A Tree Grows in Brooklyn* by Betty Smith

1949 *Nineteen Eighty-Four* by George Orwell

1950–1956 The Chronicles of Narnia Series by C. S. Lewis

1951–1993 Foundation Series by Isaac Asimov

1951 *The Catcher in the Rye* by J. D. Salinger

1952 *Invisible Man* by Ralph Ellison

1952 *Charlotte's Web* by E. B. White

1954–1955 The Lord of the Rings Series by J. R. R. Tolkien

1958 *Things Fall Apart* by Chinua Achebe

1959 *A Separate Peace* by John Knowles

1959 *The Sirens of Titan* by Kurt Vonnegut

1960 *To Kill a Mockingbird* by Harper Lee

1961 *Catch-22* by Joseph Heller

1961 *Where the Red Fern Grows* by Wilson Rawls

1962 *Another Country* by James Baldwin

1965 *Dune* by Frank Herbert

1967 *One Hundred Years of Solitude* by Gabriel García Márquez

1967 *The Outsiders* by S. E. Hinton

1969 *The Godfather* by Mario Puzo

1972 *Bless Me, Ultima* by Rudolfo Anaya

1978 *The Stand* by Stephen King

1978–2014 Tales of the City by Armistead Maupin

1979 *Flowers in the Attic* by V. C. Andrews

1979 *The Hitchhiker's Guide to the Galaxy* by Douglas Adams

1980 *The Clan of the Cave Bear* by Jean M. Auel

1980 *A Confederacy of Dunces* by John Kennedy Toole

1982 *The Color Purple* by Alice Walker

1984 *The Hunt for Red October* by Tom Clancy

1985 *The Handmaid's Tale* by Margaret Atwood

1985 *Lonesome Dove* by Larry McMurtry

1986 *This Present Darkness* by Frank E. Peretti

1987 *Watchers* by Dean Koontz

1987 *Swan Song* by Robert R. McCammon

1987 *Beloved* by Toni Morrison

1987–2003 Hatchet Series by Gary Paulsen

1988 *The Alchemist* by Paulo Coelho

1989 *Pillars of the Earth* by Ken Follett

1989 *Mind Invaders* by Dave Hunt

1989 *A Prayer for Owen Meany* by John Irving

1989 *The Joy Luck Club* by Amy Tan

1990 *Jurassic Park* by Michael Crichton

1990–2013 The Wheel of Time Series by Robert Jordan
and Brandon Sanderson

1991-present Outlander Series by Diana Gabaldon

1993 *The Giver* by Lois Lowry

1993-present *Alex Cross Mysteries* by James Patterson

1995–2007 Left Behind Series by Tim LaHaye
and Jerry B. Jenkins

1996–present A Song of Ice and Fire Series
by George R. R. Martin

1996 *The Notebook* by Nicholas Sparks

1997 *Memoirs of a Geisha* by Arthur Golden

1997–2007 Harry Potter Series by J. K. Rowling

1999 *The Coldest Winter Ever* by Sister Souljah

1999 *The Intuitionist* by Colson Whitehead

2000 *White Teeth* by Zadie Smith

2002 *The Lovely Bones* by Alice Sebold

2003 *The Da Vinci Code* by Dan Brown

2003 *The Curious Incident of the Dog in the Night-Time*
by Mark Haddon

2004 *Gilead* by Marilynne Robinson

2005 *Looking for Alaska* by John Green

2005–2008 Twilight Series by Stephenie Meyer

2005 *The Book Thief* by Markus Zusak

2007 *The Brief and Wonderous Life of Oscar Wao* by Junot Díaz

2007 The Shack by William P. Young

2008–2010 The Hunger Games Trilogy by Suzanne Collins

2009 *The Help* by Kathryn Stockett

2011 *Ready Player One* by Ernest Cline

2011–present Fifty Shades Series by E. L. James

2011 (self-published as e-book); 2014 *The Martian*
by Andy Weir

2012 *Gone Girl* by Gillian Flynn

2013 *Americanah* by Chimamanda Ngozi Adichie

2016 *Ghost* by Jason Reynolds

THE GREAT AMERICAN READ: 100 BOOKS

BY GENRE

ACTION & ADVENTURE

The Call of the Wild by Jack London (1903)

The Clan of the Cave Bear by Jean M. Auel (1980)

The Count of Monte Cristo by Alexandre Dumas (1844–1846)

Gulliver's Travels by Jonathan Swift (1726)

Hatchet Series by Gary Paulsen (1987–2003)

Moby-Dick by Herman Melville (1951)

COMING OF AGE/YOUNG ADULT

A Separate Peace by John Knowles (1959)

Anne of Green Gables by L. M. Montgomery (1908)

Bless Me, Ultima by Rudolfo Anaya (1972)

The Catcher in the Rye by J. D. Salinger (1951)

Charlotte's Web by E. B. White (1952)

Ghost by Jason Reynolds (2016)

The Giver by Lois Lowry (1993)

Great Expectations by Charles Dickens (1861)

Harry Potter Series by J. K. Rowling (1997–2007)

The Little Prince by Antoine de Saint-Exupéry (1943)

Little Women by Louisa May Alcott (1868)

Looking for Alaska by John Green (2005)

The Outsiders by S. E. Hinton (1967)

Where the Red Fern Grows by Wilson Rawls (1961)

CHRISTIAN

The Pilgrim's Progress by John Bunyan (1678)

This Present Darkness by Frank E. Peretti (1986)

The Shack by William P. Young (2007)

FANTASY

Alice's Adventures in Wonderland by Lewis Carroll (1865)

The Chronicles of Narnia Series by C. S. Lewis (1950–1956)

Foundation Series by Isaac Asimov (1951–1993)

The Intuitionist by Colson Whitehead (1999)

The Lord of the Rings Series by J. R. R. Tolkien (1954–1955)

Outlander Series by Diana Gabaldon (1991–present)

A Song of Ice and Fire Series by
George R. R. Martin (1996–present)

Swan Song by Robert R. McCammon (1987)

Twilight Series by Stephenie Meyer (2005–2008)

The Wheel of Time Series by Robert Jordan and Brandon
Sanderson (1990–2013)

GOTHIC

Flowers in the Attic by V. C. Andrews (1979)

Jane Eyre by Charlotte Brontë (1847)

Rebecca by Daphne du Maurier (1938)

Wuthering Heights by Emily Brontë (1847)

HISTORICAL

The Adventures of Tom Sawyer by Mark Twain (1876)

Beloved by Toni Morrison (1987)

The Book Thief by Markus Zusak (2005)

The Color Purple by Alice Walker (1982)

Gone with The Wind by Margaret Mitchell (1936)

The Grapes of Wrath by John Steinbeck (1939)

The Help by Kathryn Stockett (2009)

Lonesome Dove by Larry McMurtry (1985)

Memoirs of a Geisha by Arthur Golden (1997)

Pillars of the Earth by Ken Follett (1989)

Their Eyes Were Watching God by Zora Neale Hurston (1937)

HUMOR

Catch-22 by Joseph Heller (1961)

A Confederacy of Dunces by John Kennedy Toole (1980)

Don Quixote by Miguel de Cervantes (1605)

The Sirens of Titan by Kurt Vonnegut (1959)

Tales of the City by Armistead Maupin (1978–2014)

LITERARY

Another Country by James Baldwin (1962)

The Brief and Wondrous Life of Oscar Wao by Junot Díaz (2007)

The Coldest Winter Ever by Sister Souljah (1999)

The Curious Incident of the Dog in the Night-Time by Mark Haddon (2003)

Gilead by Marilynne Robinson (2004)

The Great Gatsby by F. Scott Fitzgerald (1925)

Invisible Man by Ralph Ellison (1952)

The Joy Luck Club by Amy Tan (1989)

The Picture of Dorian Gray by Oscar Wilde (1890)

Pride and Prejudice by Jane Austen (1813)

A Prayer for Owen Meany by John Irving (1989)

The Sun Also Rises by Ernest Hemingway (1926)

To Kill a Mockingbird by Harper Lee (1960)

A Tree Grows in Brooklyn by Betty Smith (1943)

White Teeth by Zadie Smith (2000)

MYSTERY & DETECTIVE

Alex Cross Mysteries by James Patterson (1993–present)

And Then There Were None by Agatha Christie (1939)

The Lovely Bones by Alice Sebold (2002)

ROMANCE

Fifty Shades Series by E. L. James (2011–present)

The Notebook by Nicholas Sparks (1996)

SCIENCE FICTION

Dune by Frank Herbert (1965)

Frankenstein by Mary Shelley (1818)

The Handmaid's Tale by Margaret Atwood (1985)

The Hitchhiker's Guide to the Galaxy by Douglas Adams (1979)

The Hunger Games Trilogy by Suzanne Collins (2008–2010)

Jurassic Park by Michael Crichton (1990)

Left Behind Series by Tim LaHaye and Jerry B. Jenkins (1995–2007)

The Martian by Andy Weir (2011, self-published as e-book); 2014

Mind Invaders by Dave Hunt (1989)

Nineteen Eighty-Four by George Orwell (1949)

Ready Player One by Ernest Cline (2011)

The Stand by Stephen King (1978)

Watchers by Dean Koontz (1987)

THRILLERS

The Da Vinci Code by Dan Brown (2003)

The Godfather by Mario Puzo (1969)

Gone Girl by Gillian Flynn (2012)

The Hunt for Red October by Tom Clancy (1984)

VISIONARY & METAPHYSICAL

The Alchemist by Paulo Coelho (1988)

Siddhartha by Hermann Hesse (1922)

WORLD

Americanah by Chimamanda Ngozi Adichie (2013)

Crime and Punishment by Fyodor Dostoyevsky (1866)

Doña Bárbara by Rómulo Gallegos (1929)

Heart of Darkness by Joseph Conrad (1899)

One Hundred Years of Solitude by Gabriel García Márquez (1967)

Things Fall Apart by Chinua Achebe (1958)

War and Peace by Leo Tolstoy (1869)

RESOURCES
FOR READERS

ON DEVICES

Plug in to literary communities from your devices.
Visit PBS's *The Great American Read*'s website: **pbs.org/greatamericanread**

LITERARY WEB

Just a few of the wonderful websites that cater to book lovers.

Book Riot: bookriot.com

Celebrating writers, readers, and genres, check out Book
Riot for reviews, recommendations, and literary lists.

Electric Literature: electricliterature.com

The literary magazine for the Internet age. Read reviews,
browse articles, and read original fiction.

Literary Hub: lithub.com

Daily news about literature and culture, with tons
of publishing and bookstore partners.

Los Angeles Review of Books: lareviewofbooks.org

A nonprofit with a magazine and quarterly publication,
the LARB also offers reviews and interviews on its website.

The Millions: themillions.com

Founded in 2003, this online magazine focuses on books,
arts, and culture.

The Page-Turner: newyorker.com/books/page-turner

Book reviews and features on literature from
The New Yorker.

The Paris Review: theparisreview.org

The online arm of the printed review, this is an excellent
space for reviews, essays, and interviews by favorite authors.

AUDIO ABOUT BOOKS

Tune into the literary podcast world for reviews of upcoming

releases, interviews with favorite writers, and literary news.

All the Books!: Weekly excitement about new book releases,
from Book Riot.

Books on the Nightstand: Conversations about books
between two publishing vets.

KCRW's Bookworm: This long-running show features
interviews with authors and host Michael Silverblatt.

Literary Disco: Bimonthly book recommendations in a
range of genres.

Slate Audio Book Club: A monthly podcast where Slate's
critics discuss new and notable books and book club picks.

SOCIAL BOOKWORMS

Books meet social media! Book clubs go viral.
Totally #amreading.

Goodreads: goodreads.com

Display your virtual "read" and "to read" shelves
and connect with other readers and authors.

LibraryThing: librarything.com

Check out other users' libraries and display your own. Even
find recommendations from readers who read like you do.

Oprah's Book Club: oprah.com/app/books.html

Still going strong, visit the website and sign up for a
newsletter for Oprah's picks.

Reese's Book Club:

instagram.com/reesesbookclubxhellosunshine/?hl=en

A book club via Instagram, with selections by actress
Reese Witherspoon.

The Rumpus Book Club: therumpus.net/bookclub/

For a fee, join the Rumpus Book Club and get a brand-new
read every month, then discuss it online with the group
and the author.

AUTHOR SOCIETIES

Alice Walker Literary Society:

www.emory.edu/alicewalker/sub-about.htm

The Brontë Society:

www.bronte.org.uk/bronte-200/join-the-bronte-society

C. S. Lewis Society of California: www.lewissociety.org

Dickens Society: http://dickenssociety.org

F. Scott Fitzgerald Society: www.fscottfitzgeraldsociety.org

The Hemingway Society: www.hemingwaysociety.org

International Dostoevsky Society: https://dostoevsky.org

International John Bunyan Society:

https://johnbunyansociety.org

Jack London Society: https://jacklondonsociety.org

The Jane Austen Society of North America: www.jasna.org

Joseph Conrad Society of America: http://josephconrad.org

The Kurt Vonnegut Society:

http://blogs.cofc.edu/vonnegut/vonneguts-life/

The L. M. Montgomery Literary Society:

http://lmmontgomeryliterarysociety.weebly.com

The Lewis Carroll Society of North America:

www.lewiscarroll.org

Louisa May Alcott Society: www.louisamayalcottsociety.org

The Lucy Maud Montgomery Society of Ontario:

http://lucymaudmontgomery.ca

Margaret Atwood Society: https://atwoodsociety.org

The Melville Society: http://melvillesociety.org

The Orwell Society: https://orwellsocietyblog.wordpress.com

The Oscar Wilde Society: http://oscarwildesociety.co.uk

The Tolkien Society: www.tolkiensociety.org/author/

The Toni Morrison Society: www.tonimorrisonsociety.org

IN PERSON

Visit historic literary places and surround yourself with literature fans.

BOOK FESTIVALS

There's nothing better than a day spent with thousands of fellow book lovers. There are countless book festivals across America. Here are a few big ones.

AJC Decatur Book Festival:
decaturbookfestival.com

Books by the Banks: Cincinnati Regional Book Festival:
booksbythebanks.org

Brooklyn Book Festival:
brooklynbookfestival.org

LA Times Festival of Books:
latimes.com/books/festivalofbooks/

Miami Book Fair:
miamibookfair.com

National Book Festival:
loc.gov/bookfest/

Texas Book Festival:
texasbookfestival.org

Printers Row Lit Fest, Chicago:
printersrowlitfest.org

EVERYDAY LITERATURE

Little Free Libraries: littlefreelibrary.org

Poetry in Motion: web.mta.info/mta/aft/poetry/

LITERARY TOURISM

#LiteraryTourism archives on Book Riot:
bookriot.com/category/literary-tourism/
Scan through pages of articles for literary tourism inspiration.

Poets & Writers Literary Places:
pw.org/literary_places
Browse a map of writing- and writer-related sites country-wide, or plug in your area to search what's nearby. You can create your own map of everything from historical sites to literary archives to writing spaces.

PUBLIC LIBRARIES WORTH A VISIT

Boston Public Library, Boston, MA:
The second-largest library in the US was also the first to create a children's section, which opened in 1895 and contained over 3,000 books.

Central Library, Los Angeles, CA:

Celebrated for its architecture and its size, this is the third largest central library in the US.

The Floating Library, Minnesota:

It's a library on a boat!

Homer Public Library, Homer, Alaska:

Sustainable by design, this library is made of recycled local material.

Library of Congress, Washington, DC:

The largest library in the world is none other than the LOC; it has millions of books and reference materials in its collection.

McAllen Public Library, McAllen, Texas:

Once a WalMart, this former-big-box retail space is now home to two football fields' worth of books.

New York Public Library, New York, NY:

The Big Apple boasts the largest public library system in the country, with 92 locations helping 17 million people each year.

Peterborough Public Library, Peterborough, NH:

This public library is the oldest in the world! It was founded in 1833, when a local reverend used public funds to create a place where anyone could borrow a book for free.

Provincetown Public Library, Provincetown, MA:

The building began as a Methodist church built in 1860, and now it's the town library and on the National Register of Historic Places; it also houses a model of a schooner, the *Rose Dorothea*, inside.

Seattle Public Library, Seattle WA:

This modern-looking building opened in 2004 and offers patrons an amazing skylight and a four-level book spiral, in addition to its collection.

WRITERS' HOUSES AND MUSEUMS

Ernest Hemingway's Birthplace and Museum, Oak Park, IL

The Eric Carle Museum of Picture Book Art, Amherst, MA

F. Scott and Zelda Fitzgerald Museum, Montgomery, Alabama

H.P. Lovecraft's Providence, Rhode Island

Kurt Vonnegut Memorial Library, Indianapolis, Indiana

Margaret Mitchell House and Museum, Atlanta, GA

Mark Twain House & Museum, Hartford, CT

The Mount (Edith Wharton's home), Lenox, MA

National Steinbeck Center, Salinas, California

O. Henry House and Museum, Austin, TX

Poe Museum, Richmond, Virginia

Willa Cather's childhood home, Red Cloud, Nebraska

William Faulkner's Rowan Oak, Oxford, MS

INDEX

IMAGE CREDITS

p. 2 *Pride and Prejudice*, first page of first edition. Used by permission of the Marion E. Wade Center, Wheaton College, Wheaton, IL. Reproduced by permission of the National Library of Scotland.

p. 4 *The Adventures of Tom Sawyer*, cover, first edition, second printing, The American Publishing Company, 1876. Courtesy of Heritage Auctions/HA.com.

p. 4 Portrait of Mark Twain. Courtesy Library of Congress.

p. 4 One of Mark Twain's later Huck Finn/Tom Sawyer manuscripts entitled "Tom Sawyer, Detective." Photo by Carolyn Cole/Los Angeles Times via Getty Images.

p. 6 *The Alchemist*, cover, first English edition, HarperSanfrancisco, 1993. Courtesy Heritage Auctions/HA.com, © HarperCollins.

p. 6 Author Paulo Coelho. © Sueddeutsche Zeitung Photo / Alamy Stock Photo.

p. 6 Page from the original manuscript for *The Alchemist*. Courtesy of Paulo Coelho & Christina Oticicia Foundation.

p. 8 Covers of *Along Came a Spider*, *Kiss the Girls*, and *Pop Goes the Weasel*. Courtesy Hachette Books.

p. 8 *Four Blind Mice*, cover. Courtesy Heritage Auctions/HA.com, © Hachette Books.

p. 8 Author James Patterson at his home office. © AP Photo/Wilfredo Lee.

p. 10 *Alice's Adventures in Wonderland*, cover, first edition, Macmillan, 1865. © Christies Auctions/Bridgeman Art Library.

p. 10 Portrait, Lewis Carroll. Courtesy Library of Congress.

P. 10 Dedication, "Alice's Adventures Under Ground," original manuscript for *Alice's Adventures in Wonderland*. © British Library/Granger Images.

p. 12 *Americanah*, 2013 hardcover edition. Courtesy Penguin Random House.

p. 12 Author Chimamanda Ngozi Adichie. Photo by Monica Schipper/WireImage.

p. 12 University of Nigeria, Nsukka. Courtesy Mobolaji Sokunbi & Akin Akinboro / The 234 Project (www .the234project.com).

p. 14 *And Then There Were None*, first edition, 1939. Courtesy Harper Collins.

p. 14 Agatha Christie in 1926. © Sueddeutsche Zeitung Photo / Alamy Stock Photo.

p. 14 Cover of the *Daily Sketch*. Photo by Hulton Archives/ Getty.

p. 18 *Anne of Green Gables*, first edition cover. Courtesy Bonhams Auctions.

p. 18 Portrait of Lucy Maud Montgomery, 1908. L. M. Montgomery Collection, Archival & Special Collections, University of Guelph Library.

p. 18 The birthplace of L. M. Montgomery. Photo by Dave G. Houser.

p. 20 *Another Country*, cover. Courtesy Penguin Random House.

p. 20 Portrait of James Baldwin. © Van Vechten Trust, via the Carl Van Vechten Papers Relating to African American Arts and Letters, James Weldon Johnson Memorial Collection, Beinecke Rare Book and Manuscript Library.

p. 20 Plaque in front of James Baldwin's Horatio St. home in New York City. simon leigh / Alamy Stock photo.

p. 22 *Atlas Shrugged*, cover. Courtesy Penguin Random House.

p. 22 Portrait of Ayn Rand. Photo by Oscar White/Corbis/ VCG via Getty Images.

p. 22 Handwritten notes by Ayn Rand for *Atlas Shrugged*. © ZUMA Press, Inc. / Alamy Stock Photo.

p. 24 *Beloved*, first edition, 1987. Courtesy Heritage Auctions/HA.com. © Penguin Random House.

p. 24 Toni Morrison, 2009. Photo by Timothy Fadek/ Corbis via Getty Images.

p. 24 Handwritten draft of *Beloved*. Copyright Toni Morrison Papers (C1491); Manuscripts Division, Department of Rare Books and Special Collections, Princeton University Library.

p. 26 *Bless Me, Ultima*, classic cover. Courtesy Hachette Books.

p. 26 Author Rudolfo Anaya in 2005. Photo by Steve Snowden/Getty Images.

p. 26 *Bless Me, Ultima*, movie tie-in cover. Courtesy Hachette Books.

p. 28 *The Book Thief*, anniversary edition cover. Courtesy Penguin Random House.

p. 28 Author Markus Zusak, 2009. Photo by David Levenson/Getty Images.

p. 28 Still from *The Book Thief* film. © 20th Century Fox Film Corp. All rights reserved./courtesy Everett Collection.

p. 31 "The Shower of Cards," illustration. © The Shower of Cards, illustration from 'Alice in Wonderland' by Lewis Carroll (1832-98) (colour litho), Tenniel, John (1820-1914) / Private Collection / Bridgeman Images.

p. 31 *The Adventures of Tom Sawyer*, title page illustration. Courtesy Heritage Auctions.

p. 33 Illustration for 1895 edition of *Pride and Prejudice*. Photo by, Universal History Archive/UIG via Getty Images.

p. 33 Engraving of Don Quixote. Courtesy Library of Congress, Prints & Photographs Division.

p. 34 *The Brief and Wondrous Life of Oscar Wao*, hardcover. Courtesy Penguin Random House.

p. 34 Author Junot Díaz, 2008. Photo by Matt Carr/ Contour by Getty Images.

p. 34 Junot Díaz's notebook for *The Brief Wondrous Life of Oscar Wao*. Photo by Jens Mortensen.

p. 36 *The Call of the Wild*, first edition. Courtesy Heritage Auctions/HA.com.

p. 36 Portrait of Jack London, 1896. JLP 588, The Jack London Collection, The Huntington Library, San Marino, California.

p. 36 "Buck" of *The Call of the Wild*. JLP 13, The Jack London Collection, The Huntington Library, San Marino, California.

p. 38 *Catch-22*, first edition cover. Courtesy Heritage Auctions/HA.com. © Simon & Schuster.

p. 38 Joseph Heller, 1965. © Inge Morath © The Inge Morath Foundation/Magnum Photos.

p. 38 Joseph Heller with his crew in the 488th Bomb Squadron. Courtesy 57th Bomb Wing Association.

p. 40 *Catcher in the Rye*, first edition cover. Courtesy Heritage Auctions/HA.com. © Hachette Books.

p. 40 Author J. D. Salinger, 1952, Brooklyn. Photo by Antony Di Gesu/San Diego Historical Society/Hulton Archive Collection/Getty Images.

p. 40 Ice skaters, Wollman Rink, Central Park, New York, 1951. Bettmann/Getty Images.

p. 42 *Charlotte's Web*, first edition cover, 1952. Courtesy Harper Collins.

p. 42 Author E. B. White with dog, 1952. Courtesy of White Literary LLC.

p. 42 *Charlotte's Web*, original illustration, 1952. Courtesy Heritage Auctions/HA.com. © Harper Collins.

p. 44 *The Lion, the Witch and the Wardrobe*, first edition cover, 1950. Illustration by Pauline Baynes. © CS Lewis Pte Ltd 1950. Courtesy HarperCollins.

p. 44 Author C. S. Lewis, 1958. Wolf Suschitzky/Pix Inc./ The LIFE Images Collection/ Getty Images.

p. 44 Aslan from the 2005 film adaptation of *The Lion, the Witch and the Wardrobe*. AF Archive / Alamy Stock Photo.

p. 47 Harper Lee, 1960. Photograph by Michael Brown ©.

p. 47 Kurt Vonnegut, 1990. Photo by Al Seib/Los Angeles Times via Getty Images.

P. 48 *The Clan of the Cave Bear*, first edition cover, 1980. Courtesy Heritage Auctions, HA.com © Penguin Random House.

p. 48 Author Jean M. Auel, 2011. Photo by In Pictures Ltd./Corbis via Getty Images.

p. 50 *The Coldest Winter Ever* cover, 1999. Courtesy Simon & Schuster.

p. 50 Author Sister Souljah. Photo © Brian Velenchenko, Courtesy Simon & Schuster.

p. 50 Sister Souljah speaking to the media, 1992. Photo by Kimberly Butler/The LIFE Images Collection/Getty Images.

p. 52 *The Color Purple*, first edition cover, 1982. Courtesy Heritage Auctions/HA.com. © Houghton Mifflin Harcourt.

p. 52 Author Alice Walker in Seattle, 2013. Dana Nalbandian/WireImage.

p. 52 Theater marquee, Broadway, 2016. Photo by Walter McBride/Getty Images.

p. 54 *A Confederacy of Dunces*, first edition cover, 1980. Courtesy Heritage Auctions/HA.com.

p. 54 Author John Kennedy Toole. Courtesy Louisiana Research Collection, Tulane University.

p. 54 Letter from Toole to Simon & Schuster. Courtesy John Kennedy Toole Papers, Tulane University.

p. 56 *The Count of Monte Cristo*, first edition cover, 1846. Photo by Kelly Welch, Courtesy Quill & Brush Booksellers.

p. 56 Author Alexandre Dumas, 1846. Photo by Apic/ Getty Images.

p. 56 Illustration from *The Count of Monte Cristo*, "My name is Edmond Dantès." Project Gutenberg.

p. 56 Chateau d'If fortress prison. © David Crossland / Alamy Stock Photo.

p. 58 Cover of *Crime and Punishment*. Courtesy Penguin Random House.

p. 58 Author Fyodor M. Dostoyevsky, 1865. Photo by adoc-photos/Corbis via Getty Images.

p. 58 Illustration for *Crime and Punishment* by Mikhail Petrovich (Baron) Klodt, Russian State Library. Photo by Fine Art Images/Heritage Images/Getty Images.

p. 61 Cover, *Bless Me, Ultima*. Courtesy Hachette Books.

p. 61 *The Call of the Wild*, first edition. Courtesy Heritage Auctions/HA.com.

P. 62 *The Curious Incident of the Dog in the Night-Time*, first edition cover, 2003. Courtesy Penguin Random House.

p. 62 Author Mark Haddon, 2016. Photo by Awakening Getty Images.

p. 62 Actor Graham Butler as Christopher Boone, London National Theatre, 2017. Photo Geraint Lewis / Alamy Stock Photo.

p. 64 *The Da Vinci Code*, first edition cover, 2003. Courtesy Penguin Random House.

p. 64 Author Dan Brown, 2016. Photo by Patrick Fouque/ Paris Match/Contour by Getty Images.

p. 64 Photo of "cryptex" made for the film *The Da Vinci Code*. Ray Tang/REX/Shutterstock.

p. 66 Opening pages of first English translation of *Don Quixote*, 1620. Courtesy Heritage Auctions/HA.com.

p. 66 Author Miguel de Cervantes. Courtesy Pictorial Press Ltd / Alamy Stock Photo.

p. 66 Illustration of Chapter 1 of *Don Quixote*. Courtesy Heritage auctions/HA.com.

p. 68 *Doña Bárbara*, first edition cover. Courtesy University of Chicago Press.

p. 68 Author Romulo Gallegos, President of Venezuela, 1947. Photo by Library of Congress/Corbis/VCG via Getty Images.

p. 68 President Gallegos with Harry S. Truman. Courtesy nsf / Alamy Stock Photo.

p. 70 Cover, *Dune*. Courtesy Penguin Random House.

p. 70 Author Frank Herbert, 1978. Photo by Ulf Andersen/ Getty Images.

p. 70 Original art for the David Lynch film version of *Dune*, 1984. © Dune / Photo © Collection CSFF / Bridgeman Images.

p. 72 Cover, *Fifty Shades of Grey*. Courtesy Penguin Random House.

p. 72 Author E. L. James, 2015. Photo by Mike Coppola/ Getty Images.

p. 72 Poster for film adaptation of *Fifty Shades of Gray*. Courtesy Heritage Auctions/HA.com. © Focus Features.

p. 74 Jack London, 1905. Photo Bettmann/Getty Images.

p. 76 *Flowers in the Attic*, first edition cover, 1979. Courtesy Heritage Auctions/HA.com and the Andrews Family.

p. 76 Author V. C. Andrews. Courtesy of the Andrews Family.

p. 76 *Flowers in the Attic*, 2014 edition cover. Courtesy Simon and Schuster.

p. 78 Cover, *Foundation*. Courtesy Penguin Random House.

p. 78 Author Isaac Asimov. © Pictorial Press Ltd / Alamy Stock Photo.

p. 78 *Astounding* magazine. Courtesy Heritage Auctions/ HA.com.

p. 80 *Frankenstein*, 1831 edition. Courtesy Heritage Auctions/HA.com.

p. 80 Title page from *Frankenstein*, 1831 edition. Courtesy Heritage Auctions/HA.com.

p. 80 Author Mary Shelley. © GL Archive / Alamy Stock Photo.

p. 80 Villa Diodati, Switzerland. Photo by Harold Cunningham/Getty Images.

p. 82 *Ghost*, hardcover. Courtesy Simon & Schuster.

p. 82 Author Jason Reynolds. Photo © Ben Fractenberg; courtesy Simon & Schuster.

p. 82 Jason Reynolds talking with Daniel José Older, 2016. Photo by Bill O'Leary/The *Washington Post* via Getty

Images.

p. 84 *Gilead*, first edition cover, 2004. Courtesy Heritage Auctions/HA.com; © Macmillan.

p. 84 Author Marilynne Robinson. Photo by Ulf Anderson/Getty Images.

p. 86 *The Giver*, cover. Courtesy Houghton Mifflin Harcourt.

p. 86 Author Lois Lowry, 2014. Photo by Logan Werlinger/Portland Press Herald via Getty Images.

p. 86 Poster for the movie, *The Giver*. © Weinstein Company/Courtesy Everett Collection.

p. 90 *The Godfather*, classic cover. Courtesy Penguin Random House.

p. 90 Author Mario Puzo, 1979. Photo by Ron Galella/WireImage.

p. 90 Letter from Puzo to Marlon Brando, 1970. © Autograph letter to Marlon Brando, Private Collection / Photo © Christie's Images / Bridgeman Images.

p. 92 *Gone Girl*, hardcover edition, 2012. Courtesy Penguin Random House.

p. 92 Author Gillian Flynn. Courtesy Penguin Random House.

p. 92 Movie tie-in cover for *Gone Girl*. © Collection Christophel / Alamy Stock Photo.

p. 94 *Gone With the Wind*, first edition cover. Courtesy Peter Harrington Books by permission of GWTW Partners, LLC.

p. 94 Author Margaret Mitchell, 1941. Library of Congress, Prints & Photographs Division.

p. 94 Poster from the movie, *Gone With the Wind*. Pictorial Press Ltd / Alamy Stock Photos.

p. 96 *The Grapes of Wrath*, Penguin Classics cover. Courtesy Penguin Random House.

p. 96 Author John Steinbeck, 1930. Library of Congress Prints & Photographs Division.

p. 96 *Migrant Mother*. Library of Congress Prints & Photographs Division, FSA/ OWI Collection.

p. 98 *Great Expectations*, first edition cover, 1891. Courtesy Heritage Auctions/HA.com.

p. 98 Author Charles Dickens, 1867. Library of Congress Prints and Photographs Division.

p. 98 *Harper's Periodicals*. Public domain.

p. 100 *The Great Gatsby*, first edition cover. Courtesy Heritage Auctions/HA.com. Image by permission of the Trustees of the Fitzgerald Estate Under Agreement Dated July 3, 1975, Created by Frances Scott Fitzgerald Smith.

p. 100 Author F. Scott Fitzgerald, 1928. © Everett Collection Historical / Alamy Stock Photo.

p. 100 Pages from original manuscript of *The Great Gatsby*. Courtesy F. Scott Fitzgerald Papers (C0187); Manuscripts Division, Department of Rare Books and Special Collections, Princeton University Library. By permission of the Trustees of the Fitzgerald Estate Under Agreement Dated July 3, 1975. Created by Frances Scott Fitzgerald Smith.

p. 103 A page from the *Codex of Leicester*. Photo © Boltin Picture Library / Bridgeman Images.

p. 103 Charles Dickens' letter opener, made from a cat's paw, c. 1866. Courtesy New York Public Library.

p. 104 *Gulliver's Travels*, first printing, 1726. Courtesy Heritage Auctions/HA.com.

p. 104 Author Jonathan Swift. © Jonathan Swift, 1875 (mezzotint), Rajon, Paul Adolphe (1843-1888) / Photo © Historic Royal Palaces/Claire Collins / Bridgeman Images.

p. 104 Engraving from *Gulliver's Travels*, 1795. Library of Congress, Prints & Photographs Division.

p. 106 *The Handmaid's Tale*, first US edition. Courtesy Heritage Auctions/HA.com © Houghton Miffin Harcourt.

p. 106 Author Margaret Atwood, 1981. Photo by Dale Brazao/Toronto Star via Getty Images.

p. 106 Handwritten pages from the original manuscript of *The Handmaid's Tale*. Courtesy Fisher Library, University of Toronto.

p. 108 *Harry Potter and the Sorcerer's Stone*, cover. Courtesy Heritage Auctions/HA.com. © Scholastic Corporation.

p. 108 Author J. K. Rowling, 2016. Photo by Ray Tang/Anadolu Agency/Getty Images.

p. 108 Sketch by J. K. Rowling. Nils Jorgensen/REX/Shutterstock.

p. 110 *Hatchet*, 30th-anniversary edition cover. Courtesy Simon & Schuster.

p. 110 Author Gary Paulsen, 2009. Photo by Brian Adams/Contour by Getty Images.

p. 110 Trade paperback edition of *Hatchet*. Courtesy Simon & Schuster.

p. 112 Conrad's *Youth: A Narrative and Two Other Stories*. Courtesy Heritage Auctions/HA.com.

p. 112 Author Joseph Conrad. © Pictorial Press Ltd / Alamy Stock Photo.

p. 112 *Blackwood's Magazine*. Courtesy Conrad First/The Joseph Conrad Periodical Archive, Uppsala University.

p. 114 *The Help*, cover. Courtesy Penguin Random House.

p. 114 Author Kathryn Stockett, 2011. Photo by Frazer Harrison/Getty Images.

p. 114 Actress Octavia Spencer accepting her Academy award for her appearance in *The Help*. © Kevin Winter/Getty Images.

P. 117 Isaac Asimov for Radio Shack, 1980 print ad. © Radio Shack / Bridgeman Images.

p. 117 Protesters dressed as characters from "The Handmaid's Tale." AP Photo/Eric Gay.

p. 118 *The Hitchhiker's Guide to the Galaxy*, first printing 1979. Courtesy Heritage Auctions/HA.com © Arthur Barker LTD.

p. 118 Author Douglas Adams, 1978. Photo by Daily Mirror/Mirrorpix/Mirrorpix via Getty Images.

p. 118 Still from the movie adaptation of *Hitchhiker's Guide*. ©Touchstone/Courtesy Everett Collection.

P. 120 *The Hunger Games*, first edition cover. Courtesy Heritage Auctions © Scholastic Corporation.

p. 120 Author Suzanne Collins. Photo by Todd Plitt © Scholastic Corporation.

p. 120 Poster from *The Hunger Games* movie. Courtesy Heritage Auctions © Scholastic Corporation.

p. 122 *The Hunt for Red October*, cover. Courtesy Penguin Random House.

p. 122 Author Tom Clancy, 1985. Photo by Diana Walker/Time & Life Pictures/Getty Images.

p. 122 Tom Clancy and President Ronald Reagan. Courtesy Ronald Reagan Presidential Library/NARA.

p. 124 *The Intuitionist*, first edition cover. Courtesy Heritage Auctions/HA.com © Penguin Random House.

p. 124 Author Colson Whitehead, 2014. © Rolf Vennenbernd/picture-alliance/dpa/AP Images.

p. 124 Sketch of the Otis elevator. Courtesy National Archives and Records Administration.

p. 126 *Invisible Man*, cover. Courtesy Penguin Random House.

p. 126 Author Ralph Ellison, 1966. Photo by David Attie/Getty Images.

p. 126 Typescript of *Invisible Man*. I:101 Ralph Ellison Papers, Manuscript Division, Library of Congress, Washington, D.C.

p. 128 *Jane Eyre*, 1848. Courtesy Heritage Auctions/HA.com.

p. 128 Author Charlotte Bronte, circa 1840. Photo by Rischgitz/Getty Images.

p. 128 First page from handwritten manuscript of *Jane Eyre*. © British Library/Granger Images.

p. 131 *Charlotte's Web*, original drawing for front cover. Courtesy Heritage Auctions/HA.com © HarperCollins.

p. 132 *The Joy Luck Club*, cover. Courtesy Penguin Random House.

p. 132 Author Amy Tan, 2011. Photo by Tim Mosenfelder/Getty Images.

p. 132 Amy Tan with Stephen King performing as part of the Rock Bottom Remainders. Photo AP Images.

p. 134 *Jurassic Park*, cover. Courtesy Penguin Random House.

p. 134 Author Michael Crichton. Photo by Ralph Crane/The LIFE Picture Collection/Getty Images.

p. 134 Poster for movie *Jurassic Park*. Courtesy Heritage Auctions/HA.com.

p. 136 Left Behind series. Photo by Urbano Delvalle/The LIFE Images Collection/Getty Images.

p. 136 Authors Tim LaHaye and Jerry B. Jenkins. Photo by Carolyn Cole/Los Angeles Times via Getty Images.

p. 136 "The Day of Judgement" painting by John Martin. © The Day of Judgement (oil on canvas), Martin, John (1789-1854) (after) / Private Collection / Bridgeman Images.

p. 138 *The Little Prince*, first edition. Courtesy Heritage Auctions/HA.com © Houghton Mifflin Harcourt.

p. 138 Author Antoine de Saint-Exupéry, circa 1922. Photo by Apic/Getty Images.

p. 138 Drawing for *The Little Prince*. Photo REMY GABALDA/AFP/Getty Images.

p. 140 *Little Women*, cover. Courtesy Heritage Auctions/HA.com.

p. 140 Author Louisa May Alcott. Bettmann/Getty Images.

p. 140 Orchard House, Alcott's home. © Andrew O›Brien / Alamy Stock Photo.

p. 142 *Lonesome Dove*, first edition. Courtesy Heritage Auctions/HA.com © Simon & Schuster.

p. 142 Author Larry McMurtry, 2006. Photo by Steve Granitz/WireImage.

p. 142 Trade paperback cover for *Lonesome Dove*. Courtesy Simon & Schuster.

p. 146 *Looking for Alaska*, cover. Courtesy Penguin Random House.

p. 146 Author John Green, 2014. Photo by Christopher Patey/Contour by Getty Images.

p. 146 *Looking for Alaska*, 10th anniversary edition. Courtesy Penguin Random House.

p. 148 *Lord of the Rings*, first complete American edition. Courtesy the Harry Lee Poe Collection.

p. 148 Author J. R. R. Tolkien. Photo by PA Images via Getty Images.

p. 148 Map of the Shire. Courtesy Bodleian Libraries, University of Oxford © The Tolkien Estate Ltd 1988.

p. 150 *The Lovely Bones*, cover. Courtesy of Hachette Books.

p. 150 Author Alice Sebold. Photo by Neville Elder/Corbis via Getty Images.

p. 150 *Lucky*, cover. Courtesy of Hachette Books.

p. 152 *The Martian*, hardcover. Courtesy Penguin Random House.

p. 152 Author Andy Weir, 2015. Photo by Jeff Vespa/Getty Images.

p. 152 View of Martian landscape. NASA/JPL.

p. 154 *Memoirs of a Geisha*, cover. Courtesy Penguin Random House.

p. 154. Author Arthur Golden, 2005. © Allstar Picture Library / Alamy Stock Photo.

p. 154 Back view of two Geishas. Photo by ullstein bild/ullstein bild via Getty Images.

p. 156 *The Mind Invaders*, cover. Courtesy The Berean Call.

p. 156 Author Dave Hunt. Courtesy The Berean Call.

p. 156 Cover, *The God Makers*. Courtesy The Berean Call.

p. 159 Page from the Fitzgerald scrapbook. Courtesy F. Scott Fitzgerald Papers (C0187); Manuscripts Division, Department of Rare Books and Special Collections, Princeton University Library. By permission of the Trustees of the Fitzgerald Estate Under Agreement Dated July 3, 1975. Created by Frances Scott Fitzgerald Smith.

p. 160 *Moby-Dick*, first US edition. Courtesy Heritage Auctions/HA.com.

p. 160 Portrait of Herman Melville. Bettmann/Getty Images.

p. 160 Original agreement between Herman Melville and Harper & Brothers for *Moby-Dick*. Courtesy Harper Collins.

p. 162 *Nineteen Eighty-Four*, Signet Classic cover. Courtesy Penguin Random House.

p. 162 Author George Orwell. Photo by ullstein bild/ullstein bild via Getty Images.

p. 162 Poster for the 1956 film, *1984*. Courtesy Everett Images.

p. 164 *The Notebook*, first edition cover. Courtesy Heritage Auctions/HA.com © Hachette Books

p. 164 Author Nicholas Sparks, 2017. Photo by Rosdiana Ciaravolo/Getty Images.

p. 164. The house on which Noah's in *The Notebook* was modeled on. Courtesy Nicholas Sparks/Hachette Books.

p. 166 *One Hundred Years of Solitude*, first US edition. Reprinted by permission of HarperCollins Publishers. Courtesy Heritage Auctions/HA.com.

p. 166 Author Gabriel García Márquez, 1982. Photo by Ulf Andersen/Getty Images.

p. 166 Telegram regarding the publication of *One Hundred Years Of Solitude*. Courtesy Harper Collins.

p. 166 Gabriel García Márquez's office in his house in Mexico City. Courtesy Harry Ransom Center, The University of Texas at Austin.

p. 168 *Outlander*, first edition cover. Courtesy Heritage

Auctions/HA.com © Penguin Random House.

p. 168 Author Diana Gabaldon. © Colin McPherson / Alamy Stock Photo.

p. 168 Clava Cairns to the East of Inverness. © Gerry McCann / Alamy Stock Photo.

p. 170 *The Outsiders* Speak Platinum Edition. Courtesy Penguin Random House.

p. 170 Author S.E. Hinton, 2017. Photo by Slaven Vlasic/Getty Images.

p. 172 Harvard Square, the setting for *The Handmaid's Tale*. Roman Babakin / Alamy Stock Photo.

p. 172 The Cloisters. © Ian Good/Shutterstock.

p. 172 Manhattan, aerial view. Photo by H. Armstrong Roberts/ClassicStock/Getty Images.

p. 174 A building in Aracataca. © EITAN ABRAMOVICH/AFP/Getty Images.

P. 174 Bilbo Baggins's home in Matamata, New Zealand. © Nolleks86/Shutterstock.

p. 175 Advice from a Caterpillar, from 'Alice's Adventures in Wonderland' by Lewis Carroll, published 1891 (litho). Tenniel, John (1820-1914) / Private Collection / Photo © Ken Welsh / Bridgeman Images.

p. 175 *Middlemarch* (colour litho). Private Collection / © Look and Learn / Bridgeman Images.

P 176 *The Picture of Dorian Gray*, first edition. Courtesy Heritage Auctions/HA.com.

p. 176 Oscar Wilde, circa 1882. Library of Congress, Prints & Photographs Division.

p. 176 First appearance of *The Picture of Dorian Gray* in *Lippincott's Monthly Magazine*. Courtesy Heritage Auctions/HA.com.

p. 178 Title page of *The Pilgrim's Progress*. Photo by Culture Club/Getty Images.

p. 178 John Bunyan, engraving. © John Bunyan (engraving), English School, (19th century) / Private Collection / © Look and Learn / Bridgeman Images.

p. 178 Commemorative illustrated edition of *The Pilgrim's Progress*. Courtesy Heritage Auctions/HA.com.

p. 178 John Bunyan's memorial, detail. © Kathy deWitt / Alamy Stock Photo.

p. 180 *The Pillars of the Earth*, cover. Courtesy Penguin Random House.

p. 180 Ken Follett, 2015. Photo by Horacio Villalobos/Corbis via Getty Images.

p. 180 Ken Follett on the set of the television adaptation of *The Pillars of the Earth*, 2009. Courtesy Everett Images.

p. 182 *A Prayer for Owen Meany*, first trade edition cover. COPYRIGHT © 1989 BY GARP ENTERPRISES, LTD. Reprinted by permission of HarperCollins Publishers. Courtesy Heritage Auctions/HA.com.

p. 182 Author John Irving. © jeremy sutton-hibbert / Alamy Stock Photo.

p. 182 Signed bookplate from 1st edition of *A Prayer for Owen Meany*. Courtesy Heritage Auctions/HA.com © HarperCollins.

p. 184 *Pride and Prejudice*, first edition. Courtesy National Library of Scotland.

p. 184 English author Jane Austen, circa 1790. Photo by Stock Montage/Stock Montage/Getty Images.

p. 184 "The Entreaties of Several," illustration for *Pride and Prejudice*. Courtesy Jane Austen's House Museum.

p. 186 *Ready Player One*, hardcover. Courtesy Penguin Random House.

p. 186 Author Ernest Cline, 2015. Photo by Jason Merritt/Getty Images for Entertainment Weekly.

p. 186 *Ready Player One*, trade cover. Courtesy Penguin Random House.

p. 189. *Jurassic Park*, cover. Courtesy Penguin Random House.

p. 189 *To Kill a Mockingbird*, front cover, first edition. Courtesy Heritage Auctions/HA.com © HarperCollins.

p. 189 *Catcher in the Rye*, first edition cover. Courtesy Heritage Auctions/HA.com © Hachette Books.

p. 189 *Catch-22*, first edition cover. Courtesy Heritage Auctions/HA.com. © Simon & Schuster.

p. 189 *Ready Player One*, hardcover. Courtesy Penguin Random House.

p. 189 *The Martian*, hardcover. Courtesy Penguin Random House.

p. 190 *Rebecca*, first US edition. Courtesy Heritage Auctions/HA.com © Hachette Books.

p. 190 Author Daphne Du Maurier. Photo by ullstein bild/ullstein bild via Getty Images.

p. 190 Silk banner advertisement for the Hitchcock film, *Rebecca*. Courtesy Heritage Auctions/HA.com.

p. 192 *A Separate Peace*, trade paperback edition. Courtesy Simon & Schuster.

p. 192 Author John Knowles. Photo by Anacleto Rapping/Los Angeles Times via Getty Images.

p. 192 Illustrated map of Phillips Exeter campus. Courtesy Phillips Exeter Academy.

p. 192 Campus of Phillips Exeter. © MAXINE HICKS / Alamy Stock Photo.

p. 194 *The Shack*, hardcover. © Hachette Books.

p. 194 Author William P. Young. Photo by Tony Bock/Toronto Star via Getty Images.

p. 194 Still from the film adaptation of *The Shack*. © Summit Entertainment/Courtesy Everett Collection.

p. 196 *Siddhartha*, Bantam edition. Courtesy Penguin Random House.

p. 196 Portrait of Hermann Hesse. Photo by Mondadori Portfolio via Getty Images.

p. 196. Departure of Prince Siddhartha (c563-c483 BC), illustration. Photo by Ann Ronan Pictures/Print Collector/Getty Images.

p. 198 *The Sirens of Titan*, cover. Courtesy Penguin Random House.

p. 198 Kurt Vonnegut, early 1970s. Photo by Bernard Gotfryd/Getty Images.

p. 198 Author Kurt Vonnegut Jr., sitting in front of his typewriter. Photo by Gil Friedberg/Pix Inc./The LIFE Images Collection/Getty Images.

p. 200 Cover, *A Game of Thrones*, first volume of the Song of Ice and Fire series. Courtesy Heritage Auctions/HA.com © Penguin Random House.

p. 200 The dramatic landscape of Iceland. Russell Pearson / Barcroft Image / Barcroft Media via Getty Images.

p. 200 HBO's *Game of Thrones* Iron Throne. Photo by Amanda Edwards/WireImage.

p. 200 Author George R.R. Martin, 2012. Photo by Clinton Gilders/FilmMagic.

p. 202 Typescript page from *Nineteen Eighty-Four*. The manuscript of George Orwell's *Nineteen Eighty-Four* is held by the John Hay Library at Brown University. The manuscript was presented to the Library in 1992 by Daniel G. Siegel. Remaining copies of the 1984 limited edition *Facsimile of the Manuscript of Nineteen Eighty-Four*, published by M & S Press, are available for purchase through M & S Press or through Amazon.

p. 202 J.R.R. Tolkien's note on the Elvish language. Courtesy Cushing Memorial Library and Archives,Texas A&M University.

p. 204 William Shakespeare, "The Chandos Portrait." IanDagnall Computing / Alamy Stock Photo.

p. 206 *The Stand*, first edition cover. Courtesy Heritage Auctions/HA.com © Penguin Random House.

p. 206 Writer Stephen King, 2013. Photo by Steve Schofield/Contour by Getty Images.

p. 206 Hardcover for *The Stand: Complete and Uncut Edition*. Courtesy Penguin Random House.

p. 208 *The Sun Also Rises*, library edition cover. Courtesy Simon & Schuster.

p. 208 Portrait of Ernest Hemingway, Paris, March 1928. Ernest Hemingway Collection. John F. Kennedy Presidential Library and Museum, Boston.

p. 208 Last page of the first draft of *The Sun Also Rises*. Ernest Hemingway Collection. John F. Kennedy Presidential Library and Museum, Boston.

p. 210 *Swan Song*, cover. Courtesy Donald Maass Literary Agency, Desert Isle Design, David Ho.

p. 210 Robert McCammon author portrait. Courtesy Donald Maass Literary Agency.

p. 210 *Swan Song* author page with quote. Courtesy Heritage Auctions/HA.com and Donald Maass Literary Agency.

p. 212 *Tales of the City*, first edition cover. Courtesy Harper Collins.

p. 212 Author Armistead Maupin, 2006. Photo by Mark Mainz/Getty Images.

p. 212 Still from the PBS series, *Tales of the City*. © PBS/Courtesy Everett Collection.

p. 214 *Their Eyes Were Watching God*, first edition cover. Courtesy Heritage Auctions/HA.com © HarperCollins.

p. 214 Portrait of author Zora Neale Hurston, circa 1940s. Photo by Fotosearch/Getty Images.

p. 214 Page from *Their Eyes Were Watching God*. Courtesy Beinecke Rare Book & Manuscript Library.

p. 216 *Things Fall Apart*, cover. Courtesy Penguin Random House.

p. 216 Writer Chinua Achebe. Photo by Juergen Frank/Corbis via Getty Images.

p. 216 Poster for the film adaptation of *Things Fall Apart*. Courtesy Everett Collection.

p. 218 Letter from Herman Melville to friend Nathaniel Hawthorne, Oct. 25, 1852. Courtesy New York Public Library.

p. 220 Harper Lee and Truman Capote, 1976. © Harry Benson/Contour by Getty Images.

p. 220 The Inklings. Used by permission of the Marion E. Wade Center, Wheaton College, Wheaton, IL.

p. 222 *This Present Darkness*, cover. Courtesy Crossway.

p. 222 Author Frank E. Peretti. Courtesy Crossway.

p. 224 *To Kill a Mockingbird*, front cover, first edition. Courtesy Heritage Auctions/HA.com © HarperCollins.

p. 224 Harper Lee sitting in rocking chair, in her hometown of Alabama. Photo © Donald Uhrbrock/The LIFE Images Collection/Getty Images.

p. 224 *To Kill a Mockingbird*, back cover, rare advance reading copy with paper covers. Courtesy Heritage Auctions/HA.com © HarperCollins.

p. 226 *A Tree Grows in Brooklyn*, front cover art. Courtesy Heritage Auctions/HA.com © HarperCollins.

p. 226 Author Betty Smith using typewriter. Photo by Ann Rosener/Pix Inc./The LIFE Images Collection/Getty Images.

p. 226 A group of women smile as they read *A Tree Grows in Brooklyn*, circa 1940s. Photo by Weegee(Arthur Fellig)/International Center of Photography/Getty Images.

p. 228 *Twilight*, trade cover. Courtesy Hachette Books.

p. 228 Author Stephanie Meyer at the 10th anniversary of *Twilight* at Barnes & Nobles at The Grove. Photo by Amanda Edwards/WireImage.

p. 228 *Twilight*, movie poster. Photo © RGR Collection/Alamy Stock Photo.

p. 230 *War and Peace*, cover. Courtesy Penguin Random House.

p. 230 Leo Tolstoy reading a book, circa 1910. Photo by Fotosearch/Getty Images.

p. 230 *War and Peace*, title page, first American edition, later issue. Courtesy Heritage Auctions/HA.com.

p. 232 *Watchers*, trade cover. Courtesy Penguin Random House.

p. 232 Author Dean Koontz. Photo by Al Schaben/Los Angeles Times via Getty Images.

p. 232 Typed letter signed "Dean R. Koontz," to a fan named Jim. Courtesy Heritage Auctions/HA.com.

p. 235 James Baldwin in his New York apartment. Bettmann / Getty Images.

p. 236 The first two volumes in the Wheel of Time series. Courtesy Heritage Auctions/HA.com © Tor/Macmillan.

p. 236 Author Robert Jordan. Photo by Liza Groen Trombi/Locus Productions, Courtesy Macmillan.

p. 236 *Eye of the World* preview booklet art. Courtesy Macmillan.

p. 238 *Where the Red Fern Grows*, first edition, front cover. Courtesy of Rachel Phillips of Burnside Rare Books.

p. 238 *Where the Red Fern Grows*, first edition, back cover. Courtesy of Rachel Phillips of Burnside Rare Books.

p. 238 *Where the Red Fern Grows*, cover. Courtesy Penguin Random House.

p. 240 *White Teeth*, cover. Courtesy Heritage Auctions/HA.com © Hamish Hamilton.

p. 240 Zadie Smith, 2014. Photo by Linda Brownlee/Corbis via Getty Images.

p. 240 Zadie Smith, speaking at Across the Pond at the New York Festival on October 10, 2014. Photo by Bryan Bedder/Getty Images The New Yorker.

p. 242 *Wuthering Heights*, first edition. Courtesy Bonhams Auctions.

p. 242 Portrait of Emily Brontë. Painting by Patrick Branwell Bronte c. 1833/PVDE/Bridgeman Images.

p. 242 Poster for the 1939 film of *Wuthering Heights*. Photo by Movie Poster Image Art/Getty Images.